Barbara Cleverly was born in the north of England and is a graduate of Durham University. She spent her working life in Cambridge and Suffolk, and now resides in Suffolk. Her first Joe Sandilands novel, *The Last Kashmiri Rose*, was named by the *New York Times* as a 'notable book of 2002'.

Praise for *Ragtime in Simla*

'Introduces an intelligent author and interesting investigator. The Indian setting is expertly exploited and the climatic scenes are full of satisfying twists.'
Mat Coward, *Morning Star*

'In an impressive debut, author Barbara Cleverly weaves an engrossing tale of serial murder and the impending decline of the British Empire into a well-written fair play mystery set in 1920s India.'
Publishers Weekly

'Don't miss this classic British crime spiced with bits of a thriller; though set in 1922, for the most part it reads like a contemporary.'
The Poisoned Pen

STOKE-ON-TRENT

D0191222

Also by Barbara Cleverly

The Last Kashmiri Rose
The Damascened Blade

Ragtime in Simla

Barbara Cleverly

CONSTABLE • London

CONSTABLE

First published in Great Britain in 2003 by Constable,
an imprint of Constable & Robinson Ltd
This paperback edition in 2015 by Constable

Copyright © Barbara Cleverly, 2002

The moral right of the author has been asserted.

All characters and events in this publication, other than those
clearly in the public domain, are fictitious and any resemblance
to real persons, living or dead, is purely coincidental.

All rights reserved.
No part of this publication may be reproduced, stored in a
retrieval system, or transmitted in any form, or by any means,
without the prior permission in writing of the publisher, nor be
otherwise circulated in any form of binding or cover other than
that in which it is published and without a similar condition
including this condition being imposed on the subsequent
purchaser.

A CIP catalogue record for this book
is available from the British Library

ISBN: 978-1-47211-155-5 (B-format paperback)
ISBN: 978-1-78211-089-3 (ebook)

Typeset in Palatino by Photoprint, Torquay, Devon
Printed and bound by CPI Group (UK) Ltd, Croydon, CR0 4YY

Constable
is an imprint of
Constable & Robinson Ltd
100 Victoria Embankment
London EC4Y 0DY

An Hatchette UK Company

www.hatchette.co.uk

www.constablerobinson.co.uk

For Annie and Roddy and Tony

STOKE-ON-TRENT LIBRARIES	
71682311	
Bertrams	09/03/2015
STO	£8.99

WITHDRAWN AND SOLD BY STOKE-ON-TRENT LIBRARIES

Chapter One

Paris, 1919

'Don't stare, Alice, dear!'

Maud Benson (Universal Companions, Foreign and Eastern Travel Division) shot a glance of concentrated disapproval at her latest charge. Her charge remained wilfully oblivious and continued to turn her head excitedly, drinking in the strange sounds and bustle of the Gare de Lyon refreshment room, still elegant in spite of four years of wartime neglect.

Alice sighed and in pursuit of a world-weary image lay back against the buttoned leather upholstery of the banquette. Like the second barrel of a shotgun, inevitably came: 'Don't loll, dear!'

Alice continued to loll and turned to her companion with a mutinous expression. Fearing that she might just have gone too far (for the moment) Maud said in a placatory tone, 'You need not, Alice, feel obliged to finish your cup of tea. The French really have no idea . . .' The monument of corseted rectitude creaked forward slightly to take up her own cup and, while deploring the dire French habit of putting the water in the pot before the tea leaves, determined, nevertheless, to set a good example. 'Always finish what is put in front of you', even if it is a cup of badly brewed tea.

Alice didn't take the hint but continued to stare enviously at the drink in the hand of the Frenchwoman sitting opposite. Frothy and pink, it fizzed seductively in a tall glass and Maud had no doubt, to judge by the appearance of the woman sipping it, that it contained alcohol. To her horror, Alice leaned forward and addressed the woman. In English public school French.

7

'*Excusez-moi, madame, mais qu'est-ce que c'est que cette . . . er . . . boisson?*'

'Alice!' hissed Maud, bristling with indignation. 'You don't address a perfect stranger! What will she think?'

The woman in question put down the enviable pink drink and, after a moment of well-bred surprise, replied in scarcely accented English and with a charming smile of friendship. 'It is called a Campari-soda. Very refreshing and very French.' And without pause she turned to a passing waiter and said, '*Monsieur, un Campari-soda pour mademoiselle, s'il vous plaît!*'

Alice's face lit up with a smile of guilty delight. Maud Benson closed her eyes and pursed her lips.

They were only three hundred miles into their journey and Maud shuddered at the thought that there were at least seven thousand more to be survived in the company of this girl. Alice Conyers. Time and again she had warned her charge, 'This is France. You're not in Hertfordshire now and the company is very mixed. You should avoid getting involved with strangers. And, above all, avoid a certain type of woman. Yes, woman. One learns to recognize the type. It's easy to connect with such people but not so easy to *disconnect*. A good rule is "never talk to strangers".' She didn't know what more she could have said. And yet . . . 'For all the good I've done, I might as well have been playing the flute!'

Discreetly, she palmed a bismuth tablet into her mouth. A martyr to indigestion, she had learned to take this precaution at the first sign of stress.

Maud recalled the briefing her Principal had given her before this assignment had begun. 'Out of the top drawer, Miss Benson. Rich family. Best of prospects. Your charge is going out to India where she is to assume the reins of power, it would seem, at the head of the family business – I'm speaking of the great commercial house Imperial and Colonial – at least, *half* the reins of power since she is, very sensibly, to share that eminence with a second cousin. Sad recent history – deaths in the family – so you must be prepared for a gloomy little companion, I'm afraid.'

(Maud felt a little gloom and becoming mourning would be preferred to this ceaseless chatter and frivolous curiosity.)

'She is not straight out of the schoolroom, she is twenty-one years old, but has led a very sheltered life in Hertfordshire. Her grandfather's executors have expressed a requirement for a highly dependable and experienced travelling chaperone and naturally they came to us.'

First impressions had been good on the whole. Though pretty enough (and this was always a concern), the girl had appeared sensible and well spoken. Her manners were those of the lady she was and rather old-fashioned. She seemed to have none of that brash giddiness that some modern young girls affected and which could give such trouble on board a P&O steamer. Her wardrobe consisted of entirely suitable clothes in mourning colours of black and grey appropriate to a girl who had recently lost not just her only brother on the battlefield mere days before the war had ended but also her father and mother to the flu the previous year. And, to cap it all, her grandfather, Lord Rupert Conyers, whose death, in the words of the *Times* obituary, 'was occasioned by a fall from his horse while hunting with the Essex and Suffolk Foxhounds' the previous December.

Maud had hoped for an undemanding run through to Bombay but was aware that the major challenge to effective chaperonage was in the three-week-long sea passage. The steamers were crowded with stylish young army officers returning to India from home leave. Many were looking for eligible wives, always in short supply in India. They had charm; they had slim, active figures and a look of suntanned alertness. Maud was well aware of the dangers and, in spite of her clever stratagems and unsleeping vigilance, had presided, in her time, unwillingly, over no fewer than three engagements (one, at least, most unsuitable) during her travelling career and had lost count of the number of broken hearts.

But she decided she need have no fears for Alice Conyers. The girl had confided early in their journey that she had the greatest hopes of marrying her second cousin, at present a junior officer in a native infantry regiment, thereby securing the dynastic future of the firm. A sensible arrangement, Maud had thought. In all the circumstances. Even a pretty and wealthy girl these days found her choice of husband very much restricted. The war had scythed down young men in their thousands and Alice had confessed sadly that she had met no one in England she could regard as a marriage partner. So, with no regrets behind her and a favourable prospect ahead, Maud thought, it should be an easy matter to keep Alice on a straight canter down the course. Provided, naturally, that she could keep 'designing women' – and she felt the description might well fit Alice's new acquaintance – at bay and fortune-hunting men at arm's length.

But Alice had left discretion behind as they had left England. Her first sight of a foreign country seemed to have turned her head. She had insisted on staying on deck on the cross-Channel ferry in spite of the stiff March breeze and had launched into a conversation not only with fellow passengers but even with several of the deckhands. Instead of writing up her diary on the train to Paris she had stared about her asking a thousand questions which had brought Maud's crochet work almost to a standstill. And now they were in Paris and the mere name appeared to work some magic on Alice Conyers. Maud was glad their itinerary had allowed for no more than three days in the capital of frivolity. Alice had spent precious time patronizing the boutiques of the Rue de la Paix when she could have been visiting the Louvre. Here she was, luggage stuffed with who knew what frou-frous, bright-eyed, alert and smiling at the world. Overexcited.

And things were getting worse. They were seated in the elaborately decorated refreshment room of the Gare de Lyon waiting for the Blue Train to be announced. Alice had sighed with pleasure and repeated the names of the towns through which it travelled on its way from Paris to the Riviera and beyond to Italy when the announcer gave them out: Lyons, Avignon, Marseilles, Cannes, Nice, Monte Carlo. She leaned forward to eye the waiters in long aprons down to their ankles as they whisked about deftly delivering plates of highly seasoned and decidedly foreign-looking food to the travellers. And now her attention was entirely caught by this Frenchwoman who had settled down opposite them, sipping her dangerously sophisticated pink drink.

No better than she should be, decided Maud. Travelling alone, what's more, and that tells you something! Typical of a certain type of Frenchwoman and a totally unsuitable acquaintance for Alice. She was wearing a wedding ring on a slim white hand but that cut no ice with Maud. Her clothes were in the height of fashion and at a guess, that dark red travelling coat with its glossy black fur trimmings and matching toque were from the

House of Monsieur Worth. Well, some French had profited from the war, apparently. Perhaps her husband – or protector – was in armaments, Maud thought suspiciously and wished she could convey these thoughts to Alice but the woman spoke good English and was certain to understand. The Frenchwoman extended slender silk-clad calves and neat buttoned ankle boots. Alice tucked her own legs under the table, conscious suddenly of her lisle stockings and lace-up shoes. She turned a defiant face to Maud.

'I'm having a Campari-soda, Miss Benson. Would you like one?'

'No, I would *not*!'

Maud didn't like to see the look of sly complicity which this provoked between Alice and the Frenchwoman.

'Pardon me,' she said. 'I am Isabelle de Neuville and I'm travelling to the Côte d'Azur. And you?'

'I'm going to the south of France too but only as far as Marseilles. I'm picking up a P&O steamer from Marseilles to Bombay. I'm Alice Conyers and this is my companion, Miss Benson.'

Madame de Neuville acknowledged Maud with an unnecessarily friendly bow and then pointed upwards to the ceiling to one of the many florid Belle Epoque landscapes with which it was decorated. Maud had, on entering, advised Alice not to look. '*Voilà*,' she said. 'That's where you're going. The painted lady represents Marseilles. The street you see is the *Canebière* where all the low life and quite a lot of the high life of Marseilles is to be found. That is where your boat will leave from.'

Alice followed her pointing finger, enchanted but a little scandalized by the series of opulent and semi-clad ladies who personified the cities along the route of the Blue Train. They smiled enticingly down at the travellers below, their allure only a little dimmed by almost twenty years of cigar smoke.

'And which one represents your destination?' Alice enquired.

'That one. Nice. And the street in the picture is the Promenade des Anglais.'

'It looks lovely! So full of sunshine and flowers! So southern!'

11

'Yes, indeed. The mimosa will be over now and the magnolia and orange blossom will be out . . .'

Maud decided that this exchange should be nipped in the bud. 'I observe,' she said frostily, 'that you are travelling without your maid?'

'Ah, no,' was the reply. 'My maid is handling the luggage. I hope successfully. But since the war, reliable domestic staff are hard to come by. Do you not find that?'

'Oh, I do!' said Alice. 'And I had noticed that all the waiters are under sixteen or over sixty!'

'Sadly it is the same all over France and not only waiters – policemen, porters, shop assistants, engine drivers . . .'

Two things occurred at this moment to bring this rather limping conversation to a close. On the one hand, Alice's Campari-soda appeared and, on the other hand, Thomas Cook's agent appeared at Maud Benson's side.

'You have plenty of time for the moment, madam,' he said, bowing politely to Maud, 'but you should take your seats. If you would accompany me?'

With relief, Maud heaved herself to her feet and gestured to Alice to follow her. Isabelle de Neuville raised her glass and smiled at Alice. 'To our journey,' she said. 'What do your English flyers say? Happy landings? Here's to happy landings!'

Alice seized the opportunity to taste her drink and annoy Maud further by not instantly leaping to her feet. Under her lowering gaze, Alice took a second sip and a third and though, truth to tell, she did not quite like the bitter aftertaste of the strange concoction, she defiantly drained her glass.

At this moment, sheepishly and with a torrent of French, Madame de Neuville's maid sidled up to her. She was dark, she was slim, she was, in Maud's opinion, unsuitably fashionably dressed for her station in life and she was, furthermore, in a shrill bad temper which she took no pains to disguise. She seemed put out to find her mistress in conversation and, after an initial look of surprise directed at Alice, she favoured her with a hostile glower. To add to Alice's embarrassment at the display and to Maud's gratification, she at once embarked on a furious and whispered quarrel with her mistress.

'There, you see!' said Maud as they followed the Cook's agent down from the peace of the Blue Train bar into the hubbub of the main station. 'Now you see what will happen if you pick up with anyone who may address you. You are abroad now. This is Paris where all the undesirables of Europe congregate. You see the kind of company you're in. Like mistress, like maid, if you ask me! Neither of them better than they should be. Maid, indeed!'

'I thought Madame de Neuville was very nice,' said Alice. 'And what lovely clothes!'

'Clothes! Are they paid for? And, if they are paid for, who paid for them? That is the kind of question you have to ask yourself when you take up with a stranger.'

'Was she,' said Alice, 'do you think, a demi-mondaine?'

She wasn't entirely sure what the words meant but had an image of risk, danger and glamour and at that moment she very much wanted to be associated with it and dissociated from the world of Maud Benson with its careful checks and counter-balances.

'*Demi*-mondaine! Huh! *Fully*-mondaine, I shouldn't wonder,' sniffed Maud. 'Most Frenchwomen are, you'll find. Now, come along!'

On arrival at the train they saw their luggage under the eye of the Cook's man and in the charge of porters in peaked caps and blue smocks loaded into the luggage compartment. They also saw Madame de Neuville and her maid no longer in altercation watching expensive luggage being loaded likewise. Alice made her way in Maud's wake, chirruping happily at the sight of the sleek and gleaming blue painted coachwork of the train, and they were handed by their agent into their reserved seats in the Pullman train under the management of the *wagons-lits* company. Alice was astonished by the elegance. She thought the attentive liveried stewards with their cream and umber kepis the most glamorous thing she had ever seen.

Their carriage was well padded and comfortable. Bobbled curtains hung at the windows, the luggage racks were tasselled. A cushion behind each head had a removable cover. Footrests could be pulled out from under the carriage seats of which there were four. Water-colour views of distant destinations hung on the partitions, a voice tube was connected to the steward.

The Cook's agent settled them in, explaining the hour of arrival and informing them that luncheon would be served from twelve o'clock onwards and that the dining car was immediately adjoining. He spent an unnecessarily long time wishing them a good journey but Maud, fully conversant with the company's advice to travellers that employees should be offered no 'douceur', made no move to reach into her bag. In a mood of increasing defiance and mischief, Alice, with flushed cheeks, extracted from her purse what she believed to be about a shilling's worth of francs and pressed them into the man's hand. He bowed and withdrew.

'I wonder,' said Alice innocently, 'who's going to have the other two seats? They are both reserved, you see. Perhaps it will be that nice French lady and her maid.'

'I sincerely hope it will not! said Maud, scandalized. 'At the very least, though she may have little sense of decorum, it is to be supposed her maid will travel second class.'

Hardly had Maud spoken before, to her dismay, the carriage door clashed open admitting a cacophony of station noises, a cloud of steam and Isabelle de Neuville. She turned, shut the carriage door, lowered the window and leaned out to where her maid, hostile and skittish, stood on the platform. She handed her an envelope. The maid tore it open and inspected the contents with indignation. Maud strained to hear what was being said, deploying her small store of French as best she could. Two or three times she caught the word *'troisième'*. Third! What could this mean? Evidently it caused much dissatisfaction on the part of the maid and icy and hostile resolution on the part of Isabelle. Third class! Of course! Isabelle had consigned her maid to third class.

Maud could understand the girl's indignation. On their way down the platform they had passed the third class carriages. Wreathed in tobacco smoke of a particularly virulent French kind, noisy with loud conversation and shouts of laughter, crowded with large and doubtless garlic-scented men in *bleu de travail*. Not the place for an elegant personal maid from Paris. Second class would have been appropriate. But such it seemed was the case and the maid, with a final imprecation (Maud hoped that the word *'merde'* did not enter Alice's vocabulary),

14

turned and marched away down the platform, heels clicking indignantly.

'Florence! *Elle s'offense pour un rien!*' said Isabelle by way of explanation. 'Very touchy, you know.'

If Alice had met Maud's eye she would have read the message, 'There! I told you so!'

Isabelle de Neuville rallied and turned with polite interest to Alice. 'You are going,' she said, 'to Bombay? For the first time? That is quite an adventure! May I ask what takes you to distant Bombay?'

Before Alice could reply, the door opened again to admit the fourth passenger to their carriage. He was a young man, perhaps in his late twenties, leaning heavily on a stick and wearing dark glasses. He needed the help of a porter to climb the step and find his seat. Any time in the last four years a wounded soldier was a common enough sight but of late there had been fewer as the hospitals discharged their last patients and, such few as there were, they once again received special attention.

The young man muttered an apology in English and repeated it in clumsy French then, obviously overcome by shyness, relapsed into silence and Alice was able to pick up Isabelle's question and reply.

'I'm going to Bombay,' she said importantly, 'because I have business there –'

'That'll do, Alice,' said Maud repressively.

'In fact I have *a* business there.'

'You make it sound very intriguing,' said Isabelle, laughing.

'Not really intriguing. There's a family business and after my grandfather's death it was left to me. To me and to a cousin, that is. My parents died of the influenza last year and though the business should have gone to my older brother, Lionel was killed in France. A month before the war ended.' Alice sighed and for a moment, reminded of her loss, she looked forlorn and vulnerable and her eyes filled with tears.

Maud Benson thought, not for the first time, that Alice's eyes were just a little too large, a little too expressive and far too blue for her own good.

Alice brightened. 'This cousin of mine, well, second cousin really – I'm going out to meet him. I've never met him before!'

'That sounds intriguing too!'

'There are lots of second cousins in the business and I've never met them either.' And Alice went on to describe as best she understood it herself the nature of the family business now, in part at least, hers. 'I don't really understand who they all are. But I've been sent a sort of "Who's Who" telling me who are the – er – *dramatis personae*,' (Alice was pleased with the phrase) 'and who'll meet me and where I'm supposed to go and where to buy clothes.' She tapped a slim leather folder in her lap. 'It's all in here and I'm supposed to read all this. But, really! There's just too much to look at!' And then, naively, 'I'm ever so excited!'

Isabelle received an impression of considerable opulence. She had never been to India but even she had heard of ICTC, the Imperial and Colonial Trading Corporation. She smiled at the excited and, she had to think, slightly inebriated English girl talking with such hope and enthusiasm of her future. So innocent. So vulnerable.

'. . . and there'll be elephants and rajahs, tigers and Bengal Lancers! Indian princes dripping with diamonds! Perhaps I might marry one of *them*!' Alice chattered on.

Maud began to nod off and was unsure how many miles they had covered when she was awoken by a waiter passing through announcing that luncheon was served. The young soldier shook himself and remembering his manners managed to say shyly that he would be delighted to escort the ladies to the dining car if they wished to go. He was smiling to himself as though at a private joke. 'Colin Simpson,' he introduced himself, 'Captain in the King's Own Yorkshire Light Infantry. Rejoining my regiment. For a month or so, prior to demobilization. Silly sort of business but if His Majesty's Government are prepared to pay my fare out and back, I'm not going to complain!' He smiled again. 'My regiment's in India at the moment actually. I too am bound for Bombay.'

Maud Benson could hardly remember a time when she had been so resentful. Her carriage companions had, quite unnecessarily, requested to be seated at the same table and had proceeded cheerfully in a babble of French and English to order every course on the menu. They had even insisted that she drink a glass of wine with the fish and another with the lamb. With predictable results. Two hours after they had sat down they were still at table talking fifty to the dozen while Maud could hardly keep her eyes open. Though unwilling to leave her protégée behind, Maud concluded that, though flushed and clearly over-stimulated, she was safe enough in the company of the rather dull and unglamorous young captain. And his presence would cancel out any attempt on Isabelle's part to engage Alice in . . . what? Maud was not quite sure but thought it might amount at its imaginable worst to – gaming or drinking. And that was most unlikely in the circumstances. In a few hours Madame de Neuville would be out of their lives anyway. Satisfied, Maud made her apologies and reeled back to their carriage to take, as she put it, 'her postprandial forty winks'.

She did not hear the sigh of relief from the three remaining at the table. She did hear the conversation resume at once and with increased animation. Three glasses of wine appeared to have loosened the captain's tongue to a point where he could boast of leopards and tigers, of shikari, of romance and danger to be found in the foothills of the Himalayas.

At the end of the meal, Colin Simpson excused himself and went to smoke a cigar in the corridor. Draining her glass of brandy, Isabelle de Neuville rose to her feet and with a gracious smile made towards the ladies' compartment at the end of the carriage. As she moved carefully along the dining car, it lurched suddenly and she had to steady herself on the arm of a waiter. Thanking him prettily, she turned, laughing, to Alice and called, 'There I told you! Sixteen-year-old train driver!'

Alice laughed back and settled to wait for Isabelle to return.

Whether it was the two unaccustomed glasses of wine taken over lunch on top of the mysterious Campari-soda which was causing the train to sway or whether there really was a sixteen-year-old engine driver at the controls, Alice couldn't decide but the condition was getting worse. Noises were getting louder as the train approached a bend before the viaduct crossing of a deep valley. Swaying and staggering and hardly able to keep her balance, Maud Benson emerged blear-eyed from the carriage.

'What on earth's going on? These French railways!'

Alice passionately wished that Isabelle would return and she took a few paces towards the ladies' cloakroom at the end of the carriage but a sudden lurch threw her on to her knees.

It was clear that something was seriously wrong. The train was bumping and banging against the parapet of the viaduct. It was worse than that. The train had smashed the parapet from which masonry blocks were, one by one, in a percussive series of deafening machine-gun explosions detached to fall many feet below into the ravine.

'Isabelle!' Alice called desperately but the floor came up and hit her. Broken glass shattered round her. A jagged splinter gashed her cheek. The ceiling of the carriage was beneath her and this was the last thing she saw before she lost consciousness.

She was spared the sickening plunge as the Blue Train – the pride of the SNCF – tumbled three hundred feet into the ravine. With an explosion of sound, the engine, pistons still racing, crashed, for a moment to be suspended between the sides of the ravine. But only for a moment. One by one the falling carriages, with a long roll of murderous noise, piled on top and as further sections of the parapet gave way further carriages fell. A despairing shriek from the train whistle continued to mark the death of the Blue Train.

In her carriage, Maud Benson struggled to regain her seat, wondering, as Alice had done, why the walls of the carriage were beneath her, becoming vaguely aware that the luggage rack opposite had buckled but never aware that it was sections of this, snapping with catapult force, that had hit her under the chin, almost severing her head.

Luggage compartments burst open, trunks and cases were spewed on to the ground. The first and second class carriages at the head of the train were little more now than an unidentifiable tangle of wrecked steel. Seat cushions, light fittings, dining-car tables and tablecloths, wine bottles even from the pantry, soon to disappear in a sheet of flame as the galley exploded. The third class carriages at the rear of the train were at first seemingly undamaged until these too were finally pulled by their own weight from the track, through the parapet and into the ravine.

As the flames died and the clanking carcass settled, the

deathly silence was broken only by the hysterical crying of a baby.

It was an hour and a half before the rescue train creaked its way cautiously from St Vincent through the Burgundy hills and came to a stop a careful hundred yards down the line from the collapsed viaduct. The employees of the SNCF, the fire brigade, the doctors and stretcher bearers hastily assembled on the train stood for a moment aghast, looking down on the disaster in the remote wooded ravine below. The Blue Train lay crushed and mangled under the weight of the iron girders and masonry which spilled under, around and above it.

Pierre Bernard, casualty officer, aged sixty-five and overdue for retirement, spoke for all. 'Maintenance! No bloody maintenance! Been going on for years! I warned them! Bloody war!'

The men stared in horror at the smouldering remains of the burnt-out carriages and crossed themselves, unable to speak. They had come prepared to save lives and tend the injured but the deep silence below was warning enough that their task was to be of a more sinister character.

An urgent message was sent back down the line for heavy lifting gear (none nearer than Lyons) and with silent determination they collected picks, spades and stretchers and set off to climb down into the ravine.

After an hour of toil, one baby still alive and unhurt had been recovered along with eighty bodies only from a death toll estimated variously at two hundred and four hundred, and the search for survivors still went on. Coming at last to wreckage which had fallen further than the rest and was untouched by the fire, the searchers caught sight of a lisle-stocking-clad leg sticking out from under a first class carriage. With picks they forced the metal seams apart and extracted the body of a middle-aged woman. Thoughtfully they pulled down her tweed skirt, put her bag and her crochet work beside her on the stretcher and covered her up. The bearers set off to make another slow trek back up to the railway line.

The next body was that of a soldier in British khaki uniform. '*Le pauvre con!*' muttered Pierre Bernard. He looked with distress at the war medals still attached to his chest. 'He survives the war to die like this! Head stove in. Take him up.'

A glimpse of red fabric behind a boulder caught his eye. 'Over here!' he called and the men followed. They stood looking with a sorrow not diminished by the number of corpses they had already handled at the woman lying like a rag doll at their feet. Her back was broken, her head smashed open by the rock next to which it still lay, the red woollen jacket and black fur trimmings sticky with congealed blood. 'Take her up,' said Pierre.

A small sound caught his attention. '*Chut! Chut!* Listen! What's that?'

Again he heard the faint cry. 'Help! Help me!'

They hurried towards the sound. A girl in a torn grey dress was struggling to rise to her knees. For a moment Pierre thought, distractedly, that she was kneeling to pick the spring flowers, primroses and cowslips, which studded the grass around her. This fancy vanished the moment she turned towards them. With a gasp of pity and horror he took in the blood-sodden dress, the mad blue eyes staring, unseeing, in a white face rendered the more startling by the stream of bright red blood which still flowed from a gash on the side of her face.

'Maud?' she said as they gathered round her. 'I'm so sorry! Maud! Oh, where's Maud?'

Chapter Two

Northern India, Spring 1922

Joe Sandilands felt the judder of the train as the brakes were applied. Eager to put the tedious journey behind him, he thankfully rose to his feet to take his hand luggage from the rack. His sudden movement triggered a fluttering response amongst the other passengers in the carriage. The two army wives roused their four children, hot and cross, who stirred about, stretching and yawning and quarrelling sleepily amongst themselves.

Joe helped them to lift down and sort out picnic hampers, toys and crayons and travelling sleeping bags, and his smiling good humour and easy ways with the children were rewarded by effusive thanks and inviting smiles from their mothers. He replied politely to suggestions of attending picnics, dinner parties, fund-raising events and theatrical performances in Simla.

'Are we there yet? Is this the Hills?' asked the youngest child for the twentieth time.

'Not yet, darling. Fifty miles to go. This is Kalka. This is where we change trains and get on to the Toy Train. Then we'll go chugging up into the Hills. Round lots of bends we'll go, through lots of tunnels, up and up into the clouds. And you'll see snowy mountains and huge trees and lots of monkeys! You're going to love it in Simla, Robin!'

'Are you coming on the Toy Train with us, sir?' Robin asked Joe.

'No, Robin. I'll be sorry to miss it but a friend is sending a car to the station to pick me up. We'll have a race, shall we? See which of us gets to Simla first?'

'A car?' said the boy's mother, Mrs Major Graham, raising her eyebrows. 'You have friends in high places then – socially as well as geographically, I mean. I understand that there are only two or three cars allowed to enter Simla . . .'

'The Lieutenant-Governor of Bengal,' said Joe, answering the question good manners forbade her to ask, 'Sir George Jardine, has kindly lent me his summer guest house for the month while I'm on leave.' He waited with curiosity to see the effect the name would have on his audience. In caste-conscious and precedent-conscious India it was always a preoccupation to establish where in the pecking order to place a new acquaintance. Joe was humorously aware that both women would subconsciously have been marking him out of ten. Policeman? One mark only. DSO ribbon, on the other hand – three marks perhaps. Quite person-able and well spoken, perhaps another three. But, borrowing the Lieutenant-Governor's guest bungalow and having a car sent to meet him! Many, many marks! Certainly up to an aggregate of ten. Good old India! thought Joe, reading the by-play and the glances exchanged between the women. He was amused to see their friendly directness now salted with a pinch of deference as they reassessed his status.

The children, supremely unaware of any change in social nuances, pounced on this new information.

'Has the Governor got an elephant?' they wanted to know.

'He has four in Calcutta where he lives in the cold weather but none in the Hills,' Joe explained.

'Will you have to wear your medals all the time if you're staying with a Governor?' asked the oldest boy.

'Oh, yes, Billie. At breakfast, at tiffin, at dinner. I shall even . . .' Joe leaned forward and finished confidentially, 'have to wear them on my pyjamas.'

Round-eyed disbelief was followed by a shout of laughter and the children were still giggling as Joe bounced them out of the carriage and into the waiting arms of their ayahs and bearers who hurried forward to retrieve their families ready for the next leg of the journey.

The Umballa to Kalka train had been crowded with English families fleeing the heat of the plains for the cool of the Hima-layan foothills. In early April the temperature was already unbearable in Delhi and government and military alike were on the move to the summer capital of India. Simla. Joe looked above the heads of the excited crowds milling around him hoping to catch his first sight of the town perched on its spur of the mountains. Though, disappointingly, Simla was still hidden from view he stood for a moment making out the line of mighty snow-capped mountains in the distance beyond the dark foothills, the morning sun striking the summits with a theatrical brilliance, rank after rank and on and up into Kashmir and far Tibet.

Joe had enjoyed the company of talkative children on the long journey from Umballa; he had even enjoyed fencing with their inquisitive mothers but now the pending arrival in Simla – so much looked forward to – was too precious to share. Joe wanted to savour it in tranquillity, and as the crowds swirled away to the Toy Train he found himself at last alone on the platform. Alone that is but for one other passenger. A tall, distinguished, heavily built man was, like him, gazing in rapt absorption at the mountains.

He seemed to be in no hurry; he was clearly not intending to take the Toy Train. He seemed, like Joe, to be savouring this moment. Joe tried to place him in the hierarchy of India. Expensively dressed in a casual linen suit. Not made in England - not made in India. France? No. Joe decided – America. Also, the man himself - English-looking but not English. His silver-grey hair was longer than any London barber would have permitted. Distinguished. Confident and attractive in his frank enjoyment of this shared moment. He caught Joe's eye and smiled.

Joe decided to test him out. ' "A fair land – a most beautiful land is this of Hind – and the land of the five rivers is fairer than all," ' he said.

' "Look, Hajji, is yonder the city of Simla? Allah, what a city!" ' finished the man in the white suit and they looked at each other, in instant rapport. 'I am addressing an admirer of *Kim*, I take it? But how did you guess that I too . . .?'

'I didn't guess,' said Joe. 'I noticed your copy of the book sticking out of your pocket.'

The stranger took out the small leather-bound volume. Balanced on his hand it fell open at a well-read page. 'Need I say? Kim's arrival in Simla!'

'Mine too,' said Joe. He pulled a similar book from his bag and demonstrated. He wondered whether the stranger had noticed the appalling condition of his copy. Every battered page was stained with Flanders earth and candle grease, and peppered with cigarette burns; some were even stained with his own blood. The cheeky, proud and resourceful bazaar boy, Kim, had been his companion through four years in the hell of France and he had never tired of reading it. Kim's spirit had encouraged, even chided him in the depths of despair; the scents and sounds and sights of a hot country he had never seen, nor expected to see, had always seemed able to distance for a while the bleak landscapes and cloying mud of the battlefields.

He looked more closely at the other. There was something familiar about him. Joe had the extraordinary feeling that he knew this man and yet he was sure they had never been introduced. As he spoke Joe's guess that he wasn't English was confirmed. He spoke with a slight accent that was neither French nor Italian. It could have been German but Joe didn't think so. He had a tall figure with a massive torso and carried himself with the confidence of an actor. The man laughed out loud at the sight of Joe's disreputable book and all at once the sound of that laugh triggered a memory. Joe had got it. He recalled a performance of *Faust* at Covent Garden when the Royal Opera House had reopened after the war. Mephistopheles had been played by a Russian baritone. He thought furiously and a name came to him.

'I think I have the honour of addressing Feodor Korsovsky,' he said. 'My name is Sandilands. Joseph Sandilands and I am a detective. From London.'

Another burst of laughter greeted this. 'A detective! You do not surprise me! Are you now going to tell me what I had for breakfast and the name of my tailor?'

'Elementary, my dear sir,' said Joe. 'You were on the Umballa train so you had a chapatti, vegetable curry and a pot of tea. Your tailor though? American? Too obscure for me but I will tell you what you are thinking . . . You're wondering how you would best go up to Simla. You're weighing the advantages of a journey on the Toy Train with its longer route and its one hundred and seven tunnels against the shorter but more precipitous cart road in a bumpy tonga drawn by a wheezing old hack of uncertain strength and speed.'

24

'Quite right, Mr Sandilands.' He pointed to the line of dejected-looking tonga horses standing by to carry passengers in relays up into the Hills. 'I was instructed to take a tonga but I fear my weight would be too much of a challenge. And yet I think the romance of the approach to Simla which I have often dreamed of would be somewhat spoiled by the summer migrants if I took the train.' He nodded to the crowds milling around it. 'And are you going to tell me which I am to take?'

Joe hesitated. This precious moment! This moment of solitude in the impressive company of the mighty hills. Did he want to share it with a stranger? He took a further look at his companion and answered his question.

'Yes. Neither.'

'I am not fifteen-year-old Kim to *walk* the fifty miles!'

'No need to do that. I would be delighted if you would accompany me. We could pass the long journey happily boring each other with quotations from Kipling!'

'Indeed! And how are you proposing to get up there?'

Joe had spotted a groom in the livery of the Governor of Bengal waiting at the entrance to the station, anxiously scanning the crowds. At a gesture from Joe he hurried forward, hand extended, and gave Joe a letter. Joe tore it open and read a note in Jardine's sprawling hand:

'Joe. Welcome to the Hills. This man will drive you to the foot of the town and then conduct you to your quarters. I came ahead of you, you see. Dinner at seven. Theatre at nine. G.J.'

'Packard. We'll go in the Governor's Packard. Where's your luggage?'

Rickshaws and tongas veered out of their path as they motored by at a steady fifteen miles an hour. At this pace Joe calculated that they would just manage to arrive in Simla by mid-afternoon. His fellow passenger settled into the big Packard with the air of one well accustomed to such luxury and even smiled and waved graciously whenever they overtook a pretty woman. He could well have been taking the air in the Bois de Boulogne, Joe thought, instead of trundling along a desert road in a temperature of over a hundred degrees. Man of the world he undoubtedly was, but Joe was amused and touched by the innocent enthusiasm with which he looked about him, curious and joyful.

The few hot sandy miles from the plains to the uplift of land which marked the beginning of the foothills passed quickly in the Russian's company. He was an entertaining companion and talked about himself with a refreshing lack of reticence. He had travelled the world and yet this journey up into the Indian hill country seemed to be a very special one for him, amounting, perhaps, to a pilgrimage.

'You know, for centuries we British have been expecting an invasion from Russia in the north,' Joe said with mock seriousness. 'We believe their armies to be poised ready to rush down through the passes of the Himalayas to sweep the British out of India and snatch it from our grasp. But here – what have we? A Russian invasion from the south? Must we think our guns are pointing the wrong way?'

Another rumbling laugh greeted this comment. 'One baritone does not make an invasion! And besides I come here for two very unmilitary reasons. One, I have been invited to perform at the Gaiety Theatre by the Amateur Dramatic Society of Simla. A great honour! Many distinguished singers and actors have performed there. And secondly, as you must have guessed, I was swept away by the romance of India and especially these hills at a very impressionable age. I was thirteen, of a diplomatic family living in London, when someone gave me a copy of *Kim* which had just come out. From then on, I knew one day I would have to make this journey . . . Listen! Is that a cuckoo? It *was* a cuckoo! And there are the trees!'

Both men enjoyed the moment when, turning a bend, a rush of cool mountain air, faintly scented with pine trees, fanned their faces. The hood of the car was down so, turning their heads this way and that, they had a complete view of the rising ground whose character changed from minute to minute. As they chugged on and up they heard the chatter of a hundred brooks spilling the spring meltwater in torrents down the hillsides. They saw the trees growing ever more plentiful, the few scrubby cacti of the plains now replaced by pine and lush rhododendron. Birds called loudly to each other and Joe thought he spotted the grey shapes of monkeys swinging through the branches of the trees.

They were not the only travellers on the road. They passed strings of Tibetan merchants on foot, men and women of the hills who stopped to gaze in amazement at the car, tongas struggling to make way for them to overtake and a good deal of foot and horse-borne traffic. Loads obviously too cumbersome to be stowed into the narrow gauge Toy Train were being carried up on the backs of men. To Joe's astonishment they passed two men labouring under the weight of a grand piano while a third walked behind carrying its legs. At the passing places when they pulled over they were greeted by cheerful young men on their way back from leave down to the plains by tonga and all asking the same rueful question: 'Hot down there, is it?' And Joe's reply was the same to all: 'Hotter than hell!'

As they climbed higher, the air grew fresher and the scenery more spectacular. Here now began to appear the majestic cedar trees of the Simla Hills, the deodars, their graceful hazy-blue branches dipping gracefully towards the slopes below. Scents grew sharper and more varied. Joe was intrigued by smells unfamiliar and familiar. He breathed in the nostalgic scents of an English garden – lily of the valley, roses, wild garlic and – like a knife to his lungs – was that balsam or wild thyme? Joe and his companion began to feel almost light-headed. The sluggishness and discomfort of the plains fell away and left them light-hearted, merry, celebratory. Rounding a bend, Feodor jumped to his feet, swaying precariously, pointing ahead. 'There it is! Driver - pull over there into that passing place and stop for a moment!'

The driver turned to them, smiling, and announced, 'This is Tara Devi, sahib, and there,' he gestured grandly ahead, 'is Simla!'

A sight Joe would never forget. In the middle distance the town spilled, higgledy-piggledy, down from the wooded summit of a precipitous hill flanked by other thickly wooded dark slopes, and beyond and above it, the lines of the Himalayas shading from green through to deepest blue and iced with a line of dazzling snow.

For a moment Joe was speechless but not so Feodor. 'Now this is an auditorium worthy of a serenade from the world's greatest baritone!' he announced and to Joe's amusement he stayed on his feet, expanded his lungs, filling them with intoxicating

27

mountain air, and with a wide gesture burst into 'The Kashmiri Love Song'.

'Pale hands I loved, beside the Shalimar . . .' Fortissimo his rich voice rolled along the narrow valley, waking flights of agitated pigeons and raising alarm calls from deer and other forest creatures. Joe joined in but found he was laughing too much to continue and, reaching the final line with its swift descent down the scale, he had to trail off and listen in admiration as Feodor's voice, echoing and bouncing from the crags, plumbed the emotional depths of that most sentimental of songs.

'Pale hands I loved, beside the Shalimar.
Where are you now? Where are you now?'

As he held the last deep note Joe almost expected to hear a thunder of applause. Instead there was a thump and a simultaneous crack and the bass note rose, tearing uncontrolled up the scale until it climaxed in an unearthly scream. A second crack cut off the sound abruptly.

Joe's soldier's instincts had hurled him instantly to the floor of the car. Turning his head, he was horrified to see Feodor Korsovsky, thrown back against the upholstery of the car, collapsing slowly across the seat.

'Drive on! Drive on!' Joe yelled urgently at the driver but his driver needed no order. Hardly had the echo of the two shots died away before he had put his foot down and the big car surged forward in a shower of gravel, bouncing across the potholes until it came sharply to a halt in the shelter of an outcrop of rocks. Scrambling up, Joe knelt on the back seat and turned to the Russian who, with arms asprawl, lay prostrate across the back seat. A glance was enough to tell Joe that he was dead and as he tore his clothing apart he saw two neat bullet holes, one just above and one just below the heart.

'Good shooting,' he thought automatically and as he slipped his hand behind Korsovsky to lift him it came away drenched in blood. The entry holes were small; the exit holes had run together in a bloody mess of torn muscle and chipped bone. .303, he thought. Service rifle perhaps. Soft-nosed bullet anyhow.

28

Pallid with alarm the driver turned towards him and, to his relief, addressed him in English.

'Where to, sahib? The Residency?'

'No,' said Joe, thinking quickly. 'To the police station. But first, look about you. Note where we are. Does this corner have a name?'

'Sahib, it is bad place. It is called the Devil's Elbow.'

Without delay the driver let the clutch up and stormed ahead, cornering dangerously to cover the few miles that separated them from Simla. With the driver's hand perpetually on the bulb of the horn, the Packard edged its way, squawking a warning, into the town.

Chapter Three

Police Superintendent Charlie Carter yawned, screwed the cap on his Waterman's fountain pen, stood up and stretched, walked to the door and shouted for tea. He strolled out on to the balcony for a breath of fresh air and paused for a moment, leaning on the rail and looking out with approval at the disciplined activity below him.

His men were changing shifts. One group of police sowars was standing chatting, taking off equipment, and one, formed up under the command of a havildar, was preparing to go on duty. He smiled with satisfaction at their businesslike appearance, their neat uniform and their alert faces. He ran an eye over the line of tethered horses, gleaming rumps stirring and bumping.

Carter wished he could join the patrol but he had to finish writing up the week's report for his Commissioner. Not that the lazy old bastard would bother to read it. And who could blame him? As usual it was almost void of incident or interest. Carter sighed. He accepted a cup of tea brought out to him on a brass tray and made his reluctant way back to his desk. He picked up the threads of his report, his meticulous account of the investigation into an alleged burglary the previous night rolling from his pen in a neat, firm hand.

The reported crime irritated him with its triviality and he resented spending even five minutes recording the fact that old Mrs Thorington of Oakland Hall, Simla, had accused her bearer of stealing a silver-backed hairbrush. It had taken him an hour to convince the old boot that it had in fact been snatched by the usual troupe of monkeys raiding down from their temple on Jakko Hill and gaining entry through a bedroom window which she herself had left open.

A clamour of voices and – surprise – the revving of a powerful engine on the road outside caught his attention. His havildar rushed excitedly into the office announcing the arrival of a motor car, a motor car going unsuitably fast for the tortuous streets of the town. Three cars only were allowed to enter Simla: cars belonging to the Viceroy and the local Governor of the Punjab, neither of whom was due in Simla until the following week, and that of the Chief of Staff, which had just gone to Delhi for repairs. Any other car owner knew very well that the rule was you left your car in the garages provided below the Cecil Hotel. So who the hell was this? Very intrigued, Carter put down his pen again and went out to see for himself.

A large pearl-grey Packard with the hood down roared the last few yards up the Mall, swung into the police compound and braked noisily in front of the police station. Carter recognized the plates and livery of the Acting Governor of Bengal. He recognized Sir George's chauffeur, wild eyes in a dust-caked face, but the two passengers in the rear seat were unknown to him. One, a dark-haired man in a khaki linen suit, had been leaning forward urging the driver on and before the car rocked to a halt he had jumped out and now stood, hands on hips, looking around him, raking the lines of sowars and horses with a searching – perhaps even a commanding – eye.

He was a tall man and carried himself with confidence. He had a brown and handsome face or at least – Carter corrected his first impression – a face that had been handsome. Intelligent, decisive but Janus-like – a face with two sides, one serene, the other scarred – distorted – hard to read. Scarred faces four years after the war to end war were common enough and Carter speculated that he was looking at a man who had taken a battering in France. The second passenger appeared to be battered beyond repair. He was lying sprawled across the back seat, his white jacket soaked with blood.

With disbelief, Carter screwed an eyeglass in position and called down, authoritative and annoyed, 'Perhaps you could explain to me who you are and what the hell you're doing here?'

Unruffled, the stranger turned to look him up and down and replied with remarkable calm, 'Certainly I could. It's rather a long story though. Are you coming down here or am I coming up to you?'

Charlie Carter rattled down the steps, putting on his cap and saying as he did so, 'I think I'd better come down to you and you might start by explaining who this dead gentleman is in the back of the Governor's car. I assume he's dead?'

'Oh yes, he's dead,' said the stranger. 'And you may not believe this, in fact I'm not quite sure I believe it myself, but his name is Feodor Korsovsky and he's a Russian baritone.'

The superintendent looked at him with disbelief. 'That's fine,' he said. 'That tells me everything I want to know. A Russian baritone – of course – how stupid of me and – lying dead in the back of the Governor's car. Where else would you expect to find a Russian baritone? And before we go any further, perhaps you would tell me who *you* are?'

'My name is Sandilands,' he began but he was instantly interrupted by the superintendent.

'Sandilands! Commander Sandilands? Ah, yes, the Governor mentioned your name to me. Told me you were a detective. From Scotland Yard? Yes? Didn't tell me you were in the habit of hauling in your own corpses though . . . This man has been shot?' He turned to the driver who explained rapidly in Hindustani what had happened and where it had happened.

'I offered the gentleman a lift in the car which had been sent to Kalka to meet me. He was the victim of a sniper about five miles down the road. .303 rifle, two accurate shots to the heart. Soft-nosed bullets – the entry wounds you see are quite small but turn him over and you'll find holes the size of your fist. To say nothing of the extensive damage done to the Governor's upholstery. May I suggest,' said Joe, 'that we travel to the scene of the crime? And perhaps we ought to go at once? The driver and I marked the spot. The trail is cold and cooling.'

The police superintendent appeared to consider. 'My name's Carter, by the way. Devil's Elbow. This side of Tara Devi. That's a damned nasty place you're talking about. To search the ground you'd need a regiment. Now, if we were in the Wild West I'd say "Take a posse" and that's exactly what we're going to do.'

He shouted orders, following which six police sowars mounted and led forward two horses for Joe and for Carter. Before mounting, Carter spoke urgently to a police daffadur with a gesture towards the body and the car. The Governor's driver was escorted into the police station to make a statement.

'We can talk as we go,' said Carter as they mounted. 'I've got a vague idea of what happened but tell me, what are you doing in Simla?'

'I'm on leave,' said Joe. 'I'm a London policeman on detachment to the Bengal Police. I was, but now I've finished my tour and Sir George has kindly offered me the use of his guest bungalow for a month. To round off my tour of duty before going back to England. You've probably heard rumours, India being what it is, of what I've been doing in Calcutta?'

He shot a questioning look sideways at Carter. The policeman was struggling to suppress a smile. He had realized that the raised left eyebrow which had been fixing him with a chilling expression of query and disdain was, in fact, permanently fixed at this disconcertingly quizzical angle by clumsy surgery.

'I've heard – and tell me if any of this is wrong – a lowly police superintendent is often at the end of the gossip chain, you know – that you are a highly decorated soldier – Scots Fusiliers, was it? – latterly of the Intelligence Corps and now recruited into the CID. An injection of brains and breeding to shake up the postwar force is what they say.'

Sandilands gave him the benefit of his left profile again but Carter pressed on, matter-of-fact and friendly, 'And that you've had a success in Bengal bringing the force there up to scratch on intelligence gathering, interrogation techniques – that sort of thing.'

'True,' said Joe. 'But, look here, Carter, I'll say again – I've finished my tour and I'm on leave. I've not come here to lecture *you* or get in your way. The last thing in the world I want is to get drawn into this.' But even as he spoke, instinctive reluctance gave way to a rush of anger. Anger for Feodor Korsovsky, so genial, so excited and friendly and so alive. And Joe had heard the last note of that wonderful voice turn to an obscene scream of pain. Yes, it was his business.

Perhaps reading his thoughts, Carter eyed him with friendship. 'I'll tell you something, Sandilands. You *are* drawn into it so you might as well settle down and enjoy yourself. I expect baritones get shot two or three times a week in London but – I'll

33

tell you – it's something of a novelty in Simla. Makes a nice change from rounding up blasted monkeys which it seems is how I spend my time nowadays.'

With the posse closed up behind them they threaded their way through the lower town and out on to the open road, breaking first into a trot and then into a canter. Carter ranged up beside Joe as they rode. 'Tell me something about this Russian,' he said. 'You had plenty of time to get acquainted travelling up from Kalka. Apart from this appearance at the Gaiety, had he any business in Simla? Any friends? Any contacts? Was anyone meeting him? I'm trying to understand why anybody would want to shoot the poor chap.'

'He didn't say anything useful,' said Joe. 'He mentioned that he was in contact with the Simla Amateur Dramatic Society who'd booked his appearance. They'd made all his arrangements, hotel and so on. But I got the impression that it was all purely professional. He didn't even mention a name. He'd taken the engagement entirely, I think, because he'd always wanted to see Simla. He'd turned down a good offer in New York to do it.'

Carter cast a sharp glance at Joe. 'Feller was a *tourist*, are you saying?' He barked out an order and four of the following sowars came forward and stationed themselves in front and on either side of Joe, all scanning the slopes ahead and on each side with increased alertness.

'Ah! You think *I* was the target? And the marksman hit the wrong man?' said Joe.

'Yes, I do,' said Carter. 'Well, it's certainly a possibility. What about you, Sandilands? Any contacts in Simla? Embarrassing connection with a disreputable past? Senior policemen pick up quite a few enemies on their way up. Especially those whose rise has been . . . would the word be – meteoric? So what about that? Something of that sort would be a great help to me, you know.'

'Sorry,' said Joe, noting the man's shrewdness with approval, 'can't supply. The only contact I have is the Lieutenant-Governor and contacts don't come much more respectable than that! No, I know nobody in Simla. And the only man who might take the trouble to line me up on a lonely mountain pass is – I'm glad to say – serving twenty years in the Scrubs.'

'But someone was lying in wait for the Governor's car. You were the expected passenger, weren't you? Was it by chance that you offered Korsovsky a lift?'

Joe nodded.

'Then, don't you agree that it's far more likely that the sniper was lying in wait for *you*?' Carter persisted. 'You were the man he was expecting to find in the back of the Governor's car.'

Something – a remark made by the Russian – was nagging at Joe's mind. He thought for a moment and then said, 'When we met and we were discussing ways of getting up to Simla he said to me . . . something like – "I've been instructed to take a tonga." Yes – instructed. I thought at the time it was an odd word to use. Listen, Carter, someone had told him, and firmly we must assume, to come up by tonga. So your sniper is lying in wait – quite possibly for hours – looking out for a tonga bearing a large Russian singer. He picked a good place. Plenty of cover and a direct shot at the very spot where I expect everyone stops on their first visit to Simla. Tara Devi. You round the corner and there it is, your first sight. And there's even a place where you can pull over and stop to get a better view.'

Carter was listening earnestly and nodding his agreement.

'So, you may be watching out for a tonga but if a car pulls over and a large man rises to his feet and serenades the hills with what is probably the most magnificent operatic baritone in the world, and that man is wearing a white suit and is outlined against a black rock, you've got your man.'

'Sounds reasonable to me,' said Carter but Joe noticed he kept his protective escort in place.

The posse swept on, attracting much attention from the few people now on the road, and rounded the bend before the ill-fated Devil's Elbow.

'We'll stop here and dismount,' said Carter. 'I'll tell off horse-holders – two should be enough – and the rest of us will do a short sweep through the rocks.' He looked up at the sky, judging the amount of light left to them. 'Better get a move on. Where did you reckon the shot came from?'

Joe pointed.

'Right then,' said Carter. 'Off we go! This is what's called a gasht. Pushtu word. Suppose if this were the British Army it would be called "an armed reconnaissance", perhaps even "a fighting patrol". Call it what you will. Equally it could be called "sticking your neck out".'

The policemen formed a line and with rifles at the port set off to sweep into the hills, Carter in the centre, a police jemadar marking the right flank and Joe reluctantly marking the left.

'I don't know what on earth I think I'm doing,' he thought. 'I'm supposed to be on leave, for God's sake! And has it occurred to Carter that of all this mob, I'm completely unarmed? Perhaps I should have said something? Ah, well, too late now.' But a further thought came to him: Feodor had been a nice man – interesting, interested, talented, looking forward to the coming weeks, harmless – yes, surely harmless, and yet someone had shot him. And, so far as he was anything to Joe, he could say that he was his friend for however brief a time. Joe could turn his back on it but – he realized – he had no intention of doing so.

The gasht moved up the hill at surprising speed and it wasn't more than a hundred yards before Joe began to blow. Tirelessly, Carter led them forward. Resentfully, Joe floundered in his wake, glad to be out on a wing, deeming this to be, if there was such a thing, the position of minimum danger. And perhaps that was why Carter had put him there.

After a sweating quarter of an hour, Carter held up a hand to call a halt and redress ranks and at once there was a call from the man to Joe's right. He shouted something Joe did not understand and Carter replied. They closed in together to meet beside the discovery of whatever it might be.

'Perhaps we have a clue,' said Carter. 'Hardly dared to hope for such a thing. Let's see what we've got!'

What they had got was the brass cases of two spent rounds. The man who'd found them was standing still and pointing at them, not, Joe was relieved to see, dashing in to scoop them up in his hand.

'We don't have the facilities to test these,' said Carter, once again reading Joe's mind, 'but we can send them away to Calcutta if it's relevant. In the meantime I'll handle them with care.' And he produced a fold of paper evidence bags from his pack. '.303,' he said. 'You were right. From a British service rifle perhaps.

'And look,' he added, 'here's something else. A cigarette end.'

'Two cigarette ends,' said Joe, pointing further up the hill.

'Black Cat,' said Carter. 'Fat lot of help! Probably the most common English cigarette in India after the Woodbine. That won't tell us much. Now if only it had been a Russian cigarette or an Afghani or a Balkan Sobranie, it might have told us something.'

They peered together at the remains of the cigarettes held on Carter's outstretched palm.

'Nervous type?' said Joe.

'See what you mean,' said Carter. 'They're only half smoked. A few puffs and they've been extinguished. Still, at least we know where the shot was fired from. Line yourself up with the black rock down there. My lady's maid couldn't have missed!'

Carter moved in closer to take a sighting between the rocks. Joe noticed that he was careful, before he did so, to look closely at the ground for footprints or other disturbance. Joe looked too, trying to make out any slight indentations where elbow or knee might have rested.

'Well, that's plain enough,' said Carter. 'See there.' He pointed to two deep scrapes in the moss about two feet apart. 'That's where the toes of his boots rested and over here . . . yes . . . there and there . . . you can just make them out – those depressions are where he placed his elbows. And here's where his knee went. Clear as day.'

'Tall man, would you say?' said Joe. 'Hard to make out, looking at the signs from above like this.'

'I'd say average to tall,' said Carter. 'Taller than me, shorter than you.' He looked along the group of interested sowars who were following developments and selected one. 'Gupta?' He did not need to explain further. The Indian came forward, dropped to his knees and adopted the classic sniper's attitude, lying slightly oblique to the line of shot. His boots fitted the scrapes perfectly and his elbows and knees the depressions.

'Arrest this man!' snapped Charlie.

A shattered silence was followed by loud guffaws as Gupta leapt to his feet in surprise and then joined in the joke. 'Thank you, Gupta,' said Charlie, writing down 'Five feet ten inches' in his notebook.

'Who in Simla would be capable of firing these shots?' Joe began and instantly regretted the naivety of his question.

'Who wouldn't?' said Carter. 'That's our problem. Place is full of Dead Eye Dicks! Army, retired army, tiger hunters – even the women are crack shots! You should see the Ladies Rifle Club at it on the range in Annandale! Still, we'll go through the motions. Get the cases and the cigarette ends fingerprinted in Calcutta then if we should ever have anything so useful as a suspect we can get them tested and do a comparison.'

'At least the cigarette ends tend to uphold the theory that Korsovsky was the intended target,' said Joe.

'How's that?' said Carter.

'Only two of them. How long does it take to smoke two cigarettes? A matter of minutes. I would guess that our killer turned up here thinking he had all the time in the world to prepare himself for the arrival of his target in a slow-moving tonga. Snipers do nothing in a hurry; they like to take up position well before the intended killing time. The time of the train's arrival in Kalka was known, easy then to calculate the arrival to this point of a tonga, but to his surprise and having had no time for more than two cigarettes, up draws a car carrying his target. He's done his job and back home for tea earlier than expected.'

The daffadur listening intently to Joe and nodding excitedly chipped in. 'Yes, sahib, sir, that is very correct. And last year, I remember, the same thing. Here at the Devil's Elbow. The young gentleman who was shot – he arrived by tonga and there was a pile of cigarette ends . . . twelve at least!'

38

Chapter Four

'That was a damned odd remark,' said Joe as they scrambled breathlessly down the hill towards their waiting horses. 'Are you going to tell me what it was all about?'

'Yes,' said Carter. 'You'll have to know what it was all about. The plain fact is that that's the second time that somebody's been shot on more or less that spot.'

'And the victim on that occasion?' said Joe. 'Don't tell me – a Brazilian counter-tenor?'

Carter laughed. 'Nothing so exotic as that, but a strange enough story all the same and a very sad one.'

They mounted and set off together towards Simla, their escort clattering and chattering behind them. Carter took up his story. 'An Englishman coming out to Simla to visit his sister. His name was Lionel Conyers. His sister Alice is a prominent local citizen, a director, and indeed a majority shareholder, I believe, in ICTC. The Imperial and Colonial Trading Company. Very rich merchant family and high up the social scale too. This young Lord Conyers had a very remarkable experience. He was a regular soldier attached to an American unit and he was caught in the retreat on the Meuse Argonne a few weeks before the war ended. Blown up and buried alive. He was only discovered two days later and by the advancing Germans. Poor chap! He'd lost his memory completely. No idea who he was or where he was and can you wonder after all he'd been through? He got hauled away by the Germans, who filed him away somewhere in a POW hospital. They didn't even know his nationality and it was some months before he surfaced again. At last they found out he was British and then by degrees who he was and sent him back to Blighty.'

'That's a terrible story but, sadly, not uncommon,' said Joe. 'I expect his sister was overwhelmed to get him back – almost literally – from the dead?'

Carter hesitated for a moment. 'Not that simple. In fact his reappearance caused an almighty muddle. You see, while he was mouldering in a German hospital he was posted "missing presumed dead". His family at that stage consisted of his grandfather and his only sister – parents both died of the flu just after the war and he didn't even know that. By the time he bobbed to the surface again his grandfather had died and left the considerable family fortune and the business to be shared between his sister Alice and her second cousin. I think she has a fifty-one per cent share in the company, he has forty-nine.'

'I see,' said Joe. 'And what was the reaction of the two directors? What, in law, was their position?'

'See what you're driving at,' said Carter. 'First thing I thought of too. Bad situation. Legal nightmare! Young Conyers seems to have been a decent sort of chap. He wrote to Alice announcing he was still alive and had taken up the family title. He also said he was coming out to see her and would make arrangements for the equitable share-out of the company. He didn't want to snatch it all straight from under her nose but he was damned if he could see why a remote second cousin should be involved. He was proposing to cut him out completely, take fifty-one per cent for himself and reduce Alice to forty-nine.'

'How do you know all this?' Joe asked.

'Alice herself told me. She showed me the letter he'd sent her announcing his arrival in Simla.'

'How did she react?'

'Well, after a period of disbelief (only to be expected, of course), apparently with joy. Her friends say she was thrilled to be getting her brother back from the dead. And then I saw her after the shooting and I can say my own impression is that she was devastated. Lost her only close relation twice, so to speak. She was, I'd say, stunned and incredulous.'

'And where was Alice and for that matter her fellow director when the shooting occurred?'

'They were together. They had by this time married, by the way. And, funnily enough, at the precise moment Alice was out shooting. She's a very good rifle shot but the only target she was hitting at the time was a bull's-eye on the range at Annandale in view of about a hundred onlookers. She rushed off from the competition to prepare to receive her brother who was expected to come up the cart road in about an hour's time. And her second cousin was one of the onlookers.'

'So what do you make of the two killings? Are they connected, do you think?'

'Well,' said Carter slowly, 'at the moment I'm thinking that the two targets are completely unrelated. I'm guessing that we're dealing with a madman. Someone killing for fun. Trying out a new rifle, if you like. What possible connection could there be between a forgotten soldier and the flamboyant Monsieur Korsovsky?'

'Beyond the fact that they were both shot in the same place. By the same sort of bullet?'

'Yes. .303, probably a service rifle in both cases. Calcutta will tell us more. They inspected the first lot of cases as well.'

'And the killer smoked the same sort of cigarette?'

'Yes. Black Cat. Same scenario exactly. Evidence of a tall – five foot ten or thereabouts – sniper though obviously with more time on his hands on the first occasion – all twelve cigarette butts were smoked right down to the end. Well, before I do anything else I ought to report to my chief. I know what he'll say – "Carry on, Carter!" He never says anything else.'

'You're lucky,' said Joe with considerable feeling. 'I wish I could say the same about my superior back in London Town. He'd let me blow my nose occasionally without consulting him but never much more than that. And while you're reporting to your Chief Superintendent I wonder if I ought to go and make myself known to the Lieutenant-Governor, my host, Sir George Jardine?'

'Yes, I suppose you should. He'll want to know. He took a very considerable interest, you might say a surprisingly considerable interest in the death of Lionel Conyers.'

'Did he?' said Joe. 'Did he indeed! Do you know him? I mean, do you know him well? Just a nodding acquaintance?'

'Well, I'm not sure,' said Carter, 'whether a humble police superintendent can have a "nodding acquaintance" with the mighty Sir George! I wouldn't dare to nod! I'd be standing at attention and though I like him I have to say I hardly know him.'

'Well, I'll tell you something,' said Joe. 'He never does or says anything without a motive. Although I was very pleased and grateful for the offer of his guest bungalow, I rather wondered why it had been offered to me . . .'

'And what conclusion did you come to?'

'He's done this to me once before. He hauled me into an investigation down in Panikhat and it just crosses my mind that he may have hauled me into this. Watch developments and you'll see that I'm right. And now I apologize because I'm quite sure the last thing you want in the world is me!'

'You're quite wrong about that, Sandilands,' said Carter. 'I'd be damned glad of somebody to talk to.'

'Well, never forget,' said Joe, 'before we both sink over our heads in this, that Sir George is a devious old bastard!'

And with these words they went their separate ways, Carter – as he put it – to set the creaking apparatus of police procedure in motion and Joe in the company of a police sowar detailed to guide him to the Governor's Residence through the intricacies of the summer capital of the Indian Empire.

Here, Joe found, was no oriental magnificence. There was no concession as far as he could see to India at all. Houses, growing in size as he rode onwards and upwards, might have strayed from Bournemouth or Guildford. The Moghul Empire might never have existed, nor yet the Honourable East India Company. Houses were tile-hung, some even had leaded windows. Balconies and french doors abounded, peaked and decorated gables and, on all sides, bogus half-timbering. House names too, smacked of the English Home Counties: Bryony, Rose Cottage, Valley View, Berkhamsted. Gardens, where they could be poked in on an available flat piece of ground, were abundant with spring flowers and, against a background pine wood smell, they breathed nostalgically of English country rectories.

The sun had sunk now behind the hills and a chill breeze knifing in from the snow fields reminded Joe that he was not in familiar Surrey but in wild country on a remote spur of the Himalayas at a height of seven thousand feet. He shivered and began to think about a hot bath and perhaps a log fire. He urged his horse along, keeping up with the cracking pace being set by the sowar, and noting the landmarks he might need to find his own way to the Governor's Residence. At last he saw a discreet sign for 'Kingswood' and they swung off the main road down a steep lane between crowding rhododendron bushes.

The Governor's house, though undeniably cosy in intent, was large and, within the limits of the architectural manner, impressive. Joe wound his way through the gardens, marking no fewer than ten gardeners at work and noting the servants in their dark green livery by the door. He handed his horse to his escort to return to the police station.

Sir George's greeting when he finally made his way to him was characteristic.

'Where the hell have you been? I've been looking out for you all afternoon! Been doing a bit of sightseeing, have you? Tasting the social charms of Simla?'

'Not exactly,' said Joe. 'Not exactly.'

'It's all right,' said Sir George. 'I'm not deaf! I am, as you may well remember, reasonably well connected. Chaprassis have been hot-footing it between here and the town hall for the last three hours. I understand there's been another shooting at Devil's Elbow. Pick it up from there. But, before you do so, tell me – what did you make of Carter?'

'Not my place to make anything of Carter,' said Joe repressively. 'But, for what it's worth, I thought – good man.'

'Somebody you could work with?' asked George innocently.

'Certainly. But, before we go any further – why do you ask? In fact, you can answer another question if you will – I was very grateful to you for the offer of your guest bungalow but I couldn't help wondering why you had offered it to me.'

'Why? Does there have to be a reason why? Thought you might be glad of it.'

'It didn't, I suppose, cross your mind that you had an unsolved shooting practically in your back garden and that a little input from the Met might not be out of the way?'

Sir George broke into a roar of laughter. 'Well, well, well,' he said. 'There's no fooling Sandilands, as they say at Scotland Yard! You've guessed my secret! Yes, Joe. It did just cross my mind that this affair might be right up your street and in my

43

devious old mind I went one further and thought, He won't be able to resist, and, dammit, from the eager look in your eye, I believe I was right! But, Joe, I say, be tactful. I'm sure I don't need to say this – I'm hoping you'll work with Carter. He's no fool and I don't think his *amour-propre* will suffer but some might resent the suggestion from me that he could do with some help.'

Joe eyed him with exasperation but with amusement too. 'I've been manipulated, I know that. And, of course, Carter has been manipulated as well. His last words on this subject to me were, "I'd be glad to have somebody to talk to." '

'And you don't mind?'

'I don't mind,' said Joe slowly, 'because of Korsovsky. I saw him killed, don't forget. I was the last person to see him alive and, it would seem, the only person in Simla to remember him. And I will remember him. He was an impressive man. Some bastard gunned him down before my very eyes.'

'And you don't hang that on Sandilands and get away with it.'

'I suppose so,' said Joe. 'I suppose so.'

'Know just how you feel,' said Sir George. 'When I was a young man in Persia I got very interested in cock fighting. I had some very good birds. Gave it all up years ago of course but now, if I see a cock fight by the side of the road, I can't just pass by. I have to see what's happening. It's the same for you. Once a copper . . . But now, tell me what happened.'

And Joe gave him an account of the events at the Devil's Elbow concluding by asking, 'Anything in particular strike you about this?'

'Beyond the obvious fact – only this: both men were on their way to Simla. Neither man got there. Someone or some people had an interest in preventing them reaching Simla. Isn't that the fact? Now who could that have been?'

'Or, as Carter believes, a mad sportsman. He said, "Someone trying out a new rifle." I can't accept that very easily. But then it's almost impossible that there should be a link between a Russian baritone and a British officer. No connection between the two.'

'Well, we shall see. And, by the way, I said in my note that we were due at the theatre at nine. It's not yet officially known that

Korsovsky's dead and he wasn't due to perform until the day after tomorrow so I would guess that all goes ahead as planned. Won't be much of an evening, I'm afraid; it's very early in the season and they won't have had much time to rehearse. The Operatic Society are doing a turn or two. Bits and bobs, you know, a sort of review to open the new season – "The First Cuckoo" or "Ragtime in Simla", something of that sort. Look, there's no reason why you should go, Joe. Why don't you recover from the rigours of the journey?'

And to an aide-de-camp entering at that moment, 'This thing at the theatre tonight, James – don't have to go in uniform, do I? Black tie be all right? Well, there you are, Joe. If you want to come – black tie.'

Bathed and changed (black tie, white mess jacket) and after an outstandingly good dinner washed down by two bottles of claret, Sir George and Joe set off together in the carriage, two attendant aides-de-camp on horseback, two syce on the box and one man running in front with a lantern. Joe lay back enjoying the busy glamour of Simla. The whole town seemed to be on the move. Rickshaws, one or two carriages, men in dinner jackets – a few in uniform – women in evening dress and long white gloves making way for Sir George who bowed and smiled absently as they went by, Sir George pointing out the sights.

Joe was enchanted by the strings of electric lights which marked out the narrow and winding road ahead. Dipping and climbing and skirting the pine-clad slopes they looked like garlands on a Christmas tree. A full April moon added a natural illumination to the scene and Joe felt his spirits reviving. He made a polite remark to Sir George on the quirkiness of the architecture of Simla, pointing ahead to the slopes of the Lower Bazaar, clinging like a swallow's nest to the hill. It rose in uneven layers, topped by corrugated iron roofs and dissected by flights of stairs climbing to the Mall above.

'It's a really terrible place, Simla!' said Sir George confidentially. 'Edwin Lutyens – architect chap – New Delhi – had it absolutely right. Took one look at Simla and said, "If one were told that the monkeys had built it, one could only say – What clever monkeys! They must be shot in case they do it again!" '

45

He burst out laughing. 'That really says everything that needs to be said but, all the same, everybody will tell you – when you come up from the plains you feel twenty years younger in Simla. It's not only the fresh air. It's the atmosphere. Irresponsible, you know. An adventurous spirit. Even at my age I feel it. No wonder people go off the rails from time to time when they get here. Most of them come up to Simla with the firm intention of going off the rails! So, my boy, mind what you're about!'

Through the thickening crowd and threading their way though the parade of timber-framed and Anglicized villas, they clattered across the Combermere Bridge and the pale bulk of Christ Church came in sight.

'There's the cathedral for you,' said Sir George unnecessarily. 'People talk about the Anglican compromise – not much compromise about that! It's as unashamedly Home Counties Gothick as you could find. You must go and look inside sometime. Frescoes were designed by Kipling's father. And if you're here on Sunday you must come and saunter about on the terrace amongst the rank and fashion.'

'I'm not expecting to have much sauntering time,' said Joe drily.

Turning a corner they came on the theatre, brilliantly lit.

'Might be a Victorian music hall,' said Sir George. 'Hindu Baroque I always say.'

With a certain amount of flourish the carriage came to rest. A syce went to the horses' heads, ADCs dismounted, carriage doors were opened and Joe and Sir George stepped down into the throng that opened up for them. As they entered the foyer an ADC leaned forward and murmured, 'His Excellency isn't here tonight, Sir George, nor the Governor of the Punjab. You're the most prominent European, I'm afraid, sir.'

'Do I have to *do* anything?'

'I don't think so, sir. Just bow and smile.'

'I spend my whole life bowing and smiling,' grumbled Sir George. 'Still, I suppose I'm paid for it! Ah, good evening Mrs Gallagher. And is this Margaret? Margaret! I would never have recognized you! So grown up, if you'll forgive my saying it. First season?'

Others pressed round him.

'May I present my sister, Sir George? Joyce, this is Sir George Jardine, Acting Lieutenant-Governor of Bengal.'

'Delightful! Delightful!' said George. 'First visit?'

'This,' said an ADC in a discreet murmur, 'is Colonel Chichester's widow who was here last year.'

'Ah,' said Sir George, 'Mrs Chichester! How delightful to see you again! Second visit, I believe? *Third*, is it? How time passes! And may I present Commander Sandilands who is staying with me – for a few weeks, I hope. Eh, Joe?'

Somewhere in the background a not very skilled orchestra was tuning and in groups of twos and fours the crowd dispersed by degrees to take their seats in the gilded boxes which surrounded the auditorium.

'Doesn't look as though they've heard about Korsovsky yet,' said Sir George as they took their seats. 'Wonder if they'll make an announcement? Well, just as long as they don't expect *me* to.'

Joe looked about him. Bright eyes, what his mother would have called 'bold glances', piled hair and silk dresses, white shirt fronts, moustached faces. Every now and then the light was reflected from a monocle amongst the audience. Joe felt himself transported back to a disappearing age. He was aware that, as Sir George's guest, he was the focus of curiosity. 'If I had a moustache, this would be the moment to twirl it!' His eye was caught by Mrs Graham, the companion of his journey up to Kalka, and he greeted her, to her satisfaction, with a conspiratorial wink.

With a few bars of what Joe believed to be the overture to *Aida*, from the six-piece orchestra, the show began. The house lights were turned out and the curtain rose on a one-act comedy played with considerable skill and to much applause by a cast of four.

'Angela,' he overheard from a near neighbour, 'really doesn't look a day over thirty.'

And the acid reply, 'I can sit in the sun and look twenty-one, while she's forty-two in the shade!'

The drawing-room comedy gave way to the Choral Society – 'List and Learn, Ye Dainty Roses' – and to a male voice choir which boomed out the 'Soldiers' Chorus' followed by a floundering cakewalk danced to a jazz record by a coltish group of only slightly embarrassed girls.

'If this was truly music hall fifty years ago, you could have one of them sent to you in the interval,' said Sir George. 'Just mention it to James!'

'Oh, sir! For goodness sake don't!' said James nervously.

'Come, come, James! We must look after our guests, you know!'

The dancing brought the first part of the entertainment to a close. Gossiping and chattering, the crowd proceeded to the foyer. Cigars were lit and, considerably daring, one or two women accepted cigarettes from their escorts. Genial and expansive, Sir George let the crowd wash about him.

The second and main part of the programme was a melodrama with a cast of eight in three acts. It had been a long day and Joe began to nod, losing the thread from time to time of the unnecessarily complicated plot. The applause, however, was warm and people were beginning to stir in their seats and gather up their wraps when a girl came on to the stage and held up her hand. The audience at once fell silent and looked at her with pleasurable anticipation. She was wearing a long, simply cut white satin evening dress with a red rose at her breast. Her hair, caught in the stage lights, was the colour of a freshly minted King George the Fifth penny and hung, shining and loose on her shoulders.

Pretty girl, thought Joe automatically. He glanced at his programme to see who this might be but there was nothing listed after the melodrama. He was turning to Sir George for some explanation when she began to speak.

'Ladies and gentlemen, on behalf of the theatre management committee I have to make an announcement.' Her voice was low and musical and carried well to all parts of the auditorium. This was a girl who was used to appearing on stage, Joe thought. Taking her time, she swept the gilded boxes with a confident gaze, gathering attention.

The audience settled into a rustling, whispering expectancy.

'A tragic announcement, I'm afraid. We've had many distinguished performers in the Gaiety Theatre and all had been looking forward to hearing perhaps the most distinguished of all – Feodor Korsovsky, booked to perform here for four nights this week.' There was a long pause. 'Ladies and gentlemen, I have to tell you that Monsieur Korsovsky was shot earlier today on his way to Simla. He was killed on the Kalka road.'

The gasp and the roar of astonishment that greeted her words drowned for a moment what she had further to say and once again she held up her hand for silence.

'At the moment,' she continued, 'there is little more to say but, in his honour and in his memory, I am going to sing a Russian song.'

The murmur of expectancy and surprise broke out again. An Indian with a stringed instrument in his hand slipped quietly into the orchestra pit below her.

'This song,' she went on, 'should properly be accompanied by a balalaika but Chandra Lal will do the best he can.' She nodded to the Indian who plucked a chord on his instrument. They nodded to each other again in an unbroken silence and she began to sing.

Her voice was untrained and soft but sweet and true. Joe knew enough Russian to make out that this was a lament. A song of sadness at a parting. A song sung, as far as he could guess, in perfect Russian. And perhaps here in the foothills of the Himalayas this haunting farewell was not out of place. It was a song of the mountains, the distant Russian mountains, beyond which a girl's lover had strayed never to return.

The song wound its way through three verses to the soft accompaniment of the strings. Joe was spellbound. Who, he wondered, could this be? Who was this girl, herself overcome by the pathos of her song and with tears, he noticed, running unheeded down her cheeks?

So, after all, someone had been waiting for Feodor. Someone in Simla was mourning him.

Chapter Five

As the last note died away the singer smiled sadly and instantly left the stage. It was clear that any applause would have been out of place and Joe noticed that, so moved was the audience, everyone stayed silently in their seats for a full minute, eyes downcast.

'For God's sake, George,' said Joe urgently, '*who* was that? I want to meet that young woman.'

George rolled his eyes. 'I don't think even James could fix that for you. You'll have to join the queue, I'm afraid. No use going backstage when Mrs Sharpe has just performed! I know, I've tried it myself. You can't move for the bouquets and the strings of eager young mashers waiting to throw themselves at her feet.'

'Mrs Sharpe?'

'Wife of Reginald Sharpe. They're both on the board of the Dramatic Society. And he's another obstacle to intimacy with your little songbird – you'll generally find him backstage like a lurking Cerberus!'

'Look, George, my interest is purely professional,' said Joe firmly. 'I want to know how well that girl knew Feodor and why she was weeping at his memory.'

'Oh, come on, Joe! Don't let your romantic imagination run away with you – there wasn't a dry eye in the house, including your own, including mine . . . but I see what you mean. James! Our guest has made his choice. Help us to hack our way through to Mrs Sharpe's dressing room, would you?'

As steam gives way to sail, the crowds hung back and moved

away before Sir George's majestic approach. Joe followed him down corridors and around to a series of poky little rooms behind the theatre – the backstage of any provincial theatre in the world – where actors and singers were calling subdued goodbyes and closing doors. A tall spare man in evening dress approached them with a questioning smile.

'Reggie!' said Sir George heartily. 'Good to see you! It went very well, I have to tell you. And here's someone I'd like you to meet. Joe Sandilands who's staying with me for the next few weeks. Joe is from Scotland Yard. Pretty useful chap to have around in our present mysterious circumstances! Would you mind introducing him to your wife? I think he has something he'd like to ask her.'

Reginald Sharpe eyed George with, in sequence, irritation, resentment and suspicion but these fell before an imperious and steady gaze down the length of George's aristocratic nose and he summoned up a tight smile. 'Of course, Sir George. How do you do, Sandilands? But look here – my wife is very tired and I'd be grateful if you could confine your, er, interview if that is what this is, to a few minutes only. I'm sure you understand.'

Joe was not quite sure what he was supposed to understand but he managed a sympathetic murmur of agreement. Reginald Sharpe knocked on a door and called out, 'My dear, you have a visitor. From Scotland Yard, no less. Will you see him?'

There was a moment's pause and then the door was flung open. She had not had time to change or to remove her make-up but she had dried her tears. A smiling and quizzical face greeted them. 'Scotland Yard? Good Lord! Was I so criminally bad this evening? And which one of you has come to arrest me? Surely not you, Sir George? How good it is to see you again!'

Introductions were made, with rather bad grace, by Sharpe. 'My dear, may I present Mr Sandilands who is a guest of the Governor? Mr Sandilands, my wife, Alice Conyers-Sharpe.'

With good humour and not a sign of the advertised fatigue, Alice Conyers-Sharpe took control of the situation. Sir George and James and her husband were all dismissed gracefully and Joe found himself alone with the young woman. Alone and, for once in his life, lost for words.

51

'Mr Sandilands? Do sit down over there and tell me why you wanted to see me. Something tells me that you have not fought your way backstage to compliment me on my awful singing.'

'Well, as a matter of fact, I have,' said Joe. 'I was moved by your love song. So was everyone in the audience. But I particularly, since I was with Feodor Korsovsky when he was killed.'

Alice nodded and he understood that the news of his involvement had obviously already reached her. She leaned forward, a look of deep concern chasing away the questioning smile. 'What a terrifying and sickening experience you must have had! It makes me shudder to think that while you were being shot at, while Korsovsky was dying, I was here at the theatre dancing the cakewalk with the Tinker Belles!' It occurred to Joe that she was the first person to acknowledge that he too, though unscathed, had been involved in a horrifying incident. He felt impelled to confide in her.

'It has, truly, left me very disturbed, Mrs Sharpe. I had known Korsovsky for a few hours only but that was enough, I think, to count him my friend. I'm here in Simla on leave but with Sir George's permission – indeed at his request – I'm going to make it my business to find his killer. And, by your reaction on stage this evening, I'm wondering whether you were personally acquainted with him? You appeared intensely moved by your song and your Russian, as far as I am any judge, was perfect . . .'

Alice nodded again and whisked aside a curtain under her dressing table, producing two glasses. These were followed by a bottle of Islay malt and, without a word, she poured two generous glasses and handed one to Joe. As she held up her glass to him in a silent toast he noticed that her deep blue eyes were large and still wet with tears. She sipped for a moment at her whisky before answering.

'I don't find your response at all strange, Mr Sandilands. I too am able to make an instant judgement about people. I know within minutes whom I am going to like, respect and trust. And you are very perceptive! That song always makes me cry. It has many memories for me. It was taught to me by my first singing master – I had a very old-fashioned English country upbringing – and he was a young Russian émigré fleeing from the Revolution. He was the penniless son of a Count from Georgia.' She laughed. 'Nothing very special about that; as far as I can see everybody in Georgia is a Count and all penniless – and he was trying to accumulate enough money to pay for a passage to America. He was the first glamorous man to come into my life. I was fifteen and ready to fall in love. I fell in love. He went to America. And that was the end of it. At least, not quite the end, because I still sing that song and I still weep.'

Her steady gaze had held his while she spoke and Joe was the first to look away.

'Your singing master?' he said hesitantly. 'His name was not Feodor Korsovsky by any chance?'

She laughed again and shook her head. 'No, my singing master was a tenor. But I would have liked to meet Feodor Korsovsky. He might have . . . you will think me very odd to say such a thing, respectable married woman that I am . . . he might have known, have heard of my tenor, might have been able to give me news of him. Korsovsky was much travelled. He had spent some time in America, I understand. Mr Sandilands, I was . . .' again her intense feelings were clear in her direct look, 'I was waiting eagerly to meet him. I am devastated that such a talent has been silenced. I will do anything I can to help you catch the man who has done this.'

'And the man who shot your brother also?' said Joe. 'Mrs Sharpe, forgive my mentioning your previous sorrow but we have reason to believe that the two killings may have been carried out by the same person. They were ambushed in the same place, shot by the same calibre bullets. Can you think of any connection, any connection at all between your brother Lionel and Korsovsky?'

She turned from him to the mirror and rubbed absently at a scar running the length of the right side of her face. 'I have given it much thought. I have no answer for you. What connection could there be but that they were travelling on the same road? There are bandits even in this part of India, you know, Mr Sandilands. Three years ago the train was stopped by a boulder on the line. Five dacoits walked along the line of carriages shooting passengers and robbing them. Carter caught them and there has been no trouble since then but others may try. On the tonga road perhaps.'

53

Faced with his silence, she shook her head and agreed with his thoughts. 'No, it's not likely, is it? I believe, and you will know the truth of this, that no attempt at robbery was made. Very well, here's my serious theory: political killings. You have heard of Amritsar?'

Joe nodded. The shooting down of over three hundred peacefully demonstrating Indians by British troops three years earlier in the town of Amritsar had been a scandal that had reverberated throughout India and Britain.

'Amritsar is not all that far from here. Someone may be seeking revenge on the British. Any British. My brother with his fair hair would have been an obvious target and Korsovsky looked British from a distance. And last month,' she hesitated, wondering how wide Joe's knowledge of the Indian political scene might be, 'last month, you may have heard that Mahatma Ghandi was sent to jail. For six years. On what many consider to be a trumped-up charge. He has many friends in Simla, Mr Sandilands, amongst whom he counts no less than the Viceroy, Lord Reading, and Lady Reading. There are both English and Indians who might try to voice their disapproval of such a sentence in a telling manner.'

'But Ghandi abhors and rejects violence, doesn't he?' Joe objected.

'Yes, indeed, he does. But one cannot always control one's supporters. And there are many in India who are ready to stir up trouble for the British by any means at their disposal. Even these green hills, Mr Sandilands, could prove to be the slopes of a sleeping volcano. The population of Simla in the summer months is forty thousand. And do you know what proportion of these are European?'

Joe shook his head.

'Four thousand. And it is the same all over India. There are millions of Indians who have never even set eyes on a white face. You could say we only scratch the surface of the continent. And, like an irritant flea, we could be swept away with one flick of our host's finger.'

'Any moment now,' thought Joe, 'she's going to start lecturing me on the Indian Mutiny.' Aloud he said, 'I'll bear this in mind, Mrs Sharpe. But I'm reluctant to begin to form any theories until I've seen the forensic evidence, however slight it may be, gathered from the scene of the crime. And this I will do tomorrow with Carter.'

'I expect you would like to see me again?' she volunteered.

Joe was taken by surprise. Her tone had been almost flirtatious. He was unaccustomed to his interview subjects requesting a second session.

She laughed, again, he suspected, reading his thoughts correctly. 'I'm sure you'll need to ask me if I was responsible for my brother's death . . . where I was at the moment he was killed . . . how I may have profited from it and so on. When you've learned all you can from Carter why don't you come to see me at my place of work – it's just off the Mall.'

'Your *work*?' said Joe.

'Oh, yes. I work, Mr Sandilands. I work hard. I am a director of a big – a very big – international company. It's based in Bombay but I prefer to run things from Simla in the summer. Now we have telegraph and telephone such an arrangement is not out of the question. Heavens! They run the whole of the Indian Empire from here for seven months of the year, one business is nothing in comparison! Take a rickshaw – all know where to find me.'

And, with a dazzling smile and an unambiguous gesture she managed to convey without any possibility of contradiction that the interview was at an end.

Much puzzled, Joe returned to the auditorium, still full of chattering people reluctant to disperse. Sir George, accompanied by James, was still holding court. Over the heads of the crowd and discreetly watching, Joe caught the eye of Carter and made his way to him.

'Well?' they both said together.

'One or two things here,' said Joe, 'which – I don't know if you agree – we really ought to talk about. When can we arrange to do that?'

'I was going to say the same thing. Look, why don't we meet again tomorrow? Go over some of the evidence with me. And, to take this thing away from the cloak of officialdom, why don't you come and have tiffin with us? Apart from anything else I'd like you to meet my wife.'

'I'd like to meet your wife. Let's do that.'

'Any rickshaw will bring you to my house.'

'I was going to say,' said Sir George as they remounted the carriage together, 'I think the time has come for a further conference with Carter but if I well understood what you and he were saying to each other just now, it seems as if that may have arranged itself. Am I right?'

On return to Sir George's residence it became clear that he and Joe had very different ideas as to how the next hour or so should be passed. Hospitable and expansive, Sir George could see no reason why they should not between them discuss the day's events over a bottle of port. Joe, nearly dropping with tiredness, wasn't even sure that he had the strength to fall into bed and he had some difficulty in convincing Sir George of this. He was suffered at last to retire to the manifest comforts of the guest bungalow.

'It's been a damn long day,' he said apologetically and, indeed, he could hardly believe that it was in the same day that he had driven up the Kalka road with Korsovsky. But the guest bungalow when he finally reached it was everything he could have asked of comfort and luxury. His clothes had been unpacked, his bed was ready, an eiderdown lay across it as a precaution against the cold Simla nights. There was even electric light. Joe fell into bed and into a restless night. Dreams and visions troubled him and more than once he woke with a shock believing himself to be hearing once more a double shot from behind encircling boulders. Visions of Alice Conyers-Sharpe perpetually intruded between him and sleep and, following him into his dreams, she bent over him, her hypnotic eyes fixed on his. 'Find him!' she said. 'You've got to find him!' Alice faded and he was climbing with Carter a sliding scree slope from which stones fell booming into an abyss below. 'Find him!' said Carter.

Twice he got out of bed to stand by the window looking down on silent, moonlit Chota Simla to the south. A very distant dog and only a somewhat less distant rattle of a trotting horse broke the silence. From Sir George's garden came the faint fragrance of jasmine and lily of the valley. He drained the carafe at his bedside, appreciating the chill water and, thankful for the absence of a mosquito net, he fell, finally exhausted, into sleep.

It was a bad night but what Sir George's staff thought suitable for breakfast went a long way to compensate for it. There was a plate of porridge, there was a rack of toast, four rashers of bacon and two fried eggs and, inevitably, a pot of Cooper's Oxford Marmalade together with an urn of coffee that would adequately have supplied the officers' mess of a small regiment. Heartened by this and grateful for the clean clothes that had been laid out for him, Joe was preparing to set off on a voyage of exploration round Simla but his eye was caught by a note from Sir George.

'If you look in your spare room, you will find your luggage and that of Feodor Korsovsky. My car has been released to me by the police and these items were with it. I thought you might like to go through his things. Carter has had a preliminary rootle around. He sends you the keys and invites you to do the same. I suppose, in due course, it will all have to be returned to K's next of kin (whoever that may turn out to be) but in the meantime you and Carter may be able to glean a thing or two. Come and see me when convenient. I shall be out all morning and certainly for the first half of the afternoon. Dinner perhaps?'

Joe was impressed. Among his mental list of things to do had been the question of the whereabouts of Korsovsky's luggage but, predictably and characteristically, Sir George was one jump ahead of him. Joe looked at his watch. Nine o'clock. He wondered at what hour officialdom in Simla got to work.

There were two large cases. Expensive luggage, Joe noticed, with a Paris label. The clothes were mostly French apart from the dinner jacket which was made in New York and the shirts which were made in London. The shoes were hand-stitched and barely worn. Amongst the toiletries was a bottle of bay rum from a barber in Duke Street, St James's. An expensive set of lawn handkerchiefs came from a haberdasher in Milan; in a black metal box was a patent safety razor from New York with a packet of razor blades, each bearing the portrait of King C. Gillette, claiming to be the inventor. It was the luggage of a very much travelled and incessantly travelling man. But the collection was curiously impersonal and was answering no questions.

Joe took out each item carefully and piled everything neatly on the floor. At the very bottom of the first trunk were one or two books and underneath that a layer of newspaper. Joe examined the books carefully, shaking them to dislodge any papers which might be hidden between the pages, but the well-worn copies of *War and Peace* in Russian, *Les Trois Mousquetaires* in French and *Plain Tales from the Hills* in English yielded up no secrets. Dutifully Joe looked at the yellowing newspaper. A French national paper, *Le Matin*, and a date in 1919. But more, evidently, than just a lining for the trunk.

A short handwritten message in French in the margin said, 'Feodor – as promised. I can't tell you how sorry I am.' And there followed initials so flamboyant as to resemble a coat of arms. G.M.? Joe thought back to his journey with the talkative Monsieur Korsovsky. He had mentioned his agent . . . Gregoire, was it? Gregoire Montefiore . . . something like that. He wondered what the agent could possibly be apologizing for. He glanced at the headlines. The French Minister for Finance was announcing strict measures to control inflation. A severe frost had decimated the vines in the Rhone Valley. Miracle baby, six-month-old orphan Jules Martin, was once again in the arms of his grandmother.

Fighting the temptation to dip deeper into three-year-old news Joe turned to the inside page where he knew he would find the Arts Diary. Yes, there it was. An article about Korsovsky. He read it quickly. After his phenomenal success in New York and New Orleans the singer was to return to Europe where he was booked to appear at the reopening of the Covent Garden Opera House in the autumn. And – a treat for French music lovers who had, after all, been the first to recognize his talents – he was to give three summer recitals in the Roman theatres of Provence.

Was this what his agent was apologizing for? It looked like a case of enthusiastic overbooking to Joe. He replaced the newspaper in the bottom of the trunk and continued his search.

Looking more closely at the trunks themselves, he noticed that under the lid of the second was a slim compartment built into the lining. He slid in a hand and took out a leather satchel containing a leather writing case. A leather writing case with Russian writing on the cover and embossed with a coat of arms. This once smart and very expensive item was the only thing which showed any signs of wear. It was, indeed, much used. On a small chain in the satchel was a key which fitted and Joe opened the writing case and took it over to the window. He settled down to go through the contents.

There were several letters of recent date still in their envelopes. There was a photograph of a family group. A bearded man, a smiling woman in a large sun hat and a little boy in a sailor suit who by a small stretch of the imagination could have been Feodor himself. There was a group photograph by a professional photographer of an operatic cast. *Rigoletto*, Joe decided after a little examination. There was a family group on a seaside terrace with a large house in the background and now Korsovsky appeared to have been joined by a younger brother and a baby in his mother's arms.

Joe took the letters one by one from their envelopes. These seemed to be letters from his agent bafflingly written in a careless mixture of Russian and French and signed with the flourishing G.M. But there was one letter with a Simla postmark. On headed Gaiety Theatre writing paper an official and impersonal typed message confirmed the arrangements for the recital. It referred to terms agreed in previous correspondence, politely said how much they were looking forward to his visit and how honoured they would be by this. It concluded with the words: '. . . you should leave the train at Kalka and come on by tonga. The Toy Train (!) is really *not* to be recommended at this time of year and is likely to be very crowded. Yours sincerely . . .' A signature he couldn't read followed.

What had been Korsovsky's words? 'I was instructed to proceed by tonga.' This, presumably, was the instruction. The instruction which had led him to his death.

'I wonder who the devil signed this?' thought Joe.

The old programme with its wine-stained front looked so ordinary Joe nearly thrust it back into the leather case unexamined. Professional procedure stayed his hand and he looked at it more closely. A performance of Rossini's *The Barber of Seville* staged in the Opera House in Nice in March 1914. With a flicker of interest Joe wondered why Korsovsky would have carried around with him just one of what must be dozens of programmes bearing his name in a starring role, a dog-eared eight-year-old programme.

He opened it, noting that the part of Figaro had, as he had guessed, been played by Korsovsky. The part of Rosina was taken by a soprano, unheard of all those years ago but now one of the glittering names on the London and international stage. But it was not the printed programme which held his attention. It was the handwritten message scrawled across the top. A message in an exuberant girlish hand. It was a quotation from the opera. The first six lines of Rosina's most famous aria 'Una voce poco fa' were copied out in the Italian but one slight alteration had been made to the text. Joe translated:

> The voice I heard just now
> Has thrilled my very heart.
> My heart already is pierced
> And it was Lindoro who hurled the dart!
> Yes, Lindoro shall be mine,
> I've sworn it! I'll succeed!

The original name 'Lindoro' had been crossed out and 'Feodoro' substituted.

'Feodoro shall be mine!' Joe mused, much intrigued.

He sat back on his heels and reflected. The message was unsigned. And surely that was unusual? In his experience girls finished off a note of such intimacy with an initial at least. Or a jokey nickname. The exuberance and youthful confidence chimed badly with this note of discretion. What had been going on? A clandestine liaison? Very likely. But an important one to the man who had carried it around with him in his trunk for eight years. He wondered who she could have been. Eight years ago in her prime or young – the writing gave the impression of youth – the lady would be in her late twenties now, possibly early thirties. Korsovsky himself, he guessed, must have been in his forties when he died. Perhaps his passport would tell him more and that would be in his notecase which undoubtedly Carter had taken from the body and kept.

Aware of the weight of material the case was now beginning to engender, Joe got to his feet. He put the programme, the photographs and the letter from the Gaiety Theatre back into the leather case and pushed it into the inside pocket of his khaki drill jacket. Deciding that the theatre would be his first call and that his approach should be a bit anonymous, he waved aside the Governor's rickshaw and set off to the town on foot.

He paused outside the Gaiety and thought how raffish and down-at-heel it seemed, like all theatres, in the daytime. The play bills announcing Korsovsky's recital had been torn down already, dustbins full of waste paper were being hauled away by teams of Indian sweepers, and others were clearing the pavings of cigarette ends and cigar stubs. With a general hangover air the doors stood open on a dimly lit interior. Finding no bell and no knocker, Joe walked in and called, 'Anybody there? Hello!'

Impatiently a figure in shirt-sleeves emerged from the booking office and Joe recognized Reggie Sharpe.

'Morning!' he said affably.

Reggie Sharpe looked him up and down. 'Yes?' And then, 'Oh, it's you, is it? Sanderson? Can I help you?'

'Yes,' said Joe. 'I think you probably can. We met last night. Commander Joseph Sandilands of Scotland Yard . . .'

Reggie Sharpe looked at him with considerable distaste. 'Can't give you long,' he said. 'So make it as short as you can. What can I do for you?'

'Well,' said Joe, not prepared to be patronized, 'what I have to ask might be confidential. I don't really choose to discuss murder in the foyer and in the presence of,' he waved an explanatory hand, 'half a dozen sweepers.'

'You'd better come in,' said Reggie Sharpe reluctantly. With ill grace he opened the door of the booking office and with an ostentatious glance at his watch he took the only chair, offering Joe a small stool. 'Now what's all this about?'

'You may know –' Joe began.

'Well,' said the other, 'I'll save you a bit of time and tell you what I *do* know. You're a policeman, though God knows what you're doing in Simla! I understand that you're acting with the approval of Sir George though again I can't imagine why and I imagine you are in concert with Carter investigating the death of the unfortunate Korsovsky. And I've yet to discover what on earth you think I will be able to tell you.'

'Perhaps I can help you. Korsovsky didn't just happen to be in Simla. His visit must have been arranged a long time ahead. There must be some correspondence between the theatre and him or between the theatre and his agent. There are two theories as to the cause of his death – firstly that it was a random shooting and has no connection with the former assassination of Conyers, and the second theory is that he was expected; someone was lying in wait for him, someone who knew his movements well enough to mount an ambush, and the information I need might conceivably emerge – to some extent at least – from any correspondence you or the theatre might have had with him. Perhaps you could enlighten me?'

Sharpe extended an angry hand and picked up a slender file of papers. 'You're welcome to look through this. It is – such as it is – the letters we exchanged with Korsovsky.'

'May I take this away?' Joe asked.

'I'd very much rather you didn't.'

'I don't need to but I wanted to spare you the boredom of sitting in silence while I read through them. Just as you like, of course.'

He began to thumb through the letters of which there were half a dozen going back about a year and opening with a letter from Korsovsky himself saying that he had always wanted to visit Simla and with due notice this might be arranged. Across the bottom of this was written 'Acknowledged' and a date. The next letter was from Korsovsky's agent naming dates and making tentative reference to terms.

'Considering his eminence, this is a very mild offer he was making you, isn't it?' Joe asked.

'Well, we certainly thought so. The Gaiety can't in the ordinary way begin to afford a man of his stature but I think it was true that for some reason unknown he wanted to come to Simla and was prepared to do it for a very modest fee.'

'I think I can explain that,' said Joe. 'He was passionately interested in *Kim* and carried the book about with him. He wanted to see where it all happened and that may have been reason enough.'

'Huh! Another one of those,' said Sharpe disparagingly. 'Kipling fans are as thick as sparrows on the ground in the season.'

'Can you suggest another reason?'

'Certainly not,' said Sharpe. 'It's no part of my job to interpret the vagaries of spoilt operatic stars.'

'No part of your job? Do you have a job? I mean – what is your concern with the management of the Gaiety?'

'I'm vice chairman. The chap who does all the work. Except that I don't in fact. My wife Alice. She's the one with the real interest in the theatre – handles the bookings, dictates the letters, checks the finance is in order. That sort of thing. You should be talking to her – I just come in one day a week, sign the letters and the cheques. You're lucky to have caught me.'

Joe was listening for any nuance of resentment or even of pride in his wife's achievements but there was none. His tone was straightforward and matter of fact.

'Your wife seems to be a busy lady . . .'

'This is just a small part of what she does. She has many irons in the fire. Talented woman, my wife, as all will tell you.'

'Do you type your letters or do you write them in longhand?'

'Sometimes one, sometimes the other. If it's important – type. If unimportant – write.'

'You, or someone,' said Joe, 'would have written to Korsovsky clinching the arrangement. Do you have a copy of that letter here or would that not have been a typed letter?'

'Certainly. Yes, it would have been typed. I think I can almost say I remember typing it myself. It'll be here somewhere.'

He took the file from Joe's hand and riffled through the papers. 'Yes, here it is.'

Joe read a carbon copy of a letter confirming arrangements for train and hotel bookings that had been made on Korsovsky's behalf, the letter concluding with the words: '. . . and again we would like to express our gratitude that you should be undertaking this trip to Simla. We are looking forward so much to hearing you perform.' It was followed by a clearly readable signature 'R. Sharpe'.

Joe produced the letter from the leather case and showed it to Sharpe.

'Good Lord!' he exclaimed and pointed to the ending of the second letter.

'You see that the two letters are in a vital particular not identical. If you typed this letter why did you advise Korsovsky to come by tonga and not by the train?'

Sharpe seemed genuinely astonished and genuinely at a loss

for a word. 'Just a moment,' he said in tones of excitement. He took up a fountain pen from his desk and a sheet of paper, signed his name and held it out to Joe. The signature was exactly like the one on the carbon copy and in no way resembled the letter from Korsovsky's writing case. 'Compare the two. Identical typewriters, identical text until you come to this last bit about the tonga. It's clear somebody wanted him to come up the cart road in a tonga but that somebody wasn't me! Somebody who had access to the Gaiety writing paper . . . That wouldn't be difficult – we're not very careful about such things. Why should we be? Who would expect something like this to happen?'

'Look at this signature,' said Joe. 'Anything familiar about it?'

'Indecipherable, wouldn't you say?' Sharpe held it to the light. 'Obviously meant to be indecipherable, for Korsovsky's eye only.' He was silent for a moment then, 'Blue-black ink, broad-nibbed fountain pen,' he said. 'Could well be my own. I leave it here on the desk. Look, Sandilands, someone could have got in here . . . when? . . . last November the letter's dated – before we all went back down to Bombay . . . typed this second letter and suppressed the first which would have been left out for posting. Perhaps they didn't even bother but just added a note to say this second supersedes the first and then they took it along to the post office. But from last November – is anyone going to remember who was in and out? It's a busy time – packing up and tying up loose ends. Lots of people in and out all day, every day.'

'Good Lord,' said Sharpe in surprise after a pause. 'Doing your job for you! Do you want me to put my own handcuffs on too?'

'That won't be necessary,' Joe smiled. 'For the moment at least. You're being very helpful, Mr Sharpe. And now, before I leave, just one more question. Can you tell me where you were yesterday between noon and five o'clock?'

'Let's see.' Reggie sighed and flipped a page in a diary lying on his desk. 'Tiffin with friends over at Mount Pleasant – Johnny Bristow's place. I keep a horse or two over there – they've got good stabling. And then they gave me a lift over to Annandale to look at a horse I was thinking of buying off Brigadier

Calhoun. Thought I could sell it on to Effie Carstairs and make a few bob on the deal. Didn't buy it. It was tubed. Made a noise like a fire engine! Took a tonga back to the theatre and got back here in time for the four o'clock run-through.'

Joe made a note of the names he mentioned and the times and closed his notebook. Leaning forward, he tweaked the Korsovsky letter from Sharpe's fingers and replaced it, along with the carbon copy, in the leather case. 'I'll keep this to show to Carter but I don't believe we need to take away the rest. Keep them available, won't you? Good morning Sharpe.'

He paused at the door and looked back to see Sharpe riffling thoughtfully through the file.

'Oh, by the way,' he said with an apologetic smile to excuse an unimportant afterthought, 'did you have any pictures, any photographs of Korsovsky? Did he or his agent send you any material in advance of the concert? To be used in posters, perhaps?'

'No. None that I am aware of. We wouldn't have the resources for that sort of publicity anyway. This isn't Paris, you know, with a Toulouse Lautrec and a printing press round every corner.'

'Well, as far as you're aware, is there anyone in Simla who would recognize him – perhaps, er, lend a hand with identifying the body? Anyone familiar with his features?'

'Not that I know of. Everybody knows his name, of course, and is aware of his reputation . . . People do go on leave, you know. Someone may have seen him on stage in London or Paris if he was performing there but no one's mentioned it. You'll just have to ask about, won't you? But then,' he added thoughtfully, 'he'd be in costume and make-up, wouldn't he? No, shouldn't think anyone would know him from Adam.'

The smirk faded from his face as he saw the implication of his words. His eye brightened, the scorn replaced by calculation as he drawled, 'Well, well, well! No one had any cause apparently to shoot down a visiting singer and no one had any means of identifying the said singer . . . but what about a visiting *detective*, a detective whose features are, it would seem, known to the highest in the land? As I understand it, Sandilands, you were sitting right next to the poor chap when someone popped him.

Now if I were you, I'd be going around grilling people to find out who knew *you* were coming up that hill! You could start with Sir George, couldn't you?'

Joe smiled and withdrew. Sharpe had told him all he wanted to know.

Chapter Six

Stepping out into the road, Joe hailed a rickshaw and gave instruction to go to 'Carter Sahib's house'. As Carter had predicted, no further instruction was required and the rickshaw proceeded to wind its way into the complicated heart of residential Simla. Houses clung to the steep side of the rising hill to the north of the town and, consulting the map Sir George had provided, he guessed this hill to be Elysium. Some houses were supported on posts, some relied on what seemed to Joe to be alarmingly ambitious cantilevers. All were surrounded by dense and prolific gardens and all, he supposed, enjoyed the superb view which opened up behind him as he progressed.

The lanes approaching these houses were narrow and several times his rickshaw had to stop and edge into the hillside as they met another coming in the opposite direction. Joe was not small, the rickshaw men were. Embarrassed to be conveyed in this way, Joe marked this with what he knew to be an over-lavish tip, greeted to his further embarrassment by a pantomime of subservient gratitude.

Carter's house when he stood before it was the epitome of Simla domestic architecture. Corrugated iron roof, painted red, two – or was it three? – verandah terraces, a profusion of climbing plants and two small, sandy-haired children digging in a sand pit under the eye of the mali. They acknowledged Joe's greeting with shy smiles and Carter's wife emerged to welcome him.

So English did she look, Joe could not suppress a smile. Sandy hair, blonde eyebrows, small bright blue eyes, freckled face and a cheerful and very English voice. Pausing only to shout an instruction over her shoulder in Hindustani, she held out a welcoming hand. 'Very pleased to meet you, Commander! Heard such a lot about you from Charlie and I can't tell you how pleased he is to have you on board! I suppose he's in charge of the investigation but it isn't often that he has a New Scotland Yard Metropolitan Police Commander under him! I say – make the most of it – it'll never happen again! All the same, you must be hot. Let me give you a drink. We'll be eating in about half an hour. Will that be long enough for you? I'll try not to be indiscreet but there's lots of things I want to ask and sometimes I think I'm married to a clam! Are you married?'

'No,' said Joe. 'Just as well perhaps, because I don't think I'd be a very good clam.'

'Good,' said Meg Carter, 'that suits me but come in here.'

She showed him into a small office of a type with which Joe was becoming familiar. Ragged files on shelves, noisy overhead electric fan, water in a water cooler, Benares brass ashtray, group photographs on the wall – it was standard Indian equipment.

'Come in! Come in!' said Charlie Carter. 'Sorry not to have been there to greet you. Didn't hear you arrive. Come and sit down and tell me where you've got to.' He pushed a cigarette box towards Joe. 'I've cabled his agent and prepared a press release. I'll have an autopsy report this afternoon confirming the cause of death and the Coroner has it in hand too. We have a problem though . . . who to identify the body? Who knew him? I've arranged for him to be photographed and I've examined the body for distinguishing features. (None incidentally.) There must be a next of kin somewhere . . .' He paused and ran a worried hand across his face.

'I've had a preliminary search through his luggage,' said Joe. 'Found this hidden in a compartment in the lining.' He produced the leather case. 'Here, we have photographic evidence of possible next of kin – a brother and younger sibling. Presumably his agent will know where they are.'

'Well, that's a start. And there's the question of a funeral. He can't just lie in the morgue for ever and we can't just shovel him underground – he was, after all, an international figure.'

'See your problem . . . should be massed choirs, banks of flowers . . .' Joe's voice trailed away.

'We don't have much in the way of refrigeration here. We must

68

talk to Sir George. These are deep waters for a country bobby like me!'

'And me! I have no real authority in the case at all. And I have to confess to you that I undertook to interview Sharpe this morning. Hope I haven't muddied the waters.' He set out his suspicions and talked his way through his recent interview with Sharpe, collecting his random thoughts as he did so. When his account reached its conclusion Carter rose and took a pace or two about the room.

'That was well done. I don't know if you agree with me but surely the most significant thing you've turned up is this change in the confirmation letter directing the poor sod to come by tonga. Find the man who did that and we've found out something which could hang a man.'

'I'm seeing Alice Sharpe again this afternoon,' said Joe. 'I may be able to glean a bit more. I gather from her husband that she's the real driving force in the theatre. She may have her own suspicions.'

They talked on until the khitmutgar summoned them to the table.

'We eat on the terrace. I hope you don't mind?' said Meg Carter. 'I never tire of looking at the view and it's nice to sit in the breeze. And anyway, our dining room is dark and our dining-room furniture repulsive.'

'Not repulsive,' said Carter defensively.

'Oh, Charlie, it is! It was old and repulsive before when we bought it off Brigadier Robinson, since when it's had six years of attention from these two.' She waved a hand at her two daughters who were sitting politely side by side with their napkins round their necks. It was an English scene and, if Mrs Carter was English, so was the lunch. Shepherd's pie and an apple tart and custard.

'Charlie tells me you've fallen for Alice Conyers? If so, I'm not surprised. Everybody does. Including Charlie. Including these two,' she added, indicating her children.

'I admit it,' said Joe. 'I thought she was delightful! And rather more than that – practical, sensible, energetic. Oh, no – I thought she was a lass unparalleled.'

'I think she is. And lucky to be alive!'

'Lucky to be alive?'

'Lucky to have survived the smash. The Beaune railway disaster! You're going to tell me you haven't heard? It's usually the first thing anybody says about Alice.'

Carter joined in. 'Yes, when she first came out three years ago she was coming down by train from Paris to Marseilles and planning to spend a couple of weeks in the south of France seeing the sights before taking the P&O to Bombay. The train went off the rails crossing a viaduct near Beaune. Terrible accident, perhaps the worst France has ever had.'

'Oh, of course,' said Joe, 'I remember it. I remember hearing about it. Just after the war. I never connected it.'

'No reason why you should but Alice was the *only* survivor – at least I think she was the only survivor. There were over two hundred fatalities. The companion she was travelling with was killed and she woke up and found herself in a French hospital, alone and miles from home.'

'What an extraordinary story,' said Joe. 'What happened then?'

'Well, under the terms of her grandfather's will she was the majority shareholder in ICTC and they were expecting her on the next boat. Nothing loath – and you'll find this is Alice all over – she wired her trustees in London to say she was quite all right and intended to continue the journey as scheduled. She spent the spare two weeks recuperating in hospital – she wasn't completely unscathed.'

'The scar on her cheek?'

'Yes, that. Plus a couple of cracked ribs, sprained this and that. Anyway, half dead though she was, she showed the enterprise we all associate her with – she made friends with a woman who was nursing her in the hospital and Alice took her on as her private nurse, lady's maid, companion – call it what you will. They managed to locate her luggage and they came out to India on the boat as planned. She's still here, the companion. In Simla as a matter of fact. Name's Marie-Jeanne Pitiot. Alice started her up in a little shop in the Mall. What's it called, Meg?'

'La Belle Epoque,' said Meg. 'Very exclusive, by which I mean very expensive. I look in the windows and hurry away before anyone charges me for the privilege – you know, that sort of establishment! All the best people shop there – it's rumoured that even H.E. has been seen shopping there.'

'H.E?'

'Her Excellency. The Vicereine, Lady Reading. She too is a friend of Alice's.'

'And who owns the shop?' Joe wanted to know.

The Carters looked at each other. 'It's in Marie-Jeanne's name, I believe,' said Carter.

'But Alice, of course, supplies her with stock,' added Meg. 'It's just another of her outlets. And it has gone from strength to strength. Marie-Jeanne's opened another branch in Bombay and they say she has one planned for Delhi next year.'

'So the accident didn't bring bad luck to everyone,' said Joe thoughtfully. 'I'd like to have a word with Mademoiselle Pitiot.'

'Well, Alice must have been very grateful to Marie-Jeanne and they have remained good friends. Alice is very generous, you know.'

'And richer than she was when she came out here,' said Carter. 'Everybody admires her business flair. ICTC was a good old-fashioned outfit when she arrived, ticking over solidly, highly respected and sound, making money. People were a bit nervous when a little twenty-one-year-old came out holding fifty-one per cent of the shares in her hand.'

'They were even more nervous at the idea of Reggie Sharpe holding forty-nine,' sniffed Meg.

'But, as it turned out, she never put a foot wrong. The first thing she did was to marry Reggie, her second cousin, and change her name to Conyers-Sharpe. The second thing was to offer retirement to the pack of distant family members who had been overseeing the company in Bombay and replace them with two Eurasians and one Indian. You may imagine how unpopular that was! But she and Reggie set to work to run the company together. Good career move. It was obviously to their mutual advantage to keep their money bags in one hand.'

'I met Reggie Sharpe this morning,' said Joe. 'Didn't like him much.'

'Not surprised!' said Meg Carter explosively. 'I can't stand him! Charlie always makes allowances but then he makes allowances for everybody. If he told the truth he'd say he can't stand him either. He's not a bit like Alice. Where Alice was and is a really good businessman, Reggie is just a pretentious ass, idle, drinks like a fish –'

'Meg!' said Carter, seriously annoyed. 'You don't know that.'

'Everybody knows that! You should hear Dulcie Pettigrew!'

'I've no desire to hear Dulcie Pettigrew,' said Carter. 'Sharpest tongue in Simla! Wouldn't believe a word she said. All the same, it is true that he is something of a layabout. There is a sort of huntin', drinkin', dancin', gamblin' mob in Simla, mostly army or ex-army, who make a business of bad behaviour and Reggie Sharpe is right in the middle of that. Johnny Bristow, Bertie Hearn-Robinson, Jackie Carlisle, Edgar Troop, oh they're all the same! I was going to say I wouldn't have one of them in the house but then, not one of them would condescend to enter our humble abode! It's a sort of twilight world – not received by H.E. and I very much doubt if any of them would be received by Sir George. They batten on the visitors, show them around, give them a good time, show them "the real India" – I can hear it all! Edgar Troop's the worst! A good deal older than the others and definitely their leader. I can't stand him but Reggie sees a lot of him, it seems.'

'The wonder of it is that Alice puts up with it,' said Meg. 'But they say they pretty much live separate lives now. Alice gets on with all the many things she has to do while Reggie surveys the world through the bottom of a whisky bottle!'

With this flourish Meg decided that the two round-eyed children had heard enough of adult conversation. She rose from the table and, summoning the help of the ayah with a clap of her hands, bustled them off for their afternoon sleep.

This flurry of activity over, Carter said confidentially to Joe, 'You must excuse Meg – though I have to say that's the reaction you'll get from any decent woman in Simla once the name of Reggie Sharpe is mentioned. Men seem to rub along easily enough with him but there's something about him that makes women bristle with rage and disgust. I could almost be sorry for him. But, of course, they all know . . .'

'Know? Know what?'

Carter stirred uncomfortably and listened for the sounds of laughter from the other end of the bungalow before continuing.

'Well, when I said "huntin', shootin' and gamblin'" just now I could have added, er . . .'

'Whorin'?' suggested Joe cheerfully.

'Exactly. That coterie may not be received by H.E. but they all find a warm welcome at Madame Flora's.'

'Madame Flora's eh? A de luxe establishment I take it?'

'Oh yes. Very recherché! And she is actually French, the madam. The place seems to be run jointly by her and her English protector – who but Edgar Troop! Troop! He's everything people mean when they talk about a "bounder". Calls himself Captain Troop but no one's sure in what outfit. He was never a captain in the British Army or the Indian Army either. He lays claim to having served in the Imperial Russian Army and it may be true. He's certainly very knowledgeable. Understands the frontier and he's well connected in tribal territory.'

'Has he any other source of income?' Joe asked. 'Apart from battening on Madame Flora? Couldn't you get him for living on immoral earnings?'

'No, it's not a crime under the Indian Penal Code. I mean – you couldn't enforce it. In a country where the avocation of temple prostitute is perfectly respectable such a thing would be ridiculous. And anyway, Edgar Troop takes people on shooting trips. Plenty of starry-eyed tourists to fall for that sort of thing. Really knows his stuff. I took the trouble to go out with him once just to check up, you know. Not ready to risk any amateurs getting themselves chewed up in my territory! I was impressed. He knows what he's doing all right. And, of course, any check – and I've run several – on his financial arrangements shows that they are completely above board and within the law.' He sighed.

'So you've no temptation or inclination to close Madame Flora down?'

'Not at the moment. I like to have the buggers where I can see them! But this is India. Lots of randy young blokes about. Lots of randy old blokes too! The air of Simla affects young and old alike, as you'll find if you haven't already.'

'If we raided the place you might find some empty chairs at the next meeting of the Legislative Council?' suggested Joe.

'Certainly! Embarrassing, what!'

'From the eminence of the clientele I would guess that the place is well run?'

'Come on a raid with me, if you like. See for yourself. No expense spared, you'll find. It's run with the efficiency of a top-class hotel and the decor is sumptuous – all red plush, gilt mirrors and subdued lighting, rude but expensive paintings on the wall, you know the sort of thing.'

'And the girls?'

'Something for every taste. European, Eurasian, local girls from the hills. All beautiful. And none under age or sick or coerced as far as I can establish. They know I'd be down on them like a ton of bricks! And in such an establishment you wouldn't prosper on the North-West Frontier if boys weren't available too for anyone who likes his vices versa.'

'Good Lord!' said Joe. 'There are huge possibilities for blackmail here.'

'Oh yes. No cases reported to me yet but if I put my mind to it I could think of at least six eminent persons in Simla at this moment whose reputations hang by a thread.'

'And bribery? Has Troop attempted . . .?'

'First thing he did. So discreetly I couldn't pin anything on him but I'm sure an offer was made to me. My response left him in no doubt as to where I stood! But it happens all the time.'

'And where is this bordello?'

'It's cleverly located! It's in the Lower Bazaar but just off the Mall and down an alleyway between two popular shopping areas. Any lady spotting her husband down there wouldn't suspect a thing. She'd assume he was on his way to the Stephanatos Emporium to buy himself some cigars or to Latif's brass foundry to order the taps she'd been nagging for for months. Or – and this is the best bit –' Carter gave a cheerful smile, 'she might even guess that he was about to buy her a bouquet of roses.'

'Roses?'

'Yes! Would you believe the cheek! The front for this operation is actually a flower shop! Madame *Flora's*, you see! You enter innocently into a flower shop but if your tastes run to more exotic blooms you are shown into the back and up the stairs.'

'This Flora – what do you know of her?'

'Very little. Mysterious woman. Never appears in public –

74

wouldn't be received, naturally. She's French – or pretends to be! I'm no expert but the accent has always seemed to be just a little bit ooh-là-là to my ear. Late twenties, very pretty, perfect manners. She just appeared in Simla out of the blue, under the protection of Edgar Troop, and opened up. With instant success. The money – and it must have taken a fair bit to launch the business – must have been hers. Troop was never in that league financially.'

Joe sighed. 'Well, this is all very fascinating but where does it leave us as far as our murders are concerned?'

'Madame Flora was firmly established and doing well about six months before Lionel Conyers appeared or failed to appear in Simla so I'd say absolutely no connection if it weren't for Reggie Sharpe. He's the connection. Drinking companion and client of Edgar Troop's establishment . . . every reason to want Lionel dead . . . perhaps Troop is branching out into the bespoke killing business.'

'But the Russian? How does he fit in?'

Carter shrugged. 'I'm still not convinced that he does. From any angle, Sandilands, you still look like a better target for an assassin's bullet than Korsovsky. Someone may have got wind of the fact that Sir George was planning to put his tame ferret down a particularly nasty rat hole in Simla.'

At that moment Carter's sharp ears warned him of Meg's return and he added hurriedly, 'And listen, Joe, don't even think of going off to inspect that flower shop by yourself! I couldn't guarantee your safety. If we have to, we'll go together – with plenty of back-up!'

Meg bustled in, happy to resume her revelations about Sharpe, and Joe was very willing to draw her out. 'Tell me, Meg,' he said, 'does Reggie Sharpe work for his living?'

'Not really. But don't forget he's on the board of ICTC and a substantial shareholder. It's common knowledge that Alice takes all the decisions. He does a bit in the ADS, I think. He used to help Alice with some of her charitable things but he doesn't even do that now. I started to work in the hospital a bit – Lady Reading's hospital – that's how I met Alice. She's an assiduous fund-raiser and works there full time one day a week when she's in Simla. I like her.'

Joe smiled. 'Yes, I gathered that much.'

'Well,' said Meg Carter defensively, 'she's easy. You can get on with her. We've worked well together. And the more she does, the more useless does Reggie Sharpe seem.'

'Perhaps,' said Joe, 'he resents her? It does happen sometimes. Bright active girl, husband trailing along behind . . . Not a recipe for happiness.'

'Oh, I don't know,' said Carter. 'It seems to work all right for us.'

Joe emerged from the Carter bungalow prepared to walk the short distance back down the lanes to the town centre but, to his surprise, the four rickshaw men who'd brought him there now reappeared, hastily putting away the dice they'd been playing with and presenting themselves again, smiling and keen to be off. Telling himself to remember rickshaws did not operate by the same rules as London taxis, Joe climbed aboard and said, 'To Mrs Sharpe's office. ICTC. It's just off the Mall,' he added helpfully but the men were away at the mention of her name.

After ten minutes scraping around corners they were back in the town's main concourse and weaving their way through the press of foot traffic. Smartly dressed ladies strolled in chattering groups pointing and exclaiming at the displays in shop windows which would not have looked out of place in Paris. Men in army uniforms marched purposefully about at a smart pace, disappearing into the town hall or the telegraph office or making their way along to the army HQ next to St Michael's Church. Indian ayahs trailed past leading files of small children, mushroom-headed in their oversized solar topees. Joe noticed with amusement that this season the fashion in topees for little girls seemed to be a white covering of broderie anglaise.

Amongst the soberly dressed English, the showy figures of chaprassis stood out, turbaned, scarlet-coated, each with his important-looking message box in his right hand, sometimes with a file of papers tucked under his arm. They walked swiftly on pointed sandalled feet from public building to public building and Joe realized that what he was looking at was the Empire at work. This dusty, narrow little street so inaccurately called the Mall was the nerve centre of British India, the scarlet messengers the electrical impulses which kept the information flowing.

Catching a glimpse of a sign advertising 'Stephanatos Cigarettes. The best in Simla', Joe, on an impulse, called out to the men to stop, indicating that he wanted to buy some cigarettes. They stopped and waited for him to do his shopping. Joe looked appreciatively at the smart façade with its array of pipes, mounds of exotic tobaccos, cigars of all sizes and brands of cigarettes he had never heard of. He entered the cool, dark and intensely fragrant interior with the anticipation of a child entering a sweetshop. The Indian assistant was eager to please a new customer and disguised his disappointment when Joe asked for a packet of Black Cat cigarettes.

'Are these a popular brand in Simla?' he asked conversationally.

'Oh, yes, sahib. Not the smartest choice but very popular with gentlemen. Craven A, Black Cat, Passing Clouds, Gold Flake, those are the ones we sell in most large numbers.'

Joe nodded. 'Oh and I'll have forty Freibourg and Treyer.'

'Ah, yes, sahib – more smart, more suitable!'

Leaving the shop he glanced down the alley to his left. At the bottom he caught the reflection of light off brass items on display piled on to tables in front of Latif's shop. And, half-way down, a discreet hand-painted sign – a circle of twining art-nouveau lilies – announced in florid lettering 'Madame Flora. Fleuriste. Paris et Simla.' Joe wandered down and examined the displays of flowers on show in the window. The theme was 'Springtime in Simla' and flowers familiar and unfamiliar to Joe were blended in subtle colour combinations, mainly the yellow of jonquils and the purples of irises.

He went inside and was met by a drowning fragrance and by the tinkle of a fountain at the back of the shop. A handsome Eurasian boy and girl looking so alike they must be brother and sister came forward to ask how they might be of service. He told them he wanted a bouquet of flowers for a lady.

'A special lady?' the boy enquired with only the slightest emphasis.

'Yes, a friend of mine,' said Joe firmly. 'No, no, I wasn't thinking of roses – give me something simpler. What about some of these springtime blooms? Those white narcissus look wonderful and what about some of those pale purple things? Wild iris, yes, I'll have some of those too.'

77

In seconds the girl had made up a bouquet with skill and flair and tied it with a distinctive broad gold ribbon.

Well satisfied with his purchase, Joe regained his rickshaw and continued on his way down the Mall. They passed a building so ludicrously out of place that Joe laughed out loud and pointed. 'What on earth's that?' he shouted more as an exclamation than a question expecting a reply. The three-storeyed, half-timbered building with its pointed dormers and turrets would have looked wonderful and entirely at home on a mountainside in the Swiss Alps.

'Sahib, General Post Office,' panted one of the men pushing behind.

They turned a corner beside the post office and bumped down a narrow alleyway between the Mall and the Ridge, coming to a halt in front of a building which could have been the little sister of the post office, smaller, less flamboyant but determinedly half-timbered and turreted. Above the large double door flanked by two turbaned doorkeepers Joe read the sign 'Imperial and Colonial Trading Corporation. Simla and Bombay.' He dismounted and handed a further generous amount to the rickshaw men, remembering this time to tell them not to wait.

An Indian, impressive in blue and gold uniform, came forward and took the card he held ready in his hand. 'Commander Sandilands. Good afternoon, sir. Mrs Sharpe is expecting you. Will you come this way?'

Joe followed him down a wide hallway hung with Indian fabrics and furnished with pieces of Indian furniture and was shown into a light and sunny room. Alice Sharpe, who was standing at the window, turned with a warm smile to greet him. She had been talking to an Indian. Tall, dark and neat, he was wearing a well-cut English suit and a green, white and blue tie. Old Rugbeian. Joe calculated that this must be Mrs Sharpe's right-hand man, the able Indian she had promoted to take the place of her English cousins in the firm. Joe looked at him more closely. Behind the conventional good looks – liquid, dark, long-lashed eyes and smooth complexion – was a shrewd intelligence which was taking stock of Joe. Joe sensed the cool gaze pass lightly over his dusty khaki drill suit, a custard stain on his dark blue police tie and the bouquet of flowers he was holding awkwardly at his side.

At a gesture from Alice the Indian went over to a gramophone which was playing a Dixieland tune Joe recognized and turned it off. He bowed and waited. Alice greeted Joe and asked if he would like tea or coffee. Joe accepted coffee and the Indian bowed again and withdrew.

With a feeling of relief that he was no longer under scornful scrutiny, Joe presented the bouquet he had been holding at his side. 'For the prettiest soprano east of the Caucasus,' he said with a flourish.

Alice Sharpe looked pleased and amused and buried her nose in the flowers, inhaling the fresh scents. 'Mmm,' she said, 'delicious but heartbreaking too! The spring flowers always remind me of Home.'

'Of home?'

'England, I mean.'

'Ah! You "get one of those mysterious fairy calls from out the void", do you?'

With a sharp glance and a smile Alice picked up the reference to *The Wind In The Willows* at once.

'Yes, just like Moley! But, unfortunately I have no Ratty to jolly me along and there is always the fear that, like Mole, I would be very disappointed if I ever did go back.'

She turned to put the flowers on a table. The formal gestures gave Joe time to take in the atmosphere of this the centre of activity of one of the world's largest trading concerns. A surprising atmosphere. Here was no heavy Edwardian mahogany-furnished, book-lined office of the kind he was familiar with in London. It was a spacious room efficiently equipped with desks and cabinets and racks of files but it was unmistakably a room in which a happy as well as busy life was lived. The white walls were decorated with paintings which seemed to Joe to be French and of the Impressionist school. The floor was covered in deep carpets in dark blues and reds, colours echoed in the three Tiffany lamps which glowed, jewel-like, in corners of the room. And Joe had never seen an office in which pride of place was held by a Decca gramophone. The latest model, he noticed, with walnut case and elegant trumpet. By the side of it was stacked a pile of records bearing the mark of a New York music publisher.

'Please, don't interrupt your music for me,' said Joe. '"Tiger Rag", wasn't it? I saw The Original Dixieland Jazz Band play that at the Hammersmith Palais a couple of years ago. I like jazz!'

A delighted smile rewarded his confidence. 'Have you ever been to America, Mr Sandilands?' Joe shook his head. 'I should love to go! It's my dream to visit New York and New Orleans. Perhaps one day I'll listen to a live jazz band on Basin Street! But here in Simla I'm considered rather odd in my taste for this "devil's music" as they call it. Oh, most people in Simla will dare to tap their foot to a Scott Joplin rag and they'll tell each other that the cakewalk is harmless and a jolly good romp, eh? what? but if the old fuddy-duddies in London on the board of ICTC knew that their profits were gained to a background of jazz they'd have a heart attack.'

The Indian returned with a tray of coffee and sweetmeats and placed it on a low table. With a searching and hostile look at Joe he bowed and went out.

'My assistant, Rheza Khan,' said Alice. 'Don't misunderstand – he's not my bearer – he brought in the coffee himself because he's in part my bodyguard and he's checking up on you. He's invaluable to me. He's my secretary and knows as much about the business as I do.'

'More than your husband?' asked Joe.

Alice raised her eyebrows. 'You've been listening to gossip already? Have you spent the morning loitering on Scandal Point, Mr Sandilands? As well as finding time to pay a visit to Madame Flora?'

Her tone was light but Joe was in no doubt that her innuendo betrayed a knowledge deeper than that of Meg Carter of the behind-the-scenes flower business. To his irritation he found himself blushing but replied mildly, 'It's one of the aspects of policing, Mrs Sharpe, that you find yourself mixing with all sorts and conditions of men – and women. Courtesan one minute, businesswoman the next.'

She gave him a searching look before picking up his original question. 'Yes, you're right. Reggie takes little interest in the day-to-day running of the business. He's happy for me to go on increasing profits on a yearly basis and he contents himself with offering expert advice on the brands of whisky we import.' She gave Joe a conspiratorial look followed by a disarming smile and handed him a cup of coffee, inviting him to take a seat on a divan.

Joe decided he was going to resist the beauty, the charm, the intelligence and obvious good nature of Alice Conyers-Sharpe. He sighed. She was standing before him, a vision of English neatness, fresh-faced, hair coiled tidily on top of her head and wearing a dark blue cotton dress with a demure white collar having all the simplicity of a girls' school uniform. And yet, there was something which pricked his suspicions. A deliberate underlining of innocence? A false note? Something she was hiding? Certainly something she had unwittingly said had made him wary and he had been so forcibly struck the evening before by the grief expressed in her song that he could not easily put aside the idea that she had known Korsovsky.

She poured her own cup of coffee and came to sit down next to him. He caught a trace of perfume, oriental and inviting – sandalwood perhaps – which surprised him. He would have expected nothing more alluring than eau de Cologne from the angelic Mrs Sharpe.

'But our unfortunate baritone, Mr Sandilands? Are you any nearer to a formal identification? Have you located his family?'

'Carter has this in hand. He is in communication with his agent and I suppose it will eventually be resolved.'

Joe spoke stiffly. He was uneasy in her presence. She was sitting too close to him for professional comfort. Her shoulder brushed his as she leaned forward to place her cup on a table and he had an irrational fear that at any moment she might put her hand on his knee. He got to his feet, walked to the window and looked out, then affected to study the scatter of records by the gramophone. She watched him, apparently stifling a smile, saying nothing. He decided to shatter her composure.

'A question, Mrs Sharpe. Where were you at 7 p.m. on Wednesday the 4th of March in 1914?'

She looked at him in astonishment. She tilted her head and closed her eyes for a moment as one giving deep thought to a vital question. Then she looked up at Joe with an easy and friendly smile. 'You did say 1914? I was sitting at the back of a classroom yearning for the bell to ring to signal the end of prep. I was at school at Wycombe Abbey. I was fifteen years old. My best friend Joyce Carstairs would have been sitting on my right but you may have difficulty in getting her to confirm this – if you can track her down – because she invariably slept through prep.'

Alice leaned forward and said, 'Are you going to tell me what this is all about? Did someone murder the headmistress? Well, heavens! We all suspected that Miss Murchison died and was mummified before the Boer War but this is the first official confirmation of our suspicions!'

Feeling foolish and a little angry, Joe produced the wine-stained programme and handed it to her, watching her closely. She was silent for a long time, absorbing the meaning of the document. Finally, she took a lawn handkerchief from a pocket and dabbed at her eyes which were welling with tears. She looked at him directly.

'This is heartbreaking! Don't you think so?'

'Certainly it must have had a very special meaning for Korsovsky. It was just about the only personal item in his luggage. Tell me what you make of it.'

'It's very touching. To have kept it for so long I think he must have been very fond of this little English girl.'

'Why do you say "English"? Why not Italian? Why not French?'

'It's obvious. Look at the writing. That is regulation girls' public school writing. It's quite different from Continental writing. Look!' She took up a pen and a sheet of paper from the desk and copied out the first two lines of verse. 'There, do you see it? Straight from Maria Plunkett's *Writing Primer For Girls*, published 1905. Green with gold lettering. I can see it now! Ugh! Allowing for differences in character and experience of course, you can still see the similarity I think?'

Joe could.

'You were quite convinced that I was hiding some connection with our baritone! Come on, confess! The fifteen-year-old I was in 1914 would have been very flattered and excited at the idea but I don't think he would have considered a little girl in gymslip and plaits worthy of much attention. And he didn't meet this girl in the Home Counties – they were having a happy time in a French opera house, apparently.'

Joe was not easy under her gentle scorn.

'Can we turn to your brother's death, Mrs Sharpe? Tell me – when and how did you discover that he had survived the war?'

'He sent me a telegram as soon as he got back to England. It reached me in Bombay in November 1919. He was still very weak and spent the next year gathering his strength, leaving family and business matters ticking over as they were. We wrote to each other, of course, and I kept him fully informed of the steps I was taking. Then, in the April of 1921, he wired again to say he was well enough to travel out to arrange his affairs in India. He'd come to some decisions. He approved of my plans and schemes.' Her face hardened for a moment. 'And why would he not? I was always much cleverer than Lionel, Mr Sandilands. Truthfully, I fear he would have undone all the good I had done, had he assumed full responsibility for the company.'

'What were his plans for you?'

'He was prepared to let me continue in an executive position, though with forty-nine per cent of control to his fifty-one per cent. He had no intention of settling here, his health was too fragile. So, in effect, I would have continued to work eighteen hours a day in the heat of India for the good of the firm though lacking the ultimate authority to steer the company in the direction I wished.' Her tone was bitter and Joe could appreciate the strength and justice of her grievance.

'And Mr Sharpe, your husband by this time . . .?'

'Would have been totally dispossessed. No, he was not happy about that and was preparing to fight the case through the courts.' She shuddered. 'It would have been a very distressing and unprofitable time for everyone. What a jolly scandal! Nothing like a family row to blossom into a cause célèbre! It doesn't bear thinking of!'

'So both you and your husband would have had a great deal to gain financially from your brother's death?'

'Of course. And there have been many to whom that thought has occurred. And many, doubtless, who must have noticed that my grief was not particularly deep.'

'You were not fond of your brother?'

'It was devastating to lose my only close living relative and for what seemed to be a second time. A very cruel twist, that. But Lionel and I were never close. He was a good deal older than I and hardly noticed me when we were growing up. I did not admire him. I knew I was . . .' she hesitated, searching for a word, 'more worthy than he was although I was constantly reminded by our parents that I was only a girl and that the family's fortunes rested on Lionel. I resented the assumption that little sisters were there to be seldom seen and never heard. Then we were divided by school and the war. He was a stranger to me. But I didn't kill him.'

'I understand you were in the view of a hundred people when he was assassinated?'

'Yes. But that means nothing, you'll find. If I wanted someone to die, Mr Sandilands, I would merely mention the matter to Rheza Khan. He would mention it to someone else who would in turn make suitable arrangements. The true killer will in all likelihood have paid to have the trigger pulled. There is no lack, you'll find, in Simla of obliging retired military types with the skill and the inclination to perform such a service for a fee. I could suggest a few names myself . . . Some, indeed, I know to be drinking companions of my husband . . . But you can be sure that the instigator of the act will almost certainly have taken the precaution of being engaged in a very public activity at the moment the shot rang out.'

Joe was silent for a moment. She was trying to tell him something without putting it into words herself. Without naming names.

'And your husband Reginald was very much in the public eye at that time?'

She shivered. With fear?

'Reggie. Yes. He was handing a plate of cucumber sandwiches to Her Excellency, Lady Reading. He could not have been more flamboyantly well positioned.'

84

Chapter Seven

Joe pondered this with disbelief, not able for a moment to react to her suggestion, so blandly delivered, saying at last, 'You're telling me that you think your husband may have procured your brother's murder?'

Alice nodded, unwilling still, it seemed, to put her suspicions into words.

'And that the instrument,' Joe continued, 'the actual assassin, could well be Edgar Troop? Is that what you're saying?'

After a quick flash of surprise she nodded again.

'And you're saying that same Edgar Troop who has, shall we say, an executive position of some significant but dubious sort chez Madame Flora?'

Low-voiced, 'Yes, that Edgar Troop!'

Joe took another turn about the room. He had imagined working tactfully and circuitously round the stark realities. He had even prepared a series of careful questions, but here was the surprising Alice firmly and unequivocally at the heart of the matter and, unlike Meg Carter, having no delusion as to the true nature of Madame Flora's establishment and seemingly with more than a suspicion as to Reggie Sharpe's true relationship with the as yet unseen but sinister Edgar Troop.

'Oh, do stop pacing about!' she said abruptly. 'Sit down and listen to me!'

Joe took a seat opposite and waited.

'I know all about Madame Flora's brothel. I know it is the source of much vice and crime in Simla and I am aware that my husband is heavily involved with it – a valued and loyal customer, you could say,' she added in a curiously flat, expressionless voice. She might have been discussing his golf handicap.

'You must find that very distressing,' was Joe's inadequate reply. Brothels formed a part of his London life but he had never held such a conversation with a lady before. He had never heard a lady pronounce the word 'brothel' and he found that it shocked him.

'Distressing?' Alice laughed derisively. 'Say rather appalling – not to be tolerated! Ours was never a happy marriage, Mr Sandilands, it was one of convenience but, initially, I did my best to pretend to the world that we had a normal married relationship. My fault, I wonder? Perhaps a bit my fault. When I arrived in India I had to fight. Fight to establish myself in a man's world. It took a lot of careful work. It filled my days and nights. Reggie is not secure – he is easily threatened. He couldn't keep his manhood intact with a woman who was his equal and was completely unmanned in the presence of a woman recognized by many to be his superior.

'But then, at the end of our first season in Simla, I discovered that my husband had contracted – was in the first stages of – a venereal disease. At first I was stunned. I thought this was the sort of thing that only happened to other people – servants – soldiers' wives – but I made him tell me who he'd got it from and where. Perhaps I was heavy-handed? Certainly I made it difficult for him. I insisted that he go and see a doctor. The MO here is very good; very co-operative and on my side. Between us we arranged for inspections – of the girls, I mean. Madame Flora didn't like it, I'm told, but she jolly well knew if she wanted to stay open she'd have to do it my way. I kept it in the background but everybody knew that I'd caused the fuss and brought about the clean-up.'

'And was the reaction favourable?' Joe wanted to know.

'Mixed,' she replied candidly. 'You know Simla . . . well, you don't yet, but you soon will. Plenty of Mrs Hawksbees around still to tittle tattle and remind one of a woman's place. You know there are still many women who would totally deny the existence of brothels. They would not recognize a sexually transmitted disease if their husband's tackle crumbled before their eyes. If you don't notice it – it's not really happening and a lady would never make reference to such matters. And then there are those who are truly women of the twentieth century. They may have been suffragettes, they may have driven an ambulance in the war . . . they know what goes on in the real world and they are with me all the way. A surprising number of them, Commander, roll their sleeves up and do a very messy job brilliantly and for no reward other than the satisfaction of knowing that they have improved things for their sisters. No matter what their colour or religion.'

'I can believe it,' said Joe simply. 'I have known such a woman.'

Alice looked at him silently for a moment with speculation.

Before she could question him he asked, 'And Reggie? How did he react to the strictures you imposed?'

'Badly. It was very embarrassing for him on two counts – bossy wife who didn't know her place and then, you know, naughty boy caught with his hand up a housemaid's skirt!' She laughed shortly and went on, 'Don't think he's ever forgiven me. Showed him up in front of his gang! I don't care! I made him use his influence with the madam and with Troop to have the girls medically examined and those suffering were to be sent to the hospital immediately for treatment. From then on regular checks were to be made and reports made to the hospital on a monthly basis.' She gave a tight smile and added, 'They think I'm a meddling nuisance but – too bad!'

Joe was stunned by what he was hearing. 'Did you confront this Madame Flora?'

Joe would have been entertained to witness such an interview. Alice put an end to his speculation by saying, 'I have never met the woman. She never appears in society, as my mother would have said. Her world and mine would never coincide were it not for the unfortunate Reggie. And I would never seek her out.'

'I understand you have some personal contact with the hospital?'

'I work there one day a week on the women's ward. I interest myself in the women whose bodies have been ravaged by poor care – or no care – in childbirth, in the child brides who, after years of abuse by their husbands, are sent as a last resort to us for repair. And I raise money and I fund the care of the unfortunate creatures who risk their lives working for people such as Troop and Flora. I talk to the patients and I have managed to learn something of the way Troop operates though

87

the girls are generally too frightened to speak to anyone outside the establishment.'

Her blue eyes blazed with indignation and rage. Joe was fast forming the opinion that Alice Sharpe was a formidable woman, a woman who must have made some implacable enemies in Simla and not least, perhaps, her own husband.

'And Reggie accepts all this?'

'He has no choice in the matter. I control the finances of ICTC. I effectively pay him a salary and I have threatened to cut it drastically if he steps out of line. To show him that I was in earnest I cut two months of his pay and gave it directly to the women's hospital. He was angry but there was little he could do about it. But I may have pushed him too far. He's a weak man and I despise him but even weak men may seek help from stronger men. I fear Reggie may have used the services of Edgar Troop to shoot my brother in order to protect his share of the company.'

And Alice Conyers' share also, incidentally, Joe thought.

Alice glared at him, resenting his silence. 'You don't believe me, do you?'

'Why do you say so?' said Joe in surprise.

'You were looking at me with the supercilious, suspicious, sceptical, cynical air that men assume so easily. Even nice men,' she added with an irritation she did not quite disguise with a spurt of humour.

'You are deceived,' said Joe. 'Many are deceived by this badly stitched eyebrow.' He raised his hand to his left eyebrow which hasty and belated surgery on the battlefield had left permanently tilted. 'In the interview room, I can tell you it has its uses but it can work against me when I'm trying to charm and impress.'

'*Were* you trying to charm and impress? But a wound! Of course, I see it now.' She raised a hand and for a heart-stopping moment Joe thought she was about to touch with gentle fingers the scar on his face but she hesitated, looked away and turned her hand to her own cheek. 'I too . . .' She traced the silvery scar trail down her face. 'But I was fortunate. I had the services of the best surgeon in the south of France.'

'Whereas my face was held together with a clothes peg,' said Joe, feeling, for the first time, that he was in tune with Alice Conyers. Wishing to hold on to this fragile rapport he said, 'It must have felt like surviving on a battlefield, surviving the rail crash.'

'Perhaps worse,' she said, 'because we were so totally unprepared for it and we were not young fighting men prepared to make a sacrifice of our lives. We were ordinary people looking forward to the south of France, to spring, to sunshine, to the rest of our lives.

'But you're right – it was like a battlefield. The blood, the severed limbs, the bodies lying like rag dolls. I was unconscious at first. I don't know for how long. When I came to and looked around all I could see was destruction and death. I'd never seen a dead body before and suddenly there I was surrounded by dozens of them. The smoke and stench of burning flesh was thick about me but even worse was the silence. And suddenly I heard a child crying. It went on and on. I tried to get up but I couldn't get my limbs to work. That was an awful moment. Mr Sandilands, I thought I was dead! I thought I was a ghost in some sort of dreadful limbo. My spirit was still there at this scene of desolation, anchored by a thread of consciousness. I've always believed in the survival of the soul and I had no doubt that I had died and was caught up between two worlds. Blackness descended again and when I woke up the child had stopped crying. I don't know how long I was lying there unconscious and bleeding . . . they say it was over an hour before the rescue train arrived.

'I was unaware of it because the next thing I remember is waking up in the hospital in Beaune with the kindly face of Marie-Jeanne Pitiot smiling at me.'

Joe sensed that she had said enough about the past but felt flattered that she had entrusted him with her sad story.

'I'm sorry,' she said. 'I really wasn't trying to put you off your questioning. We're both trying to discover the truth. I need to know who killed my brother. I desperately need to know. Do go on with your questions.'

'It might be important to know how the company stands at the moment. I mean, did Lionel leave a will? Or have the lawyers reverted to the situation as it was before he died? Who really owns the company?'

'I wish I knew! The matter is still under consideration by the firm's lawyers in London. One opinion is that as he died intestate and without progeniture all reverts to his only living relation – me. Others maintain that grandfather's wishes and provisions come into play and that the status quo obtains. I think that Reggie would remain quite content with the latter scenario but . . .'

'Should you be declared the sole heir, then . . .?'

She looked at him seriously for a moment. 'Then I would think I was at risk. Don't you think so too, Mr Sandilands?'

Soft-footed, Rheza Khan re-entered the room and stood by the door, appointment book in hand, formally signalling that the interview was at an end. Joe rose to his feet and thanked Alice Sharpe for her co-operation, the professional courtesies rolling easily from his tongue. She held out a hand and took his, looking earnestly into his face.

'I'm so glad you're here in Simla, Commander. And please let me know if there is anything at all I can do to further your enquiries into this wretched business.'

The Indian stood his ground by the door post watching Joe with eyes as dark and unyielding as obsidian. As Joe passed him he caught again the fragrance of sandalwood but much stronger than the delicate ghost of a scent that he had breathed from Alice Sharpe.

'Hmm,' thought Joe. 'So that's how it is between them!'

Joe decided to start out on foot to walk down the Mall looking out for the dress shop run by the nurse and companion Marie-Jeanne Pitiot. He was half-way along the Mall when an uncomfortable thought struck him. He patted his pockets. No, he was not mistaken. Alice Sharpe had failed to hand back Korsovsky's programme. And he hadn't even noticed the sleight of hand by which she had concealed it. He hesitated, wondering whether to go back for it. He decided to leave it for the moment. It might come in useful later on if he needed an excuse to interview Alice again.

As he stood uncertainly weighing his thoughts, a baby carriage as splendid as a Rolls Royce went by pushed by an ayah. The baby at that moment woke up and started to yell. The ayah hurried to pick up the red-faced scrap and talk to it tenderly. It gathered its strength and released another ear-splitting scream. Joe flinched.

'My God!' he exclaimed to himself. 'Of course! The baby! Little Henri!'

He summoned a rickshaw and directed the runners to take him to the Governor's Residence.

Sir George had not yet returned, to Joe's relief, so he was able to go straight back to the guest house without having to give an account of himself. As he hurried across the garden he was struck by the thought that the trunks might have been dealt with in the efficient Indian way in his absence. He'd forgotten to leave instructions to say that they should not be touched. Entering his room he found that all had been cleaned and tidied but the trunks were still as he'd left them in the middle of the room, the piles of clothes a reprimand in the centre of such orderliness.

Ignoring the clothes, Joe picked up the French newspaper which had lain at the bottom of one of the trunks. The date was 5th April, three years ago. A fortnight after the Beaune railway disaster. By the time this edition of the paper came out, he calculated that Alice would have been at sea for a day on the next leg of her voyage to India in the care of Mademoiselle Pitiot. She would not have seen it.

The headline which had been nagging at the back of his mind since his conversation with Alice now screamed at him and he remembered similar headlines carried in the English press. 'Miracle baby, little orphan Henri safe in his grandmother's arms.' He had even seen little orphan Henri looking with unfocused eyes at the camera on a Pathé News report in the cinema in Leicester Square. Yes, the article referred to the same baby. A second class passenger in the Beaune railway disaster, Henri had survived cradled tightly in his dead mother's arms and had been cared for by nurses in Beaune until he could be identified and returned to his grieving grandparents.

This article was not a fresh news item and, cynically, Joe saw it as an effort to keep the story alive but also an attempt to sum up and to bring a ray of hope however faint from the whole bleak disaster. The official list of the dead and the three survivors was given on page two. *Three* survivors? He turned hurriedly to page two. The passengers were listed by class – first, second and third – and classified again by nationality, the main lists by far being French and English with a sprinkling of other Europeans. Joe ran his finger down the page. No third class passenger had survived the crash and only one second class passenger – baby Henri. In the first class two names were listed: Alice Conyers and Captain Colin Simpson.

Alice Conyers! Joe looked again at the message scrawled by Korsovsky's agent across the top of the paper. 'As requested.' So Korsovsky had asked him to supply a copy of this paper. Why? He had assumed it was connected with the bookings listed for that summer. But his agent would have found a more efficient way of telling him his itinerary, wouldn't he? He wouldn't have trusted to the vagaries of the press to announce his bookings. No, Korsovsky must have had some other reason for wanting this paper. 'I can't tell you how sorry I am,' he had added. Why sorry? There was something in the contents that he knew would distress Korsovsky. Joe checked the lists again. No Russian names. The name of Alice Conyers was the only link he could see. Surely this was no coincidence? And yet common sense (and Alice herself) told him that there could never have been any link in the past between the singer and the little English schoolgirl leading her sheltered life in the Hertfordshire countryside. And, anyway, the girl had survived against all odds. A cause for jubilation not sorrow for anyone who knew her, surely?

'I need someone to talk to!' Joe thought. He tucked the paper away in his pocket and strode off to the front of the Governor's house where he knew a rickshaw would be waiting. He climbed aboard. 'Police headquarters,' he said.

It was five o'clock and the sun was beginning to slide towards the western mountain range when Joe was dropped off at the police station. He was shown at once into Carter's office. Carter, who had been poring over a thick file, flung it down with relief.

'You want to know who is the biggest criminal in Simla? He is!' he said tapping the file. 'Big Red! Two or three thefts a week reported and now he's branching out into physical attacks on children. Very nasty incident yesterday up at the temple on Jakko Hill. Little Lettice Murray, daughter of Colonel Murray, is said to be in a hysterical state after her awful encounter. Brave girl though! Stuck her lollipop in his eye and escaped.'

Joe looked at him in puzzlement.

'Bloody monkey! Gang leader of that pack of vermin who infest the monkey temple. Sacred to Hanuman the monkey god and I can't touch them! Mind you,' he added confidentially, 'that's not to say some of them don't disappear at dead of night sometimes! Especially when my Sikh chaps are on duty!'

'You don't . . .?'

'Of course not! No, we round them up and take them for a little excursion into the country. There's a sort of monkey paradise about ten miles from here. When they've gone whooping and hollering up the trees we sneak off and leave them there.' He laughed. 'First time we tried this we made the mistake of hanging about to make sure they were all right, having a happy time, enough food to eat and so on, and as they seemed to like the place we got on to the cart and started off back for town. Well! We'd only gone a few yards when the warning was sounded. They all came piling down from the trees and climbed back on the cart ready to go home! Just like a bunch of kids at the end of a Sunday School outing! Ah, but now – we're as clever as they are!

'But Joe, come out on to the verandah at the back and I'll order us a cup of tea. Tell me where you've got to. Save my sanity – you see, I risk being obsessed by the simians of Simla.'

Joe gave him his impressions of Alice Sharpe and an account of his conversation with her, adding, 'And remember, Alice does give Reggie good reason to resent her – hate her even. I don't know if that signifies, but it should be borne in mind, don't you think? And tell me, Carter, what do you know of her secretary, this Rheza Khan?'

Carter looked at him shrewdly. 'Clever chap. Very able. Not a Simla man so I can't tell you much about his background. I know he is from a well-to-do Indian family – father's a rajah, I believe, up in the hills towards Gilgit – and he was sent away to school in England. Perfect English of course, and perfect manners. You'll have noticed that he wears European dress. He was employed by ICTC in quite a high position, I believe, before Miss Conyers came out to Bombay. Virtually running the whole thing, according to some. No acknowledgement of that naturally. It appears that Alice came in and spent some time observing what was going on in the firm then made some pretty unpopular decisions. Under his influence many family members found themselves on a boat to Southampton! And Rheza Khan, whose qualities were, they say, immediately recognized by Alice, was promoted and now openly does the job he is best fitted for.'

'So you'd say he has strong reasons for preserving the status quo? He wouldn't have welcomed the arrival of Lionel Conyers in Simla, I'm thinking. Does he have an alibi? Though I'm assured by none other than Alice herself that the more prominently positioned you are in the eyes of Simla at the moment of the crime, the greater the likelihood that you're involved.'

Carter grunted. 'Well, by those rules, he's most probably innocent. He was on leave the week Lionel was killed. Off back in the hills celebrating his father's birthday, I think. Which is to say – no alibi! But really, if you look closely at motive, not as strong as you might think. This chap is the brains behind the company – everyone acknowledges that – and it's not likely he would have lost his job even with Lionel in the saddle. I think he'd have won over any resistance and would have gone on doing what he's doing because the plain fact is – the feller's made himself indispensable.'

'Might he have killed Lionel as a favour to Alice – to keep her in place?'

'It's possible. They're certainly very thick. And there are those who say she is too dependent on him and listens too closely to his advice.'

'*Very* thick? Just *how* thick, I wonder? Or rather, what exactly is the *nature* of their closeness? Seeing them together I *had* wondered . . .' Rather embarrassed to be heard exchanging what Carter might think of as unworthy gossip, Joe shared his suspicions.

'Well! Well! That kind of relationship!' Carter paused for a moment, smiling. 'Two attractive people so in a way I'm not surprised, but I am amazed that not a hint of it has ever come to the surface. Not even Meg has any suspicions, I'll swear it. And in Simla that's quite something!'

'I have a feeling that Alice Sharpe is very good at keeping secrets,' said Joe. 'There's something I'm uneasy about regarding

Alice. I can't get it out of my head that there is some connection between her and Korsovsky.'

'Can't see it,' said Carter. 'What have you got? This eight-year-old programme with English writing on it? Not much, is it?'

'There's more,' said Joe slowly. 'When I met Alice last night at the theatre she was suggesting that *I* might have been the killer's true target and she said something rather strange. She said, "Korsovsky looked English from a distance . . ." How did she know? I've asked about and nobody else in Simla has a clue about his appearance! They've all *heard* of him but no one has seen a photograph apparently. He might well have been five feet tall with a red beard for all they knew. She denies ever having met him. And I'm still sure that the grief she showed when she sang her Russian lament was real.'

'Mmm. Nothing in the press she could have got that idea from. What about publicity she might have seen in London before she left England?'

'He did appear at Covent Garden but not until she'd already left for India. I went to see him myself and that's how I recognized him.'

'I've got it! Catalogues from record companies. Perhaps there's a photograph of him in one of those?'

'I looked at her collection today. No opera. All jazz and ragtime.' Joe sighed. 'And there is a third connection. Look at this, Carter . . .'

Joe took the French newspaper from his pocket and showed it to Carter, drawing his attention to the agent's strange message and then to the name of Alice Conyers amongst the first class passengers.

'That's damned odd!' said Carter. 'Look, we've sent off telegrams to this Gregoire Montefiore in his Paris office to tell him Korsovsky's dead and ask for names of next of kin and so on. I'll send off another one to ask if he can remember why he sent this edition of a paper to his client three years ago. But let me look at it again.'

He looked closely at the lists of passengers, occasionally asking Joe to translate a passage he was unsure of. 'Hang on a moment! There's something else we can try for faster results. It's a shot in the dark perhaps but look here, Joe, do you see? – someone else survived the crash. Someone travelling first class.

Captain Colin Simpson. Returning to his regiment in Bombay. Perhaps he could shed some light on Alice Conyers. I don't expect so but I think we ought to try. Do you think he might be still in Bombay? What does it say about him? Anything?'

'Well it's mostly tear-jerking blather about baby Henri,' said Joe, reading down the column, 'but I thought I saw . . . Yes, here it is. Not much I'm afraid. It mentions Alice and says she left almost at once to continue her journey and then it says, "An English soldier, Captain Colin Simpson, was also bound for Bombay at the time of the accident to rejoin his regiment, the 3rd KOYLI, but his departure will be much delayed on account of the serious nature of his injuries . . . So badly concussed was the captain that he was at first taken for dead and his body had lain for several hours in the morgue before it was realized that he was still alive. He was conveyed to the hospital in Lyons where there were better facilities for treating head injuries. He was at first reported as killed but his grieving family who had been informed of this have now been reassured that he is still alive." '

'His regiment ought to be able to tell us where he's got to. I'll get off a telegram straight away. So – one to G.M. and one to the Adjutant of the 3rd battalion of the King's Own Yorkshire Light Infantry!'

Carter took a pad and a pen and carefully wrote out two messages. He called out and a young officer appeared. Instructions were given, the officer nodded in understanding, put the messages away in a leather pouch which he buttoned on to his belt and set off at the double for the telegraph office.

'Of course,' said Joe, 'no matter how much digging about we do into these little mysteries, sleuthing about, you might say, and trying to look clever, there's one step we would be negligent if we didn't take – and as soon as possible.'

'Edgar Troop, you mean,' said Carter glumly. 'Alice's accusation seems to have been pretty blunt. Yes, I agree, we would be neglecting our duty if we didn't follow it up.'

Neatly, Charlie Carter flicked a cigarette end over the verandah railing. Joe watched it sail in a graceful parabola on to the corrugated iron roof below where it exploded in a flash of sparks. 'Are you thinking, I wonder, what I'm thinking? That we might go and lean a little bit on the charming Mr Troop?'

'Yes, exactly that. Got anything better to do? Big Red can wait for another day, can he?'

'No time like the present, I'd say! I'll detail a couple of officers discreetly to accompany us but I'm not expecting a shoot-out. I'll just write a note to Meg before we go. Tell her we're going to Madame Flora's establishment and she's not to sit up for us. Should be home for breakfast.'

He bustled about making his arrangements.

'Perhaps I should write a note for Sir George,' said Joe. 'How did it go? . . . Going to Madame Flora's . . . Don't sit up . . . Be back for breakfast.'

They set off together to walk down to the town with two silent Sikh policemen padding behind.

Chapter Eight

'I don't think we can plan this interview,' said Joe. 'It so very much depends on the reaction. But you do realize, I'm sure, that we've got very little we can hang on Troop. I plan to play it very informally. Agree? Perhaps he'll be overawed by the police talent?'

'If I know anything about Edgar Troop he wouldn't be overawed by a squadron of Household Cavalry,' said Charlie dubiously.

Joe wondered as they approached Madame Flora's establishment what to expect. A tinkle of music from a honky-tonk piano? A palm court orchestra discoursing a little Offenbach? A row of black-stockinged legs kicking up an array of multi-layered petticoats?

They turned off the Mall where the street lamps had now clicked on and the brilliantly lit shop windows offered even more temptations than in the daylight. The façade of Madame Flora's, in comparison, was hardly lit at all, beyond a lamp above the front door. In the dusk Joe observed two massive chaprassis, turbaned, silent and watchful. With Joe and Carter's appearance they seemed inclined to dispute the way, moving discreetly together across the door.

'Just explain,' said Joe, 'that we've only come to buy a bowl of early crocuses.'

But the guardians recognized Charlie and, as discreetly, stood aside and following an unseen signal the door opened from within.

Within the entrance a figure in European dress rose from behind a desk and in heavily accented English gave them a smiling greeting. The accent? French? Joe wondered. Italian perhaps? He wasn't sure.

'Good evening, gentlemen. If you'd like to wait here . . . I'd be very pleased to bring you a drink if you'll say what would be your preference. We're not busy tonight. You shouldn't have to wait at all.'

Charlie Carter cut him short. 'Would you tell Mr Troop that we're here? Police Superintendent Carter and Commander Sandilands.'

Before there could be a reply a booming voice was heard from the balcony above. 'Charlie! An unexpected pleasure! And Commander Sandilands?'

Joe became aware of a large figure in a white suit, a purple cummerbund, a pair of black and white co-respondent shoes, a cigar burning in his hand.

'Stay where you are – I'll come down.'

As he descended the stairs he glanced out through a small window, observing the two silent policemen outside. 'Not entirely a social call, I see? None the less welcome for all that. Come through to the office and we'll have a small drink. Perhaps we'll have a large drink?'

He spoke to the receptionist.

The office to which he led them might have been something out of the Arabian Nights Entertainment. A difficult room to sit in with dignity, they both found, since they were offered nothing more formal than divans and cushions. As they entered the room a further door opened and closed, admitting briefly the tinkle of Indian music from the back premises.

Almost before they had sat down, following a discreet knock on the door a bottle of champagne appeared on a tray with three glasses.

'Now,' said Edgar Troop, 'I'd like to know the nature of this visit so I'm hoping you're going to accept a drink.' Troop turned confidentially to Joe. 'I don't know, Commander, how familiar you are with Indian ways – rather different here from Scotland Yard I dare say. It's impossible to go anywhere, do anything or call on anybody without being offered a dish of sweets and this establishment, although European, is no exception.'

As he spoke the door opened and a slender figure in a pink sari entered, a silver tray in her hand. A second figure in a green sari followed. Both girls, Joe estimated, were in their late teens, both tinkled with cheap jewellery, but where one had the wheaten pallor of a Eurasian, the other was ebony black. They deposited the tray on a low table and in a pose of theatrical submission, hands folded, eyes downcast, they stood by the door for an embarrassing moment until Edgar Troop with a wide gesture of a large hairy hand waved them away. With repeated salaams they backed away through the door.

'You're sure,' said Edgar Troop, 'there's nothing more with which I can provide you?'

He looked from one to the other, very much at ease, his eyes wreathed in smiles and said again, 'Anything with which I can provide you?'

'Information,' said Carter coldly.

Troop looked genially from one to the other. 'Ask your questions and if I can I'll supply the answers.'

'A simple question,' said Carter. 'What were you doing yesterday afternoon, let us say between noon and four o'clock in the afternoon?'

Troop appeared to relax. 'Easy,' he said. 'I left here at about twelve and I had tiffin with Johnny Bristow and Jackie Carlisle. Bertie Hearn-Robinson was there too for a while. Oh, and Reggie Sharpe but he had to leave to go to Annandale.'

'Where do your friends live?'

'Well, I don't suppose I have to tell the omniscient police but they – Johnny, Jackie and Bertie – share that large house on Mount Pleasant – the corner house, just past the Cecil Hotel. They're living in a chummery.'

'And they would be able to confirm this?'

'Yes, of course they would.'

'And you got there just after twelve?'

'Say ten past.'

'Was this a long-made arrangement?'

'No. It wasn't an arrangement at all. Just went round to see what they were all up to. Planning to have a game of snooker, to tell you the truth.' And, turning to Joe, 'Do you play snooker? Have you ever played snooker? It's all the rage here. Billiard game, you know.'

'I've heard of it,' said Joe.

'We should play sometime.'

'So,' said Charlie Carter, 'you were planning to play snooker though you seem to suggest that you didn't in fact do so?'

'That's quite true. When it came to the point, it was such a lovely day we thought we'd go for a drive. Jackie had got a new car and wanted to show it off to us so that's what we did.'

'Four of you?'

'No, as I said, Bertie stayed for tiffin but then had to go and do something else. Working man, you know. Reggie was due up at Annandale to look over some nag on the racecourse so we drove him up there and dropped him off then Johnny and Jackie and I went on up into the hills as far as the road was decent. We took the Mashobra road.'

'And when did you return?'

'Oh, I don't know. About three, I should say.'

'And then what happened?'

Joe had listened to Carter's level questions and sat in silence examining the room. The pictures on the wall were in the Mogul erotic tradition of centuries, that is to say bejewelled and moustachioed rajahs expressionlessly penetrated scantily silk-clad and large-eyed maidens whose thoughts, by some trick of the painting, seemed to be miles away. They seemed indifferent to the convolute and anatomically improbable positions in which they found themselves. There were though, Joe noted, some beautiful rugs on the floor, some good Tibetan cushions and a particularly fine brass hanging lamp. 'Come through to my office,' Edgar Troop had said. But whatever else this apartment might be it was no office.

Edgar Troop lounged amongst the cushions and Joe surveyed him. He was tall, nearly as tall as Joe himself, and must once have had brutish good looks. Mottled face and vinous nose hinted at the reason for his slide from peak physical perfection, Joe thought. His gaping shirt revealed a hairy chest, the top button of his trousers was undone and his braces strained over his shoulders like straps over a trunk.

Charlie Carter's insistent questions flowed on. 'And then what happened?' he repeated.

Before replying, Edgar Troop refilled his glass. 'Have another bottle, shall we?' he asked, looking from Joe to Charlie and back again. Both shook their heads. 'I get so dry,' said Troop apologetically. 'My doctor's always telling me to keep up the fluids and I do my best. But you were asking . . .?'

'What happened then?'

'Well, Johnny and I settled down to our belated game of snooker while Jackie stayed to play with his car. We had three frames – if I thought a bit I might even be able to tell you the score. Johnny won the first two and I won the third. I think. That's just about our average form. I think I got back here at about five o'clock.'

'So during the afternoon from midday until about five there was no time when you were not in the presence of others?'

'That's right.'

'And all will be prepared to bear you out?'

'I see no reason why not. But now – I've been very patient. I'm not accustomed to being grilled in my own office and more or less in the presence of my staff. I think I'm entitled to ask what the hell is all this about? Presumably you're investigating the death of the unfortunate Russkie? Now what on earth motive could I have? Just answer me that because I'm getting rather fed up with this.'

Charlie Carter ignored the question. 'Tell me, Mr Troop,' he said, 'do you own a .303 rifle?'

The question seemed briefly to disconcert Edgar Troop but he rallied smoothly. 'As a matter of fact I own two .303 rifles. One is a German sporting rifle and one a British Army Short Lee-Enfield, mark three.'

'Would you lend them to us?'

'Lend them? To you? Well, I suppose so,' said Troop. 'But I can't imagine why you'd want to borrow them. I do hire out sporting equipment, you know, to tourists – would-be shikari. Be glad to hire them out to you for the afternoon. If you really want them.'

'If we were truly investigating the death of Feodor Korsovsky,' said Charlie placidly, 'and if we were seriously wondering whether it could have been any concern of yours, the first thing I would do (and I have made arrangements to do so) would be to extract the bullet from wherever it lodged, fire a practice round from each of your muskets and forensically examine the bullet. It can be as useful as a fingerprint.'

'Well, let me know when you'd like to do that. And in the

meantime, I hope you'll excuse me but at this time of night I'm usually as they say in the theatre "front of house".'

Subconsciously Joe had become aware of noises drifting through from the entrance, roars of hearty and European laughter, the angry, chiding voice of an Indian woman, a drift of drunken song and the scamper of light feet up and down the stairs and round the balcony.

Edgar Troop rose to his feet. 'You must excuse me,' he said. 'Now come out this way. You really don't want to go back through the entrance. Never know who you might meet! Senior officers sometimes feel the urge to buy a bunch of flowers at this time of night and we pride ourselves on the discretion of our service. Go with Claudio – he'll let you out the back. And I'll bid you both farewell. Let me know when you want to pop off a few guns.'

He clapped his hands and the elegant European youth appeared at once. Troop gave a mocking salute and made towards the door. He was halted by Claudio who murmured, 'Excuse me, sir, I have a message for these gentlemen.'

'A message? For these gentlemen?' said Troop in surprise. 'Who from? Does anyone know you were coming here?'

Claudio smiled a discreet smile. 'The message is from madame. From Madame Flora, that is.'

Troop looked resentfully up. 'Now what on earth . . .? But what was the message?'

'Only to ask if the gentlemen would favour her with a visit before they left.'

Charlie Carter looked a question.

'Certainly,' said Joe. 'Wouldn't miss it for the world! Probably all in the night's work for you but I'm mesmerized by the veiled hints of oriental promise.'

'Well,' said Troop, 'if you're going, you'd better go. We've got out of the habit of keeping Flora waiting. Claudio will show you the way.'

He hurried off.

Another woman whose will will be done, thought Joe with vivid memories of the skill with which Alice had kept him at arm's length.

Claudio indicated that they should follow him. As Joe scrambled to his feet he gave a small exclamation of surprise. He leaned forward and picked something up from the floor. Handing the object to Claudio he said casually, 'Captain Troop dropped this, would you hand it back to him?'

Claudio held out his hand, looked disdainfully at the packet of Black Cat cigarettes and gave it back to Joe. 'I'm sorry, sir, you are mistaken. Captain Troop smokes only cigars. The best cigars. Perhaps your friend . . .?'

'Oh, yes, quite. Mine, I'm afraid,' said Carter and pocketed the cigarettes.

They were led down a corridor and along a raised internal verandah from where they glimpsed below them a vividly green indoor garden. The tinkling of a fountain drew Joe irresistibly over to the fretted balustrade. Small flowering trees were growing in carefully arranged profusion, lamps had been lit beneath each and the effect in the warm dusk was magical. The heat of the day was still rising from the earth of this south-facing slope and though a mountain chill would soon take its place, for this moment Joe thought he was peering down into paradise. An impression reinforced by the presence of girls sitting in twos and threes on cushions, laughing and chattering. Joe had a glancing impression of bright silks, dark eyes raised invitingly to his, white teeth and fluttering hands. The scent of strange flowers mixed with a trace of something more elusive – hashish? – rose teasingly to his nostrils as he leaned over.

He was drawn on by a look from Claudio, who was holding open a door at the far end. Joe and Carter moved through and along another corridor.

'If we had to find our way out of here in a hurry,' Joe muttered to Carter, 'could you do it? Not sure I could.'

Carter grinned and nodded confidently. 'Don't worry. I've got the place mapped.'

Claudio stopped at a carved wood door, listened, opened it and waved them in. He closed the door behind them and they were left alone with Madame Flora.

Chapter Nine

What had Joe expected? A flaunting madam of the kind he had encountered in London with gimlet eyes, bad teeth, rouged face and puffy bosom exuding wafts of Phul Nana? A corseted, iron-grey Frenchwoman with steel-trap mouth and cash box?

Carter's eyes crinkled with amusement as he watched Joe's reaction to his first sight of Madame Flora.

Joe was for a moment overwhelmed. He was taken back in time to a not-forgotten London summer which, at the age of thirteen, he had spent with two elderly uncles in Eaton Square. The uncles had set out to show him the town and make his stay a happy one. The gawky, inexperienced Borderer, neither truly Scots nor truly English in their estimation, but fully uncivilized, had been taken from gallery to gallery, to concert hall, to music hall and to the opera. And Joe had fallen in love. In love with Carmen.

He had been enchanted by the first opera he had ever seen but, even more, his awakening sexual and romantic yearnings had found a focus in the mezzo-soprano who had sung the part of Carmen. He could still call back, seventeen years on, the luxuriant dark hair, the glowing eyes that seemed to single him out in the audience and flirt with him, the voice, seductive, treacherous and reeking of death.

When his uncles had, at the end of the performance, declared their intention of taking him round backstage to meet her, Joe thought he'd never be able to breathe properly again. He remembered the moment still, the smell of the oil lamps, the shouts and laughter and bustle in the hidden and glamorous world behind the stage, and he remembered Carmen taking his hot hand in her two cool ones and leaning forward to kiss him on both cheeks.

Her soft hair had brushed his forehead and he hadn't been able to say a word.

As Madame Flora took Joe's hand in her slim, scented one he was transported back to that moment with a completeness that left him silent and astonished.

Carter covered for Joe's unaccustomed gauche reaction by breaking into a very English speech, his voice just retaining the steely edge which might be considered appropriate to keep the distance between a police superintendent and the proprietor of a brothel, however elegant. 'Always good to see you, Flora. Glad to see evidence of prosperity on every hand. I must present a friend and valued colleague . . .'

While he burbled on Joe dragged himself away from the past and focused on the woman smiling up at him. The same glossy dark hair but cut fashionably short and waving naturally about her head, large dark eyes in an olive skin and a nose of Grecian straightness – she could be southern French, Provençal, Joe guessed. A girl from Arles.

'Madame,' he said, 'je suis enchanté de faire votre connaissance. J'ai tellement entendu parler de vous depuis mon arrivée à Simla.'

'Oh, Commander,' she said, 'do let us speak in English! Captain Carter would feel we were excluding him perhaps from our conversation.'

The English was perfect with an attractive accent overlaying it. Whereas most French and certainly Parisians made a guttural, throaty sound when they pronounced the letter 'r', Flora rolled her 'r' sounds, making Joe even more certain that she was Provençal. And this distinctive sound was most likely the reason Carter had been uneasy with her accent – '. . . a little bit too ooh-là-là,' he had said.

Joe persisted. He wanted to hear her speak French. 'Madame est Arlésienne, peut-être? Vous avez un léger accent du Midi, il me semble . . .'

'Ah, oui! Vous l'avez bien deviné. Je suis, en effet, née en Provence. Et vous allez maintenant sans doute faire des observations sur l'authenticité de la ligne greque de mon nez?'

She stuck her nose in the air and offered him her profile and a smile undoubtedly inviting.

This was exactly what he'd been about to say. And he knew now that what she said about her origins was true. He reverted to English to reassure Carter who was beginning to look anxious. 'They say, Carter, that the most beautiful women in France are descended from the early Greek settlers in the south and, believe me, if you'd ever been to a bull-running feria in Arles in the summertime, you'd say so too.'

'I had not expected such gallantry from a London policeman,' said Flora.

'Even a London policeman may appreciate beauty wherever he meets it,' said Joe.

Carter cleared his throat and looked at Joe sourly. 'If you have nothing to add to that pronouncement let us turn to Flora and see what's on her mind.'

Her face clouded for a moment and, with a gesture, she invited them to sit on a gilt-legged sofa piled high with damask cushions. As they settled themselves, Joe watched her move gracefully across the room to fetch a decanter of whisky and three glasses set out on a tray. The room had none of the seductive oriental atmosphere of Captain Troop's office but was none the less of a decided and calculated style. French Château, Joe thought. Crystal wall sconces illuminated a grand sideboard bearing piles of Gien china plates and Venetian glasses, a subtle blue and white contrast in simplicity and luxury. Spindle-legged tables which would have looked quite at home in Versailles were scattered around the room, each showing off a pretty object in gold or silver. A large fireplace in which smouldered a log or two was flanked by ebony cupids and surmounted by a tall gold decorated mirror. On the mantelpiece a handsome Sèvres clock ticked comfortably. The pale green walls with panelling picked out in a darker shade gave the room an air of calm and elegance.

A strange ambience, though a convincing one and one that must have cost a great deal of money, Joe thought, an odd setting for Flora who, in Joe's increasingly fervid imagination, would have looked more at home sitting side saddle on a white horse of the Camargue, wearing a red ruched and frilled dress, one suntanned knee exposed as she and her cavalier herded black bulls through the sun-bleached streets of Arles. Against the traditional decor Flora seemed not to fit. She was wearing, not the red flounces Joe was convinced she was born to, but a dark blue silken dress which stopped a fashionable two inches below her knee. Her stockings were silk and flesh-coloured and her dark blue shoes were of kid. Around her throat was a long rope of pearls. Large pearls, Joe noted. Good quality pearls, beautifully sized and matched. In her ears were clusters of pearls and diamonds. Did she always dress as though setting out for cocktails at the Ritz, he wondered, or was the effect designed to impress them? She could have put on this outfit while they had been engaged with Troop. But, whatever Flora's antecedents, whatever her present proclivities, it was clear that business was booming. Expense chez Flora was not spared.

She poured them each a glass of whisky which they sipped politely and put down again on the table. She took a cedarwood box from the table, opened it and offered it to them. 'Turkish on this side and gaspers at the other,' she said. Joe took one of the Turkish cigarettes and in turn offered the box to Flora.

'Turkish, thank you. Not fond of Virginian tobacco,' he said. 'Will you have one?'

She also chose a mild cigarette and Joe leaned forward and lit it for her. She inhaled the scented cigarette gratefully then, after a moment, she went to the door and opened it abruptly, looking this way and that. Closing it, she returned to settle on a chair opposite them. Without doubt a piece of theatre, Joe decided suspiciously.

'You are here to investigate the shooting of the Russian singer, are you not?'

'That's so,' said Carter. 'And we are also reinvestigating the murder last year of Lionel Conyers. Do you have any information for us about either of these tragedies?' He turned to Joe. 'Madame Flora quite often gets to hear of things which would otherwise remain a mystery to the forces of law and order,' he said wryly. 'And, naturally, we are very grateful when she passes the information to us and we express our gratitude in an appropriate manner. Which is to say – we leave her in peace to tread the tightrope between the legal and the . . . not so legal.'

They smiled conspiratorially at each other.

'There is something, yes,' she said hesitantly. 'Something I find disturbing and hard to believe. Something which I think I should not tell you but yet I have to tell you . . .' She broke off in confusion and started to bite her thumbnail.

'We will be very discreet, Flora, you know that,' said Carter reassuringly.

She nodded and seemed to pull herself together. 'I hear – through my usual channels – that you are looking for the murder weapon?'

'That's true,' said Carter. 'It's a .303 rifle. The same gun could well have been used in both killings.'

'I think the gun you are looking for may be only a few steps from where we are sitting, Superintendent,' she said steadily and took another puff at her cigarette.

'Edgar Troop's pair of .303 rifles?' said Carter. 'Yes, we asked him about those and he's given us permission to take them away and test them.'

'Pair?' she said in surprise. 'Captain, there are *three*.'

She stubbed her cigarette out in a silver bowl and stood up. 'Come with me.' She glanced quickly at the clock. 'Everyone will be busy front of house at this time of day. Move quietly.'

She led them into the corridor which widened out into a small hallway. In one alcove cartridge belts and bags hung from hooks. In the other alcove in a locking glass-fronted gun cupboard were a pair of twelve-bore shotguns, other armament of smaller calibre and two rifles. .303s.

'Two?' queried Carter.

Flora shook her head and pointed to a second cupboard with a solid panelled door. She stood on tiptoe and ran a hand along the top. Showing them a small key she unlocked the cupboard and they peered inside. Behind the door, on the right, wrapped in an oily rag, was a third rifle.

Joe took it, holding it carefully by the barrel, and mimed that he wished to take the other two rifles as well. Flora unlocked the second cupboard and Joe gathered them up. Handing one to Charlie Carter, Joe took two rifles under his arm and they returned together to Flora's room. The rifles looked incongruous amongst the studied elegance of that pretty and civilized room. Not knowing what to do with them, Joe slid them under the sofa.

Carter scribbled out a note for Troop saying simply that, as arranged and agreed, they had taken his .303 rifles away to the police station for testing and handed it to Flora.

'To keep this official,' he said, 'here's a receipt for the armament but now – tell us what you're thinking, Flora,' said Carter.

She was once again hesitant. 'I hate disloyalty. Loyalty is the quality above all that I demand in my staff and yet here I am about to betray perhaps a man who has been of great service to me since I arrived in Simla, and I am not ungrateful.'

'We're talking about murder, Flora, not accusing someone of making off with the silver fruit knives.' Carter's voice acquired an official edge.

'Yes, of course. Murder,' she said more confidently. 'And I have wondered whether Edgar might be involved. He is very close to Reggie Sharpe, as you know. I have thought – with the whole of Simla – that Reggie might have been very thankful that his brother-in-law never arrived in Simla. Where would he turn? To Edgar of course! Edgar knows the ropes; he's well connected. Some of his associates are shady and worse. Yes, if he needed help he would have come to Edgar. They are always doing each other favours in their tight little group . . . and Edgar is a very good shot.'

'Flora,' said Carter, 'I want you to be very careful and ponder what you say. So far this is a private conversation but you are levelling an accusation of murder against a man who – whatever else he may be – is acknowledged as a close associate – some say a partner – of yours. We have had a suspicion identical with your own. How far are you prepared to go with this? Indeed, I wonder why you should be saying this to us at all?'

Flora drew deeply on her cigarette before replying and, briefly, her carefully made-up face was haggard in the lamplight as she said, 'I'll go all the way with you if I must.'

'Troop produces a strong alibi,' said Carter. 'And for both occasions. More or less the same thing – out with his friends. Corroborated, of course. Impossible to break. Look, have you any other reason for thinking Troop might be involved?'

She didn't need to reflect on her answer. 'Yes, Superintendent. Before the Conyers murder Edgar had been in debt. Gambling debts. He had tried to take more than was his due from the house profits and I had protested.' A look of anxiety which might have amounted to fear furrowed her brow for a moment. 'He reacted badly to that, I'm afraid! He told me what I could do with my money – very impolitely – and hinted that he knew other ways of getting it. It made me wonder, I must confess.'

'And now?' asked Carter. 'Any signs of a flush of money?'

'I don't know . . . I'm not sure. Superintendent! Commander Sandilands! Do I have your absolute assurance that you will say nothing of this? If Edgar were to find out that I . . . He is a violent man, you know that, I think. He goes about in the world in a way which I am unable to do. His influence reaches further than one might expect and I do not understand why or how far. He has friends, friends who are unquestioningly loyal, friends on whom he has special claims, I believe.'

'You mean he has the wherewithal to blackmail some influential and unscrupulous men and that he might, if pushed, use that influence to do you harm?' Joe asked.

'Do me harm?' She smiled. 'That man would put a cobra in my bed!'

Carter stirred uneasily. 'Look, Flora, we're very grateful for the information you've given us. You are in no danger from what we may divulge. You can rely absolutely on our discretion.'

'Flora,' said Joe seriously, 'I continue to wonder why you are telling us this. Are you planning to break with Troop? For good? Is this the end of a beautiful friendship? Or merely a lovers' tiff?'

'Break with Edgar? I wouldn't dare!'

'Leave it there,' said Joe, 'for the moment. But if we were to want to communicate with you without raising suspicions, without going through the Troop front-of-house presence, is there any way . . .?'

'Of course. Claudio. Contact him. He is discreet and loyal to me. And now I will show you to a side door. Edgar will grow suspicious if I delay my appearance any longer.' She smiled a sly smile. 'We have a most distinguished visitor to the house this evening.'

As they walked back to the police station in the Simla dusk, they went over the two interviews, exclaiming, swearing and laughing.

'Now see here, Sandilands,' said Carter, handing back to Joe the packet of cigarettes Joe had claimed to have found, 'you're to give me warning before you go pulling a trick like that again!'

'Well, you never know! Seemed worth the try,' said Joe. 'But the whole place seems to abound in smoker's requisites to suit all types so I don't think it got us very far. Even the madam likes to take a puff, it seems.'

'So, where do you think all this leaves us? Troop? Flora? Reggie? In collusion or at each other's throats? Who's your money on? Can we believe a word Flora says?'

'Well, considering Troop for a moment – he's quite a conspirator, our Mr Troop, but not a very practised one!'

'Oh? How so?'

'Well, first, that was an over-elaborate alibi he dished up and it depends on the testimony of three or four people. If it's true, then he has no problems but if it *isn't*, they'd have to be as well rehearsed as the chorus of the *Messiah* if they're all to give us the same story, same times, same places. Very easy to break down an alibi like that. Want to watch me do it?'

'I'll take Johnny Bristow and you can have Jackie Carlisle,' said Carter with relish.

'I shall be very surprised if there isn't a gap or two. Not sure I believed a word he said.'

'And then there's the guns! I'll get them examined as soon as we get to the station. Tomorrow we'll fire off a few rounds and send the results to Calcutta.'

'Fingerprinting?' said Joe. 'Are you all right for fingerprinting? I can –'

'Got everything we need,' said Carter confidently.

'And what did you make of Flora's fingering her partner for the double murder? Does she perhaps want him out of the way? Is she really afraid of him? You seem to know her pretty well?'

'Wouldn't say that,' said Carter uncomfortably. 'I don't think anyone really knows her. And as for being afraid – don't be taken in! Is a crocodile afraid of a rabbit? I can tell you, Sandilands, if I had to encounter one or other of them in a dark alley I'd choose Troop every time!'

'Still, there was something,' said Joe slowly, 'the wistful way she said she couldn't move about in the same circles, have the same influence as Troop . . . there was a genuine uncertainty there and perhaps fear? Don't you think?'

'Come down to earth!' said Carter derisively. 'Flora has lots of charm and poise and stunning looks with a certain amount of sexual magnetism – to which many fall prey. And, speaking of which – how's *your* blood pressure, heart rate and respiration? But don't forget she runs a grossly immoral business. She stays inside the law but she goes along with me because I *could* close her down – and there's a lot to be said for an establishment of *that* sort in a town of *this* sort. It's an alliance perhaps but not a friendship. I'm sure I don't need to say any of this – but, have a care, Joe! Have a care! Put your loose change and six-shooter under the pillow!'

'Oh, come now! I didn't think she was particularly setting out to charm and, anyway, I'm charm-proof!'

'I think she batted a pair of dampened eyelashes at you and you melted! I can see I shall have to watch your back for you, Sandilands! Now, I'll get the chaps to drop these guns off at the station and head for home. Meg will be pleased to see me. If you don't hang about you might get back to the Governor's house in time for dessert. Always assuming he's there, of course, and not out roistering at Flora's!' He laughed. 'She did say she was expecting some top brass this evening! Pity we'll never know exactly who.'

Chapter Ten

A little unsure of his welcome, Joe duly presented himself at the Residency. He couldn't remember whether Sir George had been expecting him back for dinner and it was now half-past nine. But, hospitable to the last, Sir George greeted him with a cheerful bellow as he walked across the hallway and into the dining room.

'Ah, there you are, my dear fellow! I understood that you had last been seen making your way under police escort into Madame Flora's. Shan't see him until morning! I thought. Boys will be boys! And worse – in Simla, *men* will be boys! What have you been up to, Joe?'

'I really don't know,' said Joe, 'how on earth your information service works! How the deuce could you possibly know that I'd visited Madame Flora? I only left there ten minutes ago.'

'It's very simple,' said Sir George. 'People like to keep in with me – they know I like to have information of all sorts and no better way of keeping in with me than by bringing me news as it arises. Anyway – so you've seen Madame Flora?'

'I've seen her, I've seen the charming Captain Troop and I spent quite a lot of time earlier with Alice Conyers-Sharpe and, as no doubt you already know, I had lunch with Meg and Charlie Carter.'

'Tell me – Alice – what about Alice?'

'She has all the charm, all the elegance, all the competence – a sort of ruthless competence – and she has glittering success. Popular, you might say, with all classes of the community, including yourself, unless I'm mistaken.'

'That's all very fine, Joe, but your next sentence is going to start with the word "but". Am I right?'

114

'Yes,' said Joe reluctantly, 'you're right. But there is something there I can't get hold of. I'm absolutely convinced that there is some connection between her and Korsovsky. I believe there is some connection between her and Reggie Sharpe and Edgar Troop. I'm increasingly of the opinion that Troop knows a very great deal more about these killings than he is saying.'

Joe explained his suspicions concerning the .303 rifle.

As he spoke a procession entered the room. A tray bearing a bowl of soup, a chapatti, a cold roast grouse and, on the side, a green salad.

'I guessed,' said Sir George, 'in the light of your busy evening that you hadn't had anything to eat. Will this do you? There's a good Stilton out there – shall I send for it?'

'No. This'll do me fine,' said Joe. 'Absolutely fine.' And he continued his account.

'I have a very strong feeling that some part of the secrets arise and are connected with the Beaune railway crash,' he said, telling Sir George about the newspaper he'd found in Korsovsky's luggage. 'Alice remembers practically nothing about it. She was knocked cold by the first impact apparently but remembers coming round in hospital in Beaune. It's always been said that she was the sole survivor and so she believes but we've discovered that that's not true. According to *Le Matin*, there was a British officer on the train, name of Simpson, very badly wounded in the war and badly damaged in the crash. We're trying to run him to earth to see what he has to tell us. Probably nothing to the point.'

'Well, well,' said Sir George. 'That's something, in spite of my impeccable information service, that I didn't know! One more survivor, eh?'

'And I have one other possible source: she's not exactly a survivor, nor yet is she a witness, but there is someone who may have some information that is of value to us . . . I'm referring to Marie-Jeanne Pitiot. She's right here in Simla.'

'I know who you mean. Frenchwoman – another one. Runs a dress shop. Very successful, I believe. Why might she know anything about it?'

'She's probably the person who knows Alice better than anyone, I'm told, and she was with her right after the crash that seems to have had such significance for Korsovsky. I'm planning to call on her. Not quite sure how I can question her without seeming to breach Alice's confidence, but there it is.'

'I'm confident that you will handle the interview with aplomb,' said George. 'You'll find La Belle Epoque couldn't be more different from the other French-run place in town! Height of elegance. Everything above board. Best clientele. Marie-Jeanne Pitiot has always seemed a bit mysterious to me, though,' he added.

'The ex-nurse?'

'Yes. Seems a well-bred sort of woman. Good Catholic family, I understand. Parents wanted her to be a nun. That wasn't Marie-Jeanne's intention at all and they compromised on nursing. Rather a plain girl – gawky, that's the word. I gather that marriage was not seen as much of an option.'

'Has she kept up her friendship with Alice since they arrived here?'

'Oh yes, I'd say they were very thick. She seems always to be on hand to support Alice in her more tense moments. She was with Alice at the shooting competition last year the day young Conyers was killed and it was Marie-Jeanne, I couldn't help noticing, not Reggie to whom Alice turned for comfort when they broke the news of Lionel's death. Now finish that up and have a glass of port. I'll join you. We might go into the library – it's rather more comfortable in there. Koi hai!'

They carried their glasses into the other room.

'I like this room,' said George. 'More friendly. The rooms on the floor above, of course, are supposed to be for entertaining but you can't really relax with a fifteen-foot ceiling, at least I can't. Take the big chair by the window, have another glass and tell me, if you can, what possible motive do you ascribe to Edgar Troop? Why would he want to shoot Conyers and why Korsovsky? What gain could there possibly be for him unless you're going to suggest that somebody employed him to do the dirty deed. (That's not impossible, by the way.)'

'I hadn't told you that I suspected Edgar Troop but I won't deny it – I do! It may simply be because I think he's a nasty piece of work and I know that oughtn't to influence me but it does. He's just the sort of man I don't like though I have to admit that he answered all Charlie Carter's questions with manly frankness.'

'Don't kid yourself that you saw the whole of Flora's establishment,' said George. 'I understand it goes for miles. It's one of the oldest houses in Simla. It climbs the hill, it goes into the hill, they tell me – "caverns measureless to man" you might say. I think there are about six exits; there may be as many as thirty rooms. Impossible to raid even if you wanted to. I haven't been worried about the place. You might say it serves a useful social function and gives no cause for concern – at least until recently.'

'Recently?' Joe asked.

'There's a very faint suspicion,' said George. 'We're not far from the frontier here and, of course, smuggling is a way of life, smuggling anything – gold, firearms, women. It's as old as the frontier itself but just lately it has seemed as if it's been not only more widespread but better organized. There are an awful lot of rifles washing about in the world – British Army surplus, French Army surplus, German rifles (much in demand) – the demand has always been there and now you might say the supply has caught up with it. And the collapse of the Turkish Empire has had its effect and the Arab states – not so meticulous, not above a little slavery, it would appear.'

'And if you had to pinpoint the marketplace for all this trade in Simla you'd say – Flora's?'

'It's a possibility.'

Joe frowned. 'Everywhere I turn in this investigation I confront – at the end of the passage as it were – an elegant, cooperative and even talkative woman. Eager to tell me all. And each with a faithful if mysterious gentleman friend in the background. Note this – we have Alice so eager to help, with the faithful Rheza Khan waiting in the wings to do her bidding. There is likewise the friendly but notably shady Flora, supported as far as we can tell by the no less shady Edgar Troop. And let's not forget Claudio who will, we are assured, be prepared to fetch and carry. And linking the two we have the determination on the part of both of them, it would seem, to push Troop off the back of the sledge into the jaws of the pursuing wolves – that's you, me and Carter!'

Chapter Eleven

It was early on Wednesday morning and Carter looked as though he'd been at his desk for hours. He was bubbling with information. 'Lots to report! Sit down, Joe, and hear this! Koi hai! We'll have some tea, please. And bring us some of those little Greek pastries.'

Carter's welcome washed around Joe and he wondered whether the time would ever come when he would not feel the need to question it. His fast rise to his present high position in the force had engendered suspicion and jealousy on the part of his colleagues in England and he had learned to ride the waves of mistrust and misunderstanding using only the strength of his ability to support him. His record spoke for itself. But here was a provincial policeman with no knowledge of Joe's past successes, his outstanding war record, his good family connections, accepting him for what he was – a fellow professional working to the same ends as himself with no suggestion of backbiting or rivalry.

Joe settled down for a happy exchange of information.

'Worst things first, I always say. So here's the bad news.' Carter handed a telegram to Joe. 'Korsovsky's agent – G.M. He's out of the country. We sent our telegram to his Paris office but they say he's on his way to Prague. They're sending it on. Do they have telegram facilities in Prague, do you suppose? Where is it anyway?'

'Czechoslovakia. Important cultural centre – they've got the telegraph all right but we may have to wait a day or two. Infernal nuisance!'

'Well, Korsovsky can't wait even two or three days, I'm afraid.

I've ordered the funeral for tomorrow at Christ Church. We'll just have to hope the chap wasn't a Muslim or a Zoroastrian.'

'Have you got any further with the guns?'

'Yes, we have. We've fired the rounds, got samples to compare with the fatal rounds extracted from the Governor's upholstery and they're, as we speak, on their way to Calcutta. We've finger-printed them. Lots of dabs on the two rifles that were in the glass cupboard – the two that Troop described to us. And, of course, the likelihood is that they're all his. I've sent a chap over to Flora's to get samples of his fingerprints and then we'll see. The other gun – the one in the oily rag – is a bit of a mystery. It had been wiped clean. Not a trace of a dab on it anywhere. What's the betting that's our weapon?'

Carter poured out two welcome cups of Assam tea and crunched his way noisily through a pastry.

'This is the best bit,' he said handing another telegram over. 'Simpson? Remember Simpson? We've got him! The King's Own wired me to say that he'd been demobbed from the regiment three years ago but hadn't left India. Our bloke took up a job with the *Delhi Advertiser*. He's a newspaper sub-editor. I got straight on to the paper and confirmed this. Said I wanted to talk to him about the Beaune rail disaster. Well, blow me! Five minutes later he's on the phone. Very eager to talk about it! It seems our Captain Simpson hasn't taken any leave for three years and is due some. He offered to get on the next train and come up here to Simla to meet us. Says he has something he wants to talk about concerning the crash. Of course, I agreed to this. I've booked a room at the Cecil and we can expect him here tomorrow.'

Joe looked at him anxiously.

'It's all right!' said Carter cheerfully. 'I warned him to be sure to take the Toy Train and on no account to come up in a tonga!

'And now, Joe, tell me what you've been up to. Loafing about Simla? Doing a spot of window shopping?'

'That's right,' Joe smiled. 'Loafing about on the Mall with the louche of the town. And, speaking of the louche of the town, don't we have an appointment to interview one or two of them this morning?'

Carter grinned with anticipation. 'So we have! At least not an appointment because I certainly haven't warned them that we're coming. Johnny and Bertie and Jackie and whoever else is crawling about in that gypsy encampment they call a "chummery"! Come on then, we'll walk there!'

They walked together past the Cecil Hotel and on towards Mount Pleasant and here they were confronted by a large pale corner house where Edgar Troop and others had allegedly spent the afternoon of the murder playing snooker.

The house was large and, indeed, pretentious but woefully run-down and out at elbows. Joe could not help comparing it to the splendour of Sir George's Residence and to the Anglicized charm of Charlie Carter's house under the rule of Meg Carter. The house before Joe seemed to belong to another age, an age before the dominance of the Indian Civil Service. To the days of irresponsible John Company officers with their Indian mistresses tucked away in the mysterious zenana, discreetly amassing a respectable fortune to take home on the side. This, it seemed to Joe, was India before the opening of the Suez Canal, the India of brandy pawnee and chota hazri washed down with a jug of claret.

To the right of the crumbling façade were double gates leading to a stable yard and coach house. Joe heard the clank of buckets and the restive clip of hooves on cobbles. 'Always a few horses here,' said Carter. 'They're not above a little gentlemanly horse-coping. All the old screws in Simla pass through their hands sooner or later.'

The garden was unkempt. A large car with its doors open was carelessly parked aslant in the driveway. Some window shutters were open and others closed and one or two hung on a single hinge. The honky-tonk of a tinny gramophone played from within. Servants there were aplenty but they lacked the servile discretion which Joe found he had come to expect.

As Joe stood for a moment in indecision, Carter's hand fell on his shoulder. 'Come on, we can't stand here loitering with intent. Let's have our chat with the chaps in the chummery! Why don't we step inside? It looks as though we're going to have to announce ourselves. The servants are as alert and welcoming as their masters, you'll find.'

At the door they were confronted by a tall figure in a crumpled white suit and with a solar topee somewhat askew. A silver-mounted walking-stick in his hand supported a lame foot.

'Yes?' he said without welcome.

Carter looked him up and down. 'Johnny Bristow!' he said. 'Charmin' to see you again. And are Jackie Carlisle and Bertie Hearn-Robinson at home?'

'May be. Not sure they'd want to see you. Or your friend. Who's this?' he asked, looking suspiciously at Joe.

'May I introduce Commander Joseph Sandilands of Scotland Yard?'

Joe had met men who were more impressed by the mention of his title. Johnny Bristow sighed with irritation and said, 'I suppose you'd better come in, though what you think any of us will be able to tell you about anything I can't imagine. Shouldn't you be rounding up monkeys or something?'

Joe's impression of Old India was reinforced as they entered the house. The furniture was European but shabby and knocked about. Bills and invitation cards jostled each other on the mantelpiece; not a few of these were over a year old. Inevitably, the prints of the 'Midnight Steeplechase' hung on the wall, along with a fine leopard skin and the head of a markhor. A fencing mask and crossed foils added a note of gentlemanly athleticism and there were whips, boots, boxing gloves, boxes of ammunition, not-well-secured gun cupboards, boxes of cigars sealed and opened, the remains of what had obviously been a copious breakfast amongst the debris of which could be seen a bottle of gin and a bottle of Angostura bitters.

'Give you a drink?' said Johnny Bristow. 'I usually have a pink gin about now. How about you? No? You'd better meet the others.' In rapid and competent Hindustani he gave orders to a passing servant. 'I'll get Jackie and Bertie to come and join us. I think they're out of bed. Ah – Jackie, here's Carter and Mr, er, I suppose I should say Commander, Sandilands.'

Jackie, not long out of bed, blinked myopically at them through bloodshot eyes. He was wearing the crumpled white suit which appeared to be the uniform in the chummery.

'They're here to investigate the death of that unfortunate Russkie, I expect. What they think we can tell them I really don't know,' Johnny said helpfully.

'You can tell me,' said Carter, 'where you both were at the time.'

A third figure, presumably Bertie Hearn-Robinson, entered the room.

'A clumsy device,' he said. 'You say to me, "Where were you at the time?" I tell you. You say, "How do you know that was the time?" And before I know where I am I find myself in handcuffs!'

'Perhaps we can save you a bit of trouble,' said Joe mildly. 'We've had a long conversation with Edgar Troop which would appear satisfactorily to establish an alibi and the first thing a good policeman will do with an alibi is check it and that's why we're here.'

The three men relaxed somewhat and began to talk amongst themselves. 'Well, let's have a think . . . What day are we talking about? . . . Monday, was it? That was the day I went to the dentist.'

'No, that was Tuesday.'

'Was it the day little Maudie Smithson came and made that fuss?'

'Good God, no – that was a fortnight ago!'

'It wasn't, you know!'

'Just a minute, let's get this straight. It was the day . . . or would it have been the day we tried out your new car, Jackie?'

'That's right! I believe that's right! And we all went . . . no, we didn't all go . . . I say, didn't Reggie go up to Annandale that day?'

Joe listened with exasperation and amusement. Too much gin for breakfast. Too many almost identical days. He was never going to get corroboration or denial here. And yet, on the other hand, the absence of corroboration seemed, paradoxically, to corroborate Edgar Troop's account of his movements. Surely if he had anything to hide, surely, if this careless and dissipated crew were any part of a well-structured alibi, they would have been better rehearsed than this? And yet, on the slightest hint from Troop, any one of them would remember anything and, ultimately, contradict anything as required. Joe imagined with horror standing any one of them up in court as a witness.

Charlie, who had been standing silently in the background,

now cut in. 'This is all very jolly and I'm a great believer in police interviews being carried out in the most public possible way but there are limitations and I really think I and the Commander have to ask if we could speak to you individually. Now we can either do that here or you could, as the saying goes, accompany us down to the station to assist us in our enquiries. I'll play this either way. It might be more convenient for you, to say nothing of more discreet, if you were to set aside a room for our use.'

A chorus broke out. 'Of course. Of course. Anything we can do . . . Not sure if we can remember it all but we'll do our best . . . Anyone got a cigarette?'

Finally, 'It's a bit of a mess but why don't you come into my room?' said Jackie Carlisle and he led them into an adjoining room where a servant was perfunctorily flicking about with a duster and had – not well – just finished making up the bed. There were three roorkhi chairs, a low table, a battered bureau, a wheezy overhead fan, several half-empty bottles and three or four boxes of cigars as yet unopened.

'Sit you down,' he said.

Carter flipped a notebook open on his knee. 'Tell me now, Jackie. You met here on the day in question more or less by accident and with no serious prior engagement – am I right?'

'Yes,' said Jackie Carlisle absently.

'And then you had tiffin? Correct?'

'Correct.'

'And what time is tiffin served?'

'Oh, the usual . . . one o'clock or thereabouts.'

'Then you and Johnny and Edgar and Reggie Sharpe went for a drive?'

'That's right. Bertie was there to begin with but he had to go back to work. You see, I've got this new car . . .' He waved an explanatory hand at the window. 'Well, not new exactly but new to me. Second-hand Delage.'

'Ah, yes,' said Carter. 'The Delage. We'd certainly noticed it – so conspicuously and illegally parked. Would you . . .?'

'Oh, I'll get it moved! Have to wait until I've got it fixed though,' he said resentfully. 'Anyway, we drove out on the Mashobra road. We dropped Reggie off at the racecourse to do a bit of horse-coping.'

'And until Reggie got off you were all together?'

'Yes.'

'All the time?'

'Yes, I think all the time. Edgar got out for a pee, if that counts.'

'Anybody else get out for any reason at any time?'

'Not that I remember. It was all a bit informal. You know what it's like just after lunch. I was thinking more about the car than anything else.'

And there was a good deal more in the same vein with a lot of 'as far as I can remember' and occasionally, 'ask the others, I can't remember'.

And then Carlisle resumed, 'And we dropped Reggie off and drove a bit further up towards Mashobra but the road's so bloody awful I didn't want to bump a new car about too much so we turned round – quite difficult up there, I might tell you – and we came back here and played snooker.'

'Who did?'

'Well, I did. Edgar did. Bertie was there, I think. Or – wait a minute – some but not all the time is the answer but you'd better ask him. The long and short of it is we got back here about three and played two or three frames of snooker.'

'Two? Three?'

'Three, I think. Or it may have been four. More than two, less than five. Is this any good?'

Charlie Carter listened with care and made an occasional note. His eye met Joe's and they silently signalled, This is useless! And, indeed, four (or was it by any chance five?) had met for lunch, three (or was it perhaps five?) had gone for a drive, two (or was it three?) came back for a game of snooker which, it would seem, had occupied them from three o'clock until five (or was it six?).

'Thanks, Jackie,' said Carter at last. 'That's been most helpful. Now find Johnny and ask him if he'll kindly look in. If you don't mind us using your room?'

'No. No, no. Help yourself! How about a cigar? Drink, anybody?'

'Now that's what I really appreciate,' said Charlie Carter as Jackie left the room. 'Succinct witness, all the facts at his fingertips, accurate memory of events! Christ! This is no bloody use!

We'll never get anywhere with these chaps! From about twelve noon on any given day they're all completely bottled. They're never going to remember something that happened more than two days ago. We're wasting our time, Joe, you realize that, don't you?'

'Yes,' said Joe, 'I realize that. This could, though, be the most carefully set up bit of obfuscation and by remembering nothing clearly, repeating themselves, contradicting themselves, arguing amongst themselves, they could set up the most impenetrable smoke-screen to conceal the movements of Troop.'

'It could be but I really don't think they've got the brain!'

They sat for a moment dejectedly listening to the creaking of the fan as it stirred up eddies of yesterday's curry, ancient cigar smoke and a hundred years of dissipation.

'Any point going on with this?' said Joe.

Carter eyed him apologetically.

'Got to, old man. Got to. Sake of consistency, I'm afraid.'

'Thought you'd say that,' said Joe. 'Ah, well . . . Next! Johnny, old bean! Take a pew!'

Chapter Twelve

The next morning Joe took a rickshaw back to the Mall and got out in front of a green and gold decorated shop front with its hanging sign, 'La Belle Epoque'. The shop window was empty save for a single dress of red satin displayed on a chromium-plated stand, well lit and managing to be at once exclusive yet discreetly welcoming. Joe was impressed. Impressed and embarrassed, suffering at once from an eagerness to explore and that embarrassment which overcomes the most sophisticated of men when confronted with the anguish of entering a women's dress shop alone.

'I'm supposed to be a policeman. A policeman of international repute, you might say. Clearly at my time of life I ought to be able to walk into a shop with a flourish and that's what I'm going to do!'

The shop door fell open at his gentle pressure and he stepped into a scented half darkness, the light supplied by partially concealed bracket lights set amongst fabrics on display. Side by side and talking loudly, two Englishwomen were considering day dresses being offered to them by two Eurasian girls. The transaction was overseen by a middle-aged and expensively dressed woman whom Joe presumed to be Mademoiselle Pitiot.

Without interrupting her sales talk she extended a welcoming glance to Joe. 'I don't think you would regret it, madame,' she was saying and, turning to the lady's companion, 'Do you not agree? Green is exactly the colour I would choose for madame. Mary, take this into the changing rooms and why not take the blue dress as well? Probably not the yellow – I may be wrong but I think madame would disappear in a yellow dress. Though

126

Lady Everett surprised us all with her choice of daffodil for the viceregal ball last season, did she not? Come through and try them on.'

She shepherded the party into the back premises, the assistants with armfuls of dresses, the customers eager.

This little flurry gave Joe a chance to study Mademoiselle Pitiot. Early forties, fashionably bobbed black hair, obvious and attractive French accent. She was tall and slender but would, Joe thought, never have been reckoned beautiful even in her prime. Her skin was sallow, her eyes dark brown, her nose large, but her smile was wide and friendly. Her manner towards her customers was deferential but behind it there lay a humorous conspiracy which embraced Joe.

She turned to him. 'May I show you something, sir?'

'I'm looking for Mademoiselle Pitiot, the proprietress,' he said, offering his card. 'I am Commander Joseph Sandilands of Scotland Yard and I would like to talk with her for a while.'

'Marie-Jeanne Pitiot,' she said extending a hand. 'How do you do? You are welcome, Commander. But, please, come through to my office.'

She called to an assistant for tea to be brought and led him to a small room, closing the door behind them. Sweeping lengths of fabric and piles of catalogues from two chairs, she offered him a seat and settled down opposite him on the other side of a crowded work table.

'This is about Alice?' she asked. 'And her poor brother who was shot last year? I was with her at Annandale when the news arrived. A dreadful affair! If there's anything I can do to help I'd be delighted to do so. I can't think of anything I haven't already done or said but perhaps Scotland Yard has come up with something?'

'You speak excellent English, mademoiselle,' Joe said.

'Of course! There was a time and not so long ago when I did not but then I met Alice Conyers and we struck a bargain. When she took me into her employ . . . I take it you know the circumstances of this?'

Joe nodded and she continued, '. . . Alice spoke only school French and I had very little English. On the boat out to India I taught her French and she taught me English. We still continue our lessons whenever we meet.'

'Do you meet frequently? Do you still see much of Alice?'

'Yes. We have remained good friends. She never treated me as an employee. She's a very generous-minded girl, Alice, and she often says that she owes her life to me. Quite untrue, of course. But after the Beaune crash it fell to me to nurse her and I was glad to do so. To see her coming through that was a wonderful experience for me but if she owes me anything at all from that time it is nothing to what I owe her for having established me here and helping me to set up La Belle Epoque. I owe all this,' she made a wide gesture, 'to Alice. It's no secret! She gave me money to set up the business and still takes an interest.'

'A financial interest?'

'No. I'm happy to say that the business has long been independent of any support and is flourishing. The only help she continues to give is her valued advice. And I repay Alice with – with what? – with friendship, loyalty and discretion. And in the enclosed and backbiting world of Simla, that is not to be sneezed at, Commander!'

'What do you value about Mrs Sharpe's advice?' Joe asked. This woman was probably closer to Alice Conyers-Sharpe than any other person including her husband and he was anxious to learn more of her without appearing to force confidences.

Marie-Jeanne replied without hesitation. 'She is very clever. She looks on business with a fresh eye, a modern eye. So many centuries of hidebound traditional masculine ways of doing business do not impress her. She dares to tear up the rule book. She does not have to meet – would not be *allowed* to meet other businessmen on their territory in their smoke-wreathed, gin-sodden clubs and deal with them on their terms. She makes the terms. She changes the patterns. She sees where the opportunities arise and she seizes them. ICTC was largely an export firm when she took it over – tea, cotton, indigo, rice – and it still operates as an exporter but she saw, coming fresh from England, that India was longing for the luxuries it had denied itself during the war and she set about importing them. Champagne, whisky, tinned caviar, chiffon dresses from Paris, pianolas from New York – she brings them in and they sell. And her skill is in guessing exactly what people will be wanting next.'

'This is a surprising ability, isn't it, for one so young and inexperienced? You met her yourself when she was still in the egg, so to speak. You have witnessed the transition from untried girl to shrewd businesswoman. Was this a surprising metamorphosis?'

'In a way it was not.' Marie-Jeanne thought for a moment, looking at him consideringly. 'I'll tell you something about Alice! The first surprising thing (of many) I ever noticed about her . . .'

At this moment the door opened and a tea tray was carried in and placed between them. Marie-Jeanne poured out cups for both of them and went on, 'It was her silk underwear that made me realize I was dealing with a complex young girl!' She smiled affectionately.

'Silk underwear?' said Joe in surprise.

'Yes. I was a nurse, you know, working in the hospital in Beaune and I was assigned to Alice when she was carried in on a stretcher as her personal nurse. Not a usual procedure but as she was the only survivor you can imagine that she was very precious. We would have been much blamed if we had allowed her to die. I was to watch her every moment. The best surgeons in France were summoned to her bedside but I was the one who had the initial task of caring for her as she came straight from the scene of the accident.

'My first task was to strip away her torn and bloodstained garments so that we could ascertain the full extent of her injuries. I remember she was wearing a dark grey woollen dress suitable for mourning. It was very plain, very English,' she said with a laugh. 'Of good quality but remarkably ugly and unfashionable. It was one of several similar outfits in her trunk all chosen as suitable for a well-bred English girl travelling to India. Figure my surprise, Commander, when under that drab outer layer there was revealed an emerald green silk camisole and matching knickers with a Paris label! She had stopped off with her companion Miss Benson, sadly killed in the crash, for two or three days in Paris and had dared to kit herself out with the latest in lingerie! I think that this was the first sign of her secret revolt against her narrow, restricted background. On the surface she was neat and decorous but the underpinnings bore witness to the yearnings of a young girl for romance, luxury and fashion. It made me like her a lot!'

Joe smiled. He remembered his older sister, Lydia, years ago swearing him to secrecy in the matter of a clandestine, peach-coloured, mysteriously engineered garment she had called 'camiknickers' which he had agreed to hide in his sweater drawer against the prying eyes of the housekeeper.

'The first sign of revolt?' he pursued.

'Many were to follow! She was eager for life, for new experiences. She learned so quickly, talked to anyone regardless of class or sex, charmed them, heard their advice and weighed it. Alice was like a sponge absorbing everything at great speed.'

'An energetic and formidable lady?' said Joe.

'Oh, yes. And not only energetic in her business activities – you have probably heard that she gives much of her time to good works.'

'Yes, she herself has told me of her connections with the hospital. Determined and hard-working – but tell me, is there a lighter side to Mrs Sharpe's estimable life? Does she ever have fun?'

'All the time!' Marie-Jeanne laughed. 'She loves music, especially jazz . . . she has started a girls' dance group, she is a member of the Spiritualist Society and the Dramatic Society and at weekends she –'

Joe interrupted. 'The Spiritualist Society, did you say?' His question was tinged with disapproval. In London spiritualists were all the rage, many of the old music hall performers with all their old skills intact had found an alternative way of making money by fleecing the gullible who were often in those post-war days desperate for news and contact with their departed loved ones. In Joe's experience blackmail and extortion could follow close behind spiritualist sessions.

'It's quite harmless, Commander,' she said, picking up his disapproval. 'Simla no longer witnesses the glory days of Madame Blavatski but we have our own resident medium, a Mrs Freemantle, who is well thought of.'

Joe made a note of this name and Marie-Jeanne went on, apparently ready to dispel any idea that there might be something shady going on in Simla. 'All the best people go to her seances, you know. Alice is in no way regarded as being out of the ordinary because she takes an interest. And Mrs Freemantle is very talented – I, myself, am not a believer but I have to admit that what she does is skilfully done and does no harm. At best it comforts people and at worst it's a harmless game.'

Joe made a mental note to take this up with Carter. To him, the mention of spiritualism had been a warning signal. He changed the subject, not wishing to alert Marie-Jeanne to his deepening interest.

'So, we have a clever, hard-working and successful lady with a well-rounded personality? But there is, it seems to me, one discordant note in all this . . . her marriage to Reggie Sharpe? Was that, in your opinion, a clever move?' asked Joe.

Marie-Jeanne's tender expression froze into cold disapproval. 'At the time she convinced me – she convinced herself – that it was the right, the sensible, thing to do.' She paused for a moment. 'But I infer from your question that *you* do not consider it a clever move?'

'Not my place to judge.'

'Too late!' she said. 'I think that you have met Reggie and that you have judged him – as we all have.'

'And how is that?'

'As a drunken, self-important, self-indulgent man who could never be the husband Alice deserves!' She made no attempt to hide her anger and scorn.

'You judge him despicable – do you also consider him dangerous?'

'To whom?'

Joe remained silent and looked at her steadily.

'Yes, I do,' she went on. 'I consider him a threat to anyone who would attempt to thwart him and that includes his wife.'

'And Alice is courting danger when she attempts to curb his excesses?'

'Alice is riding a tiger! Reggie is not the toothless old donkey she has persuaded herself that he is!'

Her concern, her distress, was so evident Joe found himself responding to it. 'It may be a consolation, Mademoiselle Pitiot,' he said, 'to hear that only yesterday Alice herself voiced just such suspicions to me and they are being investigated. Nevertheless, her friends would do well to look out for her. I really believe she feels in danger of her life. Please, mademoiselle, seek my help if you think there is anything untoward going on.'

'Thank you, Commander. I will do that.'

She began to stir and look towards the door to the showroom where fresh noises had broken out and was obviously eager to return to the sales floor. Joe rose and began to take his leave. He thanked her for her hospitality and made for the door, turning with his hand on the knob to say, 'I almost forgot to ask and please forgive such a bodeful question – I assure you it is purely routine – but where were you exactly between the hours of twelve and five on Monday?'

For a moment she was taken aback and then said slowly, 'You mean when the Russian opera singer was killed? I was, now let me think . . . Shall I get my day book? No, I think I can remember. I was having tiffin at the Grand Hotel with a glove manufacturer from Bombay until two o'clock – no, later than two – but you won't be able to check that with him because he's since gone on to Calcutta, and after that I went back to my warehouse to look over the latest arrivals with two of my staff. Let me think . . . It was Sumitra and Renée. We must have been there until nearly five o'clock and then I came back to the shop to close down. Do you want me to call my assistants, Commander?'

Joe shook his head. 'Later perhaps, not for the moment, mademoiselle.'

He took his leave and bowed his way out of the shop, emerging into the sunshine with a sigh of relief. Standing for a moment to get his bearings, he decided to walk the hundred yards or so to the Grand Hotel to check Mademoiselle Pitiot's story. He remembered what Carter had said – when it came to shooting, the women of Simla were crack shots and though he had never come across a less likely markswoman than the so correct Mademoiselle Pitiot, Joe was methodical. The murder had occurred at two forty-five exactly so if she had indeed been lunching at the Grand there was no way she could have been five miles away in an inaccessible spot drawing a bead on Korsovsky.

On entering the Grand he was smoothly intercepted by the maître d'hôtel, still at this early hour in shirt-sleeves, busy and not pleased to be interrupted. Joe produced his warrant card which gained him the attention he required and asked to see the reservations for Monday. The maître d'hôtel indicated a large leather-bound book open on a stand by the double doors to the restaurant. Turning back two pages he murmured, 'Monday . . . Not a busy day. By no means a full dining room.'

Joe looked down the short list. At 1 p.m. table number ten had been booked for Mademoiselle Pitiot and guest. 'This guest of Mademoiselle Pitiot – a gentleman?'

The maître d'hôtel did not welcome questions. 'A gentleman, yes. A Frenchman, Monsieur Carneau. He is a regular guest of the hotel. Mademoiselle Pitiot always entertains her business associates here.'

'You know her well, Mademoiselle Pitiot?'

'She also is a regular guest of the hotel, sir. I should say she lunches here two or three times a month.'

'And what time did they leave?'

'Somewhere between half-past two and three o'clock, sir.' And, coldly, 'Do you require to hear the menu they chose? I could have the waiter sent for . . .'

Joe left with expressions of gratitude and made for the police station to check developments with Charlie Carter. As he strolled along looking with fascination at the shop windows he came to an abrupt halt before the display in a jeweller's shop.

It was the rope of pearls that caught his eye. Amongst the riot of glittering pieces, emerald rings, sapphire necklaces, diamond clips, the rope stood out for its simplicity. It was draped around the swanlike neck of a black velvet mannequin and gleamed with the discreet allure of finely matched, high quality pearls. It was an exact likeness of the one he had seen around the neck of Madame Flora.

On impulse he went into the shop. He was relieved to see that he was the only client. A musty smell – of incense? – came faintly to his nose and when his eyes accustomed themselves to the gloom he discovered that he was in a shop very unlike the ones he was used to in the Burlington Arcade. Joe had an impression of a fabulous collection of glittering gems but also of antiquities on display. Were they for sale or were they merely for decoration, the Tibetan ghost masks, the Kashmiri embroideries hanging on the walls, the piles of sumptuous rugs, the racks of silver daggers?

As he gazed, enchanted, an assistant who had been dusting shelves in the gloomy depths of the shop came forward. A handsome young hill boy with turquoise eyes to rival the gems, he addressed Joe politely in English, enquiring what service he might offer the gentleman. Joe asked if he could speak with the proprietor. Since he came forward at once from a back room, Joe assumed that the proprietor had seen him enter.

A middle-aged man with an aquiline nose, sharp eyes and a greying beard, the owner could have been eastern European or even Turkish, Joe guessed. He nodded to Joe and said in an accented English, 'Robertson, Cecil Robertson. Tell me how I may help you, Commander Sandilands.'

Joe looked at him, startled for a moment. Robertson smiled deprecatingly. 'As far as I know, and my knowledge stretches far, Commander, there is only one Scotland Yard policeman at large in Simla at the moment. I assume you are he.'

Joe handed him his card. 'Not on official duty, you understand, Robertson. Purely personal and unprofessional.' He leaned forward and said confidingly, 'Couldn't help noticing as I passed your window that wonderful string of pearls. Just what my, er . . .' He managed a slight stammer and felt that the gloom did not do justice to his blush. 'Well, anyway, it's a lovely piece and might just do the trick, if you follow me . . . eh?'

Robertson smiled and listened.

'Well, to be blunt, how much are you valuing it at?'

'That rope would be worth a thousand rupees, Commander. It is, as you have obviously noticed, very fine. The pearls are exceptional – large and unflawed – and they are well matched. Would you like to handle it?' He smiled. 'I warn you that once you have it in your hands and feel the silkiness and weight of the pearls you will be unwilling to let it go.'

Joe shook his head. 'I'm sorry,' he said, 'but a thousand rupees, that's too steep for a London policeman like me! Ah, well,' he sighed, 'it will have to be chocolates again or perhaps a bouquet of Madame Flora's best.'

He looked closely at the man's face, watching for any change of expression when he heard the name of a client whose neck was adorned by the twin of this necklace. But he was disappointed. The man remained unflinchingly bland and polite.

Joe said goodbye, adding his regrets, and the boy assistant showed him to the door. For a moment Joe stood on the pavement looking again at the necklace. He was remembering not only the pearls around Flora's neck but also the matching pearl and diamond ear-rings.

At that moment he would have given much to turn out Madame Flora's jewel box.

He counted to ten and then swept back into the shop.

Robertson was still behind the counter giving instructions to the boy. He looked up in surprise at Joe's abrupt reappearance and obvious change in demeanour.

'One question,' said Joe. 'This *is* police business and I require an instant and truthful reply. Who, in Simla, is your best customer? And by that I mean the one who spends the largest sums of money with you – who would that be?'

'Mrs Sharpe,' he said without taking time to reflect. 'Alice Conyers-Sharpe.'

Chapter Thirteen

Eager to tell Carter about his foray into the world of fashion and his incursion into the jeweller's shop, Joe hurried along to the police station where he was greeted by smart salutes and wide smiles. A brisk order was called out for tea to be brought and he was shown into Carter's office.

'Ah, Joe! Glad you've surfaced at last! Had word from Simpson. He's on the early train and will be with us about midday. I can see you've been up to something. Your trouble is that, for an experienced bobby, you are sadly impressionable! Can it be Marie-Jeanne Pitiot who's stirred you to such a pitch of excitement?'

Joe went carefully through his interview with Mademoiselle Pitiot, saying at last, 'So it looks as though we've got yet another obliging, communicative, "do let me know if there's anything further I can do to help" woman with a solid alibi on the scene. I begin to get a bit suspicious when all the suspects are falling over themselves to be helpful. Tell you what though, Charlie, I have met someone who made my nose twitch! Anything known – and by that I mean to his discredit, of course – about a Cecil Robertson, jeweller of this town? Cecil Robertson! Such a likely name!'

'Well, for a start, that actually is his name! Scottish father, Persian mother. Not a bad pedigree if you think about it for someone who makes a lot of money out of trading in gems. I keep an eye on him. All that valuable property in small parcels, cash washing about the place, opportunities unrivalled for smuggling and goodness knows what else. As far as I can see there's never been a whiff of suspicion that his business is not entirely above board. His clients include the highest in the land.

And, if you've seen his shop, you'll understand why! It's not Cartier's, it's not Asprey's – it's more Aladdin's Cave and every bit as irresistible! Not only for buying but for selling – or even pawning as well. Expensive place, Simla. Temporary financial embarrassment not unknown and Cecil Robertson's your man!'

'And do you know who is his best customer? I asked him and, without any hesitation, he said – Alice Sharpe. Does that surprise you?'

Carter was silent for a moment, nonplussed. 'Yes, it does,' he said finally. 'I suppose in a way it ought not to because she is, after all, extremely rich but she is not at all showy. She always wears simple frocks and if I were trying to think of a particularly fine piece of jewellery that I've seen her wearing, do you know – I don't think I could mention one! I suppose she does wear the stuff – viceregal balls and that sort of thing – but you'll have to ask Meg for details. It's certainly escaped *my* attention.'

'Whereas Madame Flora flaunts her ill-gotten gains for all to see.'

'Not all. Only clients remember. Seems a bit unfair to waste all that beauty on the lower degrees and the dissolute of the town,' Carter sighed.

A police havildar slipped into the room and gestured towards the window.

'Ah, that'll be him! Our man Simpson!' said Carter, jumping up and going to look out. Joe joined him and they watched as a tonga drew up and a tall man, slim and with a scholarly stoop, got uncertainly out. He was wearing a well-cut brown linen suit, white shirt with a regimental tie and a panama hat. He leaned heavily on a stick and his eyes were concealed behind dark glasses. A waiting policeman greeted him and ushered him swiftly into the station.

Carter went to the door and flung it open. 'Simpson? Captain Colin Simpson?' he said cheerfully. 'Come in, sir. Come in. We're delighted to see you. So very good of you to come! This is Commander Joe Sandilands of Scotland Yard who's on secondment in India at the moment. I mentioned him when we spoke on the telephone. Char! Jildi!'

Carter drew forward a chair and Simpson limped his way to it and settled down. 'It's all right, Captain, I'm not blind,' he said in a firm, cheerful voice. 'But I think you'll understand why I wear these when I take them off.'

He took his dark glasses off for a moment and then replaced them at once. Joe and Carter just had time to register a right eye, brown and alert but surrounded by thick scar tissue, and a shockingly empty left eye socket. 'Apt to frighten the horses to say nothing of the memsahibs, so I keep them covered up. Souvenir of Ypres. The limp's one hundred per cent genuine.'

'Ah, yes, well, thank you for explaining that, Simpson,' said Carter. 'And we're very grateful you could get up here to speak to us with such speed. We don't have much to spare but you must let us pay your expenses – indeed, I insist.'

'Thank you but I was very anxious to come. I dropped quite a few things I ought not to have dropped and there'll be hell to pay when I get back but what you had to say rang a bell with me. Something I've been bottling up for years, you know, always intending to make a clean breast of it, and then realizing that nobody is in the least bit interested in what I have to say – can you imagine?'

'The Beaune railway disaster?' said Joe. 'It's somewhat peripheral to our enquiries, I'm afraid, so I hope you won't think you've wasted your time coming all this way to talk to a couple of strangers about something that might, in the end, have no relevance to our case.'

'Look here,' said Simpson earnestly, 'I've waited three years to talk to someone about the crash. It almost doesn't matter what you decide is the relevance of what I have to say . . . I just need to say it . . . get it out in the open . . . and that's what I've come for.'

Carter sat back in his chair, leaving Joe to continue the conversation. 'Very well, and that's good to hear. Let me start by outlining our area of interest and then perhaps you could just fill in with information as you feel able to do so? This isn't an official interrogation or anything like that – just look on it as three chaps who are trying to tug on loose ends of a puzzle until one end pulls free.

'You were travelling first class when the accident happened, I understand? We are interested in another first class passenger – an English girl called Alice Conyers – and we wondered whether you had any contact with her during the journey?'

'Certainly,' said Simpson. 'I travelled in the same compartment as Alice and at the moment of the accident we were dining together in the dining car.'

Joe and Carter looked at each other, trying to play down their relief and excitement at this.

'Can you tell us about the journey from the start?'

'Paris. Gare de Lyon. A steward found my place and showed me to my carriage. I was wearing dark glasses and walking with a stick and rather enjoying the fact that people were falling over themselves to be of assistance to me. Everyone assumed I was completely blind, of course, with the stick as well. Not proud of it but it did give me a sort of awful advantage over people. They thought I couldn't see but I actually could, and quite well. Not quite as good as being an invisible man but almost. Another advantage was that I could stare at pretty girls if I wanted to for as long as I liked and no one would think I was being rude. And in my compartment there were two girls worth staring at!'

'Two?'

'Yes. In some ways similar, in most very different. Not often you're closeted for several hours with two such good-looking young things! You'd need to have been in hospital – as I was – for two years to imagine how much I appreciated it! There was Alice Conyers, English, on her way to India. I remember she was dowdily dressed even for an English girl and then later I understood she was in mourning for her parents who were not long dead of the flu. Quite a chatterbox but a real charmer, Alice, and obviously driving her companion, a Miss Benson, mad! Now *she* was counting the miles!' Simpson shook his head sadly. 'And she wasn't to know it but there weren't all that many left for her. She died in the crash.'

'And the second young woman?'

'Completely different in style! Older, though not by much I've since thought, French, expensively dressed – Worth or Chanel or somebody of that quality – woman of the world, you'd say. She spoke good English with a very attractive French accent – when Alice let her get a word in edgeways. She was on her way to stay with friends in Nice for the season. Isabelle de Neuville – that was her name.'

'And you found yourselves lunching together?'

'Yes, though the Benson female returned to her compartment.

We were having a jolly good lunch at the same table. It worked very well, surprisingly enough for three strangers. Alice was so alive, so full of excitement at the life she was going to lead no one could resist her. Madame de Neuville was treating her like a rather spoiled little sister – she was very kind and good-humoured, I remember. She herself seemed a little sad – wistful perhaps – and I think she was enjoying Alice's artless prattle, her freshness, her optimism. Me, I was enjoying watching the pair of them!

'And then the world came apart at the seams . . . Alice was still at the table and I had gone to smoke a cigar in the corridor. Madame de Neuville had just gone off to the ladies' room when it happened. I assume you know the details?'

Joe and Carter nodded solemnly.

'We've both read the accounts of the crash,' said Joe. 'But tell us what you remember of it.'

'Yes, well, this is where I get confused,' said Simpson. 'A devastating bang – I mean truly deafening – like the end of the world! I guess that was the engine hitting the parapet. This was followed by a no less deafening series of crashes as the coaches were dragged off the viaduct and into the ravine below. There was a ruinous and continuous roar of noise. Broken glass flying. Everything turned upside down. Little Alice was screaming (and others were screaming).The dining car was split in two as it rolled down the rocky scree and most of the passengers spilled out into the ravine. My head was split open on a rock. I was unconscious and so badly injured I was taken for dead. They actually carted me off to the morgue! I'd been lying there at the scene for God knows how long when I came to. I tried to move my head and couldn't. I thought I was paralysed. I learned after that my head had bled and the clotting blood had stuck it to the rock. They had to cut me free with a knife before they could get me on a stretcher. Anyway, I came to, couldn't move, and started to call for help. There was no noise. No one crying or calling apart from me. Everything was silent except for the occasional creak of metal as another part of the wreck settled. There was a stench of burning all around me.

'I called out again. Gave out a groan more like. And that was when I heard it.' He leaned forward and paused to emphasize the importance of what he was about to say. Carter and Joe remained silent, looking at him with attentive encouragement.

'Someone was walking about. Walking quietly – I thought at the time *stealthily* – stopping at each of the bodies and then moving on. I thought rescuers must have arrived and tried to shout again to let them know I was alive. But whoever it was stopped dead. I shouted again and the steps came on towards me, nearer and nearer but not hurrying. Not hurrying to help. Ridiculous, but I began to be afraid. Tales of battlefields – looters, mad old women who cut the throats of survivors and rob them – came to me and I didn't shout again.

'I just had to wait helpless, paralysed, while the steps got closer. And then someone came just into my field of vision.'

Simpson paused for a moment and touched his missing left eye. 'This side was on top. I was lying on my right side. My spectacles were broken, lost, and all anyone looking down on me would have seen was this blind side. But I had a narrow arc of vision up to about three feet above the ground. Someone was standing beside me, looking at me but not approaching further. Standing back, you know. Not wanting to get involved, you'd say.' Simpson fell silent and looked from one to the other defiantly. 'It was the buttoned boots I saw first and the silk stockings and the dark red skirt with black fur bandings . . .'

Carter glanced at Joe in embarrassment. Simpson picked up the glance.

'I warned you not to believe a word I said,' he reminded them.

'According to reports of the accident only three people survived – yourself, a baby and Alice Conyers who is alive and well and in Simla at this moment,' said Carter.

'I know. I know. And that's obviously what you must believe.' Simpson looked embarrassed but determined and he pressed on. 'But at that time I was convinced that it was Isabelle de Neuville standing by my side. When I realized it was she and not some looter I actually called out to her for help.'

'By name? Did you say her name?'

'No, I think I just called out "Help!" Twice. And she just walked away. Just walked away without saying a word!'

'Unusual behaviour!'

'I was devastated. And later, I was so sure I'd seen Isabelle de Neuville walking about that I enquired after her. They had no clear idea of who was who for a long time of course and by then I'd been carted off to Lyons but when I described a first class passenger and what she was wearing they wrote it down and checked on it. They found her body in the morgue in Beaune. She'd died instantaneously of a broken back and head injuries. There was no way in the world Madame de Neuville could have been walking about that scene of disaster! I am left with two alternatives. I was either seeing her ghost or my mind was disturbed.'

Neither man hastened to deny this. 'It could be either,' said Carter pacifically.

'I was pretty badly beaten up in the war,' Simpson said almost apologetically. 'In fact for some months after, I was, I have to say, out of it. Out of my mind. Neurasthenia's the fancy label they put on it so, you see, you don't need to place any weight on my testimony.' His voice was self-deprecating. 'No one else would dream of doing so. In fact, you're the first people I've mentioned it to. I'm sorry. Just look on it as the ramblings of a man who's had a double dose of cranial punishment.'

'I've known men with neurasthenia,' said Joe carefully, 'and mostly, they've known the difference between that state and normality. I'm guessing you do too.' He gave Simpson a level gaze. 'I'm guessing that you're telling us what were your actual impressions as you lay injured.'

Simpson nodded. 'Yes, I'm sure in my own mind of what I saw but is my own mind a reliable place from which to be viewing the world?'

'Let's assume for the moment that it is,' said Joe. 'And let's further assume that you were not visited by an apparition. We're left with the fact that you were approached by a woman wearing Madame de Neuville's shoes, stockings and skirt and, therefore, reasonably, as you saw no further, we must assume that you did indeed see Isabelle de Neuville and that she survived the crash.'

'But only one woman survived and that was Alice Conyers,' objected Carter.

A terrible theory was beginning to form in Joe's mind. Something Marie-Jeanne Pitiot had innocently said reinforced his theory but it was so fantastical and outrageous he tried to push it away. It came back with greater force. Reluctantly he spoke again.

'There is a way to explain all this,' he said. 'But only one way. And, though I think it's ludicrous, I'll outline my idea anyway. Now – one woman only survived the crash. This is a fact. But which woman? If Simpson can believe the evidence of his one eye, it was the Frenchwoman. Imagine the scene. Miles from anywhere, no hope of rescue for hours. All dead but Simpson who, to all appearances, was dead or as good as. Just Isabelle de Neuville alive.'

Joe took a deep breath and plunged on. 'Suppose she found the body of Alice Conyers, broken-backed, dead. Alice with her hopes of a new life in a new continent, a huge fortune, a marriage ahead of her. Suppose Isabelle is dissatisfied with her own life – this is conjecture now – suppose she is fleeing Paris, running away from an irate or boring husband, from debts, from loneliness – might she not be tempted to change places with Alice? There were no witnesses. She crept around – stealthily was your word for it, Simpson – checking that the other passengers were dead. If she realized Simpson was alive she thought he was blind anyway so that was no obstacle. She takes Alice's clothes off her body, the top layer only, and she substitutes her own. If they didn't fit very well – no problem – they would be so torn and bloodstained no one would notice.'

Simpson nodded silently and Carter made no comment so Joe went on. 'But someone did notice something slightly off key about the clothes! Marie-Jeanne Pitiot was made Alice's personal nurse and she it was who had the task of stripping the damaged garments off her. She remembers being surprised to discover that under the grey serge were underpinnings of emerald green silk, if I remember it correctly. It's her theory that Alice had bought these frivolities in Paris and was wearing them as a hidden sign of revolt against her austere upbringing and I find this totally credible but, on the other hand, there is a more sinister and equally convincing reason. It would have been almost impossible for a woman injured as Isabelle undoubtedly was herself in the accident to wrestle the undergarments from a lifeless corpse and put them on herself and repeat the procedure with her own clothes. Not a task for the faint-hearted nor one for someone suffering from shock, cracked ribs and a facial wound.'

'Just about possible for her to exchange the outer garments, I would have thought,' said Carter, 'and *that* would have taken incredible determination.'

'Not so sure,' said Simpson. And, turning to Joe, 'I think you must have been in the war. A survivor. You know what battle-fields are like. This was very like a battlefield . . .'

'And people find surprising strengths despite their injuries. If their resolve is strong they can move mountains,' said Joe. 'Yes, I've witnessed that many times.'

'So,' said Simpson, taking up the theory, 'having taken her clothes and her bag –'

'Her bag?' said Carter and Joe together.

'Oh, yes, that would have been a vital part of her scheme! Alice was carrying a bag with her personal documents in it. And more than just her passport and tickets and so on – it contained her diary. She showed us all. It was one of those leather jobs with a lock and key that are so popular with girls. A five-year diary. She'd kept it up to date, she said, until she got to Paris and then life became so exciting she didn't have the time to fill it in. Well, that would have given Isabelle de Neuville plenty of background to base her character on, wouldn't it? And then there was the leather folder!' he added, memory returning with a rush. 'It contained all the information she needed to prepare herself for taking over the family business when she got to Bombay. She took us on a quick canter through that too! A day's work learning up the facts in it and anyone could make a reasonable showing as the heir apparent to the family fortune! So, what have we got? She's stolen the other girl's clothes, her documents and her identity!'

'Oh, come on, now! People would be able to *see* it wasn't Alice!' objected Carter. 'They'd take one look and know it was someone else, wouldn't they, Simpson? You said they were a bit alike but it was the *differences* you stressed.'

'That's true. Because it was the differences that were so imme-diately striking. You know – the one so sophisticated, the other so naive. But underneath the outer layers, well yes, there were similarities. Hair colour – light brown. Eyes – blue. With a

144

change of clothes Isabelle could have been Alice's older sister. There could have been only a year or two's difference in age. Alice was very childlike for her age. She was twenty-one but you'd have guessed sixteen.'

'With a change of clothes could Isabelle have *become* Alice? That's the question we have to explore.'

Simpson weighed his impressions with care, finally concluding, 'Yes, I think she could – given a certain acting ability – she could have got away with it. I'll tell you why . . . I told you Alice chattered on and on. We knew all there was to know about Miss Conyers by the end of lunch! She had no close relations left alive and the people she was to meet in Bombay, she had never met before. Good God!' he exclaimed, warming to the idea. 'Yes, she could have pulled it off!'

'A terrible risk to take,' said Carter. 'Think about it!'

'I'm not so sure,' said Joe. 'She was plunging into a completely new life where no one knew her. If there were any lapses of memory or bits of strange behaviour she could blame it on the rail crash injury. She'd need a lot of confidence, of course.'

'Oh, she had that all right!' said Simpson. 'I'd say she had a very cool head. Highly intelligent woman, was my judgement of her. But to steal someone's life and fortune like that! I can't really believe it! I liked her! I can't think she would have done such a thing.'

'Before you both get carried away,' said Carter, 'there's an obstacle you simply can't get around! Isabelle de Neuville couldn't possibly play the part of Alice Conyers because she was French, wasn't she? Pretty damn obvious! Can't think why you haven't raised it!'

Joe looked a question at Simpson.

'Her English was faultless,' he said. 'Only a slight accent. A bit *too* pure, if you know what I mean. You know how foreigners seem to speak better English than we do because they don't salt their speech with the latest slang as a native speaker does?'

'Can you be sure that she was French?'

'Oh, yes,' said Simpson smiling. 'I heard her screaming at her maid before the train started. You'd have to be French to have a vocabulary like that! Her clothes, her luggage, her mannerisms – all French.'

'Well, that's it then,' said Joe. 'That explodes our theory!'

145

'*Your* theory, old man!' said Carter. 'Still, very inventive! I enjoyed our little excursion into the realms of fantasy!'

'Why do you say with such certainty that the theory falls apart, Sandilands?' asked Simpson.

'Because the Alice Conyers I've met here in Simla couldn't possibly be French. That girl is as English as a Sally Lunn, as . . . as . . . Cheddar cheese, as the Houses of Parliament! She's English to the bone!'

'A good actress could give that impression.'

Joe shook his head. 'I agree but the best actress in the world wouldn't have the knowledge of English life that this Alice Conyers has. When I interviewed her the other day I made by chance a glancing reference to *The Wind in the Willows*. I quoted a single line – we were talking about homesickness – and she picked it up at once and put it in context.'

'When Mole went home!' said Carter and Simpson in chorus.

'There you are! You know that. And Alice Conyers knows that but no *French* girl would know about Rat and Mole and Toad and the gang. Wouldn't *want* to!' he added as an afterthought. 'It's a small thing but it's something you can't fake or prepare for. Her reaction was completely spontaneous. The girl I spoke to was English and brought up in England. I'd put my last shilling on it!'

'So Alice is Alice,' said Carter. 'Pity in a way – it would have given us a jolly good motive for the first shooting. If she were someone masquerading as Alice and she heard that Alice's brother was on his way to pay her a visit – that's the end of everything. And he would have to be removed before he arrived in Simla and set eyes on her.'

'And the second murder – Korsovsky,' said Joe, 'couldn't that have occurred for the same reason? That he would have known that Alice was not Alice? It's my opinion that he never met Alice Conyers – the real one – let's say, for the sake of argument, but he might well have known the woman pretending to be her! He could have exposed her. So he too had to be eliminated before he set eyes on her. It all fits except for the fact that the Alice we know is English.'

They fell silent again, all three thinking and speculating furiously.

146

'Hang on a minute! Call ourselves detectives!' said Carter. 'The newspaper report! Have you still got it, Joe? Good. I wonder if we've got our money's worth out of that? Get it out and we'll have another look at that list of casualties. Now just suppose that G.M.'s note of condolence – "so sorry etc." – didn't refer to Alice who was still alive and whom he had in any case never met but referred to the reported death of some other girl who was listed as a casualty. Some girl he'd had a swing round with in the south of France perhaps? Let's have a look through the list of *French* casualties.'

Joe spread the paper on the table and they all looked at it. Charlie ran his finger down the list of first class passengers, French column. There were four men each with his wife and two other ladies: a Madame Céline Darbois and her daughter Mademoiselle Arlette Darbois aged fourteen. There was no Isabelle de Neuville listed.

'This is ridiculous!' said Simpson. 'Can their record keeping have been so poor?'

'Were there any bodies unidentified?' said Carter.

'Yes,' said Joe. 'Here's one. One body without papers or any other identification. Police are asking for help in identifying this thirty-year-old man. Third class passenger. Ah.'

'Look!' said Simpson sharply. 'Look here though!'

He was pointing a finger at a name in the first class list but in the English section.

'Isobel Newton!' he said. 'Isobel Newton! Now translate that into French!'

'Isabelle de Neuville,' said Joe and Carter.

Chapter Fourteen

They were quiet for a moment after their outburst, looking intently at the printed page as though it could give them yet more information.

'I'll tell you something else,' said Carter, holding the paper up to the light. 'Do you see this? It's very faint but there's been a pencil mark by the name of Isobel Newton. To draw Korsovsky's attention to it perhaps?'

'Who is this Korsovsky you keep mentioning?' asked Simpson.

Joe told him about the Russian's death and his suspicions that there existed some link between Alice Sharpe or – as he now had to think – the woman calling herself Alice. He described the note in girlish handwriting on the programme from the Nice Opera House. Simpson picked up at once the reference to Nice.

'Isabelle de Neuville was on her way to Nice. She seemed to know the area well. Could there be a connection?'

'Certainly. We know that Feodor Korsovsky was also on his way to the south of France that summer – look, it's mentioned on an inner page . . . here it is . . . recitals in the Roman amphitheatres of Provence. That's not far from Nice, is it? Perhaps Isabelle was counting on seeing him there?'

'Bit far–fetched,' Carter said dismissively. 'And don't forget that if there was any connection between Korsovsky in 1914 and this English Isobel who was French Isabelle and is now English Alice, what we're looking at is a steaming love affair between a – say seventeen- or eighteen-year-old English girl and a Russian singing star in his mid-thirties. And this is a well-bred English girl, product of an English public school and reader of *Wind in the Willows*! Can't see it myself.'

'There is one way of finding out for certain,' said Simpson. 'I'll take a look at this Alice Sharpe. I think I'd remember which was which,' he added.

'Two problems,' said Joe. 'No one is going to take your word – excuse me, Simpson, I mean no offence – injured as you were at the time . . .'

'Not sure I do myself!'

'And secondly . . .' Joe paused for a moment. 'Remember that two men from Alice-Isobel's past have been shot dead before they could get a look at her. If you think we're going to let you come anywhere within sight of our Alice you're mistaken!'

'Good Lord!' said Carter, suddenly alert. 'That's right. Look, Simpson, does anyone in Simla know your name? Know who you are? Think carefully, man!'

Simpson thought for a moment. 'Only you two. I came straight here from the station. I haven't checked into the hotel yet.'

'That's all right then. I booked the room in my own name,' said Carter. 'Now how are we going to manage to get you close enough to her without her being able to see you? You are, after all, Simpson, rather a distinctive figure. Look, if you don't mind lying in wait in the post office you could watch out for her when she leaves her office to go home at one o'clock. She always takes a rickshaw. You can't miss her men – they wear blue and gold livery with blue turbans. Put on a topee – that'll hide most of your head – and skulk about until she goes by. Joe and I will make sure she stops in front of the window so you can get a good look at her.'

Simpson looked at his watch. 'It's a quarter to one already. Can we get ourselves in position in the time? Remember I don't walk very fast.'

'Oh yes. The post office is just down the road. Look, borrow my topee and pull the brim down. Like this. Well, it's not wonderful but if she doesn't see the stick she'll just take you for a tourist in dark glasses – we get a lot of tourist wallahs in the season. Not a few in dark glasses. The glare, you know.'

Ten minutes later Simpson was standing at the window of the post office busily writing messages on the backs of postcards while Joe and Carter lingered chatting in the middle of the Mall. A church bell tolled one when a rickshaw team hurried by and round the corner to the headquarters of ICTC. Five minutes later they came back conveying Alice Sharpe. At once Joe and Carter stepped forward with cries of delight and greeted her. At her command the men stopped and she turned first to Carter then to Joe, smiling and returning their greeting. After the brief formalities she spoke again and the men trotted on their way.

'Well?' they said eagerly when they had made their separate ways back to the station. 'Well?'

Flushed and excited, Simpson stared at them in turn, saying at last, 'I'm almost sure it was Isabelle de Neuville.'

'*Almost* sure? No better than almost?'

'I'll say pretty sure if you prefer but, look, they were very much alike and Alice Conyers had rather a chubby face which this girl hasn't got but then she might have lost her puppy fat in India, and her face would be darker and leaner after three years in the sun, wouldn't it? Sorry, I'm not being very helpful, am I? But I am trying to be honest.'

'We understand that,' said Joe. 'But look here, is there enough there for you to press this further?'

'I think so, yes . . . I really think so. Of course, I'm not swearing but you understand that.'

'She's not going to admit to a damn thing! Not the woman I met,' said Joe. 'Never! She's clever and she's tough and she enjoys taking risks – now I come to think of it she convinced me that the writing on the programme was done by an English hand. She even demonstrated by using her own handwriting! A woman with that sort of nerve isn't going to fold in the face of an accusation of this kind. She's going to laugh it off.'

'And let's not forget,' said Carter, 'particularly those of us who have to go on working in this town, that she is both popular and well connected. Alice Conyers-Sharpe would simply speak to her friend the Vicereine and the next thing you'd hear would be that Simpson and Sandilands had been put on the first train back to Kalka and that the mad police superintendent Carter had been carted off up the hill to Doolallie!'

'There has to be another way. We've got to unmask her without risking our own professional credibility. We've no proof so we'll have to resort to trickery. We're just going to have to be cleverer than little Miss Isobel and shock her into an admission.'

'Joe, what are you up to?' asked Carter suspiciously. 'You've got something up your sleeve, haven't you?'

'Yes. A little scheme. One for the dirty tricks department, you might say. And if it doesn't work no one will be any the wiser. It won't rebound on us! I'll explain, but I'm afraid it involves your dying again, Simpson!'

'. . . and I need an address from you, Carter,' said Joe. 'A certain Minerva Freemantle.'

'Mrs Freemantle?' said Carter, surprised. 'Now why could you want to see *her* of all people? Seeking a spot of unorthodox information, are we? A little cabalistic help? I hope you know what you're about, Joe! She lives in an apartment over the continental grocer's shop down the Mall. She has an excellent view of Scandal Point from there. Very convenient. A formidable lady and have a care – she too is well connected!'

Leaving Carter and Simpson to take separate rickshaws to Carter's house for lunch, Joe set off to walk down the Mall. He found the continental grocery and mounted the narrow stairs between two shops to a first-floor flat. He rapped on the door and when this was answered by an Indian servant he produced his card.

'Tell Mrs Freemantle that an officer of Scotland Yard wishes to speak to her without delay.'

A moment later the servant returned, opening the door wide, bowed him inside and withdrew through a smaller door at the far end of the long room Joe now entered.

He stepped straight into a comfortable parlour. Large windows overlooking the Mall gave an airy freshness to the room though the wine red curtains framing them might create an atmosphere of Victorian intrigue when drawn, he thought. The remains of a log fire gave off a subtle herbal scent. Juniper perhaps? Lush plants in shining copper pots were grouped on tables in the corners of the room which was dominated by a large, round and highly polished walnut table. A white cat occupying a deep armchair by the fire stretched and shot a narrow-eyed look of intense suspicion at the intruder.

She was standing by the window, an imposing woman in her early thirties. The window, as Carter had promised, afforded an excellent view of the neck of the Mall where everyone paused and stopped to gossip. Joe noted that, with the window open only six inches, sounds of laughter and snatches of conversation floated upwards by some trick of the rising air currents to reach the ears of anyone who might be standing at the window.

Minerva Freemantle was holding Joe's card between two fingers and the look in her eye rivalled that of her cat in cold suspicion. She was a strikingly handsome woman with the upright carriage of a lady whose heyday had been the stately Edwardian age. Her back was straight and her strong shoulders well fulfilled the task of supporting her ample bosom. Her glossy dark hair was curled into a neat chignon and a central parting divided her head exactly in the centre.

She fixed Joe with a haughty stare. 'You have been in Simla for four days, Commander. Quite long enough to establish that I do not see anyone without a prior appointment. And policemen not at all.' The voice was cultured, the tone cold.

Astonished by this encounter and very intrigued, Joe reached out and with suppressed laughter took her hand.

'Maisie!' he said. 'Maisie Freeman! Don't you recognize me?'

Minerva Freemantle's chin sagged towards her bosom as she gaped at Joe. 'Young man, you have the advantage of me! Am I to understand that you are presuming a previous acquaintance?'

'Acquaintance? I'll say!' said Joe happily. 'If you can call feeling someone's collar getting acquainted! Let me take you back four years, Maisie. Backstage at the Empire. Are you beginning to get it? "Merlin the Mysterious and Maisie"! Small matter of a gold watch that went missing? Memory returning yet, is it? Gold watch nicked off some poor chump in the audience who thought it would be a lark to come up on stage and offer it up to Merlin to use in his act. Amazing watch! It survived being smashed with a hammer, set alight and dunked in a goldfish bowl. Then with a roll on the drums and a distracting waggle of your backside you pulled it out of your corset undamaged and returned it to its grateful owner. Problem was – the owner wasn't so grateful when he got back to his seat and found it wasn't actually in his pocket! I wasn't the arresting officer – I was the detective sergeant lurking in the background, learning the ropes.'

After a moment of astonishment Maisie's face cleared and she gave a frank and cheerful laugh. 'Well, bugger me! Now I've got you! You had a moustache in them days! Handsome devil you were! Still are, I see . . . Christ Almighty! Must have had a rocket up yer arse to make it to Commander already! But what the hell are you doing in this godforsaken hole? Not still tracking me and Merl, are you? Like them fuckin' North-West Mounted Police what's supposed to always get their man? Well, hard luck if you are 'cos Merl died two years ago and where he's gone you wouldn't want to follow! And we was never bent anyway – as you bloody well know, bluebottle!'

'Sorry to hear about Merlin, but you seem to be doing all right on your own account.' Joe looked round the room. 'Got yourself a nice little gaff here and a nice little scam going. I hear you're well regarded in Simla, Maisie – the cream of society queuing up for a place at your table on Friday nights? I expect your conjuring experience comes in useful producing all the rappings, the materializations, the ectoplasm and whatever else you produce to amaze and entertain. But don't worry, Maisie . . .' Joe's tone signalled clearly that Maisie had every reason in the world to worry, '. . . your secret's safe with me.'

He paused.

'Just as long as . . .? Go on. What's coming next? There's always a string attached with your mob. What're you after?'

'Well, funnily, there is something you can do for me. It's very easy and right up your street . . .'

Joe explained what he wanted Mrs Freemantle to do. He outlined his scheme without giving away any information about Alice Conyers, saying simply that he wished to startle one of the sitters at her forthcoming seance into making a revelation. She listened carefully to his requirements, nodding her understanding.

'Well, Maisie, how about it? Can you do this?'

'Course I can do it! Piece o' cake! But I won't!'

Joe was taken aback. 'What do you mean, you won't?'

'Just that. You heard me. I won't do it.'

'May I ask why?'

'You may indeed,' she mocked, the elegant, clipped vowels

appearing again. 'But come and sit down while I explain and I'll give you a drink. At least for old times' sake.'

She tipped the cat from the chair and invited Joe to sit down. A moment later she pressed a whisky and soda into his hand, saying as she did so, 'Or should it be – as of old – a brandy and Baby Polly?'

She pulled up a chair opposite him.

'Before we go any further can we get two things straight as between two old acquaintances on collar-feeling terms? First – that was a put-up job with the watch. The chap who claimed we stole it was an illusionist himself – bugger was trying to get rid of the opposition! And it worked, didn't it? You couldn't quite pin it on us but you had a bloody good try and scuppered our career on the halls, damn you! Had to change tack after that but Merl was always sharp. He could see it – after the war with so many loved ones going missing and passing over the demand was there, wasn't it? The demand for someone to pass messages and receive messages from the newly dead. Sorry, I should say the ones who've gone ahead. Mediums! Everybody wanted to consult one. Merl decided that we'd move to Brighton where there was a lot of that stuff going on and cash in.'

Joe interrupted. 'Interesting to catch up with your life story, Maisie, but can we get back to my problem?'

'Selfish pig!' Maisie commented. 'Hold your horses. This is important. Brings me to the second point. Listen! We set up. Me being the medium – doesn't always have to be a woman but you remember what Merl looked like? No point frightening off the marks so he did backstage and worked the illusions.'

Maisie paused for a moment. Theatrically, Joe judged, but he didn't hurry her. He took it as a roll on the drums and waited patiently for the waggle of the backside which had made such an impression on him.

'The illusions worked. We were bloody good but that's not the point.' She paused again. 'I started extemporizing.'

'What was that, Maisie?'

'Extemporizing – cloth ears! I started saying words that weren't on the scripts. Things just started coming into my head and I said them. Out loud, just like that. And the sitters knew what I was on about, all right. I said things in those sittings I had no idea about before we started. Things that only my clients and the dear departed would know. I heard voices in my head, whispering usually, sometimes shouting, passing on messages – messages full of love and hope and reassurance as a rule. Sometimes they used *my* voice to make contact. I was scared at first and told Merl I wanted to stop but word got round and we couldn't keep them off with a stick! We put the prices up – charged double – still they came. Merl never really understood. He thought I was just clever and lucky . . . Well, I was, but there was more to it than that. Much more.'

Maisie looked at him intently. 'You see, Joe, it's a true bill. I can really do it. I have to do it. When Merl died I stopped charging fees. It didn't seem right. If someone wanted the comfort of a communication with a husband, a wife, a father and I could give it, that's what I had to do and I couldn't charge for it. It didn't stop rich folks giving me presents and some have been very generous but you don't have to have a brass farthing to ask me for help.'

'But how did you fetch up here in Simla?' Joe asked.

'No mystery. A client who was on home leave from India went back and spread the news. I got an invitation to come here, all expenses paid. I'd never travelled and with Merl gone who was to tell me I shouldn't? It's a very spiritually minded place, this, Joe. Ever since that Madame Blavatski lived here they've been keen on it. And this town's full of spirits, not all of them on the side of the light. In fact I've directed a lot of lost souls towards the light since I've been here. I look on it as my work.'

'It's very interesting, it really is, Maisie,' Joe said with only a trace of impatience. 'But I can't see why you won't help me out.'

'You can. You're sharp. I don't need to spell it out.'

Joe sighed. 'You would be compromising your art if you descended to the subterfuge I'm suggesting? Something like that?'

'Put it like that if you like. But – would you spit in church? No? Well, it would be like that if I twisted the truth like you want me to. Sorry, Joe. Can't be done.'

Joe felt his anger rising. 'Maisie, can you hear yourself? Know what you sound like? A self-righteous cow who's forgotten where she's come from! You hear a few voices, come in for some adulation by credulous idiots who can't face the truth without a

155

spiritual crutch and you think you're the next thing to the Madonna! What do you think I'm asking you to do this for anyway? To blacken someone's character? To bring eternal damnation about their ears? Of course not! Get this into your silly head will you, love? I'm with you on the side of the light! All I want to do is catch a murderer who could well kill again, to right a wrong and solve a puzzle that needs to be solved! The way you go on anybody'd think I was asking you to call up the spirit of Charlie Peace!'

He got to his feet. 'Well, I did ask nicely. You've made your decision. You can bloody well live with the consequences!'

He was at the door and opening it before she called out to him.

'Consequences? What consequences?'

He stood silently watching her.

'You're a shit, Joe Sandilands! You'd blacken my name in Simla, wouldn't you? A word in the Governor's ear about those unresolved charges against my name back in London and I'd be finished.'

She got up and paced to the window, her face stiff with resentment. After a moment she turned to him. 'Oh, all right. For God's sake, I'll do it. You'd better come round here for a rehearsal tomorrow afternoon about four. The seance is at eight o'clock sharp.'

'Right,' said Joe settling back into the chair again. 'I'll tell you how I want you to play it tomorrow afternoon then.'

'No you won't! I'm the bloody professional! It's my reputation at stake! If I'm doing it, you'll get it done and you'll know that you couldn't get it done better.'

Joe nodded his acceptance. 'I take your word for it, Maisie. Oh, just one more thing and perhaps I should have asked this first – may I see a list of your sitters for tomorrow? Make sure my target is on it.'

Maisie went to a bureau and took a sheet of paper from a drawer.

Joe looked at the list. 'I want you to go through this list with me and tell me a little bit about each person. And I don't mean the gossip you've collected at that window – I mean the reasons, if any have been given, for wanting to be here. Who are they trying to contact on the other side?'

156

Maisie knew the list by heart and recited the names from the top in order. 'The list changes every week. Some people are what you'd call the core of the meeting and we add others for variety. Major Fitzherbert. He's a regular. Trying to contact the Mem. They were inseparable. He'll likely succeed because she only died a year ago.'

'Is that significant – a year ago?'

'Oh, yes. You tend not to be lucky if the subject passed over more than about four or five years ago. They lose interest, you know – the spirits, I mean. They have work to do on the other side. They don't particularly want to be called back here all the time to sort things out for their relations. You know – "Aunty Enid – what did you do with Granny's garnets?" It's boring for them.'

'I can understand that. But Maisie – does this really work? I mean, you can tell me. It carries me out of my depth.'

'Out of *your* depth?' said Maisie derisively. 'It carries *me* out of *my* depth! But it's there and it does work. But you – you're too bound up in police procedures. You imagine that if you don't understand it, it doesn't exist! Where was I? Mr and Mrs Tilly. He's a financier. Their three boys died in Flanders. The eldest comes back quite often. Helps them to bear it. Then there's Miss Trollope. This is her first visit. She's hoping for a message from Snowdrop. Her dog.'

'Any hope?' asked Joe trying to keep a straight face.

'Yes. Now if he'd been a cockatoo or a stick insect I'd say no but dogs do come through. They put their noses in your hands sometimes to show they're there. Then we've got Colonel and Mrs Drake. They lost their twin daughters to the cholera in the plains three years ago. They've not given up hope yet. Then there's Mrs Sharpe of ICTC. Her husband never comes with her. She's trying to contact her mother.'

Joe looked away, but too late apparently to avoid giving Minerva a message he was unaware of signalling. 'Ah! So that's your mark! The Saintly Alice? Well, well!' She gave a cynical smile and went on with her list. 'And the last name is Cecil Robertson, the jeweller. I think he comes to see if he can catch me out – there's always one! But also because he's an expert on religions and he's, well, I suppose you could say he's making a study of me and my techniques. Oh, and lastly, a newcomer you can add to the list – Joe Sandilands, policeman, blackmailer and sceptic. With him in the room sneering, the spirits will take a powder and I won't blame them! Now, that's all you're getting! Bugger off! Hecate wants to get back into her chair.'

Joe got to his feet and the waiting cat sprang triumphantly back into its place.

'I'll make sure you have no cause to regret what you've agreed to do for us, Maisie, and thank you for –'

'Cut the cackle, smart arse!' she snapped impatiently. 'You don't need to turn on the smarm for me. I've said I'll do it – leave it there, will you?'

Joe put on a face of blazing honesty, one hand over his heart.

'I have your word and I trust you, Maisie. I wish you'd trust me a little.'

Maisie Freeman began to laugh. A derisive laugh that made her magnificent bosom quiver and rattled the jet beads around her neck.

'Well,' said Joe, 'why not? I did make it my business to see that that charge sheet against you in London was wiped clean. You've been in the clear for four years now!'

He dodged neatly as a whisky glass materialized and flew through the air, narrowly missing his ear.

Chapter Fifteen

The room when he returned just before eight on Friday evening projected a very different mood. The dark red curtains were drawn and a log fire burned brightly in the hearth. The lighting was discreet but adequate and supplied by two or three Tiffany lamps about the room and a row of tall white candles down the centre of the table.

The cat had been banished from the scene and Minerva Freemantle was alone in the room when he arrived. She was wearing a simple dark green velvet gown, low-cut and sleeveless, he noticed, a clear indication that no trickery was contemplated. Joe allowed his eyes to run appreciatively for a moment over the voluptuous and highly unfashionable curves of her figure, admiring the strong white arms, the waist improbably narrow between swelling bosom and lavish hips. Minerva – as he was beginning to think of her – had chosen her name well. As imposing as any Roman statue that had ever graced the temple of the Goddess of Wisdom, he thought fancifully; and guaranteed to distract the attention of any man lucky enough to be granted a seat at her table. She was still a show girl, he reckoned, and a clever one.

Unusually for India there were no drinks or sweetmeats of any kind on offer. A serious business, a seance, and not to be confused with a social occasion. All had been rehearsed and they moved easily into their routine when the other guests began to arrive. Introductions were made and brief descriptions given but they were not followed up with the usual social chit-chat. The other guests were friendly and greeted him without suspicion but with that automatic reserve which prevents people from starting up a conversation in the waiting room of a doctor's surgery. They had their own preoccupations and were not disposed to take much interest in his.

Alice Conyers-Sharpe was the last to arrive, surprised but pleased to see him.

'Well, now we're all here . . . Most of us know each other well but we welcome two newcomers to our little band this evening – Miss Trollope who has very recently lost her dear companion, Snowdrop, and who is hoping for a sign that he has safely passed over and will be there to welcome her when it is her turn to make the transition . . .'

Miss Trollope was a small, fair woman with the wide-eyed and earnest expression of a porcelain doll. She smiled nervously and received sympathetic and encouraging smiles in return. They all had animals they were fond of themselves and would hope to meet up with again in the hereafter.

'. . . and a new gentleman.' (Was there the slightest emphasis on the word 'gentleman'?) 'Commander Joseph Sandilands from London. I will let him tell you in his own words what his motivation is in joining our circle.'

She turned to him with a sweet smile. This was not rehearsed. He inferred that he was not forgiven.

'Minerva and I are old friends,' he said with engaging sincerity. 'Our paths crossed many years ago in London Town when she was already quite a star in her own field. I have long appreciated her remarkable talents. I'm here to explore the paths of truth, honesty and love. I open my mind and my heart to an approach from anyone who has passed through ahead of us to the Happy Fields and is prepared to give of his or her precious time to speak words of guidance or comfort to me.'

Everyone nodded fervently in understanding except for Minerva Freemantle whose lips appeared to twitch with suppressed emotion at this speech.

She gestured to the table. 'If we can all take our seats then? Joe, no penance, I think, if I ask you to sit between two pretty ladies? If Mrs Sharpe sits on your left and Miss Trollope on your right? There we are. Now, hold hands everyone and place your joined hands on the table where we can all see them.'

She doused the electric lamps but left the candles burning. If he had not been anxiously waiting for the performance of his own trick, Joe thought he would have begun to enjoy himself.

The atmosphere was not at all what he had expected. Seated holding the hands of a pair of pretty girls at the walnut table, surrounded by kindly faces, he was more in the mood of cheerful expectancy that came over him at the beginning of a dinner party with friends and not in the dark mood of guarded superstition he had associated with seances.

'We'll begin with our usual prayer,' said Mrs Freemantle without emotion.

Everyone except Joe and Miss Trollope knew the words and began to recite them together.

'Lord of the Universe, Spirit of Love, we ask you to look with kindness on our gathering and keep all here assembled safe from evil, from despair and from doubt.'

A silence fell but it was a comfortable silence, the silence of an audience who know the curtain is about to go up on a performance they very much want to see. Joe found that he was thinking deeply as he did in those few minutes of private prayer before a church service. The hands holding his were not the source of embarrassment or even arousal that he had anticipated but a comforting touch linking him to the rest of the group. He narrowed his eyes and focused on the candle flame in front of him. He was not sure how many minutes had slipped by when Minerva Freemantle began to speak.

'David? Is that David? Mrs Tilly, your son is with us!'

Mr and Mrs Tilly looked at her eagerly but stayed silent. Joe felt a tingle in his arms and hands and stirred his elbows and shoulders discreetly to keep the circulation flowing.

A voice, shockingly deep to the inexperienced Joe, came from Mrs Freemantle's throat. A young man's voice full of life and humour and excitement.

'Mother! Father! I've found them! Both of them! Bill and Henry are with me and quite safe now. If you can believe it they were both still in their bunker on the Somme. Didn't know which way to turn. Didn't want to desert their post even though they were supposed to have passed over! They say thank you for the last parcel you sent. Bill had the blue socks and Henry had the green ones. They send their love and we'll all be waiting for you when you come through.'

The voice faded and Joe was quite certain that he could hear chatter and laughter in the background. Mr and Mrs Tilly sat rigidly still, tears pouring down their faces but beaming with happiness.

'God, she's good!' Joe thought. 'She's bloody good! I wonder who we'll have next? And how on earth will she manage to do Snowdrop?'

Silence fell on the group once more and again Joe found himself hypnotized by the candle flame in front of his eyes. He was startled from his trance by a voice which boomed from Minerva Freemantle.

'Joe! Joe Sandilands, you old so-and-so! Ladies present so I'll watch my language. Well, there you are, old boy, and here I am! Now do you believe me?'

A soldier's clipped, jocular tones.

'Seb? Sebastian?' Joe managed to gasp. He was conscious of Alice Sharpe squeezing his hand tightly to help him through his astonishment.

'Of course it's Sebastian! We have unfinished business! I'd have won our last game, you know, if that shell hadn't wiped it off the board and me with it. I was going to move my bishop to KB3. Checkmate in three moves. Take care, old man! And watch your left flank!'

Joe couldn't speak. His throat seemed to be choked, his tongue paralysed. This wasn't in the script. His mind raced back to the summer of 1915, to the shell burst that robbed him of his dearest friend, tore open his own face and stopped a game of chess he had just realized he could not possibly win. He looked desperately at Minerva. She read his thoughts and shook her head sadly. She could not call Sebastian back again.

Excited and congratulatory looks were being directed at him from those around the table. With a final squeeze of encouragement, Alice Sharpe's hand relaxed its grip once more and Joe wondered if she thought it at all unfair that he should have made a contact on his first visit when she had tried often to communicate with her mother. He also thought about Seb's last crisp warning. 'Watch your left flank!' He looked briefly to his left flank and encountered Alice's smiling blue eyes.

'It's all right, Seb!' he said silently to himself like a prayer. 'Your message received!'

The candles guttered as a chill rush of air swept through the room. A log fell and the glow of the fire dimmed. The grandfather clock behind Mrs Freemantle abruptly stopped ticking. Somewhere in the corridor outside a cat screeched in terror and was abruptly silenced. Mrs Freemantle began hurriedly to mutter a prayer. Joe caught the words, '. . . keep us from evil . . . let no bodeful presence come nigh . . .'

Tension spread around the group. Feet shuffled, throats were cleared but the circle of hands remained intact and firm. Ears straining for the slightest sound heard it at the same moment. Tap, tap. Tap, tap. The sound of a stick in the corridor outside. It paused then tapped again. Exploring. Searching out the way. Soft footsteps shuffled after the stick. They grew louder, more confident, and came to a halt by the small door behind Minerva.

In her own voice from which she could not totally eradicate a tremble of fear, she said, 'Friends, this is very exceptional. We must not be afraid. Stay firm. We are being visited by a very strong spirit – a spirit so strong it has the power to materialize before our eyes. It wants to show itself to us. It insists on showing itself! But beware! It takes its power from negative emotions – from resentment, from hatred and desire for revenge!'

A barely audible whimper came from the throat of Miss Trollope and she squeezed Joe's hand tightly.

'This spirit is searching for someone who is close at hand. For one of us.'

The door creaked open.

'Someone whose initials are . . .' She frowned, concentrating on an inner voice. '. . . are . . . I. N. Is there anyone here who is aware of an I.N. in their life?'

Alice's hand had become icy cold and she was unconsciously moving her whole body closer to his.

No one spoke.

'There is no one here with those initials,' said Minerva. The relief was evident in her voice. 'Will you not admit your error, spirit, and leave us in peace? She whom you seek is not among us.'

'You lie! She is here!'

The voice burst from the doorway and a dimly perceived figure took on hideous shape before their eyes.

Darkly clad, the only parts of the apparition which revealed a human identity were the pale hands and the pale face. A face of such horror that Miss Trollope gurgled, released Joe's hand and slumped under the table. The deathly white features glowed with the marble colouring of a fresh corpse. A trail of blood trickled down from the forehead to the chin and as they watched in frozen fascination, dripped on to his front. Where the eyes should have been there was a black and gaping void. The apparition moved its head from side to side, slowly sweeping the table with its blind gaze. Searching. It raised a white stick threateningly.

'She's here! Isobel, you are here! Isobel Newton! You could have saved me! Why did you leave me dying?'

Alice Conyers-Sharpe made a sound half-way between a scream and a gasp, jumped to her feet and hurled herself towards the door and to the head of the stairs. Leaving a shattered audience behind him, Joe set off in pursuit. He saw her face upturned in terror as she heard him coming after her and then she lost her footing on the narrow stairs and fell with a scream.

Chapter Sixteen

Scrambling to her feet, she blundered on and fled with a bewildered cry into the street. She started to run at speed through the crowds, dodging neatly between the strolling couples, never looking back. To Joe's surprise she seemed to be making her way past the Ridge, past Christ Church and on south towards the wooded hills in which lay Sir George's Residence but at the last she turned aside and ran, still at speed, sandalled feet pattering, down a narrow lane between the backs of two rows of houses. Joe followed her into the lane and saw her disappear at last through a small arched gateway.

He went in pursuit and found himself in a walled courtyard. As his eyes grew accustomed to the gloom he became aware that a narrow flight of steps led upward from this to a higher level, a higher level from which flowering creepers and trailing roses cascaded down across the face of a pale wall. Tentatively he set his foot on the steps and began to mount.

The silence was broken by a sharp click.

Someone above him had slipped the safety catch from a pistol.

'Not a step nearer! Whoever you are, you stay right there or I fire!'

The voice was breathless and quavering with terror.

She was leaning on a parapet wall and Joe caught a glint of moonlight on the barrel of a revolver. She repeated, 'Not a step nearer!'

'This is a bit unfriendly, Alice! It's me – Joe Sandilands. I wish you no harm.'

There was a pause. 'Joe? Oh, Joe! Thank God! Are you alone?' And then, 'That creature . . . it hasn't followed you?'

'There's only me here, Alice. Let me come up, will you? Why don't we take a seat? Why don't we share a cigarette? Why don't we enjoy a moment of tranquillity together? Tranquillity! A commodity always in short supply in Simla as far as I can see.'

As he spoke, step by step he climbed the stair until at last he joined Alice on a small terrace platform shaded and scented by jasmine. Alice was just discernible in the fretted moonlight but the pistol in her hand was clear to see.

'Spare me!' he said. 'I am unarmed! At least – not entirely unarmed. Not quite sure how the evening was going to turn out, I took the precaution of filling a flask with the Governor's excellent Courvoisier! Whatever else, you've had a taxing evening! Won't you join me?'

With a sob Alice threw herself into Joe's arms and clung to him. Gently he disengaged himself and led her to sit on the low parapet wall. He sat beside her, an arm around her shoulders, waiting while she gained a fragile measure of control.

'Before we do or say anything,' she said, 'please tell me who or what on earth – or in hell – that was? Was he real? Did he exist? Did you see him too? Did everybody see him? Did you see him, Joe?'

Joe hesitated. Perhaps the truth might be most serviceable. 'He was real all right,' he said. 'He wasn't a figment of your imagination. He wasn't a revenant. He was, though, someone you know. Someone you have known. Any ideas?'

Alice looked at him with huge, uncomprehending eyes. 'I have no idea what you're talking about. I have never met such a . . . a . . . creature. And anyway, you heard him – we all heard him – he was looking for someone with the initials . . . oh, what was it? . . . I.M.? Yes, I.M. Isobel something or other . . .' She shivered. 'I shall never ever go to a seance again! It was horrid and very frightening. I had to get away! And that wretched woman, Miss Trollope! Did you see her? Fainted away completely! I really think Mrs Freemantle has overstepped herself. It's perhaps time that she moved on from Simla. I'm quite sure that when Her Excellency hears of tonight's fiasco she will insist. Don't you agree, Joe?'

Alice had recovered her self-possession; only a tremor in the voice and a trembling hand remained of the storm she had passed through.

Joe held her firmly by the shoulders and turned her face to his. 'Isobel,' he said gently, 'Isobel Newton. It's no use. You can't fool me. And before you think of shooting me to get rid of a witness, let me tell you that Carter knows and, of course, the man you met again tonight at the seance . . .'

To Joe's surprise she stopped sniffling, sat up, favoured him with a broad smile and shrugged her shoulders. 'Oh, well! It was worth a last shot, I suppose!' She gave him a level glance. 'You should have waited a little longer, Joe, I was going to make it worth your while to forget about all this. But tell me – who was that – the thing that appeared in the doorway? The only man I have ever met with whom that creature had the slightest resemblance is long dead.'

'I can promise you he isn't dead. Nor yet was he undead. His name is Simpson. Captain Colin Simpson and, by a miracle, he is as alive as you or I. It was a trick. It was a put-up job. It was a trick on you.'

'Simpson?' said Alice slowly. 'Simpson!'

'Yes. And a member of a select band. A very select band. A band of those who survived the Beaune rail crash. Now are you getting it?'

'Christ, yes!' said Alice. 'The man in the railway carriage! He still lives? Can it be? And what the hell was he doing here?'

'I'll exchange information for information,' said Joe. 'But, in the meantime . . .' He lit two cigarettes and handed one to Isobel. He unscrewed the cap of his flask and passed it across to her. 'If ever a girl needed a swig of aqua vitae, I suspect it is you so help yourself. And why don't you begin at the beginning?'

'The beginning?' said Isobel bitterly. 'The beginning is a long time ago and a long way away from here!'

'It'll do,' said Joe. 'The night is young.'

'We could begin in an impoverished Surrey vicarage if you like,' said Isobel. 'With a cold and ambitious father, a mother who died when I was eleven. Or we could begin in a bleak girls' school in the Home Counties. Or would you like to start in the south of France when our heroine is seventeen? We'd be talking about the same person. We'd be talking about me. It was a very long journey, ending – though ending is not the word – here in a private and concealed Simla garden.'

'Good God,' said Joe, looking round in astonishment. 'Garden? Private garden? Whose? Where?'

'Old Simla's full of gardens, big and small. The house this belonged to is gone but the garden remains. It belongs to Rheza Khan's family. They are a very well-to-do family – you might almost say tribe – with extensive lands north towards the Nepalese border but they've always kept what you might call a town house here in Simla.They keep the garden in order – as a sort of gesture of family piety. I come here sometimes. It's a peaceful place. Away from everybody. If I want to see someone privately it's always here and here we are – private.'

She took the proffered flask from Joe's hand and drank. She coughed and spluttered and drank again.

'Well, the beginning? Born of poor but honest parents . . . I won't deceive you, Joe. They weren't particularly poor. Thinking of my detestable father not particularly honest either but he's done pretty well for himself.'

Joe's mind was racing. 'Newton?' he said, the picture of an austere and influential bishop of the Church of England coming to mind. 'Not . . . ? Are we by any chance talking about "Retribution Newton"? And he's your father?'

'Yes,' she said, 'that Bishop Newton. The scourge of sinners. Just a rector the last time I saw him. Difficult to live with, I think you'll agree. But that's jumping ahead and I said I'd begin at the beginning. It was a detestable childhood and it got worse after my mother died. I couldn't wait to get away! But I had a stroke of luck. My father had an old friend, very rich, very much of the Church, very corseted and a great subscriber to my father's good causes. Fallen altar pieces one day, fallen women the next! You know the sort of thing. She spent every winter in the south of France and she had a pathetic, quenched companion. Her name, almost inevitably, was Mildred but Mildred got measles and lo! Horror! Tragedy! Crisis! Mrs Hyde-Jellicoe had no one to accompany her on her winter trip to Nice and after more debate, discussion (praying if you can believe!), it was decided that I should fill the vacant slot and set off for the south of France. So, suitably admonished as to how to conduct myself and much to my father's relief, off I went to carry Mrs Hyde-Jellicoe's knitting about for her.'

'And you went for it?' said Joe.

'Did I ever go for it! And, in the fullness of time, I ended up in an attic bedroom in a large Nice hotel only three flights of stairs away from Mrs Hyde-Jellicoe's first-floor suite overlooking the sea and – no telephones in those days – a voice tube from her to me so that if she felt she needed a little glass of water in the night she could blow down it. A whistle would go off in my ear and I would come padding down three fights of stairs in my school dressing gown and see what was what. Not much of a life for a girl but anything was to be preferred to the Gothick splendours of St Simeon-under-Wychcroft, Surrey.'

'Yes,' said Joe, considering. 'I can imagine that it would be. And there you found yourself, enjoying the winter sunshine?'

'Yes,' said Isobel, 'anything would have been better and one thing was – my employer was fabulously rich and there was throughout that winter and on into the spring an endless procession of her nieces, nephews, cousins, sisters, brothers-in-law, all eager to wind her wool, carry her parasol, escort her on gentle little walks down the Promenade des Anglais and all with but one idea.'

'To inherit the berries?'

'Exactly that! Amongst this mob of threadbare fortune hunters there was one who stood apart. I suppose he was a nephew – or he may have been a great-nephew. He was all right. I'd never met anyone like him before. He was a naval officer. He thought (and he taught me) that having a good time could be an end in itself. Hard to believe but such a thought had never entered my head! He was stationed in Malta. If you've got access to a navy pinnace whenever you want one, Malta's not far from Nice and it occurred to me that he had a certain advantage over the other players. He had a certain advantage over me too.'

'Don't tell me,' said Joe, 'let me guess. He proved himself to be a honey-tongued seducer? Am I right?'

'My, Commander! No wonder you occupy so prominent a place in the detective force! Nothing escapes you! And you're right. I was undone. And before I gain your undeserved sympathy for the horrors of my lot – I'll tell you – I had never until then enjoyed anything so much as being undone! He was very good fun. He was extremely amusing. He had lots and lots of rackety friends. He knew his way up and down the Côte d'Azur. His career was not very committing – I wouldn't be at all surprised in those days if you explained to your commanding officer that you were playing a rich relative you wouldn't get leave to do so! The navy was very like that in those pre-war days. So it went on but Nemesis stalked!'

'Nemesis in the form of Mrs Hyde-Jellicoe?'

'Yes,' said Isobel with a laugh. 'Came a night when the bloody voice tube didn't work or I'd forgotten to put the whistle back in it – you can imagine the tableau! The door opens and framed in the doorway, dressing-gowned and awful, my employer, his great-aunt, amazed and aghast to have imperially caught us in the act! In a trice – lost! Lost to him any chance he might have had of inheriting, lost to me, my job. I had, you see, taken my first step on the road to ruin. My employer made clear her intention of writing immediately to my father to apprise him of the fact that his daughter was a harlot! (I'd love to see that letter!) But I was damned if I'd hang about waiting for his reply. I must say Edwin – his name was Edwin – was very decent about it. I had my clothes and about thirty pounds, not much else. He gave me twenty-five pounds. All he had, I think. "Don't want you to go short, old girl," he said.

'Well, I did go short. Fifty-five pounds didn't go far even in those days on the Riviera. I had no means of making a living and when I was reduced to my last few francs I decided to do what I had seen others doing. No, not what you're thinking! Not yet at any rate . . . I started singing. There were lots of performers of different nationalities just singing in the streets. I hadn't got a wonderful voice – well, you've heard me – but I was very pretty and fresh and I seemed to appeal to rich old gentlemen. I was making enough to survive by singing in front of the cafés for a couple of hours each evening. One evening I came upon a very jolly crowd who seemed to have taken over a café in the old town. They were foreign. I listened and identified their language as Russian. Well, I knew a Russian song or two –'

'That story about your singing master?' Joe interrupted. 'It was true then?'

'Of course! I was brought up to tell the truth and I almost always do. So I thought, I'll show you! I'll get your attention!

Russians are very romantic, you know, so I started to sing the most heart-rending song I knew. It worked! They wept! They joined in the chorus! They turned out their pockets for me – not that it did me much good – they were as destitute as I was, I think! But they took me into their group, they made much of me, they gave me supper. But more than that . . .'

Her voice trailed away and Joe knew that she was thousands of miles and many years away from him.

'One of them was a singer. A real singer. Feodor Korsovsky. He took me home with him that night and for the next year we were never apart. I loved him. He said he loved me.'

'What separated you?' Joe asked. His satisfaction at having guessed that Alice Conyers had been hiding a relationship with the Russian took second place to his curiosity as the story unfolded.

Alice remained silent for a long time. 'The Atlantic Ocean,' she said finally. 'Is that big enough or should I also mention the wife I was not aware he had in New York? And perhaps the Great War which kept him away from Europe for four years? Will that do?' Her voice had taken on a sharp edge.

'He kept the programme you scribbled on . . .'

'Yes. That was quite a surprise . . . do you mind if I keep it? It means a lot to me.'

'No,' said Joe. 'I suppose that's all right. I'll ask for it if I need it.'

'So there I was alone again. Feodor had been offered a wonderful engagement in New York. He couldn't afford to take me with him so he gave me what he had and I prepared to wait until he came back. He never did. I was hurt, of course, but more than that I was angry. But I knew exactly what to do. Amongst the friends that Edwin had introduced me to there was a commander RN. Almost a caricature – red face, roving eye, probably the most entirely amoral man I've ever met but friendly and rather attractive. Finding me as it were vacant, he was very ready to take me on and, indeed, according to a good Edwardian tradition, install me in a little sea-front flat in St Raphael.

'The flat became a tremendous rendezvous for naval officers. I don't suppose for a moment that Bertie was particularly faithful to me. I don't recall that I was particularly faithful to him! I was having a really good time. But as the saying goes, All good

171

things come to an end. This was 1914 and suddenly the coast was full of French army officers as mobilization gained ground. Some of them were very dashing – Zouaves, Spahis, even a contingent of the Légion Etrangère, all with money to spend, all glad of a welcome. But none so glad as Colonel Chasteley-Riancourt. Cavalry soldier, very grand. A perfide aristo if ever I saw one! He moved me out of the St Raphael flat into a little house he owned in the hills behind Monaco.'

She paused. 'Let me look at you, Joe. What do I see? Icy disapproval?'

'Nothing of the sort,' said Joe. 'If you see anything at all you see fascination! Please don't stop!'

'Well, as I say, there we were living in Monaco. And, if Chas had a fault – what do I mean, if Chas had a fault? Chas had thousands of faults not the least of which was an inability to take his eyes off the roulette wheel and this was rather agony. I had to sit and watch thousands, millions of francs pouring through his fingers. Francs that would have been better bestowed on my little soft, scented hands! Have you ever met a compulsive gambler?'

'Yes, I have,' said Joe. 'I shared a billet with one in France. They're a race apart.'

'Chas was very much of that race. He was very Old France, you know. Conventional in many ways and what in that exalted world do you do when you find yourself short of a few francs – you peel a picture off the wall and sell it. A Fragonard, a Lancret, perhaps even a Chardin. But of course, there he was in a flat in Monaco, not much to sell so what did he do . . .?'

Joe thought he knew but, 'Go on, then,' he said, 'what did he do?'

For a moment the jaunty tone wavered. 'Well, very practical man, Chas. Not perhaps romantic but certainly practical. He sold that for which he could get the best price. He sold me. I've often wondered for how much. My purchaser was a Belgian, Aristide Mézière, an arms manufacturer, rich as only sin can make you. His idea was to export me to Paris where he had a house on the Place Vendôme, recently acquired and needing a little exotic furniture. Good God! If that had lasted I might be the Baronne Mézière now!'

'How old were you, Isobel?' Joe asked quietly.

172

'This was 1915 so I was eighteen or maybe nineteen.'

'But you never made it to the Place Vendôme?'

'No, I didn't. Fate took a hand. In those days Fate was always taking a hand! Perhaps it still is.'

She shivered slightly and looked up at Joe speculatively then snuggled closer, passing an arm under his jacket, seeking his warmth and closeness. He was conscious that she was wearing only a light silk dress and after the heat of the chase she must be cooling off rapidly. He enjoyed her touch and for a moment, perhaps more than a moment, his senses began to spin. He took off his jacket and draped it over her shoulders, putting his arm once again around her and effectively pinioning her arms to her sides. He had not forgotten that the woman in his arms was a crack shot and she was still holding a revolver in her right hand.

'Suddenly there were no men left on the Côte d'Azur. No gaiety. Everything closed down. I decided to play my own game. I sold the little jewellery I had, took my maid and left for Paris. I put on a wedding ring and became a widow. I had decided to choose and not be chosen any longer. I set up in a smart apartment in the Avenue de l'Opéra and I chose the lovers I entertained. There were plenty of officers on leave constantly from the front. By this time I spoke French as one born there and very aristocratic French. I was decidedly a *poule de luxe*, Commander!'

'And why did you find yourself on the Blue Train back to the south the year after the war ended?'

'Obvious if you think for a moment! My lovers were dead or gone back to their homes to rebuild their lives. The world had changed for ever. There were many – genuine – widows in the market for a little love and protection (amateurs!), and the competition was fierce. I was again destitute. All I had left was my good clothes. I hadn't even the money to pay for the services of a maid. I got a letter from an old friend who was recovering from war wounds in the south, in Nice. He asked me to join him. Even sent me a first class ticket.'

'And then you met Alice Conyers?'

'We were sharing a compartment. She had a great effect on me. So eager, so innocent, with everything to look forward to! She was not much younger than I was but there was a lifetime's

173

experience between us. She was on the brink of a new life with a fortune to come to her and a husband. And I – I felt as though I were at the end of my life, tired, disillusioned, used, knowing so much and having achieved so little. I envied her.'

'So much that you stole her life?'

'It wasn't deliberate. It wasn't thought out in any way. It was Fate, I do believe. An impulse. You have no idea what it feels like, or perhaps you have, Commander, to realize that you are the only one to have survived such a horror. Fate, you see, had led me to the ladies' room seconds before the crash. That saved my life. It was a small space and well padded and carpeted. I rattled around, of course, but in the confines of that space I was much more protected than everyone else.'

She touched her face. 'The mirror broke and sliced through my face, a few ribs were cracked and I sprained a wrist but really, I wasn't as badly injured as I pretended to be. When I got free of the wreckage I stood and looked at the carnage. There was no one left alive but me. A baby was screaming for a while but then that too went silent. I should have been overwhelmed, distraught, but I wasn't.'

She wrinkled her forehead, anxious to convey accurately her feelings. 'I felt elated, powerful, chosen. I of all had survived and I could do whatever came into my head. I walked about and looked at my fellow passengers. Alice Conyers, pretty little Alice was dead. Minutes ago she had everything and now she was no more than a broken doll. What a waste of a life! But I didn't steal her life, Joe. It was presented to me. I found it torn and shattered in a rock-strewn ravine. I picked it up. I put it on. It fitted. You know what Napoleon said? He said, "I didn't usurp the throne. I found the crown of France in the gutter and picked it up on the point of my sword." That's what it was like for me.'

There was a very long pause in which it seemed to Joe she was wondering whether to proceed. At last she resumed and her voice had hardened. 'You must realize that Alice Conyers was – nothing! A brainless little chatterbox. Completely without intelligence or experience. She had a certain amount of mouse-like charm but she was no more capable of running ICTC than a . . . a . . . spaniel! She could never have kept her feet in the shifting commercial politics of the firm. She would have married Reggie

174

and been completely submerged by him. He would have milked the company and it would all have been a disaster.'

'Why are you telling me all this, Isobel?'

'Please – go on calling me Alice, won't you – I've got used to it and you've made your point.'

'All right then – Alice. I don't know you very well . . .'

'We could put that right, Joe.' The invitation in her voice was unmistakable.

'I don't know you very well, Alice, but I do know this – that you'd never say or do anything without a purpose and just at the moment I'm wondering why you've told me all this. I wasn't far behind you but I hadn't got there.'

She turned to him with a frank smile. 'Because I know and you know that there's absolutely nowhere you can go with this information! Assuming you could find someone credulous enough to listen to your story, I would deny everything. But you've worked that out already, haven't you?'

'Oh, yes. There are many who would step forward to bear witness in your favour. There are many who depend for their livelihood on the continuing prosperity of ICTC. What would be their reaction if I were to attempt to clap you in handcuffs and remove you from the scene? And, anyway, what would be the charge? Would anyone thank me for being the instrument which put your husband Reggie in the driving seat? I don't think so! There are many here in Simla who admire what you do. The only evidence against you is that of a semi-blind and badly injured fellow passenger who met you briefly three years ago. And even he's not convinced he's right. I wouldn't put him on the witness stand. Your friends in high places would close ranks to preserve the status quo. You're right – we both know this, so I'm asking you again, Alice – why are you confiding in me?'

She edged closer and sighed. 'Because by finding out my identity you've put yourself in grave danger of assassination, Joe Sandilands. I have to warn you. And it's important that you know the whole story to understand why.'

Wriggling gently under the jacket, she freed her right arm and carefully placed her revolver into his hand. 'Here, take this. You have much more urgent need of it now than I. You know who I am but . . . you're not the only one.'

She shivered again and turned anxious eyes, silver in the

moonlight, to his, determined to make him understand the urgency of what she had to tell him.

'Someone else in Simla knows. Someone in Simla has always known! And they'll try to kill you now for the same reason they killed Lionel Conyers and Feodor Korsovsky.'

Chapter Seventeen

A chilling wind stirred the jasmine over their heads. Alice shook a shoulder free from the jacket and spread it over Joe's back so that they were sharing the protection of the light tweed and sharing their body heat. Her arm slipped round his waist and Joe felt a thumb inserted into his waistband. He was disconcertingly aware as she snuggled closer that her softly curved body was pressing against him, aware also of her warm breath as she whispered urgently in his ear.

'I'm telling you all this because I need help and I think you need help too. We may be able to do a deal. Let me tell you . . . When I'd been in India for nearly a year I came up to Simla. My first season here in the hot weather. ICTC had begun to turn round. Everybody knew it. I had a letter. The strangest letter! It said, "Dear Isobel." And that was all! Literally all! Someone wanted me to know that they knew who I truly was.'

'That must have given you the fright of your life!'

'It was totally unnerving. Calculatedly unnerving. I was left in suspense for two weeks and then the follow-up came. It said, and I remember the words exactly, "Dear Isobel, You are playing a dangerous game and you are going to need protection. This I can provide. Protection will be total but it will not be free. I shall require four thousand rupees a year. I will tell you how this is to be paid." And that was all.'

'Four thousand rupees a year!' said Joe, aghast. 'That's about what a senior Indian Civil Service official earns.'

'Yes, it's a lot of money but it was well calculated. It was a sum which I could without crippling difficulty raise and manage to lose in the books. Had it been substantially more there would have been a problem. But my correspondent was no fool; eager

177

only to keep the golden goose alive, well and paying – paying well but not absurdly well.'

'And how did you pay it? Surely it's traceable?'

'No. A very clever scheme. Totally untraceable. Simple and calculated not to raise the slightest suspicion. A note was delivered to the office. It told me to go along to the jewellers, Robertson. Do you know . . . ?'

'Yes,' Joe nodded. 'I've seen his shop and met the proprietor. Are you telling me he's crooked? I did wonder.'

'You must decide for yourself when I've explained the scheme. He provides the perfect cover. I was told to take cash or a money order to the value of four thousand rupees but take jewellery to only half that value. That's it. Twice a year, in April and October, I go to his shop and perform the transaction. If there are other customers present, and there sometimes are friends of mine in the shop, they simply see me take Robertson's advice on a particular piece, and pay for it with a cheque. All above board, you see. Sometimes I come away with a Burmese ruby, a choice opal, a large star sapphire. That's all I know. What Robertson does with the other half I have no idea.'

'Do you think he might be the one who's blackmailing you?'

'No. I have a feeling that he's just a channel for this exchange – I don't think he knows what's going on.'

'And what do you do with the jewellery? With your half of the Danegeld?'

She gave a mischievous smile. 'I've kept it. Every piece. It's in a safe place. Through these Simla years I've been living quite dangerously in fear of being found out at any moment. Working hard relieved the pressure. It took my mind off the threat. In a way I suppose it gave me an extra incentive to make the firm as successful as I could in as short a time as I could. Never quite knowing when it would come to an end.'

'I see,' said Joe, making no attempt to keep a mounting admiration out of his voice. 'A little running-away fund?'

'A big running-away fund. And getting bigger every year. Gems can cross borders so easily and I can sell them anywhere, no questions asked. They're the international currency in these parts. Much more reliable and acceptable than paper currency. But one day I got a letter from Lionel Conyers. My "brother", if

178

you please! I knew a good deal about him from Alice's diary. I knew that he was seven years older than her; I knew she didn't like him, perhaps was even a bit afraid of him. It seemed they hardly knew each other – hadn't seen each other for years. I turned this way and that! Risk it with the unknown Lionel? Could I ever deceive him? Play the game of "do you remember?" In the end I decided to perfect my arrangements for a sudden and discreet (and by no means empty-handed!) disappearance but to leave this till the very last minute, arguing to myself that anything could happen. I was right. In India anything could and something did! Poor Lionel! I was taken to identify the body. He was rather a mess. He'd been shot through the head. But, I'll tell you, Joe, I was so bloody relieved I had no problem in giving him a sisterly kiss.'

She was silent for a moment as if daring Joe to comment and then, 'Bystanders were much affected by this, I'm told. Many shed a tear and so did I! Do you wonder I thought myself invincible? Fate again, you see! But I was very confused. Fate this time had had an instrument. I couldn't understand why or who . . . though I had an awful suspicion. Then the day after Lionel's funeral a letter arrived at the office. "Dear Isobel, Danger averted. In gratitude for extra protection pay three thousand rupees." '

'A one-off payment?'

She nodded. 'A substantial sum, you see, but just possible.'

'And what about Korsovsky? Have your protectors communicated with you about his death?'

'No. Not yet. I found out about his theatre booking last November when it was all arranged and was very alarmed, as you might guess. He would obviously identify me the minute he set eyes on me but I knew Feodor wouldn't give me away if he was forewarned. Or even if not forewarned. One look, one wink across the heads of the crowd would have been enough! He had a rascally sense of humour and he would have relished the situation. I really loved him, Joe. Once . . .' Her voice trailed away but she shook off her memories and her voice hardened. 'My bloody protection squad! Keeping me here like a milk cow! I feel trapped, Joe! Under surveillance the whole time! But by whom?'

'Well, it has to be somebody who knows Isobel Newton rather

than Alice Conyers if you think about it,' said Joe. 'Anyone who was familiar with Alice would know that her brother would unmask you but they wouldn't know about the Korsovsky danger unless they knew Isobel from her past. And from her relatively recent past. It has to be someone who knew you in the days when you lived in France. Your gallery of old lovers? Has one of them surfaced in Simla?'

'A desperately depleted band! Not one. I check the arrivals list every day. You know that everyone arriving in Simla has to give their name and business . . . it's easy to get access to it – you could say it's almost a social register.'

'An old school friend?'

'I haven't recognized anyone. And don't forget, Joe, that anyone who knew me – Isobel – from my schooldays would remember the sixteen-year-old that I was when I left for France. I look and am a very different person.'

'Someone then who was close to you at the time of the accident, before, as it were, you had had time to slip into the role and play it as confidently as you do now?'

'Marie-Jeanne, you mean? Yes, I had considered that. I've replayed every word we exchanged in those first days over and over and I'm quite certain that I gave nothing away. I spoke entirely in English, I appeared to know who I was . . . I gave a very convincing account of myself. When they left me alone to sleep I used to get out my . . . Alice's . . . diary and learn up her life for the previous five years.' Isobel rolled her eyes. 'My God! It didn't take long to learn! My own would have filled ten volumes! And then there was the leather folder . . .'

'Containing the Company details?'

'Yes, that one. Now that held far more interest for me. Even then I began to understand and unravel the Company. Certain executive gentlemen were about to be catapulted into early retirement even before I'd left Marseilles!'

'So, as far as Marie-Jeanne was concerned, you didn't falter or hesitate?'

'No. It would have been easy enough to blame any aberration, any loss of memory on the accident, but I never needed to do that.'

'She did notice one odd thing, though.'

Isobel looked at him in surprise and alarm.

'Your green silk underwear. She thought it very strange that a soberly clad English girl would be wearing such glamorous underpinnings. Indulgently, she put it down to girlish rebellion. A hasty purchase made in Paris. Cocking a surreptitious snook at your travelling chaperone. "It made me like her a lot," she said.'

Isobel smiled and nodded. 'Marie-Jeanne *would* put that interpretation on it. She is very generous-minded and fond of me, I do believe.'

'Fond enough to protect your identity if it were known to her?'

'Yes, I don't doubt that for a moment. But she would never blackmail me. If she wanted money she would only have to ask me. She knows that. But she does not ask. She is doing very well on her own account and has turned out to be a natural business-woman. Marie-Jeanne is very . . . upright, very religious. Though not religious enough to please her parents, I'm afraid. Landed gentry, petty-minded, rigid people who didn't understand her at all. She was plain and large and the only girl among five brothers. No concessions were made for her sex – she was brought up as a boy, hunting, shooting and fighting and praying for forgiveness for all these activities on Sundays. One day they noticed that she had matured, was by no means attractive enough to be a good marriage prospect, and suggested the only thing that came into their hidebound minds – that she should become a nun. Very respectable way of getting rid of an unwanted daughter in France even in these days. She refused but placated them by offering her services in another cause dear to their hearts – the army. She became a nurse. And some years later she met me in hospital in Beaune.'

'And everything changed for her,' said Joe thoughtfully. 'She's leading a life which quite obviously suits her, a life which would come to an end perhaps if her patron, her protector, her friend, were disgraced. If the money that had launched her in business were proved to be fraudulently obtained?'

'What depths of suspicion your mind is capable of plumbing!'

'It helps to keep me alive.'

'Well, you're going to need to suspect everyone in Simla if you're to get out of this town without a bullet in your hide, Commander. I mean that! Trust no one! Well, perhaps you may turn your back on the excellent Mrs Carter but no one else.' She was silent for a moment and then added, 'And Captain Simpson – surely his life would be at risk too if my watcher, my enemy were to realize the significance of his visit to Simla?'

'We've kept his appearance very quiet. No one other than ourselves knows who he is, and be assured that Carter has him under constant watch.'

'Are you going to tell me how on earth you managed to find him? Where did he spring from? Was he always aware . . .?'

'Oh yes, he knew but the truth was so extraordinary, so unpalatable he assumed his brain was playing tricks on him. We found his name listed as a survivor in a newspaper Korsovsky carried in his luggage.'

'A newspaper? What newspaper? Why did Feodor have a copy?' Alice's voice was suddenly sharp with suspicion. Joe explained that her swift departure to India had preceded the publication of the finalized list of the dead and the survivors and that Feodor had been sent a copy by his agent largely in evidence of Isobel's reported death.

'He must have been more fond of me than I had allowed,' was her sad comment. 'But tell me, Joe, this newspaper . . . where is it now? May I see a copy? Would that be possible? I should be very interested to read an account of my death.'

'Carter has it,' Joe said, 'at the station. I can't see any reason why he wouldn't let you see it if you really wanted to.' He replied cheerfully enough but something about her tone and the barely hidden anxiety underlying it was ringing warning bells. There was more to her eagerness to read the account than mere curiosity, he thought.

'Look, Alice, if you do go to see Carter be discreet. I think for everyone's security it would be best if we all went on as though nothing out of the ordinary had happened tonight . . .'

'You're joking! The scene at the seance will be doing the rounds of the coffee houses and drawing rooms tomorrow!'

'You said yourself when I chased you up here – anyone would have fled. Miss Trollope even fainted and disappeared under the table. Some of the others looked completely horror-stricken, I recall. If Carter and I refrain from hauling you off up the Mall in manacles and continue to treat you with sycophantic deference and call you Mrs Conyers-Sharpe in public places, I think you'll find there's been no harm done and no suspicions raised. We can leave Minerva Freemantle to come up with a convincing story to cover the apparition – that's right up her street. She'll probably find her client list has doubled once the sensation-seekers get hold of this!'

Isobel nodded her agreement.

'But don't get excited,' he began, and then continued awkwardly, 'I'm making no promises. You'll be aware, of course, that I have no authority here in Simla and the decision as to whether to reveal your fraud and to whom rests with others who will, doubtless, take the appropriate action.' Joe paused, aware that the pompous and semi-official phrases contrasted absurdly with his situation. The girl in his arms was aware of it too. Hard little fingers nipped him sharply in the side.

'So – confide in me, Joe! I think you'll agree I have an interest. What *are* you going to do?' She sighed and rubbed her head against his shoulder.

'Find out who's blackmailing you, track him down and we'll have found our murderer.'

'Do you think you can do in three days what I've been unable to do in three years? I have made my own enquiries, you know. Discreetly of course. Rheza Khan is in my confidence, has always been in my confidence, and our combined efforts have been fruitless.'

'Well, at least we'll have the full resources of the law at our disposal – Scotland Yard's finest, Simla's specials and the incomparable Sir George Jardine – that's quite a line-up of talent, you know!' Joe spoke lightly and reassuringly. 'But – I have to know, Alice – to what extent is Rheza Khan in your confidence?'

'I told him why I was being blackmailed when the first demand note arrived. That I had assumed Alice's identity, that is. It was a risk but I had to trust someone. And I've never regretted it for a moment. He asks no questions – he never has. He's a Pathan, you know: natural conspirators, perhaps the best in the world. Over and over again he's shown me that I can trust him. He knows I'm not who I claim to be but he is content with that.' She stirred uncomfortably. 'Joe, I haven't told him all that I have told you about my past. He doesn't know about my . . . my career in France. He doesn't know about Korsovsky and all that.'

'Well, he won't hear about it from me. None of my business.'

'I wouldn't like him to find out. I would prefer to keep his respect. And I'm sure that at the moment I have that. He gives me discreet and unstinting help. He arranged to cover the outgoing sums of money. He covered it easily. The regularity and consistency of the leakage made it easy apparently. He runs the finances of the firm and I think he just invented other phantom employees with credible salaries. He's not concerned about who I am. I arrived in India with complete authority and I used it. To good effect. He accepts me and would do much, I believe, to ensure that . . .' Her voice trailed away and she looked thoughtful for a moment before adding, 'He has my complete trust.'

The moonlight filtering through the moving branches lit up and concealed her features by turns, reflecting her uncertainty. Joe looked with pity at the lovely, defenceless face. Who was she able truly to trust? he wondered. Who had she ever been able to trust? Used, deceived, passed from man to man and ending up literally in the arms of the law. In the sheltering arms of a man who was far from being her protector, a man who threatened her liberty and perhaps her life. And yet he recognized that he was feeling a deep urge to protect her, to keep her safe from her enemy. Time to move on.

He rose and pulled her to her feet, tucking her revolver into his pocket. 'It's getting late. I'll escort you back to the Mall and you can pick up your rickshaw. If we stay away together any longer there'll be much worse rumours circulating in Simla tomorrow.' He steered her towards the staircase. 'And as we go, I'll tell you how you can help us with this next bit.'

Joe extended a hand to steady Alice as she stepped into her rickshaw and, swept by an impulse, stood, her hand in his, and by a further impulse stooped and raised it to his lips and kissed it. They stood for a moment looking at each other in silence.

'Joe,' Alice breathed, 'I wish I knew a bit more about you. You know everything there is to know about me and I know nothing, nothing whatever about you. That's strange.'

'There's nothing to know really,' said Joe. 'I'm very pedestrian.'

Alice looked at him, considering, for a moment. 'That's the impression you try to give but I think there's more to it than that.' And then in a low voice she called to the rickshaw men to proceed.

Creaking, with the patter of running feet and the tinkle of warning bells, the rickshaw set off down the curving road, leaving Joe watching it and her disappear. 'You know all there is to know about me,' she had said. Not true, thought Joe. The rest of my life wouldn't be long enough to find out all there is to know about that very remarkable, very complex and, let me admit it to myself, that very seductive girl. What's that charge that's sometimes levied? 'Interfering with a witness'? That's one witness with whom I would so happily interfere!

He turned to go on his way but out of the shadow there came a gently mocking voice. ' "Oh, what can ail thee, Knight at Arms, alone and palely loitering?" '

Charlie Carter stepped into the dim street light. 'Loitering, Commander? Loitering with intent to commit a felony?'

Joe was quite extraordinarily pleased to see him and said so. 'Though how the hell you knew where I was I don't suppose you'll ever tell me!'

'Oh, it's not difficult! I picked up your trail after the seance. So did Alice's rickshaw men, a couple of pi-dogs joined in the chase, "and after them, the parson ran, the sexton and the squire". The whole of Simla's agog by now, I shouldn't wonder.'

'Well, whatever,' said Joe, 'I'm devilish pleased to see you! And I'll tell you – I could really do with a drink. It's been quite an evening one way and another!'

'Funny you should say that – that is exactly what Sir George said to me. Indeed, I'm under orders to bring you to him and if it's a drink you want I can think of nowhere you'll get a better one. We'll walk, shall we? Clear the brain and you can run through some of the highlights of your tête-à-tête with Alice.'

When they reached the Residence lights were burning and servants moving about.

'Sir George has had a dinner party this evening and it's only just dispersing,' said Charlie. 'There, look, that's the last carriage moving off now. Step in here with me.'

They turned together and went in through a side door. They were greeted by Sir George in white tie and decorations. It had evidently been a formal occasion.

'Flawless timing!' came his booming voice. 'Trust Scotland

Yard! Been waiting for you. Didn't know quite where you were or what you were up to. Come in here – we'll go into the library. Now, what can I offer you? Coffee? Of course. Brandy? Brandy for heroes, you know and here we are, three heroes in a row.'

He clapped his hands and shouted, and almost before he had done so glasses and a decanter appeared and a tall silver coffee pot.

'Now,' said George when they were seated, 'I've heard about the seance. Quite fascinating! Most irregular! Can't imagine how you got Charlie Carter to co-operate in your nefarious scheme but it seems to have produced a result. And now I want to know – what happened next? It is known that you disappeared into the night with the attractive Mrs Conyers-Sharpe but more than that is not known beyond the fact that you spent an unconscionable length of time hiding, I might almost say canoodling, in an unfrequented garden. And I dare say you exchanged more than words! Set your mind at rest, however – I'm only interested in the words! Whatever else passed –'

'George!' said Joe. 'For God's sake! Don't let your imagination run away with you! But it is true – I have a lot to tell you.'

'Well,' said George, 'I won't say "the night is young" because it isn't very, but here we are and we are at your service.'

Joe sipped from the proffered glass, lit the proffered cigar, crossed his legs, lay back in the cushioned armchair and collected his thoughts. 'Firstly,' he began, 'it is admitted to me, though not necessarily or even probably to anybody else, that, incredible as it may seem, there was a switch. She whom we have known as Alice Conyers, whom I shall always think of as Alice Conyers, is in fact Isobel Newton otherwise known as Isabelle de Neuville.' And he explained the events of the Beaune rail crash. His audience listened spellbound.

'That,' said George, 'is the most incredible story I have ever heard!' And to Charlie, 'Did you have even the remotest suspicion?'

'Never,' said Charlie. 'Never in a thousand years. In fact, were it not from her own lips I wouldn't believe it now. Not sure I do believe it.'

'Secondly,' Joe continued, 'Alice is being blackmailed. By someone or some people, male or female, Indian or English, who know and have known for three years her true identity. And she has paid. The blackmailers are desperate to keep her in place and will do anything including murder to do so. It's absolutely true – find the blackmailer and we've found our murderer.'

Joe explained the system whereby payments were passed through Robertson. 'And all we have to do is intercept the next payment. I've told Alice to carry on as though nothing has happened. If we all do this, the blackmailer will assume we are unaware of the switch. Now could be our moment to close in. It's likely if he or they conform to pattern, and so far the behaviour has been very consistent, that a demand will soon be made for the removal of Korsovsky. We must lean heavily on Robertson, extract everything he knows and make him co-operate.'

'You make it sound so easy,' said Charlie.

'I'm not deceived,' said George. 'I understand the problems. If we could prove it – and that's not as straightforward as it might seem at first sight – we could bring an action for fraud against Alice but as far as the further investigations are concerned, what would be the advantage of that? None, as I believe. If the blackmailer realizes his game is up then he'll disappear.'

'So you're intending no move against Alice?' said Charlie, a note of indignation creeping into his voice.

'I didn't say that,' said George. 'But I'm certainly not going to act precipitately. But I particularly ask you, Joe, Carter, to treat Alice's revelations in confidence between the three of us for the moment. This is a situation which bristles with complexity – criminal complexity, legal complexity. Indeed, just to start the ball rolling, answer me this – who has Alice (I'll go on calling her Alice) defrauded?'

'Well,' said Joe, who had been asking himself the same question, 'I conclude that she has defrauded real Alice, little Alice. Little Alice is dead so she has defrauded little Alice's heirs at law whoever they might be and little Alice's heir at law would, I suppose, be her brother Lionel and Lionel is dead so who do we come down to? Well, you may be surprised to learn that as far as I can work it out we come down to Reggie. No longer her husband of course but the joint inheritor from real Alice's grandfather's will. She fraudulently made off with fifty-one per cent of ICTC which would otherwise have reverted to him. At least I suppose that's right?' he concluded dubiously.

'Reggie!' said George explosively. 'Bloody fellow! Can't stand him!'

'Didn't think much of him,' said Joe.

'Can't stand him,' echoed Charlie.

'Well, that's fine,' said Sir George. 'We "unmask" – I apologize for the word – Alice, she is disgraced, her marriage is null and void, her position in ICTC probably completely compromised, the work she does in Simla and Bombay will fall apart and we elevate that drunken oaf Reggie to a position of trust and influence. Sounds like a jolly good evening's work, don't you think, chaps?'

'George,' said Joe, 'what on earth are you saying?'

'I'm saying, would you like to take shares in a company I'm thinking of founding? A little private company? I'm going to call it Fraudsters Anonymous or The Alice Conyers-Sharpe Protection Society. Any takers?'

With the warmest memories of his last minutes with Alice at the foot of the garden steps, Joe was tempted. With no such memories Charlie Carter was profoundly shocked. 'You can't be serious, sir!' he said indignantly. 'You can't be preparing to compound a felony! Fraud is a felony and leaving aside the moral implications I don't believe you'd ever get away with it.'

'All right then,' said Sir George, 'if you won't go all the way with me, and I acknowledge that there is a problem, let us at least agree on a stay of execution. Let us leave matters as they are. Let this complex situation roll on its way and let us exercise every sort of vigilance to follow it through until it leads us to our killer. I'm not issuing an order – I'm not quite sure if I'd be in a position to issue an order of that sort – I'm doing no more than invite your co-operation.'

He looked briskly from one to the other. 'Do I have it?'

'Yes, Sir George,' said Carter.

'Yes, Sir George,' said Joe.

Chapter Eighteen

Joe and Charlie Carter set out to walk through the streets of Simla, heading together for the establishment of Mr Robertson, the jeweller.

'You've read *Kim*, I think you said?' said Charlie as they went along the Mall.

'Yes, indeed. And it did occur to me that perhaps Cecil Robertson has too! For a moment, stepping into his shop on Wednesday morning I thought I was entering the world of Lurgan Sahib!'

'One of the best descriptions Kipling ever wrote! But I don't think Robertson does it to play to the tourists. As far as his shop is concerned time has stood still. It's been there for as long as I can remember and Robertson is not the first owner by any means. He continues a tradition. He performs an essential service. Lots of Indian families treat him as if he were a bank. Only the most informal records are kept but a satisfactory service is offered, it would seem. Many people prefer to deal personally with someone they know and can trust their money to rather than a faceless European bank with head offices in Leadenhall Street, EC1. No, he's a man of many parts, is our Mr Robertson.'

'Not above a little smuggling?'

'Certainly not above a little smuggling. But then, almost nobody who lives in these parts is above a little smuggling. Jewellery, gold, opium, hashish . . . their passage back and forth over the frontiers is as old as the Himalayas. The government of India doesn't worry too much. A little jewel smuggling this way and that doesn't do any harm, but gold – now that's a different matter. We wouldn't want to see large quantities of that disappearing north over the border into Asia. Cecil Robertson has always been totally co-operative with us. In fact he's given us two or three valuable tips over the years. We don't interfere with the movement of gemstones – mostly on their way to China – and in exchange he lets us know . . . about other things.'

'Other things?'

'Yes, boys and girls. Jewels going into China, pretty boys and girls coming back again on their way to Kashmir through Chandigarh and on eventually to the Gulf. Poor little devils! We got a tip from Robertson last year. We stopped a bullock cart . . . shots were exchanged if you can believe . . . and there they were – drugged, like a lot of dormice. So, you might say, I owe Robertson a good turn. I don't suppose that the trade troubles his conscience much, it's as good a way as any of keeping in with me – slipping a bit of information from time to time. I suppose that's the way to run an Empire. A little bit of accommodation, if you know what I mean.'

They paused outside Robertson's shop. Robertson himself emerged in his shirt-sleeves taking an elaborate farewell of a Bengali customer.

'Spare us a couple of moments, Robertson?' said Charlie. 'I think you've met my friend Joe Sandilands? Fact is, we could do with a little help. May we come in?'

'Of course,' said Robertson unctuously with something between a salute and a salaam. Joe remembered that he was said to have a Scottish father and a Persian mother and looking at that mysterious face he was very ready to believe this, supported as it was by the accent. Strange! Very much the English of a man of whom it was not the first language and yet, on the other hand, a perceptible flavour of upper class English as spoken in the Raj.

His eye slid over Charlie Carter without much interest but dwelt on Joe. 'Come in,' he said again. 'Come right through.' He said a few words to an assistant and, calling into the back premises, addressed a few more to an unseen presence who answered deferentially.

The shop, Joe recalled from his earlier brief visit, operated on two levels. Outwardly there was the stock in trade of any well-equipped jeweller's shop but behind this was an accumulation that it would be impossible to classify. Objects Tibetan, Chinese, Indian and even European. Objects doubtless from the collapse of the Russian Empire, icons and pectoral crosses and a few items of classical antiquity. Joe remembered that Alexander the Great had passed this way. He tried to suppress the unprofessional fascination which these things had awakened. His hand went out to a small carved ivory figure and he held it to the light. A large-eyed, full-breasted woman held in her hand a knot of golden snakes.

'You're right,' said Robertson surprisingly. 'From Crete, I suspect. Minoan culture. The snake goddess. Question – how on earth did it get here? I can't tell you anything about the provenance. Probably stolen from the excavations. It's not expensive. Are you interested?'

'Yes. Very,' said Joe. 'Some other time.'

'Of course. Of course. I had assumed that this was an official visit.'

He led them into an airless little room and turned on a feeble electric light. He turned some cushions aside to reveal three chairs which he indicated with a hospitable gesture. 'And now, how may I help the police?'

'What I have to say is in confidence, Robertson,' said Charlie in a bland official tone.

Robertson nodded and waited.

'It concerns Alice Conyers-Sharpe.'

'Really?' Robertson's eye flicked for a second to Joe.

'We are worried,' said Charlie confidentially. 'You may say that it has nothing to do with us but she is a prominent citizen – a good client of yours, I believe – and many people in Simla depend on her. It has been revealed to us that this lady we all so admire is being cheated. Has any idea of this sort occurred to you?'

Joe decided that Robertson was making only a show of considering this question. He replied with confidence, 'Yes. But it is not my place to question or advise or comment on Mrs Sharpe's arrangements. All acknowledge her to be a splendid businesswoman, successful, decisive and well advised. Who am I to speculate on the soundness of her transactions? So long as her requirements of me are within the law, Superintendent, there is nothing I am called upon to do but fulfil them.'

'It is known,' said Joe, 'that Mrs Sharpe deals consistently in jewels. We are making enquiries, with her knowledge and con-

191

sent I should say, into specifically the purchases she makes twice yearly in April and October. Tell us how the exchange is managed from your end, will you?'

After a moment's consideration, Robertson got up and took down a file from a high shelf. He extracted a single sheet of paper and handed it to Carter. As he and Joe eagerly pored over it he explained. 'I received that in October 1920.'

On a plain sheet of white writing paper a short message had been written in English in neat capitals. Robertson recited the message as they read. 'Mrs Sharpe will bring you a cheque for four thousand rupees biannually in April and October. When she arrives you will sell her jewels to the value of two thousand rupees. Select other jewels to the same value and place them in a blue box under the counter. Choose gems or pieces that are easily transportable and unremarkable. When a messenger asks for the blue box hand it over.'

'And this has gone on as described. I performed the fourth regular transaction at the beginning of April.'

'The regular transaction?' asked Joe.

Robertson paused. 'There was a further one, out of pattern, you might say.'

'And can you say precisely when this one occurred?'

'Yes.'

He selected another leaf from the file and handed it over. 'You will see that the value varies. This one mentions the sum of three thousand rupees. And it is dated 1st May 1921. It was shortly after Mrs Sharpe's brother was killed. I remember she was wearing black and she chose a diamond and jet mourning piece.'

Joe looked at him closely. There was no hint of suspicion or suggestion in the bland, dark eyes.

'Who collects the contents of the blue box, Robertson?'

'No one I know. It's a different messenger each time. An Indian. I suspect just someone picked up in the bazaar and given this task for a few annas. I have no doubt the messenger is carefully watched, of course, but as to the identity of the watcher or indeed the destination of the blue box, I have no idea. My responsibility ends when the box leaves here.'

'Have you a feeling about all this?' asked Charlie. 'Share your thoughts with us. You must have formed some kind of theory about the exchange. Embezzlement? Extortion? Blackmail? Generous donations to an anonymous recipient?'

Robertson's eyes gleamed for a moment. 'Probably two out of the four,' he said and appeared to be unwilling to take the thought further. 'You may be interested,' he went on after a slight pause, 'in seeing this. It was put through my door this morning.'

He handed Carter an envelope. With an exclamation of dismay, Carter took it carefully by the edges.

'I shouldn't worry about obliterating any useful fingerprints,' said Joe. 'The world and his wife will have handled it by now – everyone, I would expect, apart from our, er, customer. He's not going to make the mistake of leaving prints on it. Go ahead. Open it.'

'Let's see. "Mrs S. will buy more jewels. Value five thousand rupees. Same arrangements." Mmm . . . price has increased significantly. I take it Mrs Sharpe hasn't appeared yet?'

'Oh yes, she has. She came in very early – about half an hour before your good selves. She chose a diamond solitaire ring and she gave me a banker's draft in payment. And I have completed my arrangements in regard to the second part of the transaction.'

'Would you show us the routine with the blue box then, if you've prepared it?'

They went back into the shop and Robertson took a small velvet box from a drawer underneath the counter. They peered inside. Coiled in the bottom and glittering even in the half light was a diamond necklace.

'Very simple. Practically unrecognizable. Easy to break up and sell as individual stones,' Carter commented.

'Look,' said Joe, 'Robertson, would you have any objection to varying the routine a little? We desperately need to know – as I'm sure you've guessed – the identity of the person who is the recipient of the contents of the box. Mrs Sharpe's peace of mind, to put it simply, is at stake.'

Robertson nodded his agreement.

'What I want you to do is change these diamonds for something a lot more distinctive. Something so unique and decorative that wherever it appears again – if ever it does resurface – any jeweller would recognize it.'

'I see,' said Robertson. 'And then, delivery safely accomplished, the Simla police circulate a description of a certain piece of stolen jewellery so unmistakable that it cannot safely be worn or sold without word getting back?'

'Exactly,' said Joe.

'What if he objects?' asked Carter. 'Of course,' he added, answering his own question, 'then he contacts Robertson again and perhaps in his anger gives away more than he meant to? At least we'd have another handle on this discreet charmer. Come on – what have you got to show us, Robertson?'

Robertson hesitated then with a conspiratorial smile went into the back room and emerged a few minutes later. 'I think you would agree that this fulfils your requirements,' he said.

Joe and Carter looked and gasped.

'It's perfectly lovely,' said Carter, 'but it won't do! Nothing approaching the value you're supposed to supply. I mean – it's . . . it's . . . what do the ladies call something like this? – costume jewellery, yes, costume jewellery.'

'No it's not,' said Joe. 'I'm sure I've seen something like this before . . . on a portrait perhaps?'

Robertson smiled and nodded. 'You have it. On a portrait by Hans Holbein. Sixteenth-century German portrait painter. The Tudor royal family were much painted by him. They liked to be seen wearing rather spectacular jewels, like this one.'

They looked again. The whole arrangement was perhaps four inches across and five inches long. At its centre glowed a stone which could have been a ruby, Joe thought, had it not been so large. It was surrounded by a gold circlet inlaid with bright enamels in the form of Tudor roses and posies of glittering clear stones which Joe would have sworn were diamonds.

'The style became very popular again in Europe some years ago and these pieces began to be produced with showy semi-precious stones like peridots at the centre. They're called "Holbeinesque" in the trade.' He paused for a moment, looking at the brooch in rapt admiration. 'But there's nothing "-esque" about this one. This is a genuine sixteenth-century item. Any jeweller would recognize it if it passed through his hands. It's the Duke of Clarence Ruby.'

'If that's a ruby, isn't it a little *over* the mark?' Carter wanted to know.

'Yes. Far over. But in the interests of saving Mrs Sharpe even a minute's concern, I'm sure it is worth the sacrifice,' he said with his deprecatory smile. 'And besides I did pick it up as rather a bargain. It was the property of a prince. He bought it in London and gave it to his senior wife. She was not grateful. She hated it. Couldn't see the point of it and came and ordered me to swap it for a gold necklace she'd seen and matching ear-rings. I was happy to do so. Buy, sell or exchange, I get my commission, you know. But of course, if I were ever to sell it on the open market and it were to appear on the bosom of – let's say the Vicereine – there might be problems.'

'I see,' said Carter. 'In that case, it's perfect. Any means we have of flushing out Mrs Sharpe's unknown correspondent must be made use of, Robertson. I'm sure you understand. We're grateful for your co-operation and, look here, one more thing you can do to help – it's just a small thing – we've got the shop under discreet surveillance. When a messenger comes in for the box could you alert my men? Give them some sort of a signal?'

Robertson smiled and nodded compliance. Joe had little doubt that he was aware of Carter's discreet surveillance. 'Of course, Superintendent. Nothing simpler. The window lights are normally switched on. When the messenger asks for the box I will switch them off. The switch is here to hand under the counter.'

'That will do well,' said Carter.

With mutual assurances of esteem, they left Robertson and went out into the street. Blinking in the sharp sunlight, Joe screwed up his eyes and surreptitiously glanced up and down the Mall in an attempt to locate Carter's surveillance team. He saw the usual bustle of European shoppers, Indian servants and street urchins. Two nursemaids walked by chattering and scolding. A Hindu holy man sat patiently opposite, cross-legged, with his begging bowl in front of him. Hesitating on the pavement's edge, Carter waved away two rickshaws competing for their custom. Avoiding them, he stepped off the pavement into a puddle left over from a late night shower.

'Drat!' he exclaimed, running a fastidious eye over the spatters on his smart boots.

'You're in luck,' said Joe, pointing across the street. 'Look there!'

They crossed over to a boot black's stand and Carter greeted the swarm of little Indian boys who appeared to be loosely in charge of it. He settled into the chair and stuck out his feet.

'Clever chaps, these young 'uns,' he said. 'Movable stand, you see. They roll it around and set up shop wherever they see a puddle. Never entirely sure they don't actually create the puddles!'

Five minutes later the chattering group were prepared to release Carter's feet, now sporting boots a platoon-sergeant would have passed as acceptable. Carter offered a handful of annas to the oldest boy and, laughing, spoke to him briefly in Hindustani. They strolled on, dropping into two or three more shops on their way back to police headquarters.

Seated once again in Carter's office, Joe remarked, 'I didn't spot your men!'

'Yes, you did!' said Carter cheerily. 'There were six of them. The tallest came up to your belt and you gave them each a cigarette!'

'The shoe blacks!' Joe began to laugh. 'What is this? Simla's answer to the Baker Street Irregulars?'

'Just that! They're actually all the sons of Sir George's head gardener. Sir George set them up with the equipment and they're doing well – they make a decent living at the shoe blacking and then they're on a police retainer. It's amazing what they get to hear! People, even those you'd think would know better, seem to assume that young Indian shoe blacks must be deaf and stupid. Not at all! They're as smart as whips! And they can go practically anywhere and no one notices them. It's a good arrangement.'

'Will they know what to do?'

'Oh, yes. I passed them the word about the shop light signal. They'll follow whoever comes out with the blue box to the ends of the earth if they have to. All we have to do now is wait.'

'I don't think we'll have to wait long,' said Joe. 'There's an urgency about this last demand – don't you think? A huge amount called for . . . I'd say this could well be a last request before he calls it a day. Rumours, uncertainties may have got to his ears. I think, Carter, our man is planning to grab his loot and run. And, I'll tell you something else – Alice seems to have been caught up in the urgency too. She was out and about pretty early this morning, wasn't she? She must have got her demand note at crack of dawn, or perhaps even during the night, and gone straight off to Robertson's shop.'

'And now I'll tell *you* something, Sandilands,' said Carter. 'Before she was at the jeweller's she was here. We'd hardly opened up when she came in asking to see me. Rather an odd request. I was hoping you could shed some light on it as you seem to have got so close to her last night. She wanted to cast an eye over the newspaper list of the Beaune casualties. She said that you'd told her she could.'

'Did she now?' said Joe, an edge of concern in his voice. 'I don't like this, Carter. She's moving too fast for us. You didn't let her take it away, did you?'

'Of course not! In fact I was so suspicious of her intentions I sat with her and watched her closely while she read it.'

'And?'

'Very interesting! She pretended to read the news report of the crash first but it was clear to me that it was the list of the casualties she had really come to check on. Her eyes were continually veering sideways to the right-hand side of the page where the lists are printed.'

Carter got up and retrieved the paper from a locked file. He spread it out on the table between them. 'Now, whatever she saw printed there had quite an effect on her. She turned pale, she started to breathe faster, she was agitated. No doubt about that. I had to send for a glass of water for her. Look at it more closely, Joe. I've had another look and I must say no name leaps out at me. What do you *see*?'

Joe looked again. Somewhere concealed in this list of English and French casualties was a name which had dramatic importance for Isobel Newton. But surely not? How could she be threatened by someone who had died so long ago? None of these names had any power to harm her. So what then had she seen in these lists?

'Oh, my God!' Joe groaned. 'What bloody idiots we've been! Charlie! I now know what people mean when they call us the Defective Force! Get Simpson here! Where the devil is Simpson? You've not let him go back to Delhi, have you? We must see him!'

'No, it's all right, Joe,' said Carter in puzzlement. 'I decided it might not be quite safe to put him in the hotel after all – I put him up with me and Meg. He's at my bungalow helping Meg to peg a rug. Hang on – I'll give Meg a ring. We've got a telephone installed. We can get him over here in a few minutes. I'll send a sergeant over with a rickshaw. But tell me, Joe, what have you seen? What did Alice see?'

'Nothing,' said Joe. 'And that's the whole point. It's what she didn't see that's important!'

Chapter Nineteen

Ten-year-old Raghu Mitra stubbed out his cigarette and handed his tin of polish and his brushes and his polishing cloth to a smaller brother. Without a word spoken the two youngest boys took charge of the shoe black stall and the four bigger ones, apparently bored with the business for the moment, took out a yellow ball and began to play catch across the street to the vociferous objections of the rickshaw runners passing between them. Seconds ago the lights had gone out in the window of the jeweller's shop just as Carter Sahib had said they would.

A man emerged from the shop and set off down the Mall in an easterly direction. A Hindu in white turban, white baggy trousers and white overshirt, he strode out, looking neither to left nor right, unconcerned and unafraid. A man on legitimate business. A man of the bazaar, Raghu guessed, commissioned to carry a parcel which Carter Sahib was very interested in. And that bulge over his right hip would no doubt be the parcel in question. Whooping and hollering and bumping into the messenger, the boys chased their ball down the street. An observant onlooker might have noticed that while two boys ran ahead of their quarry, in whom they showed not the slightest interest, two lagged behind. But he would have had to be a very observant onlooker.

Nearing Christ Church, the boys put away their ball and began to play tag, weaving in and out of the crowds but always keeping their man loosely in the centre of their group, prepared to wheel and turn and change direction like leaves in the wind. Their target made straight for the big main doors of the cathedral and went unhesitatingly in. Raghu made to follow him but was chased away by a doorman. He and one brother remained playing around the doors while the two remaining boys circled the cathedral, keeping an eye on the rear doorway.

Two minutes later the Indian they had followed came out, blinking, into the sunlight. The bulge at his right hip had disappeared. At a flick of Raghu's hand, his second brother set off to follow the man. Raghu waited. After a while three Europeans came out. Two of them, a sahib and memsahib and tourists by the look of them, wandered off in the direction of the Mall. The third paused, looked to left and right, scanning the large paved concourse in front of the church, and then started to walk casually away. He had a bulge in the left pocket of his smartly cut trousers, Raghu noticed. With a piercing whistle to summon his brothers from the rear door, he set off, trotting ahead of the man back down the Mall. They were following a well-rehearsed surveillance drill devised by Charlie Carter's Havildar of Police.

As he scampered along he committed to memory the appearance of the European. Carter Sahib himself had taught him this drill. Height: medium, as tall as Raghu's father. Hair: dark and shiny. Eyes: he hadn't been close enough to see but he guessed black. Clothes: sahib clothes. Not military. Age: always a problem to guess the age of a European but he would have thought young – in his early twenties.

A quick glance behind reassured him that his brothers were following on. Raghu sat on a wall and waited until the European drew level. He shouted a greeting to the man and with gestures indicated that he thought it would be an excellent idea if the gentleman gave him a cigarette. The young man swatted him away and crossed the road. The two younger brothers now moved swiftly ahead and Raghu trailed behind. The man moved within his unseen box down the Mall and turned off into a narrow alleyway leading towards the bazaar.

This was dangerous. The shoeshine boys closed in, knowing that it took a split second of inattention to lose someone in this twisting maze of streets, though they all knew the bazaar like their own playground. The bazaar *was* their playground. But the man was hurrying now, not growing careless but confident with the confidence of someone who is on his own ground. Raghu guessed that the man was approaching his bolt hole. A turn to the left and one more to the right.

Rounding the corner, the leading brother signalled that the quarry had been lost. Raghu ran up and scanned the alley. He ran swiftly to the end and looked up and down. Retracing his tracks he pointed to a door in the creeper-hung wall. All the boys noted the door and its exact location. They began to giggle.

Raghu with a gesture indicated that they should return to base as fast as they could. And, stifling their laughter, they raced up the winding streets to the Mall, taking a roundabout way back to police headquarters.

Chapter Twenty

Joe and Carter sat side by side on the balcony, their feet on the balustrade, and settled themselves to wait.

'At last!' said Carter. 'A perfectly logical explanation which doesn't depend on anyone's arising from the dead in a cloud of sulphur and uttering terrible curses! Much more my sort of thing!'

'Oh, I don't know,' said Joe. 'If anything it's worse! It would terrify me, I can tell you! No wonder Alice Conyers looked a little pale.'

'We ought to have thought of this, don't you agree?' Carter mused. 'I mean – given all the accounts, all the evidence.'

'No. Come on, let's forgive ourselves this much. I don't believe anyone could have guessed at it from the information we had. And never forget that it hadn't even occurred to Alice herself. I think I witnessed her reaction when the awful thought first came to her but made nothing of it. It only began to cast a shadow in my mind when I noticed her unnatural interest in that list. And then it's just a question of logic. If she wasn't disturbed by the name of a person who had been killed, then what had she seen that had so profoundly shaken her? A gap, that's what! No name where a name should have been! But we'll try it out on Simpson when he gets here. Let him be the judge.'

Half an hour later a police tonga dropped Simpson at the door of the station and Carter hailed him. 'Come on up and we'll see if we can surprise you!'

The three men stepped inside the building together, Carter continuing cheerfully, 'My congratulations, by the way, on your performance last night! Here, we'll be in my office. Had to leave this morning before you were awake so we haven't had time to fill you in on what's been happening. I will just say – all that we suspected about the identity switch is confirmed. Sir George is *au courant* but back-pedalling, I'm afraid, on arresting our little quick-change artiste. Though quite rightly he thinks – and we agree – that we stand a better chance of flushing out the blackmailer and murderer if Alice is allowed to carry on as if nothing had happened.'

'Blackmailer?' said Simpson, bemused. 'Did you say blackmailer? What's this?'

'Such a lot you don't know yet! We haven't been holding out on you but things develop at a pace, it seems, in Simla. Better fill him in, Joe!'

Joe gave him the main details of his moonlit interview with Isobel Newton and as the full story unfolded and all his suspicions were confirmed Simpson began to relax and even to smile.

'Glad I was proved right,' he said at last. 'Glad I didn't put those people at the seance through such misery for no good reason! There was hell to pay when you shot off into the night, Joe, and Carter fled as well leaving me and Minerva Freemantle to deal with the riot that ensued. Quite a riot! Well, just Minerva when it came down to it because, having reduced the company to blank dismay and terror even – as arranged – I faded away into a broom cupboard. The one in the passageway with a false back. Hardly able to move, horrified by what we'd conjured up . . . I could hear them shouting and screaming and, as far as I could tell, falling over each other for ages and then it all went quiet. In the end Minerva came and got me out. She was in quite a state too! I couldn't work out whether she was laughing or crying! Even she was a bit hysterical, I think. She'd shipped Miss Trollope off home with friends and spun the story to everyone that it had all been a terrible mix-up. A crossed line from the beyond, if you like . . . a spiritual not-known-at-this-address. A vengeful entity had turned up at the wrong seance and had to be redirected! Just to make sure it doesn't happen again she's promised to strengthen the formula for the prayers she says at the beginning to ward off malevolent spirits.'

'Oh, dear!' said Joe, suddenly guilty. 'Poor old Maisie! Fences to mend there, I'm afraid!'

'But now,' said Carter, 'follow another idea with us.'

Simpson nodded.

'We want you to go over as fully and as carefully as you can all the events leading up to the crash. Yes, I know you've done it once but there was something we missed the first time . . . Something *you* missed. Can you start from the moment you arrived at the train and set eyes on Isobel Newton? Tell us everything you remember. Where she was standing, what she was doing, what she said. Everything.'

'Well, my first impression of Isabelle de Neuville – can I call her that? It's how I still think of her – was that she was a damned nuisance! I was lame and anxious to get into the first class compartment where my seat was booked and here, right in the doorway, was this Frenchwoman, blocking my way. She was haranguing her maid. In aristocratic French but shouting like a fishwife – I thought it a very odd scene . . . Odd behaviour.'

'Tell us about the maid. Was she . . . um . . . refined . . . in any way elegant too?'

'Good Lord, no!'

'Is your French good enough to know the difference? I don't mean to offend you, old man, but I know *I* wouldn't be able to tell the difference,' said Carter placatingly.

'I would. I was convalescent for a time with the Comte and Comtesse de Lausanne during the war. Used to play chess with the old man. Improved my French a lot and, well, yes, I think I'd spot a good accent when I heard it. But the maid, you say? Now she was another type entirely. Oh, pretty good to look at, don't mistake me, but not the same class as her mistress at all. Her language was coarse and she had a thick accent. A regional accent, I think.'

'A bit ooh-là-là, would you say?' said Joe with a quick look at Carter.

'Oh yes. Very pronounced cadence. Could almost have been Italian. So – swearing like a poilu – but what a beauty! Dark hair and eyes, about twenty-three or so I would guess. Mistress or maid – it was hard to know which one to look at!'

'And what were they arguing about? Can you remember?'

'Certainly! I pretended not to listen! But it was fascinating stuff! I couldn't tear my ears away. Isabelle gave her an envelope and that's when it all started. The maid tore it open and looked inside. She started yelling about her wages. Claimed she hadn't been paid for months and she wasn't going to let Isabelle get away with it any longer. Then she examined the train ticket that was in the envelope. More shrieks and screams! Third class! Isabelle had provided a third class ticket for her and she found this totally unacceptable – way beneath her dignity. And she was right, poor girl. I sympathized with her.'

'And tell us how they resolved it.'

'They didn't! Isabelle obviously was not going to give way and in the end the maid just got fed up and turned on her heel almost in mid-sentence and stormed off down the platform towards the third class carriages. At last I was able to make my way into the compartment and claim my seat.' He paused for a moment. 'Poor girl! She can't have had a very comfortable journey and, of course, it all ended in death and destruction. No one from the third class survived.'

'Think hard, Simpson. We want you to try to remember whether Isabelle called the girl by her name.'

'I'm sure she did.' Simpson frowned in an effort to recall the events of that morning at the Gare de Lyon. 'She used it several times, sort of barked it at her to bring her to heel . . . It was a common French name, um . . . Florence! Yes, that was it – Florence!'

Joe wrote the name in large letters on a pad in front of him. He looked at Carter. Carter got up and fetched the French newspaper. He spread it out on the table in front of them. 'Can you find her, Joe? Can you find Florence?'

The three of them eagerly scanned the list of third class passengers. There was no casualty by the name of Florence.

'All bodies eventually accounted for in the third class except for the one thirty-year-old man,' Joe reminded them.

'What does this mean?' Simpson asked. 'What are you trying to say?'

'Clearly the maid's name is not listed here for the simple reason that she was never on the train,' said Joe.

'Good God! Yes! I'll bet you're right! If she'd been in the third class she'd have been killed along with all the other humble citizens. None of them got out. And if she'd been killed she'd be listed – so,' said Simpson, 'she walked off down the platform and everyone assumed that she was going to the third class carriages but she must have just kept on walking! Straight out of the station!'

'But the question is,' said Carter slowly, 'where is the maid now?'

Joe looked at the name he had written down. Florence. He picked up his pen and crossed out the last four letters and added an 'a'. Flora. He drew a little flower next to the name and showed it to the other two.

'She's in Simla,' he said. 'And she's been watching us all along.'

Chapter Twenty-one

Flora took the blue velvet box eagerly in her two hands and carried it to the table in the centre of her sitting room. She returned to the door and locked it behind her. Biting her lower lip in anticipation she opened it and looked inside. Her eyes grew wide with disbelief and with a gasp of irritation she drew out the contents and held the jewel up to the light. Incomprehension was swiftly followed by anger as she tried to understand what she was seeing. She turned it this way and that, her attention caught finally by the exquisite enamelwork on the back of the brooch. If the maker had gone to the immense trouble of so skilfully decorating the back of the piece perhaps her first judgement that this was a gaudy lump of costume jewellery, a paste gem surrounded by ticky tacky and an incomprehensible joke on the part of Robertson, was wrong.

She took a jeweller's magnifying glass from a drawer and examined it in detail. She sighed. Her re-evaluation of the gem was even more disturbing than the original. What was going on? Something was going on – that was quite clear. She looked at the ruby in the centre and murmured, 'You are a messenger. You are here to tell me something of importance. But what? And who has sent you? Not Robertson, I'm thinking.'

She put her head in her hands and thought deeply for a minute or two and then, by degrees, a narrow smile began to creep across her face. She rubbed the cool stone sensuously against her cheek and she made her plans. She got up and went to the adjoining room where her dresses were stored in cupboards. She flung one open and searched through the ranks of silks and velvets. 'An opulent gem must have an opulent setting,' she told herself and she chose a simply cut black velvet dress with a low neckline. She put it on and fixed the brooch between her breasts, turning from side to side and admiring the result in her looking glass. That would do well.

Flora took a French novel from a shelf and settled down to wait.

Chapter Twenty-two

'So you're saying,' said Simpson, still struggling to understand, 'not only that I must think of Isabelle de Neuville as a high class tart but that her maid – one assumes long ago initiated into the, er, arts of the profession – is still alive and plying that trade. And has been plying her trade for the past three years here in Simla? I really can't believe this!'

'It takes a bit of believing – but it's true,' said Carter. 'And perhaps we could add that a sideline to her activities has been blackmail. Substantial sums of ICTC assets in the form of jewellery have made their way via the blue boxes into Madame Flora's sticky little hands.'

'You forget the more serious charges of murder,' said Joe. 'Remember, I'm here on George Jardine's invitation to solve a murder – two murders – and everything else is peripheral and only of urgency if it leads us to the man – the woman – the people who pulled the trigger. Alice is never going to charge Flora with blackmail – how could she? – but there's nothing she can do to prevent us arresting Flora for murder. Or as an accessory to two killings. She would have realized the significance of Lionel Conyers' arrival in Simla – would have found out about it from Reggie or Edgar Troop and made her plans to make quite sure that Lionel never caught sight of his sister. Everyone in Simla knew that Korsovsky was coming to appear at the Gaiety but only one person, apart from Alice herself, knew that the Russian could identify her as Isobel Newton. Former lover. He too had to be eliminated before setting eye on Alice.'

'But who did pull the trigger?' asked Simpson. 'I can see that Florence was the instigator but who was the agent?'

'It hardly matters,' said Carter thoughtfully. 'Edgar Troop – if we can ever break his alibi – would be my favourite for trigger-man but what about that Italian youth she keeps running her errands for her? What was his name? Giulio?'

'Claudio, I think,' said Joe.

'Yes, Claudio. But, you know, there's about twenty other rogues with that kind of skill up here. We'll probably never know which one was used until we break down Madame Flora.' He sighed.

Simpson was already rising to his feet. 'To identify the maid becomes terribly important. You'll need my help. I think I will be able to identify her.'

'Steady, Simpson,' said Carter, laughing. 'One thing at a time! We must wait a little. We wait until our irregular forces report back.'

Carter wandered out on to the balcony, leaned over the rail and glanced down. 'Not long to wait!' he said.

The police havildar joined him on the balcony. 'There are some boys to see you, sahib,' he said. 'Do you want them up here? They're very excited – do you think it would be better if . . .'

'Yes, I think it would be better if,' said Carter. And to Joe and Simpson, 'I'll go down and see what they have to tell us.'

As soon as Carter appeared in the compound, and in spite of the efforts of the havildar, Joe and Simpson watched with amusement to see him instantly surrounded by chattering boys. With difficulty he waved them to silence and, picking out Raghu, he seemed to be inviting him to speak. He did. Joe and Simpson, looking down, couldn't understand a single one of the many words that came fluting up from below but they hardly needed to. Sometimes one, sometimes two boys speaking together, sometimes all six, mimed their recent adventure. Their account was easy to follow.

Here they had waited in concealment, here they had peered round the corner, here one of them had run ahead and the rest had fallen back. Now, between them they began to play with a ball, now they feared they had been spotted. They were denied admission to the cathedral but had lain in wait at the doors. The story was as plain as print and plainer than speech. Laughing, Charlie seemed to congratulate them and, feeling in his pockets, he produced handfuls of annas and handed these out. He took a mild part in the haggling that ensued, added a few small coins and, still laughing, climbed back up on to the balcony. His irregular forces waved a cheerful and, judging by the indignation of the police havildar, a disrespectful farewell and ran together out of the compound to disappear in the busy Mall.

'Well?' said Joe and Simpson together.

'Well, indeed!' said Carter. 'I could give you three guesses as to the destination of our mysterious packet and I think you would not need as many as three! It goes without saying – the package made its way, much to the amusement of the irregular forces, into the local brothel by a back door. Into Madame Flora's! It now, presumably, lodges in the predatory hands of Flora herself.'

'What do we do now?' asked Simpson.

'We go and have a chat with the seductive Flora, of course,' said Carter.

'Would I be totally out of place?' asked Simpson. 'Indulge my curiosity! You owe me a turn for the trauma you put me through last night. And don't forget – I can identify Mademoiselle Florence.'

'Give me a moment then,' said Carter, 'and we'll go together.'

Once more he descended to the compound and was seen giving orders and they set off all three together. 'I thought it might be prudent to arrange a little armed support,' said Carter and, as they walked down through the town, Joe was aware of the discreet presence of policemen in plain clothes. For a moment he contrasted the laborious process that would have ensued had he, in London, tried to arrange a surveillance squad of six or an armed escort in plain clothes. His respect for Charlie Carter was much enhanced.

As they arrived at the flower shop the door opened and Edgar Troop came out, stopping dead with surprise and some hostility at the sight of them.

'Afternoon, Edgar,' said Charlie. 'We haven't come to see you, we've come to see madame but, as you're here, why don't you join us?'

Troop seemed for a moment inclined to bar their way. Charlie Carter pushed his way firmly past him. 'We'll announce ourselves,' he said, but Troop was just ahead of him.

'Flora!' he called. 'I'm back – at the head of a posse of policemen.'

They heard Flora's voice: 'Admit them. Always so happy to see the police.'

She came to the door. She looked welcoming and confident. Joe's eyes widened as he took in the almost theatrical elegance of her dress. A shawl of rich Persian colours, deep red and blue and indigo, was draped over her shoulders, glowing against the background of a black velvet gown. Even Charlie Carter seemed impressed.

'Hello, Flora. Good to see you again so soon. Entertaining again?'

'Charlie! Always pleased to see you and – as you see – always entertaining! But I never know quite whom I may have the honour of welcoming. Today it is yourself and Mr . . . Sandilands, I think I've got that right? But you?' She looked Simpson up and down.

Simpson bowed. 'We have not been formally introduced,' he said, 'but we have met. Once. A long time ago. No reason why you should remember me but I remember you very well.'

'This is very intriguing!' Flora smiled and waved a hand. 'Won't you come in? If we have business to discuss perhaps we should discuss it in the privacy of my room.' And to Claudio appearing at that moment, 'Tea. Tea for the gentlemen.'

'Now,' she said when they were settled, looking carefully at Simpson, 'tell me, where was this so mysterious encounter and when? In our youth?'

'When?' said Simpson. 'Well, it seems another lifetime but – three years ago. Where? At the Gare de Lyon in Paris. I was en route for the Beaune railway crash,' he pointed to his dark glasses, 'from which I emerged with a good deal more luck than all but two others.'

'Flora,' said Charlie, 'I want to ask you a few questions about that day.'

Edgar Troop, watchful and menacing, intervened. 'By what right?' he asked indignantly. 'It was a long time ago and in another continent. Of what possible interest can it be to you?'

'Oh, don't be so silly, Edgar!' said Flora. 'Edgar and I are very old friends,' she explained. 'He tries to protect me, don't you? He always has. Like a guard dog. But I don't think I need protection in the present company. The police can have no official motive for speaking to me.' There was the slightest emphasis on the word 'official'. She smiled and added, 'Though they might gain much, I think, from a friendly and unofficial interview. They need some information about the rail crash, apparently. And as you say, Edgar, far away and long ago and no one to remember what happened. I am surprised that you are aware of it, Charlie. But your questions are easily answered – I have no information! For the good and substantial reason that I was not on the train. I might have been on the train – I was planning to be on the train – but, by God's mercy, I didn't get on. All I know about the crash I learned from the newspapers like everyone else, yourself included perhaps. Now what can I tell you?'

'You were travelling –' said Charlie.

'No! I have told you I was not travelling.'

'All right,' said Charlie, 'I'll phrase that differently, you were at the time of the crash in the employment of Isabelle de Neuville, am I right? And were planning to travel with her.'

'You are right. That was the name of my employer. I left her on the station platform. She owed me money which she would not pay. She insulted me. I have not forgotten.' And she added in a murmur, 'Or forgiven either.'

'Tell me,' said Joe, 'just as a matter of interest – you parted from Madame de Neuville at the Gare de Lyon. Have you seen her since?'

'Of course she bloody well hasn't!' Edgar Troop shouted. 'She's just told you – bloody woman was killed!'

'Edgar! Edgar, I think you could leave us now. This is old news, old information. There is nothing you can add, nothing you can help me with. I am in safe hands and feel quite secure with Charlie and his friends. You may go about your business in town – you are already late for your appointment. Please do not feel that you have to stay on my account.'

With warning looks from one to the other, the guard dog turned, looking meaningfully at his watch, and left the room.

Flora continued. 'I did see Isabelle de Neuville afterwards, yes. Once more. I identified her body, Commander. I read about the crash in the papers and went to Beaune to offer my services. The police were desperate for any witnesses who could help them with the enormous task of identifying the dead. I borrowed money from . . . from an old friend of Madame de Neuville's. He was pleased to give me the cost of the rail fare – second class,' she added with a secret smile and a glance at Simpson, 'to travel down to identify her.'

'Were there any problems with the identification?' asked Joe.

'It was a chaotic scene! Distressed families and friends picking over the piles of bodies. Distraught and terrified poor souls – but for me, no problems at all. She was wearing a very recognizable red travelling dress with sable trimming and her bag and all her documents including her passport were still with the body.'

She gave Carter a level look and went on, 'But there is something you ought to know – perhaps already do know concerning Isabelle de Neuville . . . According to her passport, which was English, her real name was Isobel Newton. She took a French name as her, what shall we say . . . as her working name.'

'And how long had you been in Miss Newton's employ?' said Joe.

'For five years. I met her in the south of France in 1914 before the war. I am southern French as the commander guessed. She was living under the protection – I think that's the phrase – of a naval officer and in addition to the flat, the jewels, the motor car, he paid for the services of a maid. Myself.'

'And when she moved to Paris she took you with her. Tell me, madame, how did you enjoy life in the Avenue de l'Opéra?'

Joe asked the question with an easy smile but his intention was to disconcert and alarm. He felt himself disadvantaged by her calm. At that moment a tray of tea was carried in and placed on the table in front of Flora. Deliberately, she busied herself with the formalities of the presentation of teacups and avoided his eye and his question. Having dispensed China and Indian tea, lemon and milk in the correct proportions, she once again turned to Joe.

'To know that we resided in the Avenue de l'Opéra, my mistress and I, you must have very special knowledge of our past, Commander. Such information could only come from one source. And that source is at present in Simla. Am I correct?'

'That is correct, madame. You will realize that Isobel Newton has told me everything.'

To Joe's surprise Flora burst out laughing. 'All? Are you quite certain of that, Commander? Unless she is much changed she will have told you exactly what she wished you to know and no more than that! You won't have learned *all* there is to know about Isobel Newton!'

The tone was still light but now had a diamond-hard edge. A vengeful edge, the edge of a hatred which Joe welcomed. A show of emotion and particularly hatred in an interview was often the first crack in the façade and he thought the moment had come to widen the crack. Increase the leverage in the weak spot.

'On the contrary,' he said seriously, 'Isobel *has* confided her secrets to me. She has at great pains to herself revealed the unkind blows dealt her by fate. She has entrusted me with an account of how she came to fall from innocence and how she was subsequently manipulated and abused by those who had seemed to be her protectors.' He managed a heartfelt sigh as one saddened by the iniquities of the world.

To Joe's delight, Flora put her teacup down with a crash. Her dark eyes glowed with the intensity of jet and she shook her head slowly from side to side, never taking her eyes from Joe's. He felt himself recoil instinctively; it was for a moment as though a hooded cobra had reared up in front of him.

'Fall from innocence!' she hissed. 'That girl was never innocent! She was born guilty as sin! She was selfish to the core. She manipulated, she used, she deceived! And still it goes on. And you, Sandilands, are her latest victim it would seem! One of hundreds! How often I've seen it!'

Joe sat in silence as the dam began to burst. Flora went on, her voice rising as she spoke. 'Her own father couldn't wait to get rid of her. There was already trouble at home before he sent her away to the south of France. Silly old fool assumed that she'd be safe with his strait-laced parishioner . . . it wasn't two minutes before little Miss Isobel had betrayed her employer's trust. She was thrown out of the hotel but she ended up in a very chi-chi little flat in St Raphael which is where I began to work for her . . . Fall from innocence, indeed! She jumped! And she landed in a feather bed!' Her eyes clouded for a moment and she added in an undertone, 'I could tell you stories of besmirched innocence that would make your blood run cold.'

'And what, precisely were your duties, madame?' Joe cut her

short. 'I am wondering why, if you so despised Miss Newton, you remained in her employ? I must presume that the work was to your liking?'

'It was work! Can you imagine what is available to a girl, a lonely and unsupported girl in France? It was not to my liking, as you put it, but it was not the street. I had a roof over my head, a bed to sleep in, enough food and good clothes. If I didn't have much affection for the woman whose clothes I pressed, whose pearls I polished, I could at least put on a good face.'

'You are a beautiful woman, Flora, if you don't mind my saying so,' said Carter diffidently. 'Er . . . didn't Miss Newton feel any jealousy?'

Flora's rouged lips opened slightly in astonishment and then curved into a sly smile. 'My word, Superintendent! And to think I took you for a man of the world!' She leaned forward and spoke slowly as though explaining an intricate idea. 'It is the custom of *poules de luxe* to employ not an old hag but an attractive maid to receive their clients. If there should be any delay in service – if mademoiselle for instance has decided to sleep until midday or is caught dallying with someone she should not be dallying with – then a pretty maid can be a not unwelcome distraction.' Her voice became hard again as she went on, 'And if a client has lost his attraction or – even more unforgivably – has lost his money or mademoiselle is simply feeling lazy or indisposed, then her pretty maid may be required to exercise her own arts of seduction. To draw the fire. Isn't that what a soldier would say? I cleaned for that woman, I polished and scrubbed, I lied and I whored! And, in the end, she rewarded me with a third class ticket!'

'So when you arrived to identify the corpse you saw, of course, that it was not that of Isobel Newton but that of some other woman . . .?'

'Yes. I would never have bothered going all the way to Beaune to look at that woman's body but I thought there might just be some jewellery I knew she always wore – a ring, a necklace – that had escaped attention. She was never empty-handed, that one! She owed me a lot of money and now she was dead there would never be another way of retrieving any of it. Well, no luck there. The jewels had disappeared. The hospital was in chaos. People running around everywhere, no one's identity being checked. They left me alone with the body in a little cubicle and the first odd thing I noticed was that she was wearing lisle stockings. She had lost her shoes but the stockings were plain to see. When I investigated further I noticed her underwear. What you English call a camisole, a pink woollen vest and pink cotton drawers. Elasticated – they were called directoire knickers – a thing Isobel would never have worn.' She laughed a brittle laugh. 'She wouldn't have condescended to have been seen dead in such things! I had actually seen Isobel put on her green silk that morning. This was not Isobel Newton but a body dressed in her outer clothes. I took a closer look and then I remembered the other English girl. The one in the station bar. I came up to the bar to give Isobel a message about the luggage she'd left me to deal with and had quite a shock. She was sitting opposite a girl who could have been her twin sister! But she was very badly dressed. Expensive clothes but not smart and she was wearing just such stockings.

'What had happened became clear to me. Not so easy but not impossible to exchange outer garments. In that situation – with blood and bodies, shrieking steam from the shattered engine, fire breaking out – I can imagine the scene – our lady was cool. We all know she can be but to peel underclothes from a body and put them on to herself was too much of a task even for her. It wasn't an oversight – it was a calculated risk. And it paid off. But for me. It gave me all I wanted!'

Her smile of triumph was too much for Joe and he dropped his eyes from her face.

'I guessed what Isobel had done,' she went on.

Joe recognized this as the next stage in a confession. She had given them the truth and now felt the normal compulsion to follow it up with, if not a justification, then an account of her own cleverness.

'It was not out of character. She was using someone again but this time she had stolen a whole identity for herself. I wondered why. I wondered what was so special about this girl she was attempting to become. I left the hospital and bought a newspaper. There was an account of a Miss Alice Conyers who was the only one apart from a baby to have survived the accident. It described her as an heiress going out to India to take control of a large trading empire.'

217

'So you decided to follow "Alice Conyers" to India?'

'It wasn't that simple. I had to plot and plan and save up the fare. I looked up old clients on the Côte. Some of them had heard what had happened to Isobel and were very generous to me, for old times' sake. As soon as I'd got enough together I came out to Bombay. It wasn't difficult to track her – every newspaper was full of her. She was being a complete commercial and social success. She was even making a name for herself as a philanthropist! In Delhi I met Edgar. Probably a stupid idea but I took him into my confidence. We decided to follow her to Simla when the weather turned – she spends every summer up here – and we used his money and my experience to set up here.'

'And the blackmail money? The jewellery you extorted? What happened to that?' Carter wanted to know.

'I guessed she'd have told you about that,' said Flora with a smile of satisfaction. 'Poor little Isobel, menaced by an unknown blackmailer! Well, I can tell you, Superintendent, that she got off lightly! The demands were very reasonable in the circumstances. She truly deserved to suffer more. And never forget that we are talking about money that is not rightly hers at all. I think you do forget that!' She turned a scornful gaze on Joe.

With a defiant gesture she swept the shawl from her shoulders. Every eye was drawn to the Holbein jewel glowing richly against the black velvet. 'Here's your proof! I wouldn't want you to wreck the whole establishment in an effort to find it – I'm sure that's what you were planning to do. Such a very memorable brooch, isn't it? I wouldn't be surprised if it were posted as missing believed stolen so that you can find it in my possession!'

Simpson shuffled his feet uncomfortably. Joe and Carter looked back at her, non-committal.

'You may call it blackmail, Superintendent, but if you were to question Alice Conyers-Sharpe in your official capacity I think you will find that she will say she has merely been sending gifts to an old employee in return for a service she values greatly. She is well known to be generous. With ICTC funds,' she added waspishly. 'So, I wear this openly. I have shown it to you. As yet there is no indication that it is stolen and I assume you would apprise me of that at once if such were the case . . . Nothing to say? Then I suggest we put an end to this farce. I will detain you no longer. I know you have more important crimes to investigate.'

'Just one or two more things you can tell us, Flora,' said Joe. 'Do you remember all your mistress's lovers?'

Flora gave the question her full attention. 'I think I would recognize most of them if I saw them again but I couldn't possibly enumerate and name them! Some stand out more than others.'

'Feodor Korsovsky. Does he stand out in your memory?'

'Ah! Feodor! At last you begin to behave like a detective. No, I never met him. He had left her and gone to New York before I started to work for her. But she talked of him. She talked of him a great deal. He was one of the first of Isobel's lovers. They were together for quite a long time and she was actually faithful to him – she claims. She met him in Nice at a café frequented by singers. She always used to fancy that she had a good singing voice. Still does, I believe. They seemed to be genuinely in love with each other but he had to go off to New York and they were separated by the war. He wrote to tell her he wasn't coming back. He'd rejoined his wife who'd been waiting for him for years in America. Isobel never forgave him. For her he epitomized the treachery of all men. She certainly hated him.'

'So you realized the threat he posed to Alice Conyers-Sharpe – that is Isobel Newton's security. And you were presumably aware, as was the whole of Simla, that he was scheduled to appear at the Gaiety. You would have been able to ascertain without any difficulty the precise time of his expected arrival in the town.'

'What are you implying?' she asked, pale and controlled.

'We are implying, Flora, that you are the only one in Simla who would have the personal knowledge of Korsovsky, the motive for killing him and the means of purchasing his death. We intend further to charge you and others as yet unnamed with bringing about the murder in similar circumstances and for exactly the same motive of Lionel Conyers a year ago.'

Flora was staring at them in wide-eyed astonishment, unable to speak.

'I hope you have taken in the importance of what I have just said,' Joe added, 'and the seriousness of your situation. We come finally to the bottom of these two murders.'

'Two murders?' Flora had found her voice. 'Two murders?' she said again. A slow smile spread across her face. 'But, Commander, there have been *three* murders!'

Chapter Twenty-three

'Listen, Flora,' Carter started to say carefully, 'we are investigating the murders of Lionel Conyers and Feodor Korsovsky. We believe you to have procured with the help of an accomplice or accomplices the murders of these two men. We believe you to have had them killed to preserve intact the false identity of Alice Conyers-Sharpe in order that you might continue to blackmail her. We have no evidence – no report even – of a third murder. If you have any information to give regarding a third killing I suggest you give it at once.'

'May I make one thing quite clear, Superintendent? I have killed no one. I have not ordered or "procured", as you put it, the murder of anyone.' She laughed again, eyes shining with humour. 'Oh, dear! You're back to square one, I'm afraid. If not worse since I present you with not two unsolved crimes but three! Haven't you guessed? Can't you guess? No? Then I shall have to spell out for you a message you would much rather not hear, I think.'

'Get on with it, Flora!' said Carter, exasperated.

'Oh, my God!' murmured Joe under his breath. Fascinated, he could only watch and wait for Flora to confirm an awful suspicion and, without doubt, she was enjoying herself, teasing out the suspense, playing with them, and they could only silently sit it out.

'You should know, gentlemen, that Lionel Conyers was the second victim and Korsovsky the third. The first, oh the first victim, was killed much earlier. But the motive for all three murders is the same. To bring about and maintain the personation of Alice Conyers by Isobel Newton – if we're using official language.'

'And the first victim?' asked Carter.

'Was Alice Conyers herself!'

'What the hell are you talking about, Flora?'

She sat forward in her chair looking at each of the three men in turn, claiming their absolute attention.

'Alice Conyers was murdered. And by Isobel Newton.'

'Don't be silly! She died in the rail crash. Everyone knows that. You yourself inspected the body!' Carter was becoming angry.

'Yes! I inspected the body! I've already told you that – but I didn't tell you everything I noticed about the state of the corpse! I was left alone with it for as long as I chose to take. The official cause of death registered by the harassed doctor who had the task of processing over two hundred accident victims was accidental death due to a broken back and head injuries. A reasonable assessment considering the time available to him and the circumstances. After all – who is going to look for murder amongst so much carnage?'

She paused for a moment, fearing no interruption from her audience who were weighing every word, every nuance.

'But I was looking more carefully, with the eye of one who knew that something was not as it should be. Before even I had taken in the stockings and the underwear I had noticed that the injuries to the head were unusual. Her face was completely . . .' she reached for a word, '. . . obliterated. Smashed beyond recognition. When I had inspected the clothing and come to the conclusion that my mistress had changed places with this poor girl I took a closer look at the injuries. Not a pleasant task. I have no training in these matters and it took a lot of determination to handle a corpse in such a way but I managed. I turned the body over. Her back was injured as the doctor had said. Certainly there was much bruising to the spine and that seemed to be clearly the spot on which she had fallen. I would say that the impact of her fall was on the back. Why then was there such damage to her face?'

'Oh, come on, Flora,' said Carter, 'it happened in a ravine. Steep slope, she probably rolled about taking injuries on all sides.'

'Then why were there no injuries on any other sides? I checked. No bruising or cuts on her sides, no other injuries to her front apart from the very selective crushing of her features.

It was not a case of one glancing blow against a rock and rolling onwards . . . the face had been destroyed by a series of blows aimed exclusively at the features. If you were to take the body away from the context of the accident you would say without any doubt at all that Alice Conyers had been murdered. Now, I am aware that there will never be any way in which I could prove the truth of what I am saying but I am telling you everything that I know as a witness to help you bring to justice the one who is responsible for this trail of death. And it is not I.

'I do not think the injury to the back on the corpse I inspected would have been sufficiently serious to cause death. I would guess that Isobel, surviving almost unscathed, had come across Alice unable to move, unconscious perhaps *but alive* and a hideous idea had come to her. Here, injured and at her mercy, was a girl who had everything Isobel wanted. Perhaps she changed clothes before smashing her face. I think she did. The red tunic dress under the jacket would have had to be pulled over the head. If she had done that over those shattered and bleeding features . . . well, Commander?'

'There would have been smears and stains of blood, possibly brain tissue on the *inside* of the tunic, picked up as it was pulled down over the face.' Joe supplied.

'Yes. That occurred to me and I checked. There were no stains on the inside lining. The staining was all about the neck where blood had ponded. So – the switch had been made before Isobel had finished her off.'

Joe was thinking furiously. Wishing desperately that he could have had a look at the corpse himself. Eager to ask Flora a hundred questions and at the same time unwilling to give her the satisfaction of supplying answers he did not want to hear. Assuming her story to be true, Flora represented even more of a menace than they had imagined to Isobel Newton. Not only was her blackmailer aware of her impersonation, she was aware that Isobel was guilty of murder and surely Isobel must, at some level, through her weight of guilt, have been fearful of this.

'But what have you to say about your blackmail letters after the death of Conyers and now of Korsovsky – the so-called "protection" you offered and charged a fat price for? What is the meaning of those if it isn't murder? "We've killed off a possible menace to your continued privileged existence and we think it's worth so many rupees." Those letters!' Carter asked.

Flora smiled sadly and shook her head. 'I have already told you – I am not responsible in any way for those killings. I guessed why they had been committed and who had done them, of course I did! And I decided to make the perpetrator pay for it. The letters never laid claim to the murders – I asked for extra payments to ensure my silence, Superintendent, not to reward me for shooting (or having shot) two innocent men!' And she added quietly, 'If you are honest, Charlie, you will admit that there is nothing else I could have done. What would have been your response if I had come to you last year and denounced Alice Conyers-Sharpe as the killer of her brother, that is the man who would have been her brother if she had only been who she said she was and not the woman who had actually murdered Alice and taken her place three years ago?'

Carter's uncomfortable silence was answer enough.

'You see! If you hadn't simply labelled me mad you would have assumed my accusations were due to spite at her having harassed me and curtailed my activities here chez Flora. I'm sorry, Charlie, that your real target should turn out to be a woman whom you have always respected. How much more convenient it would have been, how much more satisfying to have flung *me* in jail.'

Flora's slanting smile was mocking and triumphant and Joe found that even he could no longer meet her eyes. 'But don't be too embarrassed by your failure,' she went on smoothly, 'you are not the first, nor yet the hundredth, man to be deceived by Isobel Newton. And you will not be the last.' She looked away thoughtfully for a moment. 'Because, you see, men are primed by nature to fall victim to her deceptions. They – all men – are so convinced of their own superiority, of their own irresistible attraction, they accept at face value and take as no more than their due a woman's attentions. There is nothing easier for a pretty and clever woman than to lead a man by his –'

'That'll do, Flora!' said Carter stiffly. 'You're talking like a tart!'

Chapter Twenty-four

The party which made its way back to the police station was subdued and thoughtful. Instead of enjoying the excitement of a showdown with its keenly anticipated arrests, they had now to rewrite in many important particulars their carefully composed plot and even perhaps to add a third crime to Isobel's charge sheet. Flora's manifest satisfaction at this turn of events made it no easier to bear. 'Bloody woman!' thought Charlie. 'Smug little trollop!' thought Joe. Simpson, eager as ever to be helpful but aware of his limitations, accepted Charlie's suggestion that he go off back for tiffin with Meg, bearing the message that Joe and Carter would follow as soon as they could.

They sank down disconsolately into chairs in Charlie's office. With a sigh he opened a drawer and held up a sheet of paper. A sheet headed with black gothic script and bedecked with sealing wax and scrawling signatures. Joe recognized it.

'A warrant?'

'Yes. Thought it sensible to be prepared. Things are moving fast and I thought I'd better get Sir George's signature on this just in case we should need it. And it's looking increasingly as though we shall need it.'

Joe didn't need to ask the name inscribed on the sheet. 'You must have been very sure of yourself and very persuasive to get him to sign away Alice Conyers' freedom?'

'Almost had to hold a gun to his head! I waited until you'd gone to bed last night, joined him in one last brandy and then hit him hard with the necessity of having the full force of the law in reserve to deal with someone so influential and so fly as little Miss Isobel. I just happened to have the warrant with me.' He smiled. 'And then when Flora came over the horizon I thought, oh good, we're not going to need this after all.'

'Look, Charlie,' Joe began slowly.

'It's all right, old son! I know how you're feeling about this. You needn't be involved. Not sure I'd want you around when I put the cuffs on! Not safe! One anguished look from those tear-filled blue eyes and you'd become a liability. Stay well away – that's my advice!'

'Is there anything we ought to review?' asked Joe with an edge of despair in his voice. 'Before we rush in? Any evidence we could collect? It seems to me we have very little, if any, solid evidence. All we have is hearsay, coincidence, speculation and accusation.'

As they trundled once more through the sequence of events, the acceptability of alibis, probability of motive, a havildar came into the room with a telegram. 'From Calcutta, sahib.'

'The bullets! About time too!' said Carter, tearing open the envelope. 'Now let's see what we've got.'

He read the messages carefully, then read them again and handed the sheets to Joe.

Joe read: 'Bullet A Killing A Gun A Stop Bullets B x 2 Killing B Gun B Stop Bullets C x 2 Gun C Stop Bullets D x 2 Gun D Stop Bullets E x 2 Gun E Stop Fingerprints guns C and D Suspect 1 Stop Gun E no prints Stop'.

'Ah,' said Joe, 'it gets worse. Seems to clear Edgar Troop of using any one of the three rifles we took away from Flora's – could have other rifles somewhere else, of course. Ironic that the only solid evidence we've got proves nothing against anybody, though.'

'Let's think about this. I suppose with all your involvement with the chaps in Calcutta it's you we have to blame – excuse me, thank – for this excessively succinct way of communicating the forensic information! The bullet that killed Lionel Conyers (that's bullet A – we took it out of his body) was fired by a gun they're labelling "A". The two bullets that finished off your Russian friend were fired by a different gun – "B". And the three rifles we took from Flora's, two service rifles and the third one in the bag, were total innocents and nothing to do with either of the killings. The two service rifles had Troop's prints all over them as you would expect but the third innocent one had been wiped clean. Now what the hell are we to make of all this?'

'Easier to start at the end, I think,' said Joe. 'Flora, knowing nothing of modern methods of ballistic recognition, was trying to implicate Troop in the murders. I expect she wiped clean the third rifle to make it look more suspicious. And I don't think we have to look any further than young Claudio to find a reason for her wanting Edgar Troop out of the picture! But then we're left with the question of the two different rifles used in the two killings. That's the worrying part . . . Same modus operandi, even the same cigarette ends left at the scene, but different rifles . . .'

'Can't see what's so strange about that,' said Carter. 'Lots of people in Simla have more than one gun. There are probably more rifles per head of population in Simla than anywhere in the world outside Texas!'

'True – but,' persisted Joe, 'we're not talking about lots of people in Simla who might shoot for fun or competition or just collect guns. We're talking about a *sniper*.' After years of keeping his head down in the trenches, the word itself still had the power to make Joe shudder. 'I know their habits. They grow attached to one particular weapon and go on using it. They know its character, its idiosyncrasies – and all rifles have them – and they don't give it up. I know of snipers, marksmen who went through the whole war using the same weapon. No . . . "Killing A Gun A, Killing B Gun B" that's where the puzzle is!'

He was remembering something that Alice had said about Lionel's killing that had struck a false note with him but before he could expand on the disturbing thought taking shape the telephone on Carter's desk gave its customary throaty purr and rattle.

'Superintendent Carter, here, Simla Police . . . Ah, yes, indeed I did . . . You have? . . . Good man! Seven o'clock this evening? Thank you very much, Patwa Singh. Thank you very much indeed.'

He put the telephone down and turned eagerly to Joe. 'We've got them!'

'Who've we got?'

Carter looked anxiously at his watch. 'The birds are flying now!' he said dramatically, enjoying the moment. 'That was the stationmaster at Kalka. I'd warned him off to tell me if any of our suspects made a booking on a train out of here. I've got lookouts covering the roads too. Hang on, Joe!'

He hurried to the door and shouted commands. Buckling on his Sam Browne, he explained: 'The whole of a first class compartment has been reserved all the way through to Bombay! Two passengers only. And paid for by ICTC. The train goes at seven from Kalka which means that Alice and a companion are probably going to catch the two o'clock local train from Simla to connect with it. In half an hour. Not much time!'

He folded the warrant and slipped it into his pocket. Before Joe could speak again the havildar returned, face bright with excitement. 'Sahib, sir! Word has come that Memsahib Sharpe passed down the Mall ten minutes ago in a tonga. Two tongas! Their luggage was in the second one! They went west towards the Kalka road.'

'They? Who was with her?' asked Carter.

'The Pathan, sahib. Rheza Khan.'

Dejectedly Joe watched Charlie Carter and his escort swing out of the police compound and set off for the railhead. At the last minute Charlie had turned about and, cupping his hand to his mouth, had shouted, 'Joe! Change your mind! Come with us!'

Joe shook his head. 'It's your affair, Charlie,' he said. 'It's up to you to make the arrest, not me. Don't forget I'm only a supernumerary. I'll stay here and mind the shop!'

Joe lingered on the verandah; bitterly he didn't want to move on to the next thing. He knew very well that care for Charlie's status in the matter was not truly his motive. Charlie had been right when he'd said he might prove a liability. He was aware that he was deeply reluctant to think of Isobel under restraint. He didn't want to be there when she was brought to book. He didn't want to witness the collapse of her long deception, the crumbling of her so carefully constructed position before the world. He went over and over the evidence. Have we got a case? Can we really persuade the world at large, to say nothing of the court, that through all these years 'Alice' has played everyone on a string? Sir George? Simla high society? Friends and colleagues in high places? Her closest friend Marie-Jeanne Pitiot? He wasn't

228

able to share Charlie's excitement and determination. And now it fell to him to report to Sir George. Joe did not look forward to this.

He stepped into the street to call a rickshaw but was surprised to find himself confronted by Edgar Troop riding into the police compound. To Joe's further surprise, he appeared to be leading a second horse. He greeted Joe with urgency. 'Glad to have caught you, Commander,' he said. 'Is there anywhere we can talk? Hurry up – we haven't much time!'

Joe hesitated. 'Here, I suppose. I don't think Charlie would mind if we sat on his verandah for a minute or two.'

Troop threw a leg over the horse's mane and slid to the ground, authoritatively calling out for a syce to take his horse. 'This'll do as well as anywhere.'

'Listen,' said Troop as they established themselves, 'I don't want to force a confidence and God knows this has nothing to do with me but I was just coming back from the chummery and I passed Charlie Carter appropriately accompanied by the full panoply of the law. Six police sowars under Charlie's havildar, no less! On his way to the station, I believe. Am I right?'

Joe hesitated before replying, saying at last, 'Well, I don't know to what extent you've put two and two together but since the world will know in an hour or so there's no reason why I shouldn't tell you that he was on his way to arrest Alice Sharpe.'

'And he expected to find her at the station?'

'Yes indeed. She and Rheza Khan have tickets booked through to Bombay from Kalka. Luggage has been sent in advance and they've taken more with them. Fact is – and again, you might as well know – the play is over and Charlie has gone to ring down the last curtain.'

'I thought that was probably it . . .' He leaned forward in his chair, speaking fast and urgently. 'Now, understand me – I have a great, though reluctant, admiration for Alice, I won't say affection, but a respect. In the eyes of the good people of Simla and in the eyes of the world at large, I'm something of a scoundrel. You'll hardly deny that you have thought so. No? Exactly. But I'm as white as the driven snow in comparison with Alice. I expect you hardly know the half of it! The fact is that she's exploited everybody she's come into contact with including myself. I've performed errands for her – and, by the way, murder has not been amongst them – and I've been paid. I am, in a way, a gun for sale but get it into your head that I had no part in the murder of Conyers or that unfortunate Russian fellow.'

Joe cut in. 'This is all a matter of evidence, Troop,' he said. 'We can safely leave it to the police.'

Troop snorted with derision. 'Alice and Rheza Khan are off to the station with Charlie in hot pursuit but don't you think it a bit odd that they should have made such a ponderous flit? With the utmost public parade? Straight down the middle of the Mall? And Charlie's gone down there, handcuffs in his back pocket? Just intercepting the miscreants at the last minute? Does that sound like the Alice we know? Can you imagine that anyone clever enough to fool the entire world for three years would make a move so inept? No! Charlie will proceed to the station to make his arrest and his birds will have flown!'

'Flown? How flown?'

'I'll tell you but – do you think this well-equipped police station could provide a chap with a drink? It's been rather a dusty day so far.'

'I don't think Charlie would begrudge us,' said Joe, turning to the whisky decanter and glasses that stood on the windowsill. 'But go on. What were you going to tell me?'

'Listen,' said Troop. 'At the back of the station is the old post office warehouse. Now empty. I couldn't help noticing that there were two horses – good horses – saddled and standing in the old warehouse. A syce was with them. Not a local man. A man, I'm prepared to surmise, from Rheza Khan's village. Now who could these horses possibly have been ready for? And I'll tell you something else. Alice and Rheza passed within a few yards of me and to all outward appearances Alice was appropriately dressed for travel with her luggage into Kalka on the Toy Train. To all outward appearances, I said. But if you have the habit, which I have, when I'm in the company of a pretty girl, and that is how I would describe Alice, you look her up and down. I speculate as to what she is wearing underneath and I'll go further – I speculate as to what she would look like if she were wearing nothing. Perhaps you do the same? And I'm never wrong about these things! Under that unfashionably long travelling dress Alice was wearing jodhpurs and riding boots. That say anything to you? It suggested to me that she was about to climb on to a horse and while Charlie Carter and others were standing by the front door waiting to interview Alice and Rheza Khan she had discreetly left by the back and by now had a considerable start.' His eyes narrowed and he took another sip of his whisky. 'Those waiting horses were good ones, I can tell you!'

'Troop,' said Joe, 'you may be right, you may be wrong. I suspect you are right but why are you telling me this? What axe have you to grind? I don't know you well but – forgive me – I have reason to believe that you are in the axe-grinding business much of the time. So, tell me, what's this all about?'

Edgar Troop suddenly flushed and turned on Joe. Venomous, he hissed, 'Alice! The mighty director of ICTC! Chosen confidante of Lady Reading! The so pitiably neglected wife of drunken Sharpe! The focus of so much womanly sympathy! Christ Almighty! Bloody woman! "Oh, Captain Troop, very kind of you. Now tell me what do I owe you?" And "Oh, Captain Troop, I have a tiny commission for you. I wonder if you'd be so kind . . . And I'm so terribly sorry if I can't know you when we meet in public . . . I'm sure you understand . . . You mustn't mind, if, when you come to see me I have to keep you waiting . . . I'm so terribly busy." Treated me like an errand boy! And she nothing but a tart if Flora's to be believed! I – and several others in Simla, I can tell you – would be delighted to see that one get what I'll call her just deserts!'

'So you're saying they've made off on fast horses, but where?'

'Well, not to Kalka, I'll bet! I think Carter and his merry men will have gone chasing off down there and it'll be some hours before they realize they're following a false trail – and you can bet a false trail will have been laid for him. By the time they double back Alice and Rheza Khan will be miles away into the hills. They're making for Borendo and the Zalori Pass and thereafter I'd guess on north through Manali. It's their back door out of this country. That's where Rheza Khan's people come from. Up there, every second person you meet is likely to be his cousin.'

'But, Troop, what's in it for Alice? What's she going to be doing empty-handed on a spur of the Himalayas?'

'Empty-handed? When was Alice ever empty-handed? Where do you suppose the jewellery paid for by ICTC and filtered through Robertson is to be found? Good jewels – I mean good by international standards and Alice wasn't collecting rubbish – don't take up much space. You can hide an emperor's ransom up your knickers! Is it in a safe at ICTC? In Alice's bottom drawer? No, it's in a saddlebag on its way up to the Zalori Pass. And remote? Not if you know the country. Come and look at this!'

He moved through into Charlie's office and pointed to a large map on the wall. 'There's Simla. And there to the south is the Kalka railhead and on south to Delhi and the P&O liner at Bombay. But north – look! You pass through these mountains – Rheza Khan's back yard – and weave your way along to Joginder Nagar. That's a railhead too and the track leads on to Amritsar, Lahore and eventually to Karachi. And in Karachi you can pick up a steamer on its way from Bombay to the Gulf and from there to London and the rest of the world. Assuming you're allowed to leave tribal territory of course.'

'What is Rheza Khan's stake in this enterprise, do you suppose?'

'Alice of course. Money and Alice – in that order. That's his stake. Do I have to spell that out?'

Joe remembered that, passing close to Alice, he had encountered a distant and teasing scent of sandalwood and that the same scent had come to him from Rheza Khan. 'I believe you, Troop,' he said heavily. 'I believe you entirely. Are you saying that Alice is in danger?'

Troop gave him a long and unfathomable look. 'I can't tell,' he said at last. 'Where she is now going, she's entirely in the hands of Rheza Khan and you know what they say? "Trust a rat before a snake and a snake before a Pathan." Alice will know that the game is up as far as Simla's concerned and Rheza will know the same but the question is – have they both the same objective? Oh, yes! They have the same primary objective, that is to say, leave the country with the swag, the fruit of three years' careful swindling of ICTC, but what then? Well, I think this is where they diverge. Alice, I believe, intends to get out of the country with her fortune and to get out in the company of Rheza Khan and then – I suppose – settle down somewhere out of British jurisdiction.'

'She told me she'd like to live in America,' Joe remembered.

'Yes, I think that would be Alice's idea. It's a country that would suit her. She'd prosper there. But I can't see Rheza, if I understand him at all, embracing a wider horizon than his native land.'

'You're not really answering my question which was – is Alice in danger?'

Troop answered immediately with the air of one who had thought this out with care. 'I don't think she's in danger until they reach journey's end. But when they do, she will, as far as Rheza is concerned, have fulfilled her purpose. I don't think Alice, clever though she be, will get out of there alive. I think she'll stay alive, as I say, just long enough to ensure a safe passage back to Rheza Khan's homeland. Women – especially faithless wives – aren't much respected up there, you know. I don't think she's going on a picnic in the foothills of the Himalayas with a couple of decent chaps like Troop and Sandilands!'

The tone was light, the tone was cynical, but Edgar Troop's face was tormented.

'Bloody girl!' he said, exasperated.

'But what now?'

'Well, Charlie is by now miles down the Kalka road. I don't know how far he'll get before he realizes he's been double-crossed and comes spurring back to Simla to pick up the trail at this end. They'll be too late. They've got to be cut off before they get to the Zalori Pass. The tribe will be waiting for them beyond that. I think we only have a serious chance of stopping them if we can get them before they make it through the pass.'

'We? Troop, you must know I have no authority.'

Troop crossed the room and pulled a rifle from the rack. He tossed it to Joe. 'That's all the authority they recognize in the hill country. I took the precaution of borrowing Reggie's best mount from the stables at the chummery. He's a bit of a handful but you look like a chap who can keep his seat. And if you're coming with me you'll need to borrow a coat of Carter's – it can get cold up there, this time of year. Here – take this poshteen. Charlie won't mind.'

He took a ragged and hairy sheepskin coat from a peg behind

the door and handed it to Joe. Joe looked at it dubiously. 'Are you quite sure it's dead?'

'Would smell even worse if it weren't. Now that's enough buggering about. They're riding already and they've got about twenty minutes on us. Are you on or not?'

Joe was already banging his way through the door.

Chapter Twenty-five

'Wouldn't quite do,' said Troop, indicating the pair of horses in the hands of a patient syce, 'for the distinguished police commander at the King's Birthday Parade on the Horseguards. Probably not quite what you're used to.'

Strong and sturdy, the two horses kicked and fretted, shaking their heads to rid themselves of flies. Joe thought they looked likely enough.

'I feel like the Colonel's son,' said Joe swinging himself into the saddle. 'Do you remember?

> 'The Colonel's son has taken a horse and a raw, rough dun
>   was he,
> A heart like hell and a mouth like a bell and a head like a
>   gallows tree.'

'Can't get away from Kipling,' said Troop as they clattered out of the yard on to the Naldera road. 'We're twenty minutes astray,' he continued as they trotted on together. 'But that won't be the end of the world. We won't go by the road. I very much doubt if Rheza knows this bit of country as well as I do. I've shot and hunted over all this stretch of land, taken picnic parties, sightseeing parties, shikari parties – this is Edgar Troop's back garden, you know. We've got to intercept them before they can get to the Zalori Pass – and taking a very large number of short cuts we ought to be able to do just that.'

Edgar Troop had roused himself. Depressions and doubts seemed to be at an end. Looking at his companion's suddenly alert eye and flushed face Joe was aware of a further reason for Troop's eagerness to lead the pursuit. Perhaps the prime reason.

'This man,' thought Joe, 'is a hunter! What's that awful phrase? – "the thrill of the chase". He's in its grip.' And much more arousing to him than any tiger or leopard hunt was the challenge of tracking a clever and dangerous human being through the wilderness. A manhunt. And just for once, Edgar Troop could appear on the side of the angels.

'Tell me, Troop, why is the Zalori Pass so important?'

'Ah, I forget you know so little about local politics! It marks the southern extreme of Rheza Khan's tribal territory. His princedom – I suppose you could call it that – has never been an easy neighbour for the British. Rheza's father, the rajah, is ambitious. Oh, he pays lip-service to the Raj, he enters into treaties, plays polo with the military top brass, his wives have entertained the Vicereine and all that. His son gives every appearance of being Westernized – Rugby-educated, suits from Savile Row, all the charm in the world – but underneath all this surface gloss they're on the boil! The old rajah broke out a few years ago and it looked for a moment as if he had it in mind to try conclusions with the army. Just after Amritsar, so everybody put it down to an upsurge of righteous indignation and merely banned him and his men from making an appearance – other than on a courtesy call, of course – south of the Zalori Pass. Very generous reaction when you think about it. Some might have thought a more punitive riposte was called for, considering what he owes the British.'

'Any particular reason for owing them special allegiance?'

'No doubt about it. This part of the world was in considerable uproar when the British decided to settle in Simla. Gurkha Wars, you've heard of that? When this pushy tribe edged its way down from the north-west, aiming to fill a vacuum it found hereabouts, the British went along with it. Signed treaties and all the usual stuff.'

'And what was in it for us?' asked Joe.

' "Divide and Rule" of course. The other tribes around here are mainly Hindu. Rheza's mob are Muslim. The theory is they'll be so busy watching each other it won't occur to them ever to join forces against the British. Seems to work. And so long as they do as they've been told and stay north of Zalori, no problems.'

'So we pick them up before they've a chance of acquiring an escort?'

'Right. And, Sandilands, if we fail to do that we must abandon the chase altogether. Any welcoming party, and I've no doubt that's what they've got arranged, will be well-armed and hostile.'

'Well-armed?' Joe's suspicions were beginning to crystallize. Drip by drip the information was filtering from Troop and none of it was pleasant.

'Up to the minute service rifles. Best Europe has to offer. In huge quantities.'

'And are you going to tell me how they get their hands on this armament?'

Troop snorted. 'If you are running the country's largest trading company with access to all its logistical arrangements there's no problem. ICTC convoys are on the roads everywhere. Most of them are carrying legitimate goods, carpets, brassware, spices, Western imports, but a percentage of them going north are carrying arms. .303 rifles mainly.'

'But how do they get their hands on them in the first place?'

'I tracked them down to source. Chap called Murphy. Armourer-sergeant and quartermaster. Crooked as they come! Condemns a batch of rifles as faulty and sends them away to be disposed of. Paperwork looks good. Only thing is – the rifles aren't faulty. And they find their way on to an ICTC mule train before they can be destroyed. One or two Murphies about, I should imagine.'

'He's been using Alice as a front for all this. Was she aware, I wonder?'

Troop shrugged. 'How can you ever tell with Alice?'

'It must have been a shock for Rheza Khan when Lionel Conyers turned up on his way to Simla to take over the business,' said Joe slowly. 'I assume he wasn't quite ready to move aside. Half-way through his operation – no time to be welcoming a new boss who might start looking into the accounts. Lionel was an older man, an ex-soldier, experienced and not (for all Rheza Khan knew) prepared to take what he found at face value. No. Rheza had every reason to stop him getting to Simla.'

'Right,' said Troop and added mildly, 'Feller smokes Black Cat cigarettes, you know. Heard you were enquiring.'

While they had been speaking, with unerring and steady

speed Troop had begun to wind his way through the thickening forest, now following the course of a roaring mountain stream, now turning aside to follow a forest track over a spur of the advancing hills, now pausing on the saddle to look back at Simla and forward into the mountains.

'The road's over to our right,' said Troop after they'd ridden for about an hour, 'behind that hill. It sets off in quite a loop there. We can make up a bit of ground. They say in these parts, "Follow the bowstring, don't follow the bow," and that's just what we're doing. And we can afford to spare the horses, indeed, we must spare the horses. We'd look an impressive pair if we ended up with a lame horse on our hands.'

As he spoke the track took a dizzying plunge down into a jungle-clad rift in the hills. The ravine stretched straight as a die for over five hundred yards and Joe followed Troop as he made his way along a forest path formed by the tramp of herds of chital deer which made a glancing appearance as they passed. Joe thought he caught sight of a band of langur monkeys and the tall trees were alive with the spring songs of birds. The hidden valley as they descended had a climate all its own. On a southern slope of the foothills, it retained the day's heat and Joe breathed gratefully the wafting sharp scent of the white star-shaped flowers of the box bushes. At the end of the valley he heard the plashing sound of a waterfall. His horse pricked up its ears and danced a few steps sideways.

Troop's eyes were alternately scanning the ground and looking on ahead. With a gesture to Joe he called a halt and silently leaned low in the saddle, examining fresh pug marks in the mud along the edge of the track. Still without a word he slipped the sling of his rifle over his head and cradled it in his arms. 'Leopard,' he said. 'It's his lucky day! We have bigger fish to fry.'

A chital hind appeared on the path ahead of them and turned in their direction calling urgently. The cry was taken up by many others; jungle fowl joined in the chorus. 'We've been spotted!' said Joe.

'No,' said Troop. 'That's a warning for us! They're telling us that there's a leopard ahead. Listen again!'

The chital began to call again on a different note. Troop smiled with satisfaction. 'And that's their "beware man" call so now the leopard knows we're here. Good! Wouldn't want to take the old bugger by surprise. Not much danger from him – leopard prefer to do their hunting at night and lie up during the day.'

They walked on, the horses not quite at ease with the scents they were picking up. At last they arrived at the waterfall. A stream burst from the cliff above and cascaded down into a rocky basin from where it overflowed into a large and steel-blue pool at their feet. As clear as gin and constantly renewed by the torrent fresh from the mountain, Joe thought he had never seen water so inviting. As he bent to drink and immerse his hot forehead he caught the reflection of Edgar Troop's red face looming over his left shoulder. At once he straightened to face him and wave him towards the water. He was for a moment shocked that he could so far have let his guard slip as to offer his unprotected neck to a man who might yet prove to be his enemy. One blow, two strong hands holding his head under water and that red face would have been the last thing he ever saw.

Troop grinned, understanding his swift movement, and bent to drink.

The insecurity of the moment impelled Joe to reflect on his situation. He was miles from civilization in the company of a self confessed 'gun for hire', a man who was in his own element and who knew the terrain and the dangers it presented. Joe began to work out the number of different ways in which Troop could kill him off and dispose of his body. And perhaps the only thing restraining Troop from doing just that was the note Joe had hurriedly written out and handed to one of Carter's sowars before leaving. And the fact that Troop needed his back-up when they eventually caught up with Alice and her escort. Joe calculated that he was probably in little danger until they embarked on the return journey with Alice and her jewellery.

With refreshed horses they pressed on, going always, it seemed to Joe, against the grain of the country. He began to appreciate the sturdy, tireless legs of the two horses as they alternately climbed up and slithered down slopes, steadily gaining altitude. Joe looked anxiously at the height of the sun. The valleys behind them were already in darkness but ahead on the uplift of land towards which they were headed he calculated they had roughly three more hours of full sunlight. Whatever the outcome of this insane dash into the mountains they would be spending the night outdoors.

A deep valley opened before them, the ground beyond it rising to a rocky outcrop.

'That,' said Edgar Troop, 'is where our routes converge. We follow this track down into the valley and up to the rocks and you see the road coming in on our right. I should think they're planning to break their journey here, spend the night and make a push for the Zalori at first light. Now, the question is – who got there first, Sandilands and Troop or Rheza and Alice? Further question – Rheza and Alice, are they alone?'

Joe strained his eyes to sweep the ground ahead, saying at last, 'Is that a building, there amongst the rocks?'

'Was,' said Troop. 'Was. Long abandoned. There's the remains of a fort there. It hasn't got a name as far as I know. We just call it the Red Fort. It's a useful landmark and overnight shelter. Used a fair bit by hunters and merchants but it's not much more than that.'

He set his horse gingerly to negotiate the rocky defile. 'Couldn't have done this earlier in the spring,' he said. 'When the snows melt it's a raging torrent but it makes a useful track at this time of year.'

Carefully the horses picked their way through the stones and down to a brawling stream crossed by a slab of rock and on the far side their path led upwards once more until, rounding a corner, they came on the Red Fort. Edgar Troop reined in sharply and gestured to Joe to stay back. 'Hello?' he muttered in a puzzled voice. 'Someone's been doing a bit of make and mend! That's curious.'

'What can you see?' said Joe.

'The gate. Somebody's repaired the gate. As long as I can remember this has just been an open archway but somebody's repaired the gate and repaired it well, too. Now who can that have been? Rheza, I guess, or Rheza on Alice's behalf. It looks to me as though we've stumbled on an ICTC staging post. And why not? No law against it, after all. Wonder if there's anybody at home?'

He searched the building ahead with his binoculars saying as he did so, 'The mast or flagstaff or whatever you care to call it

240

– that wasn't there last time I came this way . . . What's going on, I wonder?'

'Only one way to find out,' said Joe.

They moved forward cautiously, Troop in the lead, listening intently, even sniffing the air.

The building before them with its small window openings, its crenellated parapet, its watchful tower, its newly repaired gate suddenly seemed a strong place. The westering sun struck colour from the ancient walls and the building became a red fort indeed.

'Useful place, this,' said Joe. 'You can see for miles!'

'Oh, yes,' said Troop. 'These forts in the mountains are always well placed. Nobody's going to take it by surprise. When the British cleaned it up . . . oh, about fifty years ago . . . they didn't want to leave a convenient roosting place for malefactors on their back doorstep.'

'Well, that may have been their intention,' said Joe, 'but it looks about fifteen all at the moment. The British dismantle, the malefactors reassemble. Isn't that about it?'

'Yes, that's about it, I suppose.' Troop spoke slowly, his attention only half on Joe, his expression thoughtful. 'Some while since I was last here . . . last spring, I'd guess. A year in which things have been happening, it seems.'

'What sort of things?' Joe asked.

'Well, rather hard to tell but there is something. A difference between deserted and not deserted. If a place is deserted the grass grows but if it's in use the grass gets trampled. The grass has been trampled. And there – look. That's not, as you might suppose, horse shit, that's mule shit. Don't ask me how I know but I do. And if you're going for a leisurely ride through these hills you don't come riding a mule. And there have been quite a few mules. Recently. I'd guess we're ahead of Rheza and Alice but how far ahead I don't know. If anybody's going to get a surprise from this encounter I'd sooner it was them than us. First thing is to put the horses out of sight. Can't keep them silent – wish we could – but we can at least keep them concealed.'

'Is there anywhere in this battered caravanserai where we can conceal them?'

' "Think, in this battered caravanserai," ' said Edgar Troop, surprisingly,

241

'Whose portals are alternate night and day,
How sultan after sultan with his pomp
Abode his destined hour and went his way.'

'Omar Khayyam,' said Joe, much surprised.

'As you say,' said Troop absently, busily scanning the building ahead of them with his binoculars. 'Stand here, Joe, and cover me while I go and take a look.'

He disappeared into a narrow staircase which corkscrewed its way downwards and Joe heard him moving about and exclaiming from below. He was gone for what seemed a long time and Joe had a moment of anxiety. 'How little I know about this man,' he thought, 'and how I put myself into his hands. And come to that how many miles I am from anyone and anything that might reassure or be familiar.' Finally thinking, 'I'll count up to a hundred and then I'll go and see what he's up to.'

But on a count of ninety, dusty and perspiring, Troop re-emerged. 'Interesting! Interesting!' he said.

'Why? What have you seen?'

'Well, in the first place there are capacious cellars down there and somebody's taken the trouble to clean and sweep them out recently. Secondly, the cellar door was locked with an elaborate padlock. A sensible precaution, you'd think, but someone – presumably not Rheza Khan (he'd have more sense) – carefully left the key (quite a handsome one incidentally) hanging on a nearby nail. Bloody place is full of packing cases. All marked with ICTC lettering. All containing not – as you might expect – trashy Indian artefacts for the European market but far from trashy European rifles!'

'Surprised?'

'Surprised? Not in the least. Confirms all I was telling you about the Murphy system. I'd say this is the last consignment of who knows how many to make its way north of the Zalori. No, the only thing that surprises me is that it should have been left unattended. You don't just dump a hundred rifles in a cellar in the middle of nowhere and bugger off. Unless you know that someone's on his way to pick them up any minute. I reckon the mule train that dropped them off is not long gone, possibly off to the west towards the railhead on legitimate business, and Rheza is expected any moment to take charge. I'd guess his brigand cousins will arrive here tomorrow with fresh mules to pick them up. But, for the moment, we've got the place to ourselves. Wind's about right,' he added. 'We'll be safe to make ourselves a cup of tea.'

They led their horses up the slope, through the gate and round to the back of the building where they tethered them out of sight amongst the willow trees that had established a precarious foothold in the crumbling mud-brick walling. Troop slung his rifle over one shoulder and unbuckled his saddlebag, carrying it over the other. 'There's a little staircase round the corner. Let's go and man the battlements.' He led the way upwards, climbing the sunbaked masonry. 'Careful,' he said. 'Don't want to have to carry you home.'

They settled by an arched embrasure ten feet from the ground and having a sweeping overview of the approach to the fort.

'Keep a lookout, will you, while I brew up.' And from one pocket he withdrew a brick of green tea and from another a knife. He drew attention to a small charcoal stove in an angle of the wall and to a brass pot with small attendant cup on the wall behind it. 'Somebody,' he said, 'has been here very recently and thoughtfully left the tea things for us!'

He dipped water from a rainwater cistern into the brass pot and placed it on the stove. Taking pieces of charcoal from a saddlebag he set light to them and waited for the water to reach a rolling boil. Shielding his hand with a handkerchief he set the pot on the floor and began with the knife to shave flakes of green tea from the block into the pot. Watching Troop's neat, economical movements with admiration, Joe doubted if a cup of tea had ever been more eagerly awaited. The brass cup was filled from the pot and Troop brought it over, steaming and fragrant, to the embrasure where Joe remained scanning the road.

Joe found his respect for Edgar Troop mounting by the minute. 'Tell me,' he said, accepting the tea without taking his eyes from the scene below, 'where did you learn to quote from Omar Khayyam?'

'You are surprised to find even the faintest evidence of civilization in one so disreputable? My family were Baltic merchants. I was educated at the English School in Riga. Before the war, of course. I served in the army – the Russian Army. Not this mob but the Imperial Russian Army. People sometimes refer to me as

243

Captain Troop. Does me less than justice! Major Troop would have been nearer the mark.'

He rummaged around in his saddlebag and took out two small packages. 'Come and sit down. I'll take over the watch while you help yourself to some of this. Any fool can go hungry.'

'This' was a block of Caley's Marching Chocolate and a packet of Huntley and Palmer's Campaign Biscuits. They took turns to sweep the country through the binoculars, munching companionably. Joe remembered that he had had no lunch and wondered briefly what he might expect for supper. Assuming he was still around at supper time. The taste of the rough biscuit, the feel of the rifle in his hands, the jovial toughness of the man he found himself unexpectedly in harness with brought back with clarity the less unwelcome aspects of war. If only he'd been doing this with Sebastian! And was he crazy now to go unquestioningly through the familiar gestures with this stranger? They were in a situation where they would have to watch each other's back. Troop was taking Joe's ability for granted. His instructions ran to the minimum. He knew how Joe would react and that his reactions were trained and could be relied on. Joe had begun to suspect that his own background was less of a mystery to Troop than might be accounted for and yet Troop's history and motivation for Joe were still unclear. Building on the camaraderie of the moment he picked up the conversation. 'And,' said Joe, 'from the Russian Army to Simla – that seems a fair stride. How did it come about?'

'Oh, well, when all hell broke loose in 1916 in Russia the most important thing to do was stay alive! I didn't much care who won. My sympathies, I suppose, were with the Imperial Russian Army but one thing on which I was absolutely determined was that whoever else got killed, it wouldn't be Edgar Troop! I deserted. I drifted south. Even found myself in the Red Army briefly, until they found I was English. Foreigners who'd served in the Imperial Army weren't the most popular in the world with the Bolshies! I even once saw a firing squad falling in, planning to shoot me, if you can believe it! But I smoke a little hashish from time to time. I made up about twenty cigarettes which I distributed amongst my guard who were innocent kids from

Moscow. I left them all grinning and giggling – capable of nothing – and went on my way.'

'Nothing in this cup of tea that shouldn't be there, I hope?' said Joe.

'No, no! As served at Joe Lyons! But, as I say, I introduced my guards to an expensive habit and proceeded on my way, finally getting to Kashmir. A long journey. It took the best part of a year. A useful year. At the end of it I was a pretty fair shikar and a pretty fair linguist too. In Kashmir I ran into the full might of the British Empire and in particular into a good, solid-going, experienced and competent British Proconsul. He had the sense to see that a Russian-speaking, English-born, former member of the Imperial Army might be a useful individual to have on a retainer. He made me an offer. I accepted his offer and I've stayed in touch with him ever since. Oh, yes, the Troop information service has been of some use to the Raj!'

Troop grinned and added, 'I don't suppose you'll have forgotten that the talented but far from respectable Captain Troop is believed to hold a controlling interest in a thriving brothel?'

'Yes, I had heard as much.'

'Well, quite true – I do. And from the military's point of view an expensive brothel is probably the best listening post you could have! Even wily Indians like to show off at times! Plenty of valuable information reaching the ears of the Chief of Staff started on the rounds as pillow talk.'

'And what's become of this British paragon who recruited you?' Joe asked, his suspicions already formed.

'Oh, he did well. Built quite a career. Widely respected. Knighted even. His name's George Jardine.'

He paused, standing to one side of the embrasure and swept his binoculars back over the south road. He murmured a quiet oath. 'We've got visitors!' he said with satisfaction.

Chapter Twenty-six

He handed the binoculars to Joe. 'Look where I'm pointing.'

Joe focused the glass and stared. He rubbed his eye and stared again.

'Over there,' said Troop, 'where the road goes behind that big rock. Watch!'

Joe saw two figures on horseback come steadily round the rock and, leaving the road, start to climb towards the fort. Troop rubbed his glistening face with a large hand, turning to Joe with satisfaction. 'I don't want to boast,' he said, 'but I don't think there are many people who could have outflanked Rheza in this bit of country and still have had time to arrange a two-man reception committee. Quite a satisfactory moment in many ways,' he added blandly. 'Alice! She'd swindle anybody! You, me, Rheza, George Jardine if she could! But not this time! Take your stand here, Joe, and cover me. I'll go out and meet them. They'll be coming through that passage in the rock there. Expect them to be armed. Rheza, I see, has a rifle and is bound to have a pistol. Alice looks as though she's out for a picnic but don't be deceived – she'll have provided for her personal defence. I think it might easily emerge that the female of the species was the more deadly. As I say – can't get away from Kipling, can we? But I don't underestimate Rheza. A tricky little bastard in his own right and very dangerous. Had my eye on him for years. And in the meantime, we'll trust in God and keep our powder dry! Eh?'

His face was elated; he stood at the turn in the path with his hands on his hips. Joe found that his own breathing was getting faster and his palms were sweating as his excitement grew. Soon the chink and clatter of horses' hooves could clearly be heard and then voices, the deep tones of Rheza Khan and the light voice of Alice. They were speaking in a mixture of Hindustani and English.

'So far, so good!' Joe heard her say. 'Be glad to rest for a bit.'

With Rheza Khan leading they rounded the turn in the path and entered the curtain wall of the little fort. Rheza Khan looked sleek, cool and efficient. It was hard to believe that he had just ridden thirty miles in the sun. He wore well-cut breeches and boots, a light tweed shooting coat and a white drill shikar helmet. Alice, riding behind him, matched him in style with jodhpurs, a white silk shirt and a wide-brimmed felt hat hanging down her back on a chin strap. Her abundant copper hair hung loose.

'Good afternoon, Rheza! And good afternoon, Alice,' said Edgar Troop, stepping forward. 'Are you going somewhere?'

'Troop!' Rheza Khan jerked his horse to a slithering halt and sat and stared in astonishment.

Alice burst into a babble of indignant and angry speech. 'Edgar! What the hell are you doing here? What the hell! Rheza – quick!'

'Don't try anything silly, Rheza Khan,' said Troop. 'And you too, Alice. Don't do anything silly. I'm not alone.'

'Not alone?'

'No,' said Edgar. 'You're a genius girl, Alice, and you, Rheza Khan, I'll pay you the compliment of saying you're not to be despised either, but I wouldn't be likely to come to this brigands' roost without a little armed support!'

Theatrically, Joe shot the bolt of his rifle and they both spun around and stared up at him. 'Forgive the expression, Alice,' said Joe from the window embrasure, 'but the game's up! And just to make this entirely official, I will say – you're under arrest. And, to dot the i's and cross the t's, you should know that although you so skilfully sent Charlie Carter many miles and many hours out of his way, he's a persevering man is Charlie. He'll know where we are and, faint but pursuing, he'll be joining us. In a very bad temper, I should think. He won't be here for tea. I don't think he'll be here for supper but he could well be with us for breakfast!'

Edgar Troop intervened. 'And until then – what to do with

you two? No one knows better than you, Rheza, that this dilapidated establishment has capacious cellarage, not all of which is occupied by assorted military hardware. I'll apologize in advance for the poverty of the accommodation but that is where you will wait for Charlie.'

Joe knew Alice in many moods. He had seen her poised and competent with the great and good of Simla on the stage of the Gaiety Theatre; he had seen her on equal terms with George Jardine; he had seen her soft and yielding in a small, moonlit garden, but here was a different image. On the verge of making her escape, the fruits of three years spent looting ICTC in her saddlebags and now only the biddable and despised Edgar Troop and the deceivable London policeman between her and her rewards. In a flash, white-faced and as vicious as a leopard, she slid from her horse and stood, it seemed, at bay and in no mood to give up.

'Under arrest?' she said derisively. 'On whose authority? And on what charge? We're not in the Mile End Road, as perhaps I can remind you! "Would you mind coming down to the station" and that sort of routine! I'll tell you, Joe, and I hope I won't need to repeat it – I'm not going anywhere with you! Not now; not at any time.'

'To answer your questions,' said Joe, 'there is a warrant out for your arrest. A warrant signed by Sir George Jardine. I am a duly appointed deputy police superintendent. And the charge? For the time being a holding charge only. Fraud. But I don't need to tell you that more lies behind that. It's a well-worn phrase but I'll use it again – the game's up.' He turned to Rheza Khan. 'And while we're at it, I'm pulling *you* in for murder.'

'Murder?' said Rheza Khan derisively. 'What are you talking about? The murder of that inflated Russian barn-door cockerel?'

'Is this a confession?' asked Joe. 'If so, I'll be interested to hear it in due course. And I'm going back a little bit further than that. I'm going back to the death of Lionel Conyers. I don't need to tell you, of course, that the murder weapon used on both unfortunate victims was a .303, probably a British Army Short Lee-Enfield – of which there are not a few below and one of which you have with you, I see.'

Alice shot a look of blind astonishment at Rheza then looked back at Joe, more nearly disconcerted than he had ever seen her.

There was a pistol holster on Rheza Khan's saddle and his hand moved towards it.

'We don't want any unnecessary bloodshed,' said Edgar Troop, 'so oblige me by keeping your hands where we can see them and – to shut down all unwelcome possibilities – you do the same, Alice. Cover them while I get their guns. Joe.'

Joe watched while he collected a .303 rifle from Rheza Khan and slipped the pistol from its holster. Unloading both, he threw them out of reach and told Rheza to dismount. An expert search of his clothing turned up no further firearms and he turned his attention to Alice. She reached behind her back and handed over a revolver by its barrel.

'Here, take it,' she snapped. 'And you can keep your brothel-keeper's hands off me!'

Taking no notice, Troop proceeded to pat down her clothing, a dispassionate, professional procedure, but the figure-hugging silk shirt, jodhpurs and soft leather boots concealed nothing that should not have been there. His inspection completed, Edgar gathered up the guns then took charge of the horses and with reins looped over his arm led them round the fort to picket them in the shade. Rheza Khan's horse had a neat bedding roll on the crupper, Alice's had two deep leather pannier bags. Her eyes followed these with anxiety.

Returning to them, Edgar said cheerfully, 'Can't offer you much but if you'd like to step into our parlour my colleague would gladly supply a cup of tea. Before we bed you both down in the cellar for the night.'

Making the prisoners walk ahead of them, Joe and Edgar went back to the lookout room and while Joe kept them covered, Edgar, with half an eye to the window and the approach road, poured out cups of tea and offered one to Alice. She ignored the outstretched hand. Turning to Joe, she said almost casually, 'This cellar in which you're planning on keeping us locked up for the night – what did you say it contained?'

'Military equipment,' Joe replied, 'to be precise, army rifles. .303s. Brand new. On their way north. Rheza Khan could tell you more but there's a consignment of a hundred. The last of who knows how many other consignments which have passed through this fort under ICTC markings on an ICTC pack train – you tell me! *You* may not be able to tell me how many down to the last hundred but I'll bet your precious accountant here knows. It's not going to inflate your reputation with your society friends in Simla and elsewhere when they hear that you've been gun-running to a volatile tribe right on their doorstep.'

With chalk-white face and eyes narrowed to slits, Alice turned from Joe to Rheza Khan and back again. Joe leaned forward and spoke earnestly, 'Alice, listen! This is the end of the road for you. There only needs to be the whisper of a rumour that ICTC have been supplying dissidents in tribal territory for the British authorities to act with ferocious speed.'

Edgar Troop intervened. 'And there's more to it than that, Alice. Times change, the management changes. ICTC drifts into the hands of the competent Mrs Conyers-Sharpe, the ramshackle remains of the Russian Empire drift into the hands of the Bolshevik establishment but the game remains the same – Russian eyes turn to northern India, British eyes, my own amongst them incidentally, are turned where they have always been – to their northern neighbours. You know this, I know this, but above all, George Jardine and others know it. And to those concerned to preserve a precarious balance, the arrival on the scene of five hundred? a thousand? more? modern rifles is a matter of acute concern.'

With care and with something approaching pity Joe was studying Alice's face as these revelations unfolded. As he watched there came to him a moment of blinding clarity. 'Is it possible,' he said, a note of wonder in his voice, 'that you were unaware of this? You, Rheza Khan, is it possible that you managed to conceal your gun-running operation from all, including your boss, the managing director of ICTC? Is this possible?'

Neither said a word.

'Could it be,' Joe went on, turning to Alice, 'that, preoccupied with your own *jewellery* run, you weren't aware of the other smuggling going on?'

'And I'll add something to that,' said Edgar Troop, speaking slowly and with ferocity. 'Lionel Conyers, your "brother", gunned down with surgical precision on the Kalka road – Korsovsky likewise a few days ago – and what did they have in common? The only thing they shared was the lethal knowledge that the managing director of ICTC, the pretty façade, was not who she claimed to be. The authorities have searched high and

250

low – I understand I even came under suspicion myself! (suspicion carefully planted!) – looking for the trigger man. Once aware that you were being blackmailed all assumed that the blackmailer and the murderer were one. Not so! Tell me,' he added, with something approaching geniality, turning to Rheza Khan, 'is it not a fact that no one has been as anxious as you have always been to keep Alice in place and supplying you? You're a fine shot, Rheza, all acknowledge this and the killings would for you have been money for old rope. I'm not certain whether Charlie Carter had time to get around to establishing your whereabouts at the time of Korsovsky's killing – he's been rather busy harassing me and Reggie and the other chaps at the chummery. I hope for your sake that you're not thinking of counting on your boss for an alibi!'

He turned a scornful look on Alice. 'Poor little Alice, you ran into someone even more manipulative than you are yourself! How does it feel to be led by the nose – to be used?' Edgar Troop asked softly. 'To be used by this tailor's dummy in his old school tie? How does it feel, I wonder?'

The question floated in the air while all stood silent and as though frozen. Expressionless, Alice spoke at last. She was gazing through the window, her face a blank. 'Just how it has always felt,' she said bitterly. 'When I look at my life I realize that I have known nothing else. I've been abused, deceived and betrayed by men for as long as I can remember. *C'est normal, quoi*? It's what I have come to expect. And it's what I prepare for.' She looked back at Rheza Khan. 'But you? What was special about *you*, I wonder? I believed you. I believed in you. I thought perhaps – at last – I had found a man.'

Rheza Khan had remained still, apparently unconcerned, slightly smiling. 'No, Alice,' he said at last, '*I* had found *you*. And I'm sorry to say this but your period of usefulness, for which I have been more than grateful, is over. And, as they say – "I shall always take an interest in your future career," but it's going to be no concern of mine. The frontier is about to explode and I think the omniscient Sir George has heard rumours – but no more than rumours. The arms are in place. But arms by themselves are nothing; arms are nothing without money. To exploit them there are men to pay, men who not only need pay but need food and clothing and all the things that go with a successful armed uprising – and, believe me, I'm not backing an *unsuccessful* uprising! And, at this moment, Alice conveniently arrives! Pockets full of jewels! I've worked out their value once or twice. Very negotiable and designed to provide Alice and – if you can believe it – my humble self as well with a comfortable lifestyle somewhere far from this border. But I have men, good men and well-mounted who only await my signal to descend on this ramshackle fort. And what do they find when they get here?' He laughed, it seemed, in genuine amusement. 'A superannuated Russian moujik, a puzzled London policeman and a hysterical little girl who's going to have her toys snatched away.'

'Oh, dear,' said Edgar. 'We seem to be listening in to a lovers' tiff! Better not to intrude, eh, Joe? I'll go and unlock downstairs and they can have all the time in the world for their recriminations! And Rheza Khan can spend some time wondering just how he's going to do any signalling from the cellar.'

He turned and, leaving Joe covering them, clattered off down the spiral staircase. Joe gestured to Rheza to move further over to his left away from Alice. He sensed that Alice was dangerously disturbed by what she had just heard and he didn't want to risk a wild cat attack. Not while they were under *his* supervision. Alice tossed her head, understanding him. She took hold of her felt hat and, holding it in front of her, began in a leisurely fashion to fan her face, in a theatrically provocative and dismissive gesture.

The grating of a heavy door down below was the signal. Moving steadily away from Alice as directed, his eyes fixed on Joe's revolver, Rheza Khan worked his way round to Joe's left. Moving backwards slowly, he stumbled on the uneven floor and leant over to balance himself. In a lightning movement he pulled a slim knife from the inside of his riding boot. At that same moment a voice burst like a shell in Joe's head: *Watch your left flank!* and he hurled himself to his right, firing instinctively as he fell a round that caught Rheza Khan in the right thigh. The knife, a flash of silver, sliced through the space Joe had a split second ago occupied to sink itself in the doorpost. From the floor, Joe watched, horrified, as Alice took her hand from inside her felt hat and pointed. The small revolver was only just visible in her palm. 'No! No! For God's sake, Alice! Don't do this!' Joe called urgently, but with a tight smile and deaf to his protests, she took unhurried aim and fired.

The pistol banged noisily in the confined space and awoke an echo across the hill. Rheza Khan had only a brief moment to register complete surprise before the bullet hit him straight between the eyes. His body slithered to the ground between them. Joe lay on one elbow, his gun trained on Alice, and she stood, still smiling, her gun now pointing at him. 'Stand-off, Joe?' she said. 'If you're wondering why I shot him and not you, well . . .' She shrugged her shoulders. 'At least you've never concealed the fact that you were out to get me. And you're such a gentleman! You could have had me, you know, and I do believe it mightn't have been such a penance but you're not an exploiter. Perhaps the only one such I've ever met. And I'll trust my judgement further. I don't think you would ever kill a woman. Certainly not by shooting her in the back which is going to be your only option!'

She ran to the window embrasure and, turning, jumped up on to the wide sill. She stood for a moment outlined in the window and gazing down across the baked and empty hillside. She looked defiantly over her shoulder. 'I didn't know about the rifles, Joe. And I never asked Rheza Khan to kill anyone for me. I was brought up to tell the truth, remember!'

She twisted her body neatly and let herself down from the sill, hanging on until she was steady, and then released her grip. It was a long drop but she landed with balanced grace. She looked up, hair glowing red in the slanting sun, smiled at Joe and was gone. Helplessly, Joe watched from the window while feet clattered up the stairs and Edgar Troop called from outside the heavy door. Joe shouted to him to come in.

'What the hell?'

Troop looked from the body to Joe and, startled, looked around for Alice.

'Rheza Khan had a knife hidden in his boot,' said Joe pointing to the door post. 'Just missed me. Alice didn't miss though! She shot him. She had a gun.'

'She bloody didn't have a gun!' Edgar exploded. 'God, Joe, you saw me search her! The only bumps under her clothes were legitimately there!'

'You omitted to search her hat! She took it out of her hat!

253

When she said she was always prepared for betrayal, she wasn't kidding.'

'You let her get away! Idiot! Where the hell's she gone? Did you do this on purpose?' He bounded to the window, cocked his gun and leaned out covering the path up to the fort. 'I'll get her when she makes her dash for the road.'

'You won't, you know!' said Joe. 'You couldn't shoot her, any more than I could. *You* know it and *she* knew it.'

'Don't count on it!' Troop snarled.

The clatter of horses' hooves pounding on the loose scree and excited whinnying rose up from below. Troop leant despairingly over the wide windowsill. 'Bloody hell! That's our horses! The bitch has spooked our horses! Get down there, Joe, and get them back while I cover the road.'

Joe ran downstairs and took stock of the scene in the rear courtyard. Cut reins – three sets, he noted – were dangling from a willow tree but of horses no sign. With a few slashes, Alice had rendered three unrideable and, tearing down a willow branch, had thrashed them out on to the bare mountain, sending them skittering off back the way they had come. The fourth? Bent twigs showed him where she had ridden through the scrub away from the fort in the opposite direction from the approach road. He guessed her plan was to circle widely, out of rifle range, back to the main track and then on – to where? Would she take the road back to Simla or would she continue on for a while, branching left to Joginder Nagar?

He continued down the road in a desultory way for a while, fatuously whistling and calling for horses long out of earshot. He was not looking forward to facing Edgar Troop again and the idea of spending the night cut off from civilization with him in this dreadful place was infinitely depressing.

The sound of a rifle shot behind the fort as he trudged back up the road startled and alarmed him. He made slowly towards it, approaching carefully at the last until, peering round a corner of the building, he saw Edgar Troop returning from the scrub carrying his rifle and a bunch of wild sage in one hand and a fat golden pheasant in the other.

'This is our supper,' he said, catching sight of Joe, good humour seemingly restored. 'Better than the bully beef tin I had in my saddlebag. No luck with the horses? Didn't really expect it. Silly buggers'll be half-way to Simla by now! Come on – I'll get the fire going if you pluck the bird. Not much improved by being hit amidships with a round from a service rifle but still better than bully beef.'

Back in the main room of the fort only a stain on the floor remained of Rheza Khan.

'What have you done with him?' Joe asked.

'Down in the cellar with the other rats,' said Troop cheerfully. 'Now all we have to do is get through the evening as best we may. We'll take it in turns to watch through the night until first light and then we both stand guard and hope that when we hear horses coming up the road, they're carrying Charlie Carter and his mob and not Rheza Khan's followers coming to check the contents of the cellar and wondering why they've not been whistled up by the boss!'

The pheasant was tough but full of flavour and night fell suddenly as they cut it into strips with Edgar's knife and shared it out. Edgar won the toss and decided that Joe should take the first watch. Rifle in hand and a prey to many misgivings, Joe sat looking over the empty hills as twilight turned to moonlight, and listened to the sounds of forest creatures all around, snuffling and padding under the open window. Here and there he spotted the gleam of strange eyes.

Somewhere out there, he thought in sudden dismay, is Alice. Alone, virtually unarmed and miles from civilization. Reliant on a tired horse. Come back in, Alice! Don't be alone! We'll think of something! I know we will!

As he watched, the night was assailed by a wavering, blood-chilling scream which brought Joe to his feet, alarmed and in terror. From a corner beyond the circle of firelight came Edgar Troop's gravelly voice, 'Jackal, Joe! Take it easy!'

Joe gathered Charlie's poshteen tight about his shoulders and shivered on.

He took up his second watch when the night was at its blackest two hours or so before he could expect to see the first flush of dawn over the rim of the eastern hills. He rubbed his gritty eyelids and peered, unbelieving, into the darkness. No, he was not mistaken. There was light in the distance where no light should be. A moving light. No – lights. He watched on. The eerie sight of a swarm of glow-worms wriggling its way through the hills and onward towards the fort startled him into full wakefulness. Hurriedly he shook Edgar who leapt, instantly alert, to the window. He snatched the binoculars from Joe, saying at last, 'We've got company! Lots of it, I'd say. Judging by the spacing of those torches – at least fifty men.'

As the glow-worms drew level with the fort the bobbing torches were suddenly extinguished and there was movement which told Joe that men were spreading out to cover the fort. Joe asked uneasily, 'Ours or theirs? And if ours, how are we going to attract their attention? They might take us for enemy and open fire.'

'They might be a party of Rheza Khan's people coming to take delivery of a bundook or two. Possible but not likely. Too many of them. But get the torch out of my right saddlebag. Got it? Signal something. Anything.'

Standing in the window embrasure Joe began to signal.

'What are you sending?' said Troop.

'Well, anyone who was on the Western Front might recognize it – something we used to use in the trenches. "O . . . K" – something we picked up from the Yanks. I think it stands for "orl korrect".'

At once someone at the head of the advancing column began to signal back.

'What's that?' said Troop anxiously.

'Dee dah, dee dah, dee dah. Ack, ack, ack,' said Joe. ' "A" for "Acknowledged". Didn't they have the Morse code in the army of Imperial Russia?'

'If they had, there wouldn't be anyone down there who'd know it and if there was anyone down there who knew it, they wouldn't have a torch and if anyone down there knew it and had a torch it wouldn't occur to them to reply, if I know anything about the Imperial Russian Army.'

Soon they heard the clatter of advancing hooves and then the jingle of curb chains and the clash of equipment. Just below the fort the column halted and two men cantered up the hill alone.

'Who goes there?' said Joe.

'Friend.'

'Advance one and be recognized,' said Joe remembering the formula.

'This is getting all very Sandhurst!' said Edgar Troop.

They walked out to meet their visitors, a young British officer and a bearded sowar, his lance pennant fluttering in the wind off the hill.

'Good God!' said the advancing figure in cheerful tones. 'I don't know what I was expecting to find but I wasn't expecting to find you, Edgar! You tricky old bastard! Before we say any more, be good enough to tell me – just for the time being, of course – which side you're on. I like to establish these things.'

'Where's Charlie Carter?' said Joe.

'Here!' said a voice, and a weary and dishevelled Charlie Carter rode into the circle of torchlight.

Chapter Twenty-seven

Sir George Jardine, resplendent in a quilted smoking-jacket whose pocket bore the insignia of a long defunct Cambridge dining club, was ensuring that all the final touches were complete and in order. He was giving a small dinner party. A dinner party for four. A *partie carrée*, he called it to himself. The perfect size. And no women.

An amontillado with the turtle soup, a light burgundy with the saddle of mutton (he'd ordered up four bottles from the cellar and now gave instructions for two to be opened), a montbazillac with the fabulous water ice for which the Residence was famed and a good Stilton assisted down by a glass of 1910 port by Williams, Standring. 'Yes! That should be enough.' And he gave instructions that his guests as they arrived be shown straight to the library, the windows of which stood open to the balcony and the balcony open to the moon and to the murmurs of the town.

The first to arrive was Joe Sandilands. 'Good evening, Sir George,' he said easily. 'This is very kind of you. A little cooler this evening, perhaps?'

'That's all the flannel you're allowed, young Sandilands,' said Sir George. 'I won't anticipate but I'm expecting some direct and straight-from-the-shoulder explaining.'

Joe had long learnt that it was unwise to let Sir George get away with anything and he said, 'Dash it! I was hoping for a good dinner. The last few days have been rather austere. A few campaign biscuits don't go a very long way.'

'Have a glass of sherry,' said Sir George, 'and don't try it on with me!'

Next to come and arriving together were Charlie Carter and

Edgar Troop, the latter perhaps a little embarrassed to find himself comfortably at the heart of the Simla establishment and in company with citizens of such impeccable respectability. His 'Good evening, Sir George' was a little over-affable as Charlie Carter's had been a little over-deferential.

'Good evening! Good evening!' said Sir George. 'Delightful occasion! Thought we'd have dinner straight away.'

He picked up and tinkled a little silver bell. 'Sherry? Or if you prefer a madeira? I find it a little heavy these spring nights but do please help yourselves.' And, to Joe, 'Saw your friend Jane Fortescue today. Asked to be remembered to you.' And to Charlie Carter, 'Those girls of yours did well in the potato race at the gymkhana yesterday. Sorry you weren't there. I really enjoyed it.' And to Edgar Troop, 'While we're waiting, do please take the long chair. Kind to saddle sores, you'll find.'

None of them spoke, all looking at him warily. 'So good of you fellows to come at such short notice. Perhaps I don't need to tell you – you're all in serious trouble. You're not under arrest, of course, but the only reason why you're not under arrest is that with Charlie in handcuffs, there'd be no one to arrest you!'

They all took their seats around the table and, as though by rehearsal, shook out in unison large table napkins.

'But to start at the end and work back from there . . . one of you gunned down Rheza Khan? No particular loss! Deplorable fellow! Arms aren't the only thing he's moved across the border. Scallywag if ever I knew one but nevertheless an episode that stands in need of some explanation. Influential man, Rheza Khan. Considerable following in the Hills. Vast consignment of arms on its way north under the eyes of the police and, worst of all, a deplorable young woman, guilty beyond question of pulling off the most bare-faced fraud in the history of the Indian Empire and more than suspected of complicity in no fewer than two murders –'

'Possibly three,' said Joe.

'We shall get on a little bit faster, Sandilands,' said Sir George repressively, 'if you don't interrupt. As I say, this bare-faced miscreant allowed, possibly even encouraged, to slip quietly away under your benign gaze.'

'Not *my* benign gaze,' said Charlie happily, appreciatively sipping Sir George's admirable burgundy. 'I wasn't there at the time.'

'No indeed! Forty miles away at the time, I understand, searching railway sidings. Looking the other way? I've marked you down as an accessory,' said Sir George.

'Could I ask,' said Edgar Troop, 'how you know these things, sir?'

'You're not stupid, Troop! Apart from myself, possibly the only person in this room who is not – so I don't need to tell you that any group containing half a dozen or so in this town is likely to contain one of my agents. Charlie, I understand, had twelve policemen with him – need I say more? You must not assume you are the only man in Simla with interesting things to tell me.'

'But there were no witnesses conveniently placed when Alice shot Rheza Khan,' Joe said mildly. 'Apart from myself, of course, so you'll just have to hear and accept my version of the killing, sir.'

Sir George sighed impatiently. 'Very well, Sandilands. Why don't you tell us your version of the events? Your memory of them? Illuminated, no doubt, by hindsight.'

All listened intently as Joe recounted the outline of his carefully rehearsed story.

Turning to Edgar Troop, Sir George asked, 'Now, tell me, Troop, how much of this litany of lapses are you able to corroborate? Tell me first – did you leave undiscovered the knife in Rheza Khan's boot?'

'I am responsible, yes, sir,' said Edgar uncomfortably. 'I searched both prisoners.'

'It was a most remarkable knife,' Joe explained. 'Very slender with a six-inch blade. It fitted down the seam of the boot – the handle was part of a boot pull-on – it was virtually undetectable. Very clever!'

He fell silent at a glower from Sir George. 'And the next virtually undetectable item was a gun. You allowed Alice to retain – uninspected – a hat containing a revolver but, as it transpires according to Joe's account, this lapse had laudable consequences. If we are to believe it –' he paused for a moment, 'and why would we not? – she saved Joe's life by pulling this gun and shooting Rheza Khan dead. Then, while he and Edgar run around like headless chickens, Miss Alice leaps nimbly through a window and makes off into the sunset, saddlebags stuffed with her ill-gotten gains, having had the forethought first to run your horses off? Am I getting it right, Edgar?'

'More or less, Sir George, more or less.'

'And the question which we should all be asking ourselves – and perhaps Joe will have an answer – is why should Alice, in unexpected possession of a gun and with two chaps at her mercy to choose from, put her bullet in her comrade in crime rather than in the police officer whose avowed intention is to haul her back in chains to face justice?'

All remained silent waiting for the next thrust.

'I'm sure we're all grateful to Alice. She saved us a little trouble in shooting Rheza Khan but will someone tell me why she should do that? Her associate, her partner? Her interests and his were one, were they not? I'll tell you why,' he went on, answering his own question. 'She'd raised Rheza Khan up to a position of special power in the firm. He'd started out in a relatively humble position, in spite of his background and family wealth, in ICTC. Alice spotted his potential; she saw he could go all the way. And he did. He had authority and prestige, money and unshakeable status. Without Alice's support he would have been nothing in Simla commerce and society. He owed all to her and she trusted him without question. It was more than she could easily bear that he should have – and with great success – played his own game. Another man to have failed her. Used her and failed her. It cost him his life.'

' "Tis the strumpet's plague, To beguile many and be beguiled by one," ' Joe murmured. 'I think there was more to it than the knowledge that he'd deceived her in the matter of the gun-running.'

'Ah, yes, Sandilands, your theory that there was some romantic alliance between those two? I hear no evidence of that from any other quarter but it wouldn't surprise me. Nasty piece of work, Rheza Khan, though quite seductive I would have thought.'

Edgar Troop poured himself a further glass of wine and passed the decanter to Charlie Carter. 'I don't believe it,' he said. 'I don't believe that Alice was romantically interested in Rheza

Khan. In fact I'll go further – I don't think she was interested in men at all.'

'Are you perhaps obliquely telling us that on some occasion or occasions unspecified you found her inappropriately uninterested in *you*? Now, Joe, perhaps you have something to add to this debate? Very taking little thing, Alice.'

'I pass,' said Joe.

Sir George's generous grey eyebrows rose in query. 'The deputy police superintendent passes! We must return to you, Edgar, for further illumination.'

'I believe,' said Edgar Troop shaking his head, 'she had many admirers. And, yes, all right, I'll agree, myself amongst them.' He turned to Joe. 'Yourself amongst them too possibly, Sandilands?'

'All right,' said Sir George, 'since this seems to be the fashion, I will add myself to this list. But, to get a dispassionate view, Carter, since you seem to be the only man in Simla proof to her charms – what have you to say on this subject?'

'I agree with Edgar. The only person she was at ease with in Simla, the only person she did not deceive and manipulate, was her friend Marie-Jeanne Pitiot.'

'Are you suggesting . . .?' The eyebrows rose again.

'I think I have an insight into that particular relationship,' said Joe. 'When we were staging the seance routine I remember Minerva Freemantle saying that Alice returned week after week in the hope of contacting her mother. Alice herself told me that her mother had died when she was eleven, leaving her to be brought up by her cold, uncaring and ambitious father. The first in a long line of men to betray and abuse her. Marie-Jeanne is much older than Alice – I think she sees her as a mother-replacement. Perhaps the only person in India or the world that she can truly trust. And since Alice has totally disappeared I would think it sensible to keep a watch on Marie-Jeanne because it is to her that Alice will go, I think, to find shelter.'

Charlie Carter added eagerly, 'That's taken care of, Sir George. I have had men posted outside her house for the last three days and I have had the house and her warehouse searched.'

'Your stable-door-shutting techniques are second to none,' Sir George said. 'And what does Marie-Jeanne have to say about all this? I assume that you have interviewed her?'

'Seems to have nothing to hide – well, we know she hasn't because the search was pretty thorough. Says she hasn't seen Alice for at least a week. She wanted to know if we were keeping her a prisoner, surrounding her house with troops, and gave us notice that she's intending to leave Simla tomorrow. She has a long-standing engagement in Bombay and has booked her ticket. She said she wouldn't object if a policeman accompanied her if I wanted to send one along. I think she was being ironic, sir.'

Clever, confident Marie-Jeanne. Helpful on the surface, Joe thought but, given her strong loyalties to Alice, surely she would make some attempt to help her friend? Joe decided that there was one more call he should make before his time in Simla was up.

Sir George sighed. 'Go on, Carter, tell us what other steps you have taken to trail after your light-footed quarry.'

Businesslike, Carter replied, 'Alice has two ways of getting out of the country. On the narrow gauge rail from Joginder Nagar and on to Amritsar or doubling back to Simla and getting out in a tonga or the Toy Train to Kalka and on to Delhi.'

'Was there no sign of her on the Simla road when you came hot-footing it to the rescue up the mountain?'

'No, sir. But it would have been very easy for her to hide herself along the route when she caught sight of the patrol.'

'Yes,' drawled Sir George, 'well, you were certainly visible. From miles away, I should think. A squadron of Bengal Lancers, Slater's Horse I believe, armed to the teeth and clattering along in the dark preceded by a dozen flare carriers and, if I know anything about those popinjays in Slater's, singing the Eton Boating Song! Yes, she'd have seen you coming. So she could by now, three full days after the drama, be safely back and hiding in Simla or anywhere else for that matter. What about the other exit?'

'All passengers taking the train from Joginder Nagar have their identity checked, sir. So far no European woman has tried to get on the train.' He passed a list of passengers to Sir George.

'And what about the exits from Simla?'

'They likewise are being watched. The papers of every passenger are checked both in Simla and Kalka. I have men stationed on the tonga road and they too check all passengers. So

263

far nothing.' He passed over another list. 'Not many *leaving* Simla of course at this time of year which makes our job easy. Mostly people are flooding *in*.'

Sir George inspected the list. 'Mmm . . . six tax-inspectors, five opium smugglers, four French nuns, three box-wallahs, two brigadiers,' he paraphrased, 'but no partridge in this pear tree. Keep shaking the branches, Carter!'

'Doesn't surprise me,' said Edgar Troop suddenly grim. 'You're looking in the wrong place. She had two more hours of daylight when she rode off into the wilderness. Not long enough to reach any civilized part or even shelter. She would have been riding a tired horse through dangerous country whichever route she took. Bandits . . . wild animals . . . rough terrain. Wouldn't care to do it alone myself, even armed to the teeth. Alice didn't have a rifle with her – she only had her little pop-gun. Wouldn't scare off a monkey let alone a leopard. So, the other chance which none of you has mentioned is that Alice may be dead!' He looked from one to the other and suddenly his large red face was haggard in the candlelight. 'She may well be dead,' he repeated. 'Can't think why you don't all acknowledge it.'

There was a moment's silence as all did acknowledge it.

'Hmm,' said Sir George. 'If so –

> 'Now boast thee, Death,
> In thy possession lies
> A lass unparalleled.'

Chapter Twenty-eight

Summer 1922

In the moment of waking, Joe Sandilands could not work out where he was. A distant and regular underfloor throb accompanied by the cry of a passing sea-bird told him that he was on board a ship. But what ship and why he could not for the moment decide. A dazzle of sunshine reflected in the ceiling a few feet above his face told him that it was early morning, the breakfast tray at his elbow – a dish of croissants and a white china coffee pot – reminded him at last that he was on one of the few remaining French liners which ran from Bombay to Marseilles. A slight but insistent headache reminded him that, celebrating his escape from the confusions of crime-prevention in India, he'd had too much to drink the night before.

He was glad to be on a French boat. P&O were grand and formal but French boats were domestic, comfortable and informal. Furthermore, not many English people travelled this way and, in all the circumstances, on his present journey Joe was glad of the anonymity until, from Marseilles, he could run straight home to England by train and into the safe and predictable confines of his regular London life. 'I've had enough India,' he'd said to himself. 'Yes, definitely enough India.' He searched his mind. Any regrets? He found he was delighted – relieved and delighted – to be out of the shade of George's umbrella. 'Another month and I'd have become a performing poodle at the Residence!' He spared a moment to think of Charlie Carter. 'The Good Centurion' he decided. 'A *bon copain* if ever I had one. Could we have worked on together? Years of steady police work in the sun?' It was for a moment a tempting thought. But at the last, London beckoned. 'Okay. That's it. Charlie'll be okay.'

And Edgar? What about Edgar Troop? The eternal mercenary.

The gun perpetually for sale. The world was changing. Would there always be a place for the likes of Edgar? He decided that there would. There must have been hundreds of Edgars in John Company's India, designed to survive. Yes! Edgar would survive.

A glance to the right to take in the adjoining bedside table with its twinned breakfast tray told him that he was not alone and an exploring hand, encountering a warm female presence, confirmed this. Tentatively he whispered, 'Good morning.' And, after a moment's thought, '*Bonjour, ma belle.*'

He arranged himself on one elbow and with an only slightly unsteady hand poured himself out a cup of coffee and began to sip. The excellence of the coffee, if nothing else, would have confirmed that he was not on a steamer of the Peninsular and Oriental Steam Navigation Company. The quality of the champagne too had been exceptional and the amounts served by the captain, at whose table he'd dined, copious. They had all drunk too much, the passengers apparently determined to make their first night on the Indian Ocean a memorable one. The captain had held a small reception for a selected eight guests. As they began to arrive, some singly and some in couples and all French, the captain relaxed on hearing Joe chatting comfortably with them in their own language.

'My dear Commander,' he had said, 'how fortunate we are that you speak French so well! Believe me, it is a most unusual accomplishment in an Englishman. Your countrymen can speak Hindustani, it would appear, and any one of a hundred native Indian languages with ease but French they do not deign to learn. And, like a good host, I had taken the trouble to invite the one other English passenger we have aboard to join us tonight so that you would have one person at least to talk to. I understand you also have travelled recently from Simla?'

As Joe nodded cautiously the captain had caught sight of the last guest to appear and had extended arms in welcome. Joe stared in amazement, the five other male guests in open admiration. With a warm smile of recognition for Joe, she listened carefully to the captain's introductions and acknowledged that she and Joe were already well known to each other. After this auspicious beginning and after four hours sampling the hospitality of the *Duc de Bourgogne*, and along with the prevailing holiday mood, it had seemed entirely natural that, on escorting his partner back to her cabin, she should have offered him a brandy and that he should have accepted.

Joe looked around him more carefully. He was in a first class cabin, spacious and well-equipped. Discreetly he wriggled out of bed, drew aside a small lacy curtain from a porthole and looked out on a sunny deck. An aggressively healthy couple strode past, two young French naval officers presumably returning from leave lounged, smoking, against the rail casting speculative glances about them. A small party of schoolgirls on their way back to school in Europe pattered by. Joe enjoyed the sunshine and the French noises and the French smells. He enjoyed not being under British jurisdiction for a brief spell and being off duty. He had enjoyed the night; he looked forward to the day.

His sensual reverie was interrupted by a yawn and a rustle behind him.

'Coffee? I smell coffee!'

A tousled head rose from the pillow and Joe turned to watch with appreciation as white shoulders shrugged off the light cotton sheet. 'Pour me some, for God's sake, Joe! Shan't be able to focus on anything until I've had a cup. Not drunk it all already have you, you insatiable devil?'

'Yours is over there on the table.' Joe nodded towards the tray.

'What? You expect me to get up and get it myself? Is that it? But you'll see my bum!' The indignation turned to resignation. 'Oh, well, I suppose it doesn't matter now.'

She slid naked out of bed and began to hunt about fretfully. Relenting, Joe picked up a bathrobe from the floor and went to drape it around her. He kissed her ear. 'Maisie, for a showgirl you're remarkably modest,' he said, pouring out her coffee.

She scooped long, silky hair from her face the better to glower at him. 'I was never a fan-dancer, Joe Sandilands! In public or in private. And you get out of the habit after a while. There hasn't been anybody since Merl, in fact.' She gave a throaty laugh. 'And not a lot *during* Merl, if you see what I mean!'

'Well, I'd never have guessed and I feel honoured that you should . . .' Joe began gallantly.

'Arsehole,' Maisie commented equably. 'No need for all that. Pigs is equal. We're doing each other a favour. It's going to be a long voyage and I don't play cards. And with all these randy young Frogs hopping about the boat, pepped up with sea air and champagne, I'll be rather glad of a steady old London bobby on guard at my cabin door.'

'That's all very well, Maisie!' Joe's voice was suddenly menacing. 'But who's going to guard the guard? Now put down that cup!'

They met some hours later, Joe more suitably clad for a promenade on the deck. Maisie had chosen to put on a white cotton day dress edged with broderie anglaise and was resisting the hot Indian Ocean sun with a wide straw hat and a parasol. As such she did not stand out from the French ladies demurely pacing the deck in chattering pairs and groups. Slipping his arm through hers, Joe duly admired, saying 'Now let's go for a little walk and show ourselves off.'

After two circuits of the deck they settled on the shady side of the ship on reclining chairs and ordered drinks. 'I don't know what it could be,' said Maisie, 'but something seems to have given me a thirst!'

From below there drifted up the sound of the ship's orchestra rehearsing for the evening's dance. 'We've not had much time for conversation,' said Joe, 'what with one thing and another. Let me catch up on you, Maisie. Tell me why you left Simla. And why you're on this boat.'

Maisie grimaced. 'You did it again, didn't you? Interfering bastard! Made life impossible and I had to move on!'

'Impossible? Surely not? Sir George assured me that he was grateful for all that you'd done and he certainly wasn't intending to make your life difficult.'

'George wasn't the problem! You changed things with that materialization of yours. Turned me into a freak show. Everyone wanted to come to a sitting for all the wrong reasons. Minerva Freemantle – purveyor of frissons (would that be the word, Joe? Frissons?) to the gentry. That bloody apparition brought in the sensation seekers and scared off my genuine clients. Oh, they would have come back again, I think, and it would all have blown over in time but . . . well . . . I'd had enough of Simla. India was beginning to get on my nerves. The place is coming to a boil, Joe, I can feel it.' Maisie shuddered in spite of the heat. 'I don't look far into the future – can't afford to – but it does sometimes force itself on you.'

The slow foxtrot from below swirled to a finish and was immediately followed by a livelier sound. A jazz quartet was tuning up and after a short warm-up they launched into a very creditable version of 'St Louis Blues'. Two small children with their nursemaid came skipping by, wriggling delightedly to the music. Two nuns in light grey summer habit seated themselves in deck chairs, each with a book, each with a breviary.

'And why this boat?' Maisie went on. 'Well, it wasn't for the band! Like you – for the anonymity that's in it, I suppose. No one knows me – no one would try particularly hard to talk to me on a French boat. Peace and quiet, that's what I wanted.'

'I wouldn't count on that, Maisie, looking the way you do – I'd only have to relax my vigilance for a moment and the French Navy would lay you aboard.'

Maisie resumed, 'Three weeks of peace and quiet.' She gave him a sly smile. 'And you had to come along and wreck those plans too! But you, Joe, what are you doing here? You disappeared from Simla and there were all kinds of rumours circulating. Some said Alice Sharpe wasn't dead and she'd run off with you, a victim to your rugged charm!'

'No such luck! No, George found a little job for me to do up on the north-west frontier and what I'm doing here is escaping back to reality. Like you, Maisie, I'd had enough. Too claustrophobic. Too foreign. And I got fed up with being used.'

'George, you mean? Nothing personal in that, you know, the old bugger manipulates everybody.'

'Well, it's not what I'm used to. Charlie Carter once called me Sir George's pet ferret. He wasn't so far wrong. And that might not have been so bad . . . I can look after myself down rat holes. But it's bloody annoying to surface with a dead rat in your mouth to be told by the boss that what you've caught is a mouse, all's well and thank you very much.'

'Not sure who your rat is. Rheza Khan? I don't know all the details but I had heard that you – and Edgar Troop of all people – had saved the whole of northern India from a native uprising, a Russian invasion and God knows what else.'

'That's George's official line and in part true. That's why he's so convincing. An uprising – yes, it could have happened – they'd certainly equipped themselves. George had been keeping an eye on them all along. He seized on this chance of coming down on Rheza's father like a ton of bricks. That squadron of Slater's was only a beginning. There was a Gurkha battalion ready to back up. Massive confiscation of arms and a finger wagged at the rajah. "See what your son has been up to – gun-running and two murders on his slate!" Rheza's father took the hint. Enough menace to keep him quiet and north of the Zalori for a few years I should think. George has played down Alice Sharpe's role in all this.'

'Alice Sharpe's role? I thought that girl must be at the bottom of things! And was it true, then, that story about the shikari trip that went wrong? How *did* she die?'

'Well, you can't just allow the owner of the country's biggest trading empire to disappear in the night without trace. Too many questions. Too many unresolved problems and that's just what George won't tolerate. The Jardine version which is now largely put about, again, is convincing because most of it is true and verifiable. Alice, who as everyone knows is a superb rifle shot and had rather taken under her wing the visiting police commander from Scotland Yard, decided to introduce him to the delights of a shikari party in the Simla Hills. Of course she hired Edgar Troop to be their guide. Who else? There'd been talk of a man-eater raiding in one or two of the remote villages up towards Joginder Nagar and they thought they'd try their luck. Unfortunately Alice wandered off from the camp during the night – against all advice, of course – and was found to be missing in the morning. Frantic searches, Carter and a police squad called in, rewards posted but no trace of Alice. ICTC ticking over until a representative can be shipped out from London and all that.'

'*Is* Alice dead?'

'That part of George's story is based on the truth. She rode off into the night, miles from anywhere and has never resurfaced. Edgar rated her chances of survival pretty low. And the chances of finding a body in that bit of country are slim.'

'Why on earth did she ride off?'

'Because I'd just arrested her for fraud and as an accessory to the murders of Lionel Conyers and Feodor Korsovsky but

270

mainly because she'd just put a bullet between the eyes of Rheza Khan.'

'Now why would she want to do that? Good Lord! Rogue of the worst kind, I'm sure, but that seems a bit extreme. Especially when she had you and Edgar standing by, fingers on the trigger.'

'It was very personal. She trusted him all the way and he betrayed her. She had no idea he was using her as a front for his gun-running. It was the one thing Alice couldn't stand. All her life, she told me, she'd been used and betrayed by the men she loved. But I think her worst betrayal, the one she never got over, was Korsovsky's.'

And slowly at first but with growing eloquence as the details of Alice's story came back to mind, Joe filled in the details as far as he understood them of Alice/Isobel's early life and the part Madame Flora had played in it. He explained the impersonation at the root of everything and how deception and murder had flowed from it. He went over everything again from the devastating experience of sitting alongside Korsovsky when he had been shot at Tara Devi to the disappearance of Alice and ending with George's meticulous sanitizing of the story for public consumption.

Maisie's eyes widened in astonishment as his story unfolded. 'That's the most extraordinary story I've ever heard! Definitely calling for another drink.' She called a passing steward. 'You're telling me that Saintly Alice is a fraud and she's pulled the wool over everybody's eyes for three years?'

'Yes, beyond any doubt and she has admitted it. Rheza Khan to a limited extent, Troop and Flora were the only ones in Simla – or the world – who knew the truth.'

'What? Not even Reggie? Her husband!' Maisie gave a throaty gurgle. 'I can see a few difficulties there!'

Joe smiled. 'I know what you mean! And how interested I would be to have heard Alice's bedtime stories!'

'I had no idea! And I thought I knew everyone's secrets in Simla! But hang on a minute, Joe . . .' Maisie bit her lip and narrowed her eyes in concentration finally saying slowly, 'Look, I know you're the detective and as smart as a new rupee, so I feel a bit daft even suggesting this but – it doesn't add up! There's one or two things you've just said that strike me as a bit odd.'

271

She looked at him speculatively. 'And perhaps that's what you intended? *You're* not happy about it, are you, Joe? The murders, I mean? Alice obviously didn't do either of the killings herself but was she guilty of ordering Rheza Khan to kill both those men?'

'She was and she wasn't,' said Joe.

'What's that supposed to mean? Come on, Joe! You can do better than that!'

'I'm afraid that it means justice has not yet been done. It means that I got only half of it right. It means that there's a killer still on the loose.'

Joe paused for a long time, looking along the deck at the passengers enjoying the sunshine. He said at last, 'Let you into a secret, Maisie. The killer is right here with us on this boat.'

Chapter Twenty-nine

To her credit, Maisie did not look round.

'Maisie, I want you to go over this with me. Tell me if you think I'm reading too much into it, making an already mystifying situation even more complex than it really is.'

'All right – just so long as you only expect me to call on my common sense. I can't involve any higher authority so don't think of it! Can't be done – not on a personal level. It would be like asking the name of the next Derby winner.' Maisie paused and looked searchingly at him. 'Are you – are we – in danger, Joe?' she asked.

'I'm not sure. We could be. This is rather a wild scene! There are no guarantees.'

'I think you'd better explain.'

Joe began slowly, 'It goes right back to the two killings. The modus operandi as we call it in the trade.'

Maisie nodded. 'You don't have to spell every word. I'm not illiterate. Merl's brother (horrible man!) was a sniper in the war. Bored the pants off us talking about his experiences and I must say there's not a lot I can still remember about what he had to say but there are one or two things in your account he would have picked up on and argued about till he was blue in the face. You said Lionel was hit in the head – one shot? – and Korsovsky was hit in the chest – two shots? Well there you are!'

'Maisie, you're amazing!' said Joe with feeling. 'It's a foul trade. Merl's brother would have said – and I would have agreed with him – that snipers always choose the same target area. I'm not talking about a snap shot across No Man's Land – some fool putting his head above the parapet – but a serious, long-range, carefully planned killing. That's what we're talking about. We came to recognize snipers from their technique; even gave them nicknames. And the area they choose is the chest. Much bigger target, you see, less chance of getting it wrong. And if they have time they make sure they've pulled it off by firing two rounds. The killing of Korsovsky was cool, controlled and done by the book. I think it was done by a completely different person from the first killing. Lionel was killed by one shot. To the head. I inspected the scene of the ambush with Charlie Carter and I can tell you it was a pretty amazing piece of shooting! I'm a good shot but I wouldn't have risked a single head shot. Not at that range.'

'And you say the guns were different?'

'Yes. I think Merl's brother would have had a comment to make on that too.'

'Killings were only a year apart – he'd have used the same rifle. Merl's brother went through the whole war with the same gun. God! – he knew the sensitive parts of that bloody gun better than any woman's. Still he did sleep with it for four years.'

'So what I'm saying is that the first murder was done by Rheza Khan. It's his style. A first-rate shot, arrogant sod! A hard target – the head – and only one shot necessary. We know he was five feet ten or thereabouts – a couple of inches shorter than me I would guess – and that he smoked Black Cat cigarettes. His motive was strong. I don't think he did it with Alice's knowledge though, let alone her approval. I'll swear she was genuinely surprised when Troop and I brought it to light in her presence. I'll go further – I'd have sworn she genuinely put down both killings to her blackmailer, whoever that was.'

Joe paused for a moment, his thoughts on the last few minutes he had spent with Alice, his nostrils seared with cordite, his ears singing from the gunshot echoing in that small stone room and, above all, he remembered her saying over her shoulder before she jumped: 'I never asked Rheza to kill anyone for me, Joe.' He remembered her almost proud insistence on the fact that she had never lied to him. He had set this aside in the face of the one enormous outrageous lie of her impersonation. But suppose she had been telling him the literal truth all along?

He spoke aloud her farewell sentence, changing the emphasis. 'I never asked Rheza to kill *anyone* for me, Joe,' became, 'I never asked *Rheza* to kill anyone for me, Joe.'

'But did you ask someone else to kill for you, Alice?' Joe asked.

'Listen, Maisie! How does this sound? Lionel gets killed without Alice's knowledge by Rheza for the reasons we know. Now, a year later, Korsovsky is expected in Simla. Alice wants him dead.'

'To protect her identity? Couldn't she just have done a bunk with her ill-gotten gains? She had plenty of warning – the theatre had booked him back in November. All she had to do to avoid being recognized was stay in bloody Bombay in April. Doesn't wash, Joe.'

'That wasn't the reason she asked for his head on a plate. No. There was a darker reason. Revenge. She hated him with all the fury of a woman who had truly loved him and been rejected, deserted. I know she was capable of this. I've seen her kill a man for the same reason. The moment she discovered Rheza had cheated and betrayed her he was lost. I watched her face as she shot him. I even pleaded with her not to do it. She didn't hear me. She was set to kill: concentrated and unswerving. And she smiled while she shot him.'

Joe shuddered. 'And then she turned her gun on me. I'll never know why she didn't kill me.' He described the last few charged minutes before Alice escaped.

Maisie snorted. 'There's two reasons and neither of them is that she was overwhelmed by your masculine allure! You were a good insurance policy, Joe! There was no point in upsetting Sir George by gunning down his guest and agent and she left you feeling flattered – aren't I right? – that she'd kindly not pulled the trigger. Just in case you ever met again your last memory of her would be that she had – I can't say *saved* your life – but had failed to take it. You owe her one, Joe. She knows that. You know that.'

'And the second reason?'

'Drama. Playacting. Showtime. Takes one to know one! That's what Alice or Isobel or whoever she is has really been doing all the time. If you've got it right she spent five or six years whoring her way through France and, by God, you learn to put on a performance on that kind of stage!' Her face clouded for a moment. 'I've known one or two tarts who could have played Drury Lane if they'd had the vowels. And this one had. I always

275

thought there was more to Alice Sharpe than the virtuous veneer. God! Think about it, Joe! That sugar-icing, touch-me-not respectability underpinned by a tart's skills in handling men – it's an unbeatable combination!'

'It certainly had all the men in Simla twisted round her little finger.'

'And she made the most of it! Playing a part – that's what this woman is all about. I bet she doesn't know who she really is, she's been through so many changes of mask!'

Joe remembered his first sight of Alice, in the spotlight, tears streaming down her face for a lost lover, he remembered her body pressed shivering against him, her breath warm against his cheek as she whispered that his life was in danger and melodramatically gave him her gun. He saw her framed in the embrasure at the Red Fort before she leapt towards freedom. 'Playacting all the way,' he said sadly. 'You're right, Maisie.'

'Still – acting's one thing, killing's . . . well, that's a bit real-life, like. This Korsovsky – it was such a long time ago. 1914, that's eight years. I was deserted in the war and if I ever set eyes on the bugger again I'd shake his hand and thank him for the forethought! Would any woman still want to kill a deserting lover – even the love of her life – after all that time?'

'Alice would. In fact, I'll go further,' said Joe feeling his way through his argument. 'We know from Korsovsky's papers that he was due to appear in the Roman theatres of Provence shortly after the Beaune rail crash. Was it a coincidence that Isobel Newton was travelling to the south of France at that very time? This was the first time he'd returned to the place where they met since his desertion. The first chance she'd had to get close to him again and, perhaps, even to kill him. The rail crash intervened and she had other things on her mind but, waking or sleeping, I don't think the overpowering need to be avenged ever left her.'

'And you're saying that she asked – or blackmailed – she could have blackmailed, Joe – somebody in Simla to gun him down? Some feller who happened to be the same size as the first assassin was known to be and who smoked the same cigarettes – everybody had heard, on the quiet of course, a description of the chap they were looking for first time round.'

'She would have had to find someone the right size, yes. That

276

would have been tricky to fake – but the cigarettes?' Joe smiled. 'That *was* a fake! I think she sent a non-smoker! A non-smoker armed with a pack of the same Black Cats. The killer puffed unenthusiastically at a couple of fags and stubbed them out. We worked out from the timing of Korsovsky's arrival in the Governor's car that there hadn't been time to smoke more than two cigarettes and that would account for one of them being put out hastily and half smoked. But not both! Those stubs were left there for us to find as were the spent rounds and the deeper than necessary scrapes where boots and elbows had rested. So the bumbling police would assume that the maniac sniper had struck again. And then Alice spreads the rumour that it's a deliberate political provocation – quite a credible theory in the present climate.'

'But who, Joe? Who shot Korsovsky? You know, don't you? Are you going to tell me?'

'No.' Joe smiled irritatingly. 'Are you ready for Act 3 of this performance? I think it's time for the killer to speak.'

Chapter Thirty

The jazz quartet had pressed on with its rehearsal, gathering strength and gathering an audience. All deck chairs within earshot of the ballroom were now occupied and white-jacketed stewards slipped to and fro at speed delivering long iced drinks in bright colours, the green of menthe, the fiery orange of grenadine and the yellow of citron. The group broke into a fast-paced 'Broadway Rose'.

'Maisie,' said Joe, 'look at those two nuns over there. Tell me what you see.'

Maisie looked. 'Stupid cows,' she said, 'sweating it out under all those layers of cloth! And why do nuns always wear glasses? Does becoming a nun do your eyes in or do you have to be short-sighted in the first place before they'll take you on? At least those two have had the sense to order drinks. One of them, the big one, is drinking fizzy mineral water by the looks of it and the little one is drinking something her Mother Superior would never approve of, I should guess! What is that pink drink anyway?'

'Looks like a Campari-soda to me. Distinctly intoxicating,' said Joe.

'Should we tell her? Perhaps the waiter got her order mixed up and she's too inexperienced to realize! Can't be doing with a legless nun aboard!'

'It's all right. That one can take her liquor!'

'Tell you something else, Joe,' Maisie added, her voice suddenly bright with excitement and suspicion. 'Just look at her right foot!'

'Her foot? What do you mean – her foot?'

'Look at it! It's been tapping to that jazz rhythm for some time now. I've never seen a syncopating nun before, have you?'

'See what you mean! Come on then, Maisie – into battle! Let's go and renew an acquaintance!'

They strolled arm in arm along the deck and paused in front of the two grey figures. To the gentle click of rosary beads a French voice was whispering through the office for the day. As Joe turned to look at them and opened his mouth to speak they both looked up, calm and friendly.

'*Dieu soit loué!*' said the smaller of the two easily. '*Mais c'est le Commandant Sandilands et Madame Freemantle!*' She leaned close and whispered in English, 'I had wondered when you'd condescend to recognize us! Don't tell me! You're running away together! Oh, how romantic that is! Don't worry! Your secret's safe with us!'

'Wish I could say the same, Sister Alice,' said Joe affably. 'And how do you do, Marie-Jeanne.'

'We were just saying – it's getting very crowded up here and rather too hot,' said Alice, seemingly undismayed. 'Why don't we go below? The Richelieu lounge perhaps will not be so full of people. I'm sure there are things you and Mrs Freemantle would like to confide in private.'

'We were rather more expecting to put you two in the confessional,' said Joe. 'But – lead on, will you? We'll follow. Not anticipating that we'll lose track of you out here in the middle of the ocean.'

They settled down on buttoned leather seats around a small table screened by the fronds of potted palms from the rest of the room. As a steward approached Alice immediately opened the conversation. 'First things first,' she said. 'Get us some drinks, will you? Campari-soda for me, Perrier water for Marie-Jeanne. And you? Port and lemon for the old artiste, perhaps? Whisky-soda for the copper? Put it on my bill. Why not? And the second thing – which you should not forget, Joe – is that this is a French ship. But, of course, I hardly need to remind you of that! I can see that for you and Mrs Freemantle the choice would ensure discretion. Imagine the wagging tongues on a P&O ship! For us also the choice is significant. The captain is in command here, and though you may find it hard to believe, Scotland Yard has no authority whatsoever over this little part of the French Republic. Marie-Jeanne and I have papers, perfectly valid papers, which would satisfy the most pernickety *juge d'instruction* that we are who we say we are – simply two sisters of the Carmelite order on our way from India to . . . well, let's say somewhere west of Suez. Give us any trouble whatsoever and I won't hesitate to complain of interference to the captain.'

Joe had no doubt of this and he had no doubt that any Frenchman would hasten to take the part of a religieuse, especially a pretty one, against an Englishman if she accused him of harassment.

'I acknowledge the difficulties, Alice, and don't worry, we'll stay as far away from you as is possible on a ship this size until we reach Marseilles. And then, while we go on north to London I expect you and your friend will – let me guess now – transfer to a transatlantic liner and on to New York? New Orleans?'

A flash of humour behind the spectacles told him his guess was right. He found it very disconcerting to be talking to Alice, whom he had known in some quite intimate situations, now hidden from him in the folds of headdress and the concealing habit. He found the lack of thick copper-coloured hair confusing and wondered briefly if she'd cut it off the better to enter into the spirit of the playacting. Marie-Jeanne on the other hand looked as though she'd been born to play this role, her quiet air of puzzled sanctity convincing and disconcerting.

'I was about to ask how you had managed to slip out of Simla but I think I can work that out,' Joe said. 'The passenger lists from the station . . . what was it? – ". . . four French nuns, three box-wallahs, two brigadiers . . ." Sir George wasn't joking when he read out the list? You were the French nuns?'

'Well, I was one of them, Joe. The other three were girls from Marie-Jeanne's staff. My only worry was that they were enjoying the performance so much their over-acting would give us away but all was well. ICTC had supplied habits to the convent and we still had some in stock. Your men were looking for a single Englishwoman. They didn't look twice at a flight of French nuns! There are always some going or coming through the station anyway – it was hardly an unusual sight.'

'And the swag, Alice? The loot? The ill-gotten gains? Stashed away in your luggage in hollowed-out bibles?'

'Something like that,' she smiled. 'Trade secret, Joe! Don't ask!'

'How did you manage to get back into Simla?' His mind going back to that dark night, he added, 'We all thought you must be dead. I was horrified for you.'

'Thank you, Joe. I appreciate that. I decided to play safe and return the way I'd come. It wasn't easy in the dark, in fact it was awful! I didn't stop – just slogged away on that good horse at a slow pace. The worst part was coming across your rescue party, flares and all, clattering along in the dark. Not that they were likely to catch sight of me – I saw them coming a mile off – but you'll never know how tempting it was to rush forward and ask their help. So many of them. So solid. So cheerful. It was agony to hear their silly, familiar voices getting further and further away and the blackness and silence rolling in again. Leaving me shivering and alone.' Her voice wavered.

Maisie groaned and kicked Joe's ankle.

'All's well that ends well,' said Joe brightly, 'and it certainly seems to have ended well for you, Alice. Tell us where you holed up in Simla. You disappeared without trace. And some very clever fellows were watching for you: Charlie's regulars, George's irregulars. Quite a decent reward discreetly on offer as well.'

'I was in the convent of course. The Mother Superior was very understanding when I explained that I was being pursued, misrepresented and threatened. I have been a very generous patron of the order, you understand, Joe. She repaid a portion of my kindness. And glad to do so. I still have friends, you may be surprised to hear.'

'And then Mademoiselle Pitiot joined you later, travelling openly to Bombay to keep a long-arranged business appointment.' He turned his attention to Marie-Jeanne. 'With another glove salesman, I wonder? The kind who disappears before he can confirm your alibi? Like the gentleman you had lunch with on the day of Korsovsky's death?'

'No,' she said placidly, 'not a glove salesman. The recent purchaser and new owner of Belle Epoque. The sale was arranged some while ago. No mystery there!' Marie-Jeanne went on absently telling the beads of her rosary.

'Not impossible, I suppose, to locate your guest,' Joe went on ruminatively. 'But to be honest I didn't even try. I did, however, talk with the maître d'hôtel of the Grand. I checked their bookings and, of course, there it was: a table for two for lunch at one o'clock in the name of Mademoiselle Pitiot. The maître d'hôtel, who knows you well, remembers you arriving and showing you to table number ten which you had particularly requested. He reports that the lunch party didn't break up until after half-past two as would have been normal. The murder occurred several miles away over rough country at precisely two forty-five.'

Marie-Jeanne continued to fix him with a melting look of innocence. 'This is what I told you, Commander. I commend you on your thoroughness because it establishes that what I told you was the truth.'

'Thorough? Yes, Marie-Jeanne, I was thorough. Belatedly thorough. Before I left Simla I returned to the Grand. I insisted on having table ten pointed out to me and on interviewing the waiter who had personally served you throughout the meal.'

'Oh, yes?' said Marie-Jeanne without curiosity.

'Table ten is right at the back of the dining room, screened from the rest of the diners by potted plants – a sort of little kala-juggah all on its own and conveniently close to the rear door. Your guest must have been a bit puzzled when you left the lunch table – but only a bit. Filled with anticipation of the best the house had to offer it may have been a moment or two before he realized that the pretty girl who returned and sat down opposite him was no longer the hard-headed bargainer but something younger and more pliable. One of your assistants? Identically dressed? Why should he complain? The waiter spoke very admiringly of her. It was discreetly done according to him and did not surprise him. It's not unusual for him to preside over clandestine meetings of an amatory nature and his estimation that this was what was taking place was reinforced by the large tip he was given at the end of the meal. The lunch was a great success apparently and the pair rolled away through the back door a good deal the worse for copious amounts of food and two bottles of burgundy. The time was well past half-past two, nearer three, he says, and if you had indeed been present, Marie-Jeanne, there would have been no time to allow you to get out to Tara Devi in time to lie in wait and shoot Korsovsky. But you weren't there, were you? You'd ridden a distance of five miles through the hills by then, and were setting up your ambush. Puffing half-heartedly at a couple of Black Cat cigarettes and firing two dum-dum bullets into my friend's heart.'

After a long silence Alice found her voice. 'None of this matters any longer, Joe,' she said. 'Don't you see? No one is going to want to hear such things – not any more – not even George Jardine. Why don't we just acknowledge that you're a very clever chap? I'm sure that's what you want to hear. And why don't we leave it at that?'

She made to rise. She seemed suddenly uneasy, eager to end the conversation.

'Well, *I* want to hear it!' Maisie broke in angrily. 'The whole world *ought* to hear it! And it's a crying shame if there's no way two conniving, murdering creatures can be brought to justice because they've got the means and the nous to get themselves away over frontiers and over seas! Joe, are you just going to let them get away with it? I hate the thought that these two can just set up somewhere else and use the money they've got their hands on! If they'd stolen a gold watch you'd be down on them like a ton of bricks!' she finished acidly.

'I have to. There's no way they can be pursued as things stand at the moment. India to the USA – that's too far for British justice to stretch, I'm afraid.'

They were both looking at him with sly triumph. A sudden surge of anger and distress for Korsovsky shook him.

'But Feodor was well known and much loved in America,' he said. 'It mightn't be difficult to get the attention of those who would want to bring his killers to justice. Why the hell did you have to kill him, Alice? You could have just left Simla – you could have avoided him.'

Alice seemed not to know how to reply and it was Marie-Jeanne who answered. Laying a protective hand over Alice's she said, 'Alice told me last November that this man was to come to Simla. I don't know how much of Alice's history you know, Commander? Perhaps you are not aware that this Russian, this glamorous, much-fêted figure was, like most Russians as far as I can tell, a smooth, sentimental, self-serving . . .' She paused and finally brought out the word explosively, '. . . shit! He met Alice when she was visiting the south of France under the guardianship of a family friend and managed to seduce her. And she a schoolgirl at the time. He promised marriage of course. He didn't reveal that he was already married to a Russian lady who was living in New York. At the first sniff of a European war he went back there and wrote a letter to Alice telling her all. I have seen it. I know that this is true.'

'That's enough, Marie-Jeanne. He knows all this. I told him. He doesn't need to know any more. We must go now.'

Alice's voice was curt and Joe was again aware of a lapse of confidence. The awareness was followed by the sudden gratification which accompanies the realization that an opponent at cards is bluffing. There was one more thing that Alice wanted to remain concealed, something that could still do her damage if he guessed it. And he thought he had guessed her weakness.

'No, stay a little longer. Here come our drinks,' he said cheerfully. 'Marie-Jeanne, do go on but remember that I met Korsovsky and formed a good opinion of him. It would take much to convince me that he would behave badly to the innocent young girl I'm sure Alice was in those days.'

Alice gave him a look of guarded suspicion but Marie-Jeanne was eager to continue. 'You will see how misplaced was your good opinion, Commander! Alice didn't tell him that by this time she realized she was pregnant. This was dealt with in a discreet clinic in France but the scars of this emotional and physical abuse have stayed with her unhealed – corrosive even. She hated him and for good reason. Alice has been more than kind to me, I owe her more than I can say and it was a small thing to repay some of what I owe by removing the cause of her torment. I was brought up to shoot – a skill in which I excelled my brothers though of course like my many other qualities it went unacknowledged.'

'But not unremarked, Marie-Jeanne,' said Joe. 'I and many others were deceived by the marksmanship. We assumed that the killing had been done by a sniper of formidable talents.'

A slow smile of satisfaction acknowledged the compliment. 'It was a man of just such talents who taught me. My father's gamekeeper had been a soldier. He had fought the Rifis in

Morocco and survived. I have a good eye and the target was not a difficult one,' she finished modestly.

Maisie gave a snort of disgust. 'Your *target*, as you call him, was a living man and your *talent* splattered his blood and flesh all over Joe. And I'd still like to know why. Because I'm not convinced by all this nonsense about doing it for poor little Alice.'

Marie-Jeanne looked stonily beyond Maisie, loftily refusing to acknowledge her presence let alone her right to speak out in criticism.

Undeterred, Maisie pressed on, a sudden gleam of understanding in her eyes. 'You were doing it for yourself! Why does anyone kill? You were looking after number one! You knew this Russian was the love of her life . . . if he'd resurfaced in Simla who knows what might have happened? She told you she hated him but you're clever – you weren't deceived! Love? Hate? They're very close. I'm guessing – and I think *you* guessed – she'd have had her bags packed and been off on the next boat with him! Leaving her old friend and protégée Marie-Jeanne to face the music. You love her, Marie-Jeanne, don't you? She's your whole life. There was no way you could risk letting her meet Korsovsky again! She never asked you to kill him for her. You did it for yourself!'

A slight flush on Marie-Jeanne's pale cheeks was the only sign that Maisie's darts had hit their target and she remained tight-lipped and scornful. Her silence seemed to incite Maisie to deeper fury. 'Men! We've all wanted to line them up in our sights and pull the bloody trigger, haven't we, love! Who were you really killing? Who were you really seeing when you squinted through your sights? Your father, your brothers?' She paused for a second and added, 'All the men who've ever looked at you and then looked hurriedly away again? You talk about it as though the act of killing were a gift, a selfless offering to this evil-minded little tart here – it wasn't! There was nothing generous or even dutiful about it. You enjoyed it!'

'Maisie! Maisie!' Joe had been the only one to notice that Alice had visibly winced when Maisie used the word 'tart'. He was right then. Alice had not told Marie-Jeanne about her past. Incredibly, the devoted Frenchwoman still believed that Alice was Alice Conyers. She would never have told Joe the story of her emerald green underwear had she known of the deception and now, after all that had happened, she was still unaware. And this was what Alice was so anxious to keep from Joe. He had only to reveal who she really was to wreck for ever the only relationship which had any meaning and value to her. She did not want him to give her away to Marie-Jeanne.

In a wash of comprehension Joe began to understand the relationship between these two women. So different and yet so closely linked. He saw that to Marie-Jeanne Alice was still the battered and damaged little girl she had rescued from the Beaune rail crash. The girl she had put together again. Healthy, successful, beautiful but ultimately still in need of protection from her previous life, still in need of a refuge. And to Alice, Marie-Jeanne was that refuge. Someone who asked no questions and who in all circumstances gave her the shelter so brutally denied by others. Marie-Jeanne's unquestioning belief in her was vital to Alice. Her message to Joe was, 'Don't give me away.' And Marie-Jeanne, so close to Alice, had still no realization of the switch. Alice was Alice Conyers.

He looked steadily into the blue eyes and thought that this was perhaps the first time he had seen the real girl. The nun's habit, the spectacles were no longer even a distraction. The eyes were pleading with him, fearful, trying to convey her message. Maisie had foreseen this moment. What had she said? – 'You owe her one, Joe. She knows that. You know that.' And now, wordlessly, she was reminding him. Suddenly Joe was weary. Weary of the blackmail, the deceptions, the heat. He wanted to be finally free of this woman, owing her nothing, all contact severed. He resented the emotional and professional demands India had made on him and in that moment Alice represented for him the writhing layers of Indian intrigue and he wanted to be rid of it. He wanted his London life with a cold wind blowing off the Thames, the Lots Road power station puthering out smoke, the bells of St Luke's, Chelsea, waking him. He wanted to be back in bed with Maisie.

He got to his feet. 'I can't forgive you, Alice Conyers.' The slight stress on his use of her adopted name told her what she needed to know. Joe was acknowledging and cancelling his debt. 'London bobbies aren't in the absolving business and you'll have to look to a higher authority for that. You've got away with it as far as I'm concerned. For now. For here.' He took Maisie's arm and with a nod to each woman he walked away.

At the door Maisie, whose disapproval had been conveyed by the tension in her arm and the tight line of her lips, finally rounded on him. 'I see what you're at, Joe, and – all right – there's not a lot you can do,' she hissed in his ear, 'but it riles me that they can get away with murder. I can't leave it like that.'

She shook off his restraining arm and walked with dignity back to the table to confront the silent pair. They waited, wide-eyed, for her to speak. Maisie paused, head slightly on one side, eyes unfocused as she listened with attention to inner voices. At last she began to speak in a low voice which Joe, standing uncertainly in the doorway, could only just make out.

'I never did get the chance in Simla to pass on messages which came to me from someone who was desperate to communicate with you, Mrs Sharpe, because of an identity mix-up – you'll know what I mean, I think. Hannah. That was the name of the departed. Hannah Newton. No one of that name in our circle, was there? A relative perhaps? She seemed very concerned. In fact she had some dire warnings for a young person still on this side of the veil. Awful warnings! My God! I wouldn't be in your shoes, madam, for all the tea in Assam!' Maisie shook her head sadly and shivered with dread at things only she could see. Joe saw Alice's lips almost imperceptibly form the word 'mother' but she managed to stay calm and silent.

Back in Maisie's cabin Joe asked, 'Hannah Newton? Isobel's mother? Now how the hell did you find that out? And those warnings of doom! Laying it on a bit thick, weren't you? Alice is a true believer, you know – she'll never have another moment's peace after that little performance! Where did you get all that from, Maisie?'

'Trade secret, Joe! Don't ask!'